K-9 HEROES

BOOKS 1, 2, 3

K-9 HEROES

RADA JONES

APOLODOR

APOLODOR PUBLISHING

BECOMING K-9

A BOMB DOG'S MEMOIIR

RADA JONES

BOOK 1 IN THE K-9 HEROES SERIES

CHAPTER 1

WHO KNEW training humans was so hard? You'd wonder why. They aren't that stupid. It takes them a while, but they eventually learn when you want out, you're hungry or you're thirsty. They can even talk to each other by making noise with their tongue. How weird is that? Even my brother Blue, who's the slowest of us all, knows that the tongue is for lapping water and panting to cool down.

Mom cocked her head and licked my nose.

"That's the best they can do, dear. They have no tails, their ears don't move, and most don't even have enough fur to raise their hackles. No wonder they're confused and need us to guide them. And that's what we do; that's our life's work. But we need to choose them carefully."

Mom was on her sixth litter and very wise. Beautiful, too, with her long muzzle, amber eyes, and smooth, shiny fur, all black but for her golden legs and loving pink tongue.

She glanced at Yellow, who chased his tail instead of paying attention, and growled. He hung his head and sat in line with the rest of us to listen.

It was a lovely summer day as Mom homeschooled us in Jones's front yard. The warm wind tickled my nose. I bit it, but I caught nothing. I tried again, but Mother threw me a side glance, so I closed my mouth and sat still.

"Boys and girls, today's the day. People will come to check you out and choose which one to take home. They don't know it, but it doesn't work that way. You choose your humans, but choose them wisely. Sniff them all, then pick the ones that smell like food if you want a good life. You may sometimes get bacon, maybe even grapes. Humans say dogs don't eat grapes, but that's poppycock. They just want to keep them for themselves. My grandma was a pure-bred Alsatian, and she loved Riesling. I never had Riesling, but Concord isn't bad."

A shiny strip of drool dripped from Mom's mouth. She licked it off and inspected us. We were seven: three boys and four girls. But that doesn't much matter when you're just ten weeks old. The only difference is how you pee. The boys don't know how to squat so they need something to lift their leg to, like a bush or a mailbox. How stupid!

"Why don't you just lift your leg, if that's what you need to do? What does the bush have to do with anything?"

Mom bristled.

"Leave them alone, Red."

I tried, but it was hard. I was the runt of the litter, so I had to prove myself all the time. Mom said I had a Napoleonic complex.

"What's that?"

"It's when you're the smallest, so you have to be meaner to show them that size doesn't matter."

I told you Mom is brilliant. She came all the way from Germany when she was just a pup. Our human, Jones, has two passions: German shepherds and history. Mom was his first German shepherd, and he spent lots of time teaching her things most dogs never heard about.

He still does, even now that she's old. He sits in his recliner and reads to her as she lays by the fireplace. Sometimes I listen in. There was a story about a dude named Hitler. Not a nice guy, but for loving German shepherds. Another one about that short guy Napoleon who tried to conquer the world while wearing funny hats. And one about some place called Afghanistan.

"That's a bad war, Maddie," Jones said, scratching the four white hairs in his beard. "Those Taliban, they are not nice people."

He calls her Maddie, but her real name is Madeline Rose Kahn Van Jones. He is Jones. The Van is for Van Gogh, some orange dude who got so mad he bit off his own ear. The rest is just for show, since people pay more for dogs with long names; they call that a pedigree. Mom's pedigree is longer than her tail.

As always, Mom was right. People came to see us, and they brought their spouses, their kids, and even their dogs to check us out and choose which one to get. Like, really? Jones said that only one out of twenty German shepherd owners is smarter than his dog. I don't believe it. I bet he fudged the numbers to feel better. You think you own a dog? Who feeds who? Who cleans after who? Who does the work, everything but making decisions? You, human, in case you didn't know it. You don't buy a dog; you hire supervision. But I digress.

My littermates and I wore colored collars so humans could tell us apart. There was no need, really, since we were all different, but humans couldn't see it. What color did I wear? Red, of course. I was small, but I was the queen of the litter, whether the others liked it or not.

A fat man in a Hawaiian shirt stopped to stare at me. He called his female.

"Look at this red one! Isn't he cute?"

She hobbled closer, leaning on her crooked stick. I love sticks, so I tried to take it. She didn't want to let go, but I insisted. They laughed.

"Let's get him."

Jones cleared his throat.

"Red is lovely, indeed, but she's a very active little person who needs a lot of attention. How much time do you plan to work with her every day?"

"Work with her?"

"Yes. Walk her, train her, and play with her."

They stared at him like he'd lost his marbles. He smiled.

"May I recommend Brown here? He's lovely, easygoing, and eager to please. He'll be happy to lay on the sofa watching TV. Or Miss Green? She's a polite little lady who gets along with everyone and never disappoints."

Brown left. So did Green, Yellow, and even White, while I stayed, waiting for my forever home.

"Take it easy, Red dear," Mother said when there were only two of us left—Black and me. "You need to soften up a bit; otherwise, you'll be left without a family. People look for easygoing dogs to fit into their lives, not for somebody to take charge. Though maybe they should, really, but they aren't smart enough to know that."

Her German accent made her words feel harsh. Have you ever listened to Germans? It's like they're constipated while they also have a cold. They keep clearing their throats, so their words come out like bullets from a machine gun. I don't speak German, but I love watching old war movies with Jones.

"What do you mean, Mom? What should I do?"

"Lick their hands, sweetheart. Wrap yourself around their feet and stare at them like they hung the moon."

"Are you serious?"

"Of course."

"But they're stupid!"

"Come on, Red, don't be so judgmental. You're just a pup, and you have so much to learn. A nice family will give you a good life. They'll love you, play with you, and spoil you. Knowing you have a good, safe home will lift a weight off my soul."

You think I listened? You've got to be kidding.

That's how I ended up in the military.

CHAPTER 2

WHEN THE LAST family stopped by to pick up Black and I was left behind, Mom got upset. She licked me all over to give me a nice bath, but I knew she wasn't happy.

"That's OK, Mom. I'd rather stay here with you and Jones than go with those stupid humans. They don't even have tails. Even worse, they don't have the common sense of a cat."

Mom shook all over like she'd been out in the rain. She was dry, but that's how she disagreed. Why shake just your head when you can make a stronger statement?

"You can't stay here, Red. We aren't a breeding program; we're just a little family business. Jones can't afford to keep us both. I'm old, and I'm not worth much to anyone but him. I'm afraid you'll have to go."

"Go where?"

"Wherever he finds you a job. He loves you, and he'll do his best, but I'm afraid you won't get to be a spoiled pet living the good life with a nice family."

"I don't want to be a spoiled pet living with a nice family."

"What do you want, Red?"

"I want...I want to go for long walks and smell new things and eat bacon and be free."

Mom sighed.

"I'm sorry to break it to you, baby, but you're a dog. Dogs no longer run free. Our ancestors gave that up thousands of years ago when they decided to share people's fire and eat their food. These days, our life revolves around humans. I hope yours will be kind, loving, and smart enough to appreciate everything you have to offer."

"I'll bite them if they don't. I have sharp teeth."

Mom looked away, and for a moment, I thought she was hiding tears. But that can't be. Number one, dogs don't cry. And number two...I forgot what number two was. So I went to chew on Jones's boots for a while, trying to remember. Chewing always helps me focus. But I couldn't remember, not even after I finished the left heel. Even worse, they weren't real leather, so that night, I got sick all over the kitchen. Mom cleaned it up, and Jones never knew. Well, not until he wore the boots, that is.

I was thirteen weeks by then, and my brothers and sisters were all gone, so I got to chill with Mom and Jones. That was the life. We went for long walks every morning, then we napped and re-napped. In the evenings, we watched old movies and munched on crunchy buttered popcorn.

But then the days got shorter, and the sun lost its power. One day, as Mom and I played in the yard, waiting for Jones to drive us to the park, a burst of wind shook off a bunch of yellow leaves that fell on us like rain.

"The fall's here," Mom said.

"The fall of what?"

She cocked her head to think better.

"Good question, Red. The fall of leaves, I guess. It gets cold, so the leaves turn yellow and red, then fall off."

"What do the trees do?"

"They wait for spring to come back. That's how life goes."

Jones turned on the radio.

"To everything, there is a season; to everything, there is a reason."

Mom perked her ears, then lifted her muzzle to the sky and started howling with the music.

"There's a time to be born, and a time to die; a time to plant, and a time to reap; a time to kill, and a time to heal; a time to laugh, and a time to weep."

The song stirred something inside me. I lifted my nose to the sky and howled with Mom. I didn't understand the words, but the melody came from deep in my soul, and I couldn't stop singing like I couldn't stop breathing.

Jones's jaw dropped. He stared at us, then shook his head and laughed.

"I didn't know the Byrds sang the song of your people, but I'd be darned if it doesn't make sense."

That evening he looked up the song.

"I got something for you, girls."

When that haunting song filled the house, Mom and I sang along. Jones joined us.

"A time to kill, and a time to heal; a time to laugh, and a time to weep."

I didn't know it then, but my time to leave was coming.

CHAPTER 3

A FEW DAYS LATER, two men in a Jeep came by. The short one was old, the young one was tall, and they both wore khaki.

Jones took me out to meet them, and Mom followed.

"Thanks for coming, folks. This is Red. She's an opinionated young lady with a high prey drive, and she's fearless."

I glance at Mom.

"What's he saying?"

"That you're good at catching fast things, dear. It's a compliment."

It doesn't really feel that way, with him looking gloomy and all, but I don't have time to ponder. The young man slaps his hip in command and screeches:

"Hey, Pup. Come here."

I sit on my butt and ogle him down my nose.

"Like really? You think I'll have any random Tom, Dick, or Harry tell me what to do? Young whippersnapper, if you want us to get acquainted, you'll have to do the work."

The short one laughs. He's small and wiry, with warm eyes and a few white hairs floating above his pink head.

"She's got a personality, doesn't she? All thirty pounds of her, and she's tough as nails."

He offers me his hands to sniff.

He had Michigans for lunch. That's our North Country specialty—hot dogs with garlicky meat sauce and raw onions. They're delicious, but you want to spit out the onions, especially if you plan on a date. But he doesn't look like he's into dating. He's old and smells like sweat, cars, and something acrid.

Mom's nose wrinkles.

"That's gunpowder, Red. See their uniforms? This is the Army. There's nothing further from freedom than the Army. Are you sure you want to do this? You'll go God knows where with God knows whom, and you'll work your butt off. You'll never be a pet."

"What if I don't want to go?"

"Bite him, dear, like you did with that other guy who wanted you, the one who smelled like cats. Otherwise, your Army career is staring you in the face. Is this what you want?"

"How would I know?"

Mom nods.

"True that. You rejected every chance to be a pet; I don't know what else Jones can find for you."

I sniff Shorty again. He's nothing to write home about, even if I knew how to write, but he's OK. And he's lonely. I sense no kids, no wife, no pets. Just stale beer, wood smoke, and gunpowder. He needs someone to look after him.

I stare him in the eye, and he stares back. Nobody blinks.

He bursts laughing.

"She's something else, this one. We'll take her."

Jones nods. Mom's ears flatten, and she suddenly looks sad and old.

"Let's go, little girl," Shorty says, reaching for my collar.

I bare my teeth and growl. He stares at me with wide eyes.

"What's up, Baby?"

I point to Mom.

"I need to say goodbye."

He steps back.

I lick Mom's nose, pretending I don't see her shiny eyes.

"I love you, Mom. I'm sorry if I disappointed you, but I need to be who I am. I love you."

"I love you too, Red. You didn't disappoint me, just the opposite. You're just like your father, Rocky, who got wounded in Afghanistan. He earned a purple heart. He's a hero. None of my other kids turned out like him. I'm so proud of you."

"Thank you, Mom. I'll be back."

"I hope so. In my old age, I'd love to get to see my kids again. You, especially."

I lick her nose and sniff her for the last time, then I say goodbye to Jones, who's biting his lips to stop from crying. People are weird. He chose to send me away, and now he's all upset. Why? Who knows? I walk to Shorty and sit next to him. He nods.

"You're ready? Let's go then."

He opens the door. I try to jump in, but it's too high, and I fall on my face. The young whippersnapper laughs and then helps me up. His smell raises my hackles.

As we drive away, Whippy asks:

"What are we going to call her? Red?"

Shorty laughs.

"Oh, no. This beautiful young lady deserves better than that. And she's not even red, she's black and tan. Mostly black. From now on, she'll be Guinness. The queen of beers."

As we drive through the potholes, I lay my nose on my paws and think about Mom and Jones. I miss them terribly, and I know they miss me even more.

"I'll be back, Mom."

I hope that's true.

CHAPTER 4

THE TRAINING WAS FUN. Except for obedience training, of course. Being told what to do has never been my bowl of kibble. But I liked Shorty, and I enjoyed making him happy. More importantly, I was hungry, and training came with food. Gone were the days when Jones filled my bowl with High-Performance Grass-Fed Beef kibble three times a day, not counting the buttered popcorn that came with the movies. I now had to work for my food.

My training started as soon as we got to Shorty's house, a small blue ranch at the edge of town.

I started at the front door and sniffed everything: boots, remote controls, ashtrays. The green velour sofa smelled like tobacco, beer, and Shorty. Nobody else. I moved from the kitchen to the bathroom, where I scored. The large brush behind the water bowl smelled delicious. Tasted good, too, so I lay down to brush my teeth.

"Guinness, come," Shorty called.

I was busy, so ignored him. He was welcome to come over if he needed me.

But then he shook the food container, and my stomach growled, reminding me I hadn't eaten since breakfast. So off I went.

That's how I learned to sit, stay, down, and heel. I didn't enjoy it, but as Mom said, I had rejected every chance to be a pet. I had to work for a living.

It wasn't all work, though. We took long walks every morning, though Shorty needed a lot of encouragement. It wasn't his fault. He's missing his front legs, so he had to walk on his hind paws all the time. It was hard to watch, really, but he did a good job, considering. After training, we stretched on the sofa, drank Bud Light, and watched action movies. That's how I learned to appreciate beer. Shorty poured a few drops in my dish every time he opened a can. At first, I tried it just to be polite, but then I got into it. I liked the way it tickled my tongue. So did Shorty. By bedtime, he'd slur his commands, but it didn't matter, since I had learned to hear his thoughts. He still spoke a lot.

One evening he showed me the picture of a stiff couple staring straight into the camera. Dressed in black and unsmiling, they looked like they'd never chewed on a juicy bone or tried a good mud bath. But Shorty's eyes got wet.

"This is my mother."

His mother didn't look anything like my mom. She had cold eyes and a thin mouth. Even worse, she had no tail; but then neither did Shorty. It must be genetic.

"And this is Dad."

Shorty choked up and blew his nose in the kitchen towel.

"When I was a kid, he used to take me clamming in Maine. We'd go camping there every summer and look for clams in the mud. I've still got his clamming fork. Let me show you."

He came back from the garage with a short pitchfork with ugly flat teeth.

"Isn't she beautiful? Forty years later, and she's still as good as new. Have you ever seen anything like it?"

I hadn't really, and I was doing just fine, but I slapped my tail on the floor to be polite. The last thing I wanted was to hurt Shorty's feelings.

"Guess what, Guinness? We're going clamming."

That sounded interesting. I'd never seen clams before, but I knew mud, and I loved it. I still do. The rotten eggs smell. The way it farts as it squishes between your toes! And the lovely coating that spikes your fur! I was all in.

We loaded the Jeep with food, a tent, and a stinky gas stove. I sniffed everything and knocked down a thing or two, getting in Shorty's way at every step to slow him down and help him make good choices.

We started north before sunrise. The sun went up, then back down, as we munched on chips and listened to the radio where dude after dude complained about their cheating females and their old trucks breaking down. I wondered about cheating. Is it like when Black tried to steal my food? I had an easy fix for that. I just bared my teeth and growled, and he left me alone. I wanted to ask Shorty, but he was busy singing along in his creaky voice.

"I love country music. It keeps me going on long rides and reminds me how good I've got it."

And a long ride it was. By the time we got there, it was too dark for clamming. We put up the tent, drank beer, ate Bush's beans, and watched the stars blinking up above. Shorty loved them.

"See, Guinness, when we die, our soul becomes a star. It looks down upon Earth and waits for our loved ones to come and join us. I know Father's there; I just don't know which one he is. When I die, I'll join him, and we'll go clamming together again."

I sniffed them looking for Shorty 's father, but they were too far and too many. I smelled nothing but the beans, the seaweed, and Shorty's socks.

"See that shiny one there? That's the North Star. It shows you the north. It will help you get home if you ever get lost."

He started explaining how I can find it by adding five times the distance between these two stars to the direction of those other two. At first I thought he was kidding, but nope, he was darn serious. Smart humans can say the most amazing things. Watch the stars? How about following your nose? I can't even walk while staring up at the sky. Humans!

We slept in the tent, keeping each other warm, then walked to the beach at sunrise. The tide had covered the sand with sea creatures entangled in garlands of green seaweed. I don't do greens, but I found two small crabs and a tiny silver fish. The sand coating gave them a satisfying crunch. I found another fish for Shorty, but he was busy digging in the mud, so I ate that one too.

Sweat ran down Shorty's face as he dug with his pitchfork. He looked exhausted. Time to help him, I thought. Before you could say kibble bits, I dug a hole as big as our tent, and I called him over. He shook his head.

"There are no clams there, Guinness. That's way too deep. We don't dig for the sake of digging. We look for clams, you see?"

He showed me a sandy rock that smelled like the sea.

OK then. I brought Shorty a rock even bigger than his, but he laughed and threw it away. I got it back, but he ignored it and kept digging.

When he was done, he covered his clams with seaweed to keep them moist though he didn't need to. We walked to the tent in an icy drizzle that seeped into our bones and made us shiver. If those clams could shiver, they would have. But Shorty made a fire, and we warmed up, drinking beer while waiting for the water to boil.

As always after a few sips, he started talking.

"I've been with the Army for thirty years, Guinness. Good years. I bought a house and paid off my mortgage; I even set aside a little money. Father would be so proud of me. I wish I could tell him. I think about him every day, but here, up north, I feel him with me."

His voice cracks. I lay my head on his thigh, and he scratches me behind the ears.

"You know your father, Guinness? Do you miss him?"

I only know what Mom told me, and I don't miss him. How can you miss someone you never met? But I feel Shorty's pain, so I lick his beer.

He laughs and starts cooking the clams. He brought scallions, parsley, and other useless green stuff, but he also got chorizo - a sausage with an attitude.

He pours them all over the clams, then sprinkles over a yellow powder that makes me sneeze. He laughs.

"That's Old Bay, Guinness. Father said you can't cook seafood without Old Bay. That's what makes it real."

If you say so. I'd be just fine with just the chorizo, but who am I to disagree with Shorty's father?

That evening we ate clams, we drank beer, and listened to country music. Shorty was happy and pleased with himself, and I didn't want to hurt his feelings. But those clams? They smelled like Old Bay, and they had more sand than the fish I found on the beach.

In the morning we packed up and went home. I had a splendid time. I just wish I could tell my Mom that I found a good home after all.

CHAPTER 5

I woke up one morning to discover that the world had turned white. I couldn't believe it.

Nothing but white everywhere. Blanketing the ground, outlining the trees, covering the house. More white kept falling from the sky. I opened my mouth to catch it, but it vanished. It was soft and so cold it felt hot. The world was white and quiet.

That filled me with so much joy that I needed to jump out of my skin. I loved that white, and I wanted it all. I rolled in it, I dug into it, I ate it. I was in love.

Shorty watched me from the door, his thin hair messed up from sleep, his smile cracking his face from one ear to the other.

"You like it, huh? It's snow."

He bent over and picked some, molded it into a ball, and threw it at me. I jumped to catch it, but it disappeared amongst the whiteness. He threw another. This time I got it, but it was like grabbing the wind. I chomped on it, and it disappeared.

He laughed and threw another, then another. I leaped to catch them, sliding and falling and jumping again. I'd never had so much fun.

"You know what, Guinness? How about we skip training today, and we take a snow day. What do you think?"

"Seriously?"

"Yep."

I leaped and barked with joy. He put on his boots and his coat, then came to play with me. His face turned pink with cold, but his eyes warmed with laughter. I'd never seen him happier. Before long, we'd flattened the snow and turned it from fluffy to slippery. Running got tricky.

I was just gathering myself after a face-plant when a green Cadillac stopped by the driveway, and Shorty's smile vanished like the snow I'd chomped on.

The driver was a woman, old, crooked and unsmiling. I went to greet her, since she looked familiar, but she ignored me. Her fierce eyes were glued on Shorty.

"Hello, Mother."

"Hello, Alfred."

She stared at him. He stared back. She had his narrow down-turned eyes, but she lacked his warmth and his softness.

"I came for the last time."

"I see."

"I had to. God reminded me that he will take me soon, but I have to finish my work here first. I can't go to Him without giving it one more try."

"I'm sorry you bothered, Mother. Especially in a snowstorm."

She leaned toward him, her hands on her hips, her voice thunder.

"Alfred, it's not too late to renounce your evil ways and turn your heart back to God. He'll take you back to His flock if you repent."

"Repent for what?"

"You know that better than I do."

"Mother, I've got nothing for you. I believe, and I pray, and I do my best to hurt nobody and be the best man I can be. There's little else I can do, for God or for you."

"You're not a man. You know what you are."

"I am what I am because God made me this way. I didn't ask for it."

"My only son. An abomination. Refusing to see the sin of his ways. Refusing to repent. What did I ever do to deserve this?"

"Good question, Mom. Now, if you'll excuse me, I have work to do."

"Work? You're just playing with that filthy dog. So, you refuse to answer God's call, repent, and become a faithful man."

"Mother, I am a faithful man. And she's not a filthy dog. Her name is Guinness. She's the best K-9 I ever had the privilege to train. Now, if you'll excuse us..."

The woman spits in the snow, and that drives me nuts. I don't spit—I drool, and I occasionally puke when I eat the wrong thing —but I know what spitting means. She's disrespecting Shorty, just like a dog who'd pee in my territory to show me that I don't matter. This is Shorty's home, and this woman has no business being rude. I get that, even though I don't understand her words.

She raises her fist in the air.

"You are an abomination. God..."

I'm done with this nonsense. That's enough. This woman will not disrespect Shorty while he's in my care. I growl, bare my teeth, and lunge at her.

"Gather your nonsense and go away. Now!"

Her stare moves from Shorty to me. I get in her face, close enough to get her in one leap, and bark out a storm. Her eyes widen.

She's scared. Good. That's the idea. Get out of here, lady, and leave my Shorty alone.

"Alfred!"

I bark even louder to drown Shorty's voice calling me back. Obedience is one thing; responsibility is another. Shorty is my responsibility. He's my human, and I won't let anyone hurt him, not even his mother.

I'm about to take a bite of her flowing black skirts, just to clarify my message, when she climbs back in her Cadillac and slams the door shut. She takes off, blowing a cloud of snow behind her. I don't blink until she's out of sight.

I turn back to see Shorty's as white as the snow. The joy drained out of him like the air out of a spiked balloon. He looks old, sad, and frail. I know he'll tell me off for ignoring his order, but I don't care. It was for his own good. That's what we, dogs, are here for. To protect our humans whether they like it or not. I won't obey an order that could hurt my human. But he says nothing, and I feel bad.

"Sorry, Shorty. I just tried to help."

We go back in. He takes off his coat, shedding snow all over the linoleum floor, then pours me a bowl of kibble.

"Thanks for getting her off my back, Guinness. You made it easier."

Seriously? He's totally deflated. Easy is not what comes to mind. But, little by little, he gathers some color. By the time I finish breakfast, he's back to being himself.

"That was my mother, you know. She never got used to who I am, and she couldn't stand that Father loved me anyhow. They separated when I was just a teenager. She didn't want me, so she left me with Dad, but she never gave up. Every once in a while, she still comes back to remind me that I'm a useless failure and that God hates me."

I don't get that. I don't know God, but I don't see anything wrong with Shorty. He's my favorite human ever. I love him even better than I loved Jones. Jones was Mom's human, and I just got to tag along. Shorty is mine and only mine. And he's terrific, baldness and beer and all.

"I tried to be the best person I could be, but that wasn't enough for her. I can't be who she wants me to be: A family man with a wife and children, reading the Bible in church every Sunday. But that's not me. I'm lucky to have the Army for a family.

And you. I've never seen anyone silence Mother before. Not even Father. I think I'll keep you around."

As I go to take a nap, I wonder at how strange humans are. Mom accepted me as I was, even though I wasn't who she expected me to be. She loved me just the same. What's wrong with humans? What can't they love each other as they are? I don't get it.

I love Shorty even when he snores, farts, and makes no sense. That's what love is all about, isn't it?

CHAPTER 6

AFTER OBEDIENCE, we moved to combat training. That was so much fun! I got to bark, bite, and fight boogeymen all day long. I woke up every day looking forward to my training. I didn't want it to end.

Shorty was glad to see me so excited about learning. Still, he never failed to remind me that combat is more than physical. It's a calling.

"What you do matters, Guinness. You aren't a pet to lay around, watch TV, and eat snacks all day long. You are a professional and an officer. Your mission is to keep the good guys safe and lock away the bad guys. Be proud of your work and give it all you've got."

So I did.

We trained in an enormous hangar full of tools: rock-filled plastic jugs sounding like explosions when they hit the floor; leather rags; treadmills, and deafening whips louder than gunshots. My favorite was the bite trainer, but I'm getting ahead of myself.

Training K-9s for combat starts with building frustration and bite work. You'd think biting is easy since you've been doing it since you grew teeth. But a professional K-9 bite is nothing like eating Jones's boots or even like chewing on the cat. Professional biting is a complex skill that takes work to master. Here's a mini-tutorial if you want to try it:

#1. Don't bite with your incisors, your front teeth, nor on one side. Bite with your molars, the big teeth at the back of your mouth.

#2. Fill your whole mouth with whatever you're biting, whether it's a rag, a bite pillow, or a perpetrator (that's what we call the bad guys).

#3. When you bite, push forward to grip deeper instead of pulling away. Your incisors will rip and shred, allowing the perpetrator to escape, while your molars will crush and hold the prey.

#4. Never let go.

It may sound easy, but Shorty and I spent weeks and weeks on my bite work. We started with a leather rag, then moved on to the leather pillow. Never burlap. Why, you ask? Because wet leather gets slippery, forcing you to tighten your grip. That's how you build champions, Shorty said.

Once he was happy with my bite and grip, we started training on the bite sleeve—leather too, of course. Shorty put it on above his clothes to teach me to target my bite on the perp's arm and hold on to it. Once I learned that, he started screaming, shouting, and trying to shake me off. He even cracked the whip above my head to make me let go. Are you kidding? I bit even deeper and held on for dear life. The best game ever!

After I got good with the sleeve, we moved on to the boogey-men. They're decoys wearing thick padded suits who pretend to be perpetrators. They appear out of nowhere and threaten you. Your job is to grab them, pull them down, and hold them there until your handler pulls you off.

But I didn't know that until the day Whippy came to help with the training. Shorty drove us to the forest.

"The boogeyman is where you separate the grain from the

chaff. No matter how you check the dog's breeding and test their environmentals, you may still get surprised."

"What are environmentals?" Whippy asked.

"The dog's response to whatever happens around him. Some dogs get scared and back up. Some get mad and push forward. You won't know which is which until you try."

"Why?"

"When a dog faces a threatening challenge he's never seen before, he has no learning to support him. He only has his instinct and the genes he inherited from his ancestors. You won't know what those are until you try them."

"Are you saying she'll fail?"

"Of course not. Guinness will pass with flying colors. I'm not so sure about you."

Whippy snickered and left, then Shorty and I took a walk and fell upon the boogeyman threatening us with a whip.

I started barking like I'd seen a cat and leaped forward, dragging Shorty on his leash, but the boogeyman disappeared in the bushes.

"Good girl, Guinness. Nice job."

"Not really. The creep escaped," I growled. I rose my hackles to look scarier, and I sniffed along the bushes looking for the boogeyman, but he'd vanished. I stayed on high alert though, and when he returned, I was ready.

I leaped and caught him. I filled my mouth with his arm, biting hard, and grabbed him with my legs to pull him closer. I'd give my tail for opposable thumbs, I thought, as I crushed his arm through the padded suit and pulled him to the ground.

"Jesus," the boogeyman gasped.

The smell of onions confirmed what I knew: the boogeyman was Whippy. I growled like a Harley Davidson with a broken muffler and bit even deeper.

He lashed me with the whip, and the pain took my breath

away, but I didn't let go. He hit me again. My left ear was on fire, but I bit even deeper.

"Don't hurt her, you moron," Shorty shouted. "You're not supposed to hit her, just to make noise and scare her, then pull away."

Whippy didn't listen. He slammed his whip against my head again, then kneed me in the throat, but I didn't let go. When I felt his imbalance, I pulled him to the ground, then jumped on him and kept him there.

Shorty pulled me up by the choke collar until I could no longer breathe, and I had to let go. I sat panting by his side as he checked on Whippy.

"Are you hurt?"

Whippy stood up and spat to the side, but he was okay. I never tasted blood, and that padded suit wouldn't let my canines go through.

My ears were on fire though. I cried when Shorty touched them. Even worse, I couldn't reach to lick them, no matter how hard I stuck my tongue out.

We drove back home in silence. Shorty sent me inside and closed the door.

"Why did you hit her?"

"I had to defend myself."

"No, you didn't. This is not what you do. Your job is to teach the dog and build her confidence, not to hurt her. I thought even you knew that much!"

"It's nothing but a bruise. She'll be better in no time, looking forward to the next session."

"She might, but you won't. I'm done with you. Find yourself another trainer."

"Are you kidding?"

"No. I don't want you near my dog ever again."

"You can't train her by yourself."

"That's none of your business. Get lost."

Whippy left. Shorty and I split a beer, and as always, he started talking.

"I'm sorry your ears hurt, Guinness. That won't happen again. There, this helps."

He got some ice cubes in a plastic bag and put them on my head.

I ate them as soon as he looked away. I love ice cubes—they're cold, slippery, and crunchy. I spat out the bag.

"What a loser, to find joy in hurting those weaker than him."

"I beg your pardon?"

"You're still a pup, Guinness, and you still have a lot to learn. That's what I'm here for. To make you into the best K-9 you can be. Someday you'll save somebody's life."

That would be nice. In the meantime, however, I'd like to kill Whippy. I don't think anyone will miss him.

CHAPTER 7

Shorty said I graduated combat training with flying colors. I looked everywhere, but nothing was flying but the crow I'd chased from the bushes, and he was black.

Shorty laughed.

"You're a big girl now, Guinness. Time to look for a job. What would you like to do?"

I hate that question. That's what Mom asked before I joined the Army, a lifetime ago when I was just a puppy. Now I'm a real German shepherd. Nobody ow-oohs over me and rushes to pet me, even though I'm beautiful, Shorty says. My best feature is my tail—long, shiny, and expressive, just like Mom's. That's how I talk to Shorty. That, and my ears. I can't imagine how people can make it through life without tails. Even cats have them, for dog's sake, though they use them all wrong. Instead of wagging their tails when they're happy, they wag them when they're mad. No wonder we don't get along. But I digress.

"Can we go places?"

"We could, but we won't be going to many fun places. We'd go to danger zones where life is hard, and death stares at you from everywhere. We may never come back."

"Bummer."

"On the other hand, you've already aced obedience, tracking, and apprehension. You could further your training and learn to detect explosives. After that, you'd be an MPC, Multi-Purpose Canine. The best-trained dogs ever."

"I'd like that."

"I'll put in an application. I think they'll take us since there's a desperate need for explosive detecting canines. We need them everywhere: in the Army to protect our troops, in police work, at the border, and for TSA to look for bombs and firearms. When they see your record, they'll beg us to join. We should find out in a week or two."

But we didn't have a week or two.

The phone rang in the middle of the night. At first, I thought I was dreaming, since the phone never rings in Shorty's house. His voice was thick with sleep when he answered.

"What?"

He sat up and glanced at me.

"Of course, she's here. Where else could she be?"

We were alone, so I knew he was talking about me. Cool! I never get phone calls, I thought. Who would call me? Then my heart skipped a beat. Did something happen to Mom?

"When? Yesterday? So why didn't you call us then?"

I crawl closer to listen in, but I hear nothing.

"Where?"

Silence.

I miss Mom. Her warm tongue licking away my sorrows, her amber eyes looking into my soul, her wisdom, her love. I seldom thought of her when I was training, but the thought she may be in trouble breaks my heart.

"We'll be there in an hour."

"An hour? Why an hour? Why not now?"

Shorty hangs up and looks at me.

"Your first mission, Guinness. A little girl disappeared last night. Her mom put her to bed, but she was gone in the morning.

Nobody knows what happened. Did she wander out and get lost, or did someone take her? You need to find her."

Me? But I don't do kids! They scream, pull your tail, and stick their fingers in your mouth, and you're supposed to think they're cute! Poppycock! They're just untrained human puppies, but you can't even growl to tell them off, let alone bite them!

Shorty opens the door to send me out as he gets dressed. My hackles are up, and my legs tremble. I'm terrified. As I pee on the bushes, I consider running away. This is too much and too fast. A kid? Really?

I can make it to the forest. Shorty can't catch me. He's improved since I've been training him, but he's old, and he only has two legs. I could live on grass and whatever grows on trees. Bacon maybe?

But I remember what Shorty said about my mission. I trained all this time to save a life someday. Is today someday?

I drag my tail back inside. Shorty's all kitted-up with his helmet and his body armor. He slips my armored vest over my head and buckles it, then starts the Jeep, and I jump in. My heart races. For the first time in my life, I'm scared.

Our lights break a tunnel in the darkness as Shorty drives faster than he should. I smell his excitement and fear, and I feel better knowing that he's scared too.

"That's not how I thought your first job would go, Guinness. But it is what it is. Technically, this is not our problem, but the police folks asked for our help. Apparently, their Malinois isn't getting anywhere."

I sit up a little. There now. Wouldn't that be fun to show this Malinois a thing or two! And save the kid, of course.

"Her parents put her to bed at eight. This morning she was gone. The doors weren't locked—it's that kind of neighborhood. Police have been looking and got nothing. The odds of finding her alive drop by the minute, but they wasted a day before they called us. Moronic neophytes!"

That's strong language for Shorty, who's a mild-mannered man, more into clamming than into fights. But I store that for the next time I meet a Malinois.

The pale house sits in a lovely neighborhood: tall houses surrounded by greenery, attached garages, playscapes, plenty of room to roam. The car lights find a narrow driveway flanked by trees, then the house standing like a ghost amid the turmoil. All around it, police cars blink like Christmas trees. Lights are on everywhere; the whole neighborhood is awake and watching.

Shorty parks outside the yellow tape and shows his ID to the uniforms guarding the entrance. They let us through as cameras flash and people shout questions. They all look forward to seeing us at work, and I choke with fear. I so wish I knew what I'm doing.

CHAPTER 8

With its gleaming floors and tall windows, the house would be lovely if it weren't for the yellow tape across the doors, the people crawling all over to get samples, and the smell of doom.

The odor doesn't come from the house. It comes from the people. To dogs, people smell like they feel: happy, anxious, angry, or scared. Every one of these people works feverishly and sweats fear, and the scent of doom is so thick it chokes me.

Shorty stops in front of a wide uniformed man, whose shoulders are heavy with shiny things, and salutes. The man's neither young nor good-looking, but he exudes authority. Even I can feel it, and I don't give a hoot about authority.

"Thanks for coming, Shorty. I wish they called you sooner."

"So do I, Colonel. This is Guinness, my partner."

"She looks young."

"She is. This is her first mission."

"I see. Well, we can only do the best we can."

Shorty's jaw clenches so hard that I can see the little muscle twitching.

"Which way?"

The man points to the stairs.

"Go, Guinness."

I sniff my way up the stairs, stopping on every step. I've never looked for a person before. I only tracked widgets. You know, the round metal things that go on screws? Shorty taught me how to follow them by their smell. The day I found every single one, he gave me a whole bag of buttered popcorn. Boy, what cramps I had that night! And then diarrhea. And it wasn't pink and sweet-smelling like that time I ate a whole bar of soap. This one was brown and smelled like poop.

After a few steps, I get in a groove. I gain momentum and accelerate, dragging Shorty behind me. He's panting, but he keeps the pace, and we get to the second floor. As I sniff, odors flow through my nostrils into my brain, where they flash like the images from a movie trailer. Old sneakers. Orange. Bubble gum. Baby shampoo.

I turn right. This is the girl's room: An army of stuffed animals; pink walls with unicorns jumping over rainbows. I sniff the pink carpet, the tiny shoes, and the ruffly dress crumpled on the pink armchair. Painfully pink, I think, and I move on to the wardrobe.

A black K-9 in a bulletproof vest stares at me from behind the mirror. I bare my teeth—he does the same. I growl—he growls back. I sniff him. He smells like baby shampoo. What a sissy, I think, and move on to the open window.

Something's different here. New odors of onions, sweat, and fear float in from the old oak tree by the window. There may be ten feet to the ground, but the tree is easy to scale. Even I could do it, and I don't have opposable thumbs.

I glance back. Shorty stands at the other end of the leash, his burning eyes glued on me.

I sit, giving the signal. He unhooks the leash.

"Go."

I leap out the window onto a thick branch, eight feet from the ground. I lose my balance, but I hang on and crawl down the fork to the trunk, where I sniff the onions again. I creep to a lower branch, thankful for all those times Shorty had me walk the narrow plank in agility training, then jump to the ground. I hope Shorty can follow, despite his leg shortage. But whether he does or he doesn't, I have to do what I have to do. I track the scent across the lawn, then through the garden to the forest, sniffing at every step. By now, I'm making good progress, so I speed up, and I leap down the path, stopping to sniff every once in a while.

Oops! The trail's gone. I lost the scent. There's nothing left. It's like whoever was here just flew away. Jeepers!

I turn around and head back, looking for where I lost the trail, but I can't find it. It disappeared. I'm thinking about returning to the house and starting over when I recover the track where the path nears the stream. They must have crossed here.

Sure enough, I pick up the scent on the other side. It's stronger now. I glance back for Shorty, but he's nowhere to be seen. I lost him somewhere, but I have no time to wait. I run down the narrow path between the trees, farther and farther. I see a glimmer of light, and I reach a small cottage. The lights are still on, even though it's got to be almost tomorrow.

I peek through the window—a small room with a table, a narrow bed, and some chairs. And there's my girl.

She sits in a highchair, her pink pajamas sprinkled with cloudy sheep, her cheeks wet with tears, staring at the banana in front of her.

The fat man next to her leans against the table to touch her cheek. She shivers.

"Eat your banana."

"I don't want it. I want my mommy. When can I go home to my mommy?"

"Very soon, if you're a good girl."

"I'm a good girl. I want my mommy."

"Then eat your banana. There, try that."

He sprays a cloud of whipped cream on the banana and brings it to her mouth. She licks it.

"Good girl."

He traces her wet cheeks with his finger, then dips it in whipped cream and holds it to her mouth. She licks it off, and he starts panting like he's been running. He kisses her hair, then her forehead, then her mouth, as her eyes grow wide and scared. He smells like fear, onions, and something else. It's like he's in heat.

"I have something better than that banana for you."

I don't know what that is, but I feel I can't wait anymore. I must go in now.

But I can't!

I've never done this before. I never fought a perpetrator, just the boogeymen. And never alone. I can't do this without Shorty.

What if I went back to get him? He'll never find me otherwise. I'll just get him and return. I look back. Nothing but silent darkness, but I'll follow my nose and find my way.

I head back to get Shorty.

The girl screams.

CHAPTER 9

HE'S TRYING to take off her pajamas, and she won't let him.

He slaps her, and she screams a blood-curdling cry of terror like I've never heard before. I shiver, my heart pounds, and my brain catches fire.

I'm all alone, and I've never done this before. I can't do it. I need to get Shorty right now.

That's the last thing I remember before I blow through the window and grab onto his arm.

He squeals like a pig and lets go of the girl to punch me in the nose. He sticks his fingers in my eyes, and I wish I could bite and break them, but I can't. I can't let go of his arm.

The girl screams. I'd like to tell her not to worry. I've got it. She's all right now that I'm here. But I can only growl, since my mouth is full of the man's thick arm. Every time he moves, I bite harder, like Shorty taught me.

Now what? What do I do? Where's Shorty? He was supposed to be here and get me off him!

The man punches me again and again, but I won't let go. I hang on to his arm with all my weight, trying to pull him to the ground, but he holds on to the table and leans over to grab a knife.

I clutch onto the ground with my claws and pull back, struggling to drag him away, but he's too heavy.

He lifts the knife and plunges it to stab me in the chest. I'm ready for pain, but the blade can't cut through my bulletproof vest, and it feels just like another punch. I bite even deeper.

I taste his blood as he lifts the knife again. This time a searing pain in my hip takes my breath away, since my vest doesn't cover my legs. He sees me flinch, and lifts the knife again. The pain is so sharp that it sets my paw on fire. I slip off his arm and crash to the ground.

He leans over me, his bloody knife ready. An evil grin splits his ugly face as he lifts the blade. I roll over, then leap and grab onto his throat. He drops the knife and falls to the ground.

I hold on to my bite and jump on his chest. He starts snoring, and I can't believe he fell asleep while we're fighting. He's got to be faking it. I get ready to bite deeper.

"Let go, Guinness. I've got him."

Shorty's words come out clipped with his ragged breath. He must have run all the way here. Boy, am I proud of him!

"Are you sure?" I growl.

"Yep."

I let go. The man doesn't move. As he lies snoring on the floor, I limp to the girl in pink pajamas. Streaks of tears cut through the whipped cream on her cheeks, but her face lights up into a smile.

"Hey, it's all good, baby. You're going home."

"Doggy?"

"Sort of. I prefer being called a K-9. It's more respectful, you know."

"Doggy!"

Oh well. I get close enough to lick the whipped cream off her cheeks, but I don't touch the banana. I hate bananas.

"Great job, Guinness." Shorty puts away his weapon, then kneels to check my wounds as two uniforms handcuff the fat man, then take him away on a stretcher.

"Nothing major, Guinness. Just flesh wounds. I bet you won't even need stitches. I'm so proud of you!"

"Thanks. Can we go home now?"

"Soon."

It turns out he lied. It took hours and hours of talking to the officers, then waiting for the photographers to take pictures. The little girl was long gone by then. She cried when her mommy took her away.

"Doggy, Doggy."

"That's all right, Rose. We'll get you a puppy."

"Doggy?"

Shorty and I were left behind to deal with the mess.

"Good work, Guinness. You too, Shorty," the colonel said. He shook Shorty's hand, then offered me some peppered beef jerky.

"Thanks, Colonel. We can only do the best we can."

The colonel laughed.

"Your best wasn't too shabby. I think the girl will be alright. Guinness got here just in time."

"How about the perpetrator?"

"The EMT's think that he'll make it too, though he won't be singing anytime soon."

"Good."

"He's got a history. He's done some time for attempting to kidnap a kid a few years ago. They just let him go last month. This time they'll throw away the key."

What key? And why would you throw it away? What if you need it later? But I have no more energy left to think about some useless key. I'm hungry and thirsty, and my wounds hurt. Even Shorty, who never complains, looks exhausted. His face is ashen and his hands shake as he cleans my cuts.

"Looking good, Guinness. Thank God it wasn't much of a knife. By tomorrow, you'll be as good as new. Good job, partner."

The sun is up by the time he drags himself to bed. No wonder he wouldn't wake up.

CHAPTER 10

IT GOT dark again by the time I woke up. I was desperate to pee, and my belly growled. I needed food, but I didn't want to be rude. Shorty had a long day for a human. He needed his rest.

I waited and waited until I couldn't wait anymore. I went to wake him up.

He lay motionless, staring at the ceiling. I whined, but he didn't move. I barked, but he didn't blink. I licked his hand. It was cold and stiff, and it smelled funky. That's how I knew he was dead. He smelled just like Whiskey, Jones's cat.

That tabby was the worst feline I ever met. He was bigger than me and acted like I didn't belong in Jones's home. Never a nice word or a polite greeting. No matter how gently I jumped on him to invite him to play, he'd fluff himself like a striped toilet brush and hiss, moan, and try to scratch my eyes out.

"He's deaf, dear," Mom said. "He didn't hear you say good morning. When you touched him, he thought you crept behind to scare him."

"What an ice-hole," I said, licking my bloody lip.

Mom gasped.

"Red! Where did you learn this kind of vocabulary?"

I hung my head, flattened my ears, and did my best to look contrite, but she wouldn't relent.

"Where did you hear this? I want to know."

Like really? Where do you think I did? Where do I ever go by myself? Nowhere, ever. Even at the dog park you watch my every move. I learned it at home, of course.

"From Jones."

Mom sits up straight and crinkles her nose to bare her teeth like she does whenever Jones invites her for a bath. She's not crazy about baths, Mom, even though she never hesitates to give me one. But there's something about shampoo that raises her hackles.

"That's not true, Red. Do you know what we call people who say things that are not true?"

"Malinois?"

If you're a German shepherd, being called a Malinois is the worst insult. Everybody knows they are fickle and neurotic. Even Mom. Whenever we misbehaved, she'd growl at us: "Don't act like a Malinois."

Not today. She snorts, and I lie my nose on my paws, doing my best to look repentant. I hope she'll get over it, but no. She's on a roll. I love Mom dearly, but I wish she wouldn't get into these funks. She's got this thing about good manners, especially for the girls. She'd do anything to make an exemplary young lady out of me. Not gonna happen, Mom. Not to me.

"Those who don't tell the truth are liars. And that's an insult. You don't ever want to hear that from anyone. Never. Got it, Red?"

I give up. I roll on my back, presenting my belly in submission. Mom gathers her tail and stomps out, looking dignified, but I bet you she went out to chill. Because deep inside, she knows I'm not lying.

Whenever Jones watches sports, Mom takes off somewhere for a beauty nap. She finds sports noisy and boring. That's when Jones shouts things unsuitable for a lady's ears. He agitates, sputters, and hollers at the fat people playing ball with some sticks as they trample all over each other.

"JD, you lousy piece of crap. You could catch that one if you got off your butt, but no. You lazy fudge!" Except he didn't say "crap" or "fudge."

I didn't watch the TV. I watched him, storing every word for future use. That's where I learned the stuff Mom disapproves of.

But we were talking about Whiskey.

One morning, Jones came out of his bedroom, his eyes red and swollen, his voice broken like the dinner plate I ate the other day. I grabbed a stick and went to cheer him up, but Mom pulled me aside.

"Let him be, Red."

"Why? What's up with him?"

"He's upset. His old buddy Whiskey died."

"How?"

"I don't know. Whiskey was a nasty old coot, really, but he was Jones's best friend, and Jones is heartbroken. He needs time to mourn."

"Why?"

"Because he'll never play with him again, hear him purr, or curl with him for a nap. That's so sad."

That sounded like excellent news to me, but people are weird. I snuck into the bedroom to check out Whiskey. He laid on his pillow as usual, staring at me with wide-open yellow eyes. I talked to him, but he wouldn't answer. Like, what's new? I went closer to sniff him. He was cold, stiff, and smelled funky. Just like Shorty.

Mom sighed.

"That's the smell of death, Red dear. Everybody dies sooner or later."

"What happens when they die?"

"I don't know. People think they'll go somewhere warm, green, and peaceful. Like an all-inclusive resort where you get together with all those you loved and lost. God is supposed to make the bookings."

"Is that true?"

"I don't know, Red, but I'd be surprised. There's no such thing as a free lunch, let alone a free, all-inclusive vacation. Moreover, I wonder why nobody ever comes back. Can it really be that good? And the funny part is that they don't even take their bodies with them. The body stays here to get burned or buried. Like really? Without a body, how can you eat, run, and have fun? You don't even have a tail to wag!"

No tail? That's awful. I hope they're wrong.

"What do you really think happens, Mom?"

"I don't know, baby. I'd love to think we'll all get together to chase squirrels and howl at the moon someday, but I doubt it. I don't think there's anything left. When you die, you die, and it's over."

I went back to smell Whiskey. I looked in his eyes, stepped on his toes, and bit his ear. He didn't even hiss. He was gone.

Jones sniffed as he dug a hole under the old pine tree. He wrapped Whiskey and his toys in his bed, placed him in the hole, and covered him with dirt.

I watched. Mother watched me watch him.

"Don't dig him out, Red."

"Why not?"

"Do you want him back?"

"No."

"So why dig him out?"

Mom was right, as always. I didn't dig out Whiskey, and he never came back.

But Shorty was different. I wanted him back. I wanted our evenings, our beer, and our clamming. I decided I'd dig him out, wherever they put him. But I couldn't. When people came to take him away, they locked me in a cage and left me there. I waited and waited, but nobody came to free me. I was sad and bored, and I needed to pee, so I started barking and wouldn't stop until some woman came.

"What?"

"Can you tell me where they took Shorty?"

She left and came back with a bowl of water and some food.

"There."

"Thanks, ma'am, but that's not what I asked. This is not about food; it's about Shorty. I need to dig him out. Where is he?"

She shrugged and left.

I lay in my cage, waiting, like forever. Nothing happened until Whippy, Shorty's former sidekick, came to see me. For the first time in my life, I was glad to see him.

"Where's Shorty?"

"Sorry, Guinness. Shorty's dead. He won't be back."

He didn't look sorry. He looked pleased, if anything. I felt my hackles rising, but I kept my voice low and sweet.

"I know that, you twit. Mom taught me long ago. Where is he, please?"

"You and me, we'll work together."

"Work together at what? Do you even know how to dig?"

"You're ready for the next stage of your training. I'll make sure you do a great job."

I sighed. I wanted to rip off Whippy's throat, right there and then, but I was in the crate, and he was out. And if I killed him, how would I find Shorty to dig him out?

I put my nose on my paws and thought of what Mom said. I so hope she was wrong. I hope Shorty is someplace green and peaceful, clamming with his father. I hope he told him about paying off his mortgage, whatever that means, and about how the two of us saved a little girl. But somehow, I don't think so.

CHAPTER 11

IF YOU THINK BEING a K-9 is glamorous, think again. The gunfights and the exciting apprehensions only happen in the movies. K-9 life is all about training, training, and more training. I spent day after day looking for explosives, from fertilizer to old-fashioned TNT and new plastics. Honestly, it isn't all that it's cracked up to be. I'd rather look for a burger, a bone, or even a ball, but for some strange reason, all the ATF folks look for are explosives.

But it wasn't all bad. The best part about it was that the Army took Whippy off my back. He wasn't happy.

"But Colonel, I recruited her, then trained her alongside Shorty. Now that he's gone, I'm the only person she trusts. Any other handler would have to start over. Get acquainted with her. Gain her confidence. Build a relationship."

I wonder what he's thinking. I haven't seen him since he was the boogeyman and whipped my ears. And that's too much.

The colonel is the same guy who ran the search that night we looked for the little girl. It feels like a lifetime ago. I wonder if he's got any beef jerky left. Even more, I hope he can see through Whippy's lies.

The colonel shakes his head.

"Hogwash. You aren't qualified to handle her, nor do you have the skills. She's just a puppy, but she's already too smart for you. And she's stubborn as a mule. In a couple of months, she'll tell you exactly what to do with yourself."

"But sir…"

"No but. She'll work with Silver."

Silver? Why not gold, I think, but I don't have time to wonder. The colonel dismisses Whippy and makes a phone call. He then comes to me, pats my head, and slips me a strip of jerky. I'm still drooling when someone knocks at the door.

"Bridget Silver, sir."

"Come in, Bridge. Meet your new partner."

The slight brown woman studies me from my ears to my toes with unblinking dark eyes. She's small and neat, and her dark hair sticks tight to her head. Her uniform is pressed, unlike Shorty's, which always looked like he slept in it. I sniff her. She smells odd, like she's frozen.

"I didn't request a partner, sir."

"I know. You got one anyhow."

"May I ask why?"

"This K-9 lost her handler a few days ago, just as she finished combat training. Shorty was a good man and a great handler, but the stress was too much for his heart. He died the day after their first mission. This K-9 is green but very talented. She has a lot of potential as an explosive detecting K-9. I can't think of anyone better to handle her than you."

"But sir…"

"Bridge, she needs a handler. You need a purpose. Bear died a year ago, and you're still moping. You're in the Army. We have work to do; we can't afford to mope forever. We have a country to protect, people to take care of, and enemies to put to rest. It's time you got back to work."

"But, sir, I work. I've been with Human Resources, and I…"

"I know exactly what you do, Bridge. I've watched you. You're doing the least you can do, get engaged as little as you can, and avoid any social contact to go home and mourn. It's like you're sleepwalking. That's enough. I thought I should give you a break, but that didn't help. If anything, you got worse. You'll get back in action, or you'll quit. Up to you. If the Army is no longer for you, there are other things you could do. You could garden, cook, open a doggy daycare..."

"Sir, I swore off dogs."

"Well, you'll have to swear them on again. Or quit."

I didn't understand all that, but I got the idea. That's how we, dogs, operate. We don't understand many words, but we know feelings. We smell them. I can smell fear, hate, love, anger, and guilt without even trying. Mother is even better. She can tell loneliness, pride, despair, and many others she didn't get to teach me.

Right now, I can smell Bridge's reluctance, sadness, and fear, though I don't understand it. What's she afraid of? The colonel? Getting fired? Me? She didn't blink when she met the colonel's eyes, but she avoided mine.

"You really mean it, sir?"

"I do. I care for you, Bridge, but the life you're living is no life. I won't let you bury yourself alive. I've been patient long enough, and after all this time, you're no better than you were when Bear died. Time to poop or get off the pot."

Bridge glances at me.

"How long do I have to decide?"

"A week. You take her for a partner and get back in action, or you're out."

"That's a sucky choice."

"It is. But you've squandered your other choices. And you may get a sucky choice, but not a sucky dog. This K-9 comes from champion lines. Her sire, Rocky, got a purple heart in Afghanistan. She passed basic training with flying colors. On her rooky mission, she and Shorty saved a kid when others failed. I turned down other handlers who want her. I'll have no trouble finding her a handler, but I'll have a lot of trouble finding you a better dog."

"Yes, sir."

Bridge nods and turns to me. For the first time, her black ice eyes look straight into mine.

"Let's go... What's her name?"

"Guinness. Her name is Guinness."

CHAPTER 12

ONE THING IS SURE: Unlike Shorty, who had trouble keeping his mouth shut, Silver's not a talker. She didn't utter a single word as she drove her green Subaru out of town. The sunset glows over green fields, muddy meadows, and bubblegum-pink apple orchards. We're almost out of town when she turns in the driveway of a tiny blue house smelling like wood smoke and raccoons. She parks under an old pine and lets me out.

I leap in the tall grass and squat under the junipers. I've never been here, but I can tell junipers from far away. I like them, though they're kind of pushy. They're the kind of scent that throws itself at you and fills your nose, like garlic, dead fish, and poop. Speaking about poop: Did you know that every kind of poop smells different? They taste different too, but I won't go into that right now. I can tell horse manure from rabbit pellets, goose guano, or dog poop from a mile away. Poop is one of my areas of expertise, and I can't resist showing off. But I digress.

Silver's house is tidy and frozen, just like her. It's like nobody really lives here: clean wooden floors, gray walls, sparse furniture with nothing out of place: no lonely shoes, no scattered clothes, no open books, no leftovers. Nothing.

Silver drops her bag on the sofa and gets me a bowl of water. I slurp it down, and she brings another.

"Guinness, I hope you don't take it personally, but I can't take you."

I slap my tail on the floor.

"OK."

"I'm sure you're a great dog and all, but I'm done with dogs. I used to have a partner, you see. His name was Bear. He was more than my dog; he was my best friend. We were a team working on detecting explosives. I trained him since he was a pup. We worked, we walked, we did everything together. He was a great dog. There, that's him."

She shows me a framed picture on the wall. Silver, smiling, holding some sort of cup and a dog. He's not bad looking, with sharp dark ears, fierce eyes, and a sable coat, but there's something about him. Something's off, but I can't put my paw on it.

"This is Bear. He died last year, saving my life."

All of a sudden, the room smells like sorrow and guilt, and she looks ready to burst into tears. But she can't do it in front of me. I'm just a stranger, and she has to save face.

She blows her nose and turns to me.

"What makes it worse is that he died because of my mistake. He tried to warn me, but I didn't listen. He died to save me."

Her eyes turn red, and her face crumples like she's about to lose it, but she turns away and heads to the kitchen, where she starts opening cupboards.

"There's no dog food in the house. We could go back out to get you some, but it's hardly worth it for one night. Do you eat anything else?"

"Bacon?"

She shakes her head.

"Popcorn? Cereal? A sandwich?"

She takes out a bag of popcorn and starts the microwave, then opens a can of Labatt's. She sets the popcorn in front of me and takes a swig of beer.

I stare at her.

"Break," she says, giving me permission to eat.

I stare at her. She stares back.

"How about a little beer? I've had a stressful day."

Her lips twist into the shadow of a smile, and she pours me a little beer. I slurp it. She shakes her head and sets the popcorn on the table.

"If we share the beer, we may as well share the popcorn too."

She turns on the TV, and we watch the news. Wars. Famine. Disasters.

"That's terrible. How about a cooking show or a movie?" I ask.

She scrolls through and finds "*Homeward Bound.*"

"How's that?"

I like it, even though that cat, Sassy, is a bully. But I like Shadow and especially Chance. I can totally relate to him eating that underwear. Sadly, neither Jones's nor Shorty's looked that appetizing. By the time old Shadow limps back home, just as you thought he died in that hole, we finished the second bag of popcorn and another Labatt's, and there isn't a dry eye in the house.

She lets me out again. I sniff around to check on things, then I go bless the junipers. It's late, and the black sky is studded with more blinking stars than I can count. I sniff for Shorty's, wondering if he's up there clamming and waiting for me. Then I look for Bear. Is he waiting for Silver?

I return inside to find a folded towel by the sofa.

"This is your bed. It's not much, but it should do for one night. I'll take you back tomorrow morning."

She leaves. I curl on the towel. What will she do if the Army kicks her out? It's none of my business. She's just a stranger. All I know about her is that she drives a Subaru, drinks Labatt's, and misses a dog named Bear. I'd better worry about myself. I hope I don't end up with that loser Whippy. That thought is so depressing that I go back to thinking about Bear. What on earth was wrong with him?

Then it dawns on me. Bear wasn't a German shepherd; he was a freaking Belgian Malinois! That's what was wrong with him! Unless you have four paws and a tail, you won't know about the eternal rivalry between shepherds and Malinois. It's worse than that between the Cowboys and the Giants. We both compete for the title of being the best K-9s. There are even a few morons who think the Malinois are better, but they're wrong. Those neurotic, single-minded, high-strung Belgians lack the balance, the finesse, and the elegance of German shepherds. I'd love to show that Bear a thing or two.

I lie my nose on my paws, and I'm about to fall asleep when I hear steps next door. I jump up and bark, but it's only Silver, looking like a little girl with her tight bun undone and her Hello Kitty pajamas.

"Come," she says, getting my towel. "It's warmer in the bedroom."

I follow her, even though I'm not cold. I curl up on the towel by her bed as she gets under her blankets. I sigh and lie my nose on my paws.

Oh, Shorty, how I miss you! I can't wait to dig you out.

CHAPTER 13

Silver didn't sleep much that night. Neither did I. She kept tossing, turning, and sniffing. I got up and looked everywhere for whatever she was sniffing for, but I couldn't find a thing. There was nothing there, I tell you. If there was anything, I'd find it since a K-9's nose is a hundred times better than a human's. There was nothing there but old sneakers, wood smoke, popcorn, and beer. I looked for Bear's scent, but it's been too long. There's no smell other than hers. It's like nobody ever comes inside this house, not even the plumber. Compared to this, Shorty's place was like a bus stop. People came in and out all the time—the UPS guy, the FedEx guy, a neighbor bringing a beer. Not here.

I wake up before sunrise, as I always do, and I watch her. After fretting the whole night, she finally fell into a restless sleep. She turns from side to side, panting like she's running. She moans, then screams:

"No, Bear. No!"

She's having a nightmare. I lick her face to make her feel better. It's salty.

"It's alright, girl. You're OK."

She opens her eyes and stares at me. For a moment, she smiles like everything's all right with the world. Then it's over.

"You aren't Bear."

You bet your assets. I'm not some neurotic Malinois, even if he's a bomb sniffer and a hero and all that. I'm Guinness Van Jones, German shepherd, K-9 extraordinaire.

But I don't have the heart to say that. I just lick her face once more, and that's like opening the hot water tap. She cries and cries and can't stop.

I don't know what to do. Licking her didn't help. I look away, pretending I can't hear her, but she won't stop. She carries on until my bladder's about to explode, so I walk to the door. She lets me out.

I water the bushes, then sniff around. Oops! Someone was here last night, and I know exactly who—one of these stinky black-and-white fake cats. One spray from those skunks and your nose is out of commission for days. I caught one once when I was young and didn't know any better. It was terrible. Jones washed me in tomato juice. Twice! I was red and salty, but I still stank. I was so embarrassed that I hid under the bed and wouldn't come out. Mom and Jones had to sleep in the guest bedroom for a week.

I consider going after the skunk to get sprayed. I bet you two strips of bacon against an empty bowl of kibble that I'd distract Silver from anything else. But what if she drops me off at the headquarters and I can't even use my nose to find Shorty? Not a good plan.

I stay out as long as I can. When I return, she's stopped crying and washed her face. I look for something to say, but the only thing that comes to mind is: "You've got to be crazy to get so worked up about a darn Malinois." I don't think that would help, so I just act like nothing happened.

She pours Cheerios and milk in two bowls. No sugar. Really? You can afford to gain a pound or two, lady. And so can I. Oh well. I inhale mine, then finish hers while she gets into her uniform.

We drive back the way we came: same fields, same houses,

same bubblegum orchards, now basking in the morning sun. But now she's talking.

"Listen, Guinness. It's not that I don't like you or that you're not a good dog. I think you'll be a great dog someday. But I'm done with dogs. I think I'll get a cat."

I choke. Are you serious? Have you ever even met a cat? I remember that self-centered Whiskey who thought the whole world revolved around him—ill-tempered ice-hole. I sure hope he's not anywhere near Shorty when it's my turn to join him. I clear my throat.

"What an interesting idea. Cats are different."

"Yep. Unlike dogs, they don't get attached to people; they get attached to places. A cat would never die to save me."

You've got that right, sister.

"I don't know what I'll do next. I hope the colonel doesn't throw me out, but I think he will. He prides himself on being true to his word. He's not trying to be mean; he thinks he's helping, but he's wrong. The Army is my safe place where I know everybody. I know who to talk to and who to stay away from. Here I can be myself."

I don't think being herself in the Army does her any good, but what do I know? I used to think Shorty was lonely, but he had his clamming, his father looking after him, and me. Silver has nothing.

"I have a little pension. It's not enough, mind you, but it's better than nothing. I may start a nursery and grow plants. Bushes, flowers, trees. They aren't great company, but at least they won't blow up with a bomb. As for you, you'll be OK. You look great, in person and on paper. The handlers will fight for you."

That reminds me of Whippy. For the first time ever, I wonder if Mother was right. Maybe I should have chosen a lovely family to care for. But it's too late now. I belong to the Army, bless it. I'll have to handle whatever comes my way.

When we get to the headquarters, Silver parks away from the door to give me a chance to check out the bushes. I appreciate it since many humans forget. I do my thing, then we walk to the reception and wait.

Silver sits and wrings her hands. Her worried dark eyes meet mine, and I can see she's changed. If nothing else, she's no longer frozen. She looks like she'll burst into tears.

"I'm sorry, Guinness. No can do."

I lay my nose on my paws and look away. It's her loss. Anyhow, she's nothing like Shorty. No clamming, no country music, no bacon. But, even though I feel rejected, I hope she gets over her freaking Malinois someday.

"Malinois suck."

She stares at me in disbelief.

"What?"

I shrug.

"Sorry. I need to learn to keep my mouth shut. But we German shepherds don't think much of Malinois. Maybe it's professional jealousy, but I wouldn't throw my life away for a Malinois. Especially not a male. They think they hung the moon, but they're nothing but neurotic gigolos looking for their moment of fame."

Her jaw drops. I flatten my ears, and I look away in embarrassment.

"You can go in now."

I follow Silver to the office feeling like a loser. She didn't need my snarky comments, and they didn't do me any good either. But it's too late. We step into the office to find the colonel sitting behind his desk like he never left it. He glances up from his pile of papers and frowns.

"I gave you a week."

"You did. But there was no point to it, really. Might as well get it done and move on."

"I see. What's your decision?"

Silver glances at me, and I look down. Oops! There's half a cookie under the desk. I wonder if I can grab it while they aren't watching. I'm sorry I belittled her dead friend, but a cookie is a cookie. One has to have priorities. I sniff it. White chocolate and raisins, my favorite. I sneak closer.

"I decided I can't do this. I've tried so hard and suffered so much. I decided to return her and move on."

"I'd lie if I said I'm not disappointed. But it's your life and your choice."

I sneak and grab the cookie. It's yummy. Is there another? Nope. This is it. I lay my nose on my paws, trying to figure out how to whip Whippy into shape. I hope Silver finds a way to deal with her guilt.

"But then I changed my mind. I'll take her."

Take her? Take her where?

"So you commit to training her and handling her for her career?"

"I do."

"Why?"

"I thought you wanted me to do it."

"Sure. But why?"

"I'm not sure. Because she can read my thoughts and she was there when I needed her? Because it's time to move on? Because she always speaks her mind? I don't know. Either way, I'll take her."

"Good. Guinness, your explosives training starts tomorrow."

CHAPTER 14

WE STOPPED at PetSmart on the way home. I was delighted. I love shopping, especially for food. I looked for fried chicken. They didn't have it. Blue cheese, maybe? Nope.

This wasn't all that it was cracked up to be. I left Silver struggling to decide on a bed, a shedding brush, and a backpack, and I went in the back to check out the spa. Mud bath, anyone? Nope. Just a standard poodle with a freshly shaved beak having her hair dried. Her white barrel chest and the pom-poms on her hips made her look like a giant popcorn kernel. I choked with laughter. She glared at me.

"I beg your pardon?"

"Sorry. Just something I remembered."

I took off, acting like I was looking to adopt one of the cats in the aquarium. I pretended I didn't hear the poodle's snide comments to a Pekinese having his nails done.

"German shepherd, of course. How pedestrian. She wouldn't know chic if it hit her in the muzzle."

The Pekinese yapped something, but I don't speak Chinese. Moreover, the orange cat started hissing, and her compatriots followed. Wouldn't it be fun to get one for Silver, I thought? And I could chase it, too. I tried to squeeze back through the employee door when Silver clipped her leash to my collar.

"What are you doing here? I thought I lost you."

I smiled and bared my teeth to the orange. He hissed like a defective hairdryer.

"Just making new friends. You?"

Silver shook her head.

"Let's get you some food."

Great idea, I thought. But then I saw they had nothing there but kibble. No chicken, no bacon, not even popcorn. Nothing but kibble. Like, seriously?

"You like chicken or lamb?"

"Chicken? Where?"

She pointed to a bag of kibble. No, thanks.

"I prefer popcorn. Or a sandwich."

"You can't live on popcorn and sandwiches."

"Try me."

She bought a forty-pound bag of kibble with the picture of a Malinois on it. I smirked.

"Now, now, Guinness. Get over it. It just happens to be the large breed food with joint protection. It's not my fault they put the picture of a Malinois on it."

True that. But that's how advertising works. They make you think they'll give you happiness, but they sell you what they have. Like those stupid dogs, crazy about tick protection. Or the smiling humans sweating on their bikes. That's how they snag you. Even I fell for it. I wanted to make Shorty happy, so I tried to get him a blue pill, but I couldn't find his credit card.

We get home. Silver lays my bed in the bedroom and opens a Labatt's.

"Yes, please."

"That's not good for you," she says, pouring a little in my bowl. "Who taught you to drink beer?"

"Shorty. But he drank Bud Light."

She takes something out of the freezer and pops it in the microwave, then pours a cup of the new kibble in my bowl.

"There."

I sniff it from far away.

"Why don't I wait until your stuff is ready. Tell me, what changed your mind?"

She shrugs.

"I'm not a cat person. And the nursery's nothing but a pipe dream. I don't have a green thumb. I even hate mowing the grass."

I check her thumbs. Sure enough, they're both brown.

"So?"

"There aren't many things I'm good at. I don't garden; I don't cook; I'm not good with people. But I'm good with dogs. I can hear their thoughts."

"And?"

"I thought about what you said in the waiting room. You're right. Bear was the center of his universe, not me. It just dawned on me that he didn't die to save my life. He died for his neurosis. Anyhow, here we are."

The microwave beeps, and she takes out something smelling worse than dog food.

"What is it?"

"Beef Merlot with broccoli."

"Are you sure? Did you sniff it?"

"Well, you're the sniffing specialist around here. You tell me."

I sniff again. There may be a little beef and even some dead broccoli, but I can't recognize a dozen other things. You see, we dogs smell things differently than humans. Humans smell the composite and come up with a label. Like when you walk into Grandma's house for Christmas and the scent bowls you down, you think apple pie. I smell apples, cinnamon, butter, sugar, and nutmeg. I put them together, and I think apple pie. But the things in her meal? I don't know what they are, but I don't believe they're food.

"Read the label."

"Water. Onions. Modified corn starch. Beef flavor. Seasoned cooked beef and binder product. Maltodextrin. Potassium chloride. Potassium phosphate."

She throws the plate in the trash, then takes another sip of Labatt's.

"How about popcorn? Or you can have my kibble."

That evening, we lie on the sofa as she scratches my ears and tells me about the job.

"You won't have any trouble sniffing; you're a natural. The hard part is knowing when to signal me. They'll present you with all sorts of odors. Some matter, some don't. You'll have to learn those that have anything to do with explosives and point them out to me."

"How?"

"You sit by it. You don't paw at it, you don't rip it apart, and you don't bite it."

"Why not?"

She scratches her head with her front paw. How odd! I always use my hind paws or my teeth.

"Guinness, do you know what a bomb is?"

"I do. I watched war movies with Jones. It's something that blows up to destroy everything around it."

"Precisely. That's why you don't touch the bomb. You point it out to me, and I call the specialist who deactivates it. Your job is to find it, theirs to get rid of it."

"What if I miss it?"

"You won't. That's why we'll train. You won't miss it once you know what you're looking for."

I hope she's right. But how will I know what to look for if I've never seen it?

"Relax, Guinness. That's what training is all about. You'll be a shining star, I know it."

I take in a deep breath and mumble to myself: Don't let the bastages get you down.

"What?"

"That's what Jones said when things weren't going well. Except he didn't say 'bastages.'"

"He was a wise man."

"He still is. I surely hope he's not dead. If he died, who'll take care of Mom?"

"How long since you saw them, Guinness?"

"I last saw them in summer, when Shorty took me. I was a few months old."

"Not too long then. You know what?"

"No."

"If we make it through the training, we'll go visit them before we get deployed."

"Deployed?"

"Yes. That's when the Army sends us somewhere to look for mines and protect our soldiers."

"Where?"

"The Middle East, probably. Iraq or Afghanistan."

"Have you been there? How is it?"

"Different. The good news is that it's warm. And we'll be together with our brothers in arms."

"What's the bad news?'

"The bad news is that the enemy wants to kill us. And they often succeed."

CHAPTER 15

THE NEXT DAY we started explosive detection. I was so busy that I forgot about Iraq, Afghanistan, and enemies.

We came to this massive hangar with a gleaming white floor covered by rows of metal cans. There's nothing but cans, six feet apart, as far as the eye can see. And two other K-9 teams. Two rows ahead of us, a yellow Lab drags a tall black man on his leash. Further along, a sable Malinois glares at me down his nose then moves on, pulling a blonde woman in his wake. Yikes! I'm getting tired of these freaking Malinois.

They've clearly been here before. The K-9s swiftly sniff their way from one can to the other, dragging their handlers behind. What the heck, I can do that with the best of them, I think, and I launch in hot pursuit, but Silver holds me back.

"Not so fast, Sparky. You first need to learn what to look for."

She takes me to a line of cans standing by the wall at the far side of the building.

"Check these out. These are the smells you need to find."

I sniff the first one. Acrid and chemical. Totally unattractive. I move to the next. This one is even acrider but less chemical. So is the following. And the next.

I'd be lying if I said they smell like crap. Crap smells good. But this? Nah. Not a single one in the lot is worth finding if you ask me. I wouldn't roll in any of them if you paid me in popcorn. But maybe for bacon…Oh well. If that's what Silver wants me to find, I'll find it.

We start on the grid, looking for the awful odors that Silver had me learn. I sniff gently, wary of having my delicate nose scorched by those miserable fumes.

Mamma Mia! This is heaven! The first one's manure. Then cat litter. Then bacon!

I paw at the can of bacon, struggling to open it. Silver freezes.

"Guinness! What are you doing? You're supposed to sit!"

"Relax, it's not a bomb. It's bacon! I'm trying to get it. Don't you want some?"

Silver sighs.

"There's no bacon in there, Guinness. Just the smell of it."

"How do you get the smell without the bacon?"

"Well, there is a little bacon, but not much. And it's not there for you to eat."

"Then what is it there for?"

"It's there to do exactly what it did. Distract you from your work. We waste our time talking about bacon when you have a hundred cans to check and find what we talked about: dynamite, TNT, water gel, RDX, urea nitrate, and hydrogen peroxide."

My bad. I hang my head and flatten my ears. I was not a good dog.

I start again along the row of cans, smelling each one and trying to ignore the fascinating smells. Rose Dove! I love rose soap, even though it gives me diarrhea. Mowed grass. Dead fish, aged. Heavenly!

I reluctantly move on.

Oops! Someone peed here. It's got to be the yellow lab.

I glance to see what he does. He's clearly ahead in his training, and I can use all the help I can get. He sniffs, then sits by a can a few rows down. His handler pets him and gives him a snack.

I stare at Silver.

"How about a snack?"

"As soon as you find what we're looking for."

I try to memorize the can the lab sat by, but they all look the same. I move on. Pepperoni. Gasoline. Olive oil.

Oops! This one's different. It smells like garlic, but it's not. It's faint, but sharp and persistent. It lingers, scratching the inside of my nostrils. I sit.

"Good girl, Guinness. Nice job," Silver says, offering me a snack.

I smell it. It's kibble.

"Seriously? After all this work? I can get that at home."

"No longer, baby. No more free food for you. From now on, you'll have to work for your food, just like everyone else."

"How about some popcorn, at least?"

"Not here. We have to go by the book."

"Tonight?"

Silver hides her smile. I take the kibble and move to the next can, then the next.

That evening we eat popcorn and watch *Babe*, the shepherd pig. Silver thought it would motivate me with my training.

"He's got a heck of a way with sheep," I say, as he parlays his flock into reorganizing.

"He's a pig, not a shepherd. Unlike you, he doesn't have shepherding in his DNA. But he's doing a good job. He uses his strengths to overcome his weaknesses."

"I guess I'm envious. I'd rather work with sheep than with cans. They're more fun. They escape, and you get to run after them. You can run after them even if they don't escape. And you're outside."

"Me too. But remember, this is just the beginning of your training. As soon as we're done with the cans, we'll go outside."

"When?"

"After you learn all the smells. You've got to be 100 percent accurate."

"What's that?"

"When you find every explosive, no matter how strong or how faint the smell is, and you never make mistakes."

"When will that be?"

"In a few weeks, hopefully."

"And afterward?"

"We'll get our assignment and go to real work."

"Where?"

"Wherever they send us. In an airport, checking people's luggage, with a police department, or with the military. Wherever they need us the most. The demand for explosive detection K-9s went through the roof after 9/11. There's never enough of them, even though we import oodles from Europe. You'll be in big demand, Guinness."

"I don't want to be in big demand."

"What do you want, then?"

"I want to have fun. Learn things. Go places."

"We'll do that too. I got an idea. If you are as good as I think you will be, we'll go compete in NORT."

"What's NORT?"

"The National Odor Recognition Test. That's like the Olympics of explosive detecting K-9s. The best K-9s in the country and their handlers compete to recognize odors, perform searches, and find firearms and ammunition. We'll also learn the newest trends in homemade explosives."

Compete? That's me, all right. I'll get to show them who's boss.

"Will there be any Malinois at NORT?"

"Probably."

"Let's go then!"

CHAPTER 16

I DIDN'T REALLY EXPECT to win NORT. Neither did Silver, I'm sure. She just wanted to challenge me to get better while I tried to show her that a German shepherd is better than a Malinois any day of the week.

It turns out that NORT wasn't just for German shepherds and Malinois. At NORT, K-9s came in all sizes, colors, and shapes: Labradors, Dutch shepherds, golden retrievers. There were even some pathetic creatures that didn't look like dogs. I was just about to pounce after some sort of misshapen cat with crooked legs and a dogged attitude when Silver pulled me back.

"Stop that, Guinness. You'll get us disqualified. You're not supposed to attack your competitors."

"Competitors? Are you serious? That thing over there is competing in NORT?"

"Don't be racist, Guinness. This is not the Westminster Dog Show. Here, breed doesn't matter. What matters is how good you are. So what if he's a mixed breed? His focus and his nose may be better than yours. What will you think if he wins?"

If he wins? What will I think if he wins? I will be humiliated forever. I'll never be able to hold my tail up again. Lose to that?

I snapped to attention and followed Silver's commands like I meant business. I didn't even glance at the evil little thing when he passed by and growled at me as if he were a real dog. Phew! What an abomination! I was bigger than that when I was twelve weeks old. Prettier, too, I bet. I never had a pig snout and a thin, bald tail like a giant rat. I told him all that, by the way. I held my head up and waved my tail in dismissal, without ever looking his way. When he started yapping like a maniac, I pretended I had nothing to do with it. His poor handler didn't know what hit him, but Silver gave me the "I know you're up to something" look. She suspected it was me, but she couldn't be sure. Humans, even the smart ones, don't get these signals. How could they? They have no tails, and they can't even move their ears. It's a wonder they can communicate at all. Either way, that mutt was gone before the finals while I qualified. Silver was ecstatic.

"Good job, Guinness. Few dogs ever get a NORT Finalist certificate."

That didn't impress me one bit, since I can't read. I don't even have a wall to hang it on. But I was happy for Silver. That meant a lot to her. Personally, I'd rather have a bone. Maybe coming?

"What will they give us if we win? A cake? A bone? A hamburger, at least?"

"The first three get medals. The winner gets a trophy."

"A trophy?"

"Yep. Like a cup."

"A cup of what?"

"Just a cup. With ribbons and such."

Ribbons? Are you serious? And a cup? I don't need a cup. I have two bowls, one for water and one for food, and they work just fine. Humans are silly, I tell you. What's the point of giving a certificate to someone who can't read, a medal to someone who already has a tag on their collar, or an empty cup to someone who has two bowls? And it's not just me. I'll bet you two bones against a rolled newspaper that the other K-9s can't read either.

Oh well. I wasn't competing for the cup, anyhow. I was

competing for bragging rights and for Silver. So, I forgot about the stupid cup and pushed on.

There were six of us left in the finals. Me, a chocolate Lab, another German shepherd, and three Malinois. Three of them! Overachievers!

The first test was to take our handlers through the field of smelly cans, identify the explosives and sit by them to signal our handlers.

As we sit in a windowless room with the other teams waiting for our turn, I smell Silver's stress sweat as she eyeballs the Malinois.

"Guinness, don't forget that accuracy trumps speed," she whispers.

I lick her hand to make her feel better.

"Relax."

"There are sixty cans with twenty odors, and you have to find every single one of them!"

"Roger that."

She pets me, but her hands are cold and clammy. Fortunately, we don't have long to wait. They call us, the door opens, and we're in the field of metal cans.

"Now's your time, Guinness."

I feel her heart pumping at the end of her leash as I pull her from can to can. Detergent. Ancho chiles. Gasoline. Cloves. Turpentine. Hickory. Garlic.

I sit next to the can of TNT.

Silver raises her hand to signal, and the referee nods.

"Go, Guinness."

I burst ahead, pulling Silver with me. Latex. Alcohol. Lard. Iodine. Coffee.

I sit next to the fertilizer. Silver raises her hand. The referee nods.

"Go, Guinness."

Milk. Lanoline. Onions. Cinnamon. I sit next to the hydrogen peroxide. Silver raises her hand. The referee nods.

Lemongrass. Acrylics. Bacon.

I ignore it and push forward.

Popcorn.

Like really?

I sit next to the gunpowder, which is the last can in the field. Silver raises her hand, the referee nods, and just like that, we're out, and Silver hugs me with tears in her eyes.

"We won?"

"Not yet, but you did a fantastic job. I'm so proud of you!"

I resist the urge to pull away. I'm not much into PDA, to be honest, but I don't want to hurt her feelings. I clear my throat.

"Is there some bacon in my future?"

"As soon as we get home."

We wait until they call the results. The Lab's out. So is the other German shepherd and one of the Malinois.

There are three of us left for the final phase. No matter what, Silver will get a medal, and she's happy beyond belief.

I'm happy too. Not for the medal. For the bacon.

And I'm looking forward to showing those Malinois what's what.

CHAPTER 17

I WOKE up and remembered it was the day of the NORT finale. I did an upward dog, then a downward dog, then I shook. I was ready.

I came to the kitchen looking for breakfast.

"You slept like a log," Silver says, pouring milk over my Cheerios.

"Sugar?"

"It's not good for you." She adds a spoonful of sugar, and I inhale my breakfast, wondering about sleeping logs. I've never seen one wake up, not even when I peed on them. I thought they were dead. It turns out they're just asleep. Go figure.

"How about you?" I ask, cleaning up the milk I spilled on the floor.

"I'm fine."

I don't think so. Silver's tidy as usual, with her tight bun and her clean uniform, but her tired red eyes and her crumpled face show me she didn't get any sleep.

"What's wrong, girl? We did OK! I even got you a medal!"

"You did great. But that was yesterday. Today's the real deal. We'll have a mission search, a box search, a vehicle search, and then the field search. The cans were easy. This is going to be tricky. You'll have to look into every nook and cranny, and you won't even know what you're looking for."

"Piece of cake, baby. If those stinky Malinois can do it, I can too. Just watch me."

Silver shakes her head. That's what people do. If she were a dog, she'd shake all over, like Mom, to show me that I'm full of it.

"I'm glad you're feeling confident, Guinness, but too much confidence is dangerous. This is all about paying attention and being thorough. Being cocky may trip you up. A little paranoia will take you further."

"What's paranoia?"

"It's when you think that everybody's out to get you."

Are you kidding? I don't think they are; I know they are. My paranoia's just fine, thank you.

The Malinois and I take turns through the searches. I find some fertilizer in a box, a couple of spent cartridges in the hangar, and a suspicious device that turns out to be an IED inside the car's tire. All that's left is the field search. We all load into a truck—the Malinois, their handlers, Silver, and me—and we get moving.

The truck drops from pothole to pothole, creaking like it's about to fall apart. I sit between Silver's legs, grabbing on to the floor, and study my two opponents. The one on the left is slate gray with sharp dark ears and fierce eyes. He'd be handsome if he weren't a Malinois. Well, maybe he's handsome anyhow.

He eyeballs me and slaps his tail on the floor.

"Hello, baby. How's it going?"

"Fine, thanks. And you?"

"Frank, are you fraternizing with the enemy or just trying to distract her?" asks the one on the right. He's almost black but for his pink tongue hanging sideways to his knees.

"Shut up, Jesse. She's not the enemy; she's just the competition. We may as well be civil. What's your name, beautiful?"

"Guinness. Guinness Van Jones."

"Are you Dutch?" Jesse asks.

"Of course not. I'm a German shepherd." I lift my chin to show off the elegant line of my long black muzzle. "You boys Belgian, I presume. Are you related?"

"Yep. Jesse's my littermate. We enrolled together. We're a military family. Father was a Marine."

"So was mine."

"Don't say! Hey, what are you doing tonight?"

Who knows? Eating bacon, I hope, but I don't have to answer since the truck stops.

"The first team out!"

"See you guys later." Jesse pulls his handler to the field.

We sit and wait. The tension is thick enough to bite through when Jesse returns and mumbles something in Belgian to his brother.

Frank's next. He drags his handler out, and we wait again. Jesse lays his muzzle on his feet, pretending to sleep.

"How was it?" I ask.

He opens one yellow eye.

"Lousy. There's a whole field out there full of crap you need to search. You'd better have a system; otherwise, you'll lose track."

He's right. I jump out of the truck in a fenced grass field full of things. Piles of tires. Debris. A shed. Scattered barrels. A mountain of boxes. A bunch of trees and bushes.

"Crap," Silver mumbles. I'm not sure if it's a command, but it sounds like a good idea.

"Search!"

System, he said. I'll show you system.

I start left and sniff everything to the fence, then turn around and come back to the other wall, stopping by to check everything on my way. I smell the tires, crawl under a bush, sniff the boxes. I sit.

Silver raises her hand, and the observer nods. She finds the gun hidden inside a box and takes it.

"Search."

I sniff around the shed, then go inside and sniff the toolbox. I get out again, and I smell the fence as I get to it, then turn around again, in a grid pattern. I sit by the pine tree.

Silver signals.

The observer nods. Silver picks up the ammunition hidden in the branches, and we move on forward, always in a tight grid pattern. We find a bag of fertilizer in a box, a box of ammunition inside a truck tire, then a grenade under a rusty wheelbarrow.

I'm done, but to be extra-sure, I scan the field again, in the opposite direction this time. That's it.

I sit and look at Silver.

"Are you sure?"

I slap my tail to the ground. Silver calls it.

"We're done, sir."

"Congratulations."

The boys don't speak to me on the way back. They pretend to be asleep, but I know better.

The bacon was delicious, crisp, flavorful, and crunchy. Silver sat on the sofa holding the cup and watched me eat as my medal clanged against my bowl.

"Have some," I said. "It's better than that empty cup! Or at least pour a beer in it!"

"I'm so proud of you, Guinness. Is there anything else you'd like besides that bacon?"

I lick my bowl clean.

"Now that you mention it, there is one thing."

"What?"

"I'd like to visit Mom."

CHAPTER 18

WINNING NORT was the high point of my training. Even more so after Silver started drinking her coffee out of her cup. I felt like I got her something useful. Plus, we were on vacation. We went out for long walks and watched movies with popcorn every evening. Life was good.

Until the day Silver had a long talk with the colonel, and she came out looking grim. We drove home in silence. I wondered what was up. She poured us a beer, then looked at me with teary eyes.

"Guinness, you know I love you."

My hackles went up. That was no good. Whatever was coming was awful news. I took a deep breath and steeled myself to get it.

"What is it? Something wrong with Mom? Are you about to die too? Have you changed your mind and decided to get a cat instead of me?"

Silver shook her head.

"Guinness, have you ever thought about having puppies?"

"Poppies? I'd rather have some bacon."

"Puppies. Like small dogs."

"I had puppies. My littermates: Yellow, Black, Green, Brown, White, and Purple. They were fun. I was Red."

"No. I mean having your own puppies."

"They were my own. My own brothers and sisters."

"Would you like to be a mom?"

I freeze.

"Are you kidding? I can't be Mom."

"Why not?"

"I'm not smart enough. And I don't have the patience. Mom's a genius. I'm nothing like her. If you're going to get me something, get me a cat. Chasing them is a good sport."

Silver sighs.

"Good then. The colonel told me you'll have to get spayed before we deploy."

"What's spayed?"

"Guinness, the Army is a full-time job. You've got to give it all you've got. They can't have working K-9s having puppies on the base. That's why you'll have surgery before we go, to make sure you don't have puppies."

"Is that like having a bath?"

I hate baths. I'd swim all day, and I'd roll in the mud forever, but a bath? No, thanks. It's not the water; it's the shampoo. I work hard every day to hold on to my good smells. Whenever I find something smelling sexy, I'll roll in it, whether it's dead fish, horse manure, or poop. But if they give you a bath, it's all over. You end up fluffy and smelling like perfume. Embarrassing! Don't get me wrong now, I love soap, especially Rose Dove, even though it gives me diarrhea. That's why I limit myself to half a bar.

Silver sighs.

"Not quite, but it's not much fun. But I'll have some bacon for you when you come through."

"Come through? Come through what?"

She takes me out, even though I don't need to go. I wonder if it's just to change the subject. But then we drive to the vet, and I forget. She hugs me and sniffs.

"You're going to be all right. This is the best vet this side of the

Atlantic."

She's gone before I can ask anything else, and a girl in scrubs leads me to an exam room, giving a wide berth to a barking bulldog wearing a lampshade.

"What happened to you, Bully? They ran out of lamps?"

He sputters toward me, but his leash holds him back.

"Don't forget you're plugged in," I say, then they give me a shot, and I fall into a burst of colors. I'm twirling faster and faster inside a swirl of rainbows. I remember Shorty telling Whippy about his old dog crossing the rainbow bridge, and I wonder. Will I cross it too? If I don't return, who'll take care of Silver? She's my responsibility. I should have planned who to leave her to.

I wake up to Silver watching me. That, I like. What I don't like is the lampshade around my neck. What's with these people and their lamps?

"How are you, Guinness?"

I'm groggy, and my tongue is so dry I can barely mumble. But I don't want to worry Silver.

"Good. You?"

She pets my head, but she looks like she's far away.

"Does it hurt?"

"Sort of. But I'm mainly hungry. Did you say bacon?"

She shakes her head.

"One day, you're going to die from a heart attack. You need to learn to like vegetables. And fruit."

"I do."

"Which?"

"Grapes. Raisins. White chocolate."

When we get home, she cooks my bacon. It smokes and sizzles, and I slobber as the scent fills my nose.

"There. But that's just for tonight. Starting tomorrow, we'll eat healthily."

I ignore her words but I inhale the bacon, every little crumb of it. She fills my water bowl and sighs.

"You know, Guinness, I always wanted children. That's like puppies for humans."

"I know. I met one. It tasted great. It was covered in whipped cream. So what happened?"

"When I was sixteen, I had a boyfriend; I became pregnant. That's like expecting puppies."

"And?"

She looks away to hide the tears streaming down her cheeks. She sighs and hugs herself.

"I was too young. The baby died inside me, and he wouldn't come out. They had to take him out to save my life. I could never have kids after that."

Her sorrow is so raw that I can feel her suffering, even through my fogged brain.

"I'm sorry, Silver." I lick her face as best I can from inside that darn lamp shade, and I almost scoop out one eye, but she doesn't complain.

"To my people, being a woman was all about having kids. If I couldn't have kids, it was like I stopped being a woman. My boyfriend left me. Even my mom ignored me to focus on my sisters. That's how I got into dogs. Dogs didn't care whether I had kids. They loved me just as I was. So I joined the Army as a K-9 handler. That was my best decision ever. My second one was to take you."

I don't understand what she says, but I feel her pain. And I'm sorry.

But I'm fogged and tired. My belly is on fire like they ripped something out, and that darn lamp shade cuts me away from Silver and the world. I can't even lick the burn in my belly. So I lick her once more, then I lay down to rest. She sniffs.

"Thanks, Guinness. I hope this won't leave you hollow like it left me."

I'm sorry she hurts. My belly's on fire, but her pain is in her soul. That's got to hurt worse.

CHAPTER 19

THE DAYS GOT SHORTER and the leaves started turning. Vacation was over, and it was time to go. I wasn't ready to get deployed, but I don't think anyone ever is. Not even Silver, though she knew what was coming.

She packed Bear's picture, my medal, her trophy, and some popcorn. She added some clothes for herself and my bulletproof vest. I have no other clothes, so I pack light, but I'm always dressed for the occasion.

The trip to Afghanistan was long and not much fun. After all the movies I'd seen, I couldn't wait to fly, but it turns out that I was cargo. I spent long hours locked in a crate with no view and no entertainment other than the engine noise. And the odors.

Odors being one of my areas of expertise, I started sniffing the cargo and making up stories about them to pass the time.

There were gasoline and oil and all the usual mechanical smells, but there were some fascinating scents here and there. The peppered pastrami and pickles to my left got me drooling like crazy and made my stomach growl. Somebody bringing home a gift of food, I thought. The golf bag next to me gave a faint whiff of cat pee. They must have locked the cat with the bag, and the cat made sure it won't happen again. From somewhere up in front, I sniffed a full set of essential oils: bergamot, chamomile, eucalyptus, lavender—the whole lot. One of those naturopaths hell-bent on curing cancer with tea-tree oil?

All of a sudden, I sniff a dog.

Really?

I sniff again. I'll be darned if that's not a Labrador, somewhere behind me.

"Hey! Buddy!"

Claws scratch the floor, then someone barks.

"Hey. Where are you?"

"A few bags ahead, I think. How's it going?"

"Awful! I need help!"

She sounds miserable. I am too, but I'm a German shepherd, so I can't show it. It would be beneath my dignity. I'd rather chew on my tail and struggle to hold my bladder than ask for help.

"What's your problem, buddy?"

"I've been locked in this cage for ages. I'm hungry, I'm thirsty, and I need to pee."

"Roger that. Same here. Who are you?"

"I'm Corporal Butter. I'm a K-9 en route to Afghanistan. You?"

"Name's Guinness. Guinness Van Jones. We'll get there, buddy. Just relax."

"I can't relax. I need to pee."

I swear silently and cross my legs.

"Me too. But it may take a while. How about peeing in a corner?"

"I can't pee in my crate! I've never done that, not even when I was a puppy!"

I've never done that either, but it ain't looking like any juniper bushes are coming my way soon. I sigh and squeeze into a corner to squat, but I change my mind. Boys raise their legs and pee sideways. What if I try it?

I focus on the cat-smelling golf bag, and lift my leg. That feels weird, with the plane moving under me and all. Oh well. I let go, and the golden stream flows out my crate and sprays the bag like it's a mailbox. Hah! There may be a few drops inside, but that's nothing. I'll call this a success.

"Hey, Butter?"

"Yes."

"Are you a girl?"

"Of course."

"Me too. Have you ever peed like a boy?"

"No."

"How about trying? I just did, and I feel so much better. And my cage is almost clean."

I hear shuffling, scratching, and movement, then running water; finally, a sigh of relief.

"Thanks, Guinness. This is much better. I'm still hungry and thirsty, but I'm better. I hate soiling myself."

"Is this your first deployment?"

"Nope. My third. You?"

"My first. What do you do?"

"I sniff explosives. No matter where you go in Afghanistan, tons of IEDs, Improvised Explosive Devices, are ready to explode. Even when they don't kill anyone, they prevent people from living their lives, working their fields, and sending their kids to school. After we clear them, they get to live a better life."

"You must feel so proud."

"Sometimes. But I mostly feel tired. My handler and I have done this so many times that it's getting old."

"You like your handler?"

"I love him. I love his wife and the kids even more. It was hard for us to leave our family and come back here. I hope to retire soon."

"What will you do when you retire?"

"Take long walks? Play with the kids? Chase cats? I don't know, but I can't wait to find out."

I lay in my crate with my nose on my paws, thinking about Silver. What will she do if she retires? She has no kids. No hobbies. She doesn't have anyone but me. And for some reason, that reminds me of Mom.

CHAPTER 20

Silver kept her word. After NORT, we went to visit Mom. It was both wonderful and strange to see my old home, the yard, the trees, the leaves turning. It was like I'd never left.

Silver rang the doorbell. Mom warned us off, and her voice made me feel all warm and squishy inside, even though I knew she thought we were the mailman.

Jones opened the door wearing his old red sweater, the one with the elbow hole I ate when he forgot me in the library. He looked at Silver, then at me. His jaw dropped, and he broke into tears. I put my paws on his shoulders and licked them off before anyone could see them.

"Red!"

"Who?"

The door flung open, and Mom flew out. She was smaller than I remembered; her black muzzle had turned gray, and her amber eyes cloudy, but her lovely pink tongue licked my nose just like she used to.

"Mom!"

"Red! It is you!"

"Mom!"

We jumped, barked, and played together, rolling around in

the yard like puppies. Jones wiped his eyes with his sleeve, then blew his nose. Silver pretended not to notice.

"Thank you for bringing her, Miss…"

"Sergeant Silver."

"Thank you for bringing her, Sergeant Silver. This means a lot to Maddie and me. Red was our last pup since we're both too old to carry on. How's she doing?"

"She's doing fantastic. She just won NORT, which is like the Olympics for explosives detecting canines. There."

Silver handed him a picture of me trying to eat the medal dangling around my neck. It's not my best picture, since I had to cross my eyes to see the medal, but she's very proud of it. She framed it and put it on the wall next to Bear's photo.

"I brought this for you. There she is, winning NORT."

Jones choked, and I didn't know if he was laughing or crying. Mom licked my face.

"I'm so proud of you, Red."

"I love you, Mom."

As we got ready to leave, Jones asked Silver, "Did you know she can sing?"

Silver looked at him like he'd lost it.

"Guinness?"

"Yep. Watch."

He fumbles with his phone, and just like that, the call of my people stirs my soul. Mom lifts her muzzle to the sky and starts singing. I can't help but follow, and Jones joins us.

"A time to be born, a time to die; a time to plant, a time to reap; A time to kill, a time to heal."

"A time to laugh, a time to weep," Silver sings along, wiping her eyes.

That was the last time I saw Mom.

Thinking of her makes me choke. I sigh and turn in my cage, trying to find a better spot, but, after all this time, I'm running out of spots.

"Guinness?"

"Yes, Butter."

"What are you going to do in Afghanistan?"

"Whatever they tell me, I guess."

"Are you an explosive sniffing dog? Will you go looking for land mines?

"I think so."

"We may work together."

"That would be nice. I could use a friend."

"Me too."

I wake up as they drag my crate through the door. I get a glimpse of a concrete floor and dark green walls before they store me with the rest of the luggage.

"Guinness?" Butter calls.

"Yes?"

"You OK?"

She sounds really close, so I peek through the holes of my crate, looking for her in the pile of luggage. I can't see her, but I can smell her, a soothing smell of Labrador. I love Labradors. They are the kindest, nicest, friendliest dogs in the world. Better than German shepherds, you ask? Well. We German shepherds don't think about ourselves as dogs. We're people.

"I'm hanging in there. You?"

"Me too. Hey Guinness?"

"Yes?"

"We girls ought to get together. Look me up when you land. I'm an explosive detecting canine. My handler's name is Brown. You?"

"I'm an MPC, multi-purpose K9. My handler's name is Silver. They also call her Bridge."

"Bridge? The Malinois's Bridge?"

"Maybe?"

"That dog blew himself up just to show everybody he was right. What an ice-hole. Bridge is lucky to be rid of him, even if she doesn't know it. She's a lovely girl. You'll be all right with her."

"Thanks, Butter. See you soon, I hope."

Somebody loads my crate on a trolley.

"Same here, girlfriend. Stay safe."

Minutes later, Silver comes to check on me.

"You OK, Guinness?"

"Splendid. You?"

"I'm sorry, Guinness. I know it was a long trip, but it's almost over. I'm glad to see you're all right."

Me too, I think, as they roll me somewhere like I'm luggage.

CHAPTER 21

THE FIRST THING I notice about Afghanistan is the heat. I've never seen heat like this before, not even when people complained, sweated, and walked around in their underwear. All but me, of course. My coat is my uniform, swimsuit, and winter coat, all in one. I dress the same at −10 as I do here, at 105. I'm very proud of my shiny black coat, but right now, I'd trade it for something skimpy and sleeveless, even if it were ruffly and pink. But that's not an option, so I just lie in my crate, panting like a train engine.

After the heat, the next thing I can't miss is the dust covering everything: roads, cars, people. It's everywhere, like snow in winter, but it's not white and pretty. It's dull beige, like desert camo, and it doesn't melt. It's so light that I raise a cloud if I swig my tail, and so thick that I see nothing beyond twenty feet. Whenever I sniff, it gets into my nose, and I sneeze. And right then and there, I know the dust is my enemy.

I bare my teeth and bark at it, but it only gets thicker. I growl and try to bite it, but it's like biting air. I get nothing but a parched throat and a bad taste in my mouth.

"You'll get used to it," Silver says, as someone loads my crate in the back of a dusty truck. "You'll get so used to it you'll stop noticing it."

I don't think so. This nasty thing is so pervasive that I know I'll find it in my you-know-what when I get around to cleaning it.

Another crate gets loaded next to mine.

"Guinness! Is that you?"

"Butter?"

I sniff, trying to ignore the dust. Sure thing, it's Butter. I get to see her for the first time. She's light gold, the color of Irish butter, with silky ears and shiny brown eyes.

"I'm so glad we're together. Oh, my, aren't you good-looking," Butter says, eyeing me through the grid of her crate. "That elegant black muzzle with brown eyebrows and jowls. Nice markings."

"You're not so bad yourself."

I'm so embarrassed that I feel like blushing, but I don't know how. That's a Labrador for you. These Canadians would make you feel good even if your tail grew out of your forehead. We German shepherds have a more Teutonic approach.

"Nice coat," I say. "Ears too. When will they stand up?"

Butter laughs.

"Cut the crap, Guinness. I'm a Labrador. My ears don't stand up."

"Oh. I see. Well, they're pretty just the way they are."

"Thanks, kid. I'm so glad to be back on the ground. We're on the last stretch here. Just a couple more hours, and we should reach our base in Kandahar."

"I thought we were going to Afghanistan?"

"Of course. We are in Afghanistan. Kandahar is one of its provinces. The deadliest one. More American soldiers—K-9 and humans—died here than anywhere else in this country. Helmand comes next."

"Hell-man?"

"Helmand. Another province. I hope we get deployed together. Wouldn't that be great?

"I'd love that."

She falls asleep, but I can't. I stare through the grid of my crate, but there isn't much to see. We drive through miles and miles of dusty, empty roads between dusty, empty fields, leaving behind a cloud of dust. It's hot too, but the truck's open, so the heat's not bad. But, as far as the eye can see, there's nothing but scorched earth and dust. Every now and then, a tiny village with dust-colored mud houses, then more dust and desolation.

"I hate dust."

Butter opens her left eye.

"We all do, Guinness. But, against the dust, there's no winning. You can't fight it, you can't kill it, you can't ignore it. You need to accept it."

Every cell in my body wants to fight it, but I lay in wait, pretending to agree. Butter falls asleep again. We carry on through miles and miles of dust until the truck stops in front of a green metal gate topped with spikes. That's the only break in the ten-foot-tall mud wall, covered with rolls of evil-looking razor wire that seems to go on forever. The gate opens to let us in, then slams shut behind us, and my heart jumps. I hate being locked in.

Butter sighs with relief.

"We're safe now."

"Safe from what?"

"Guinness, we're inside the wire. This is our home, the one place we're safe since everything and everyone gets checked when they come in. Outside the wire, there's a big bad world. You never know where the strike will come from. Everybody there hates us. The roads and the fields are full of IEDs waiting to blow us up. The villages shelter snipers who are looking to kill us. Anyone there, from old men to kids, may throw a grenade or blow themselves up to kill us. There is no safety outside the wire."

I can see she means it. She speaks from a place of conviction, but I'm not so sure. I don't know if she's right, and everyone out there is trying to get us, or if she's paranoid. No wonder, after three deployments. But I don't want to hurt her feelings, so I keep my mouth shut.

"See, Guinness, that's why we're here. People can't smell worth a damn unless it's apple pie or hot pizza and wings. Bombs? Not so much. That's why they need us, K-9s, to find the IEDs and point them out to our handlers as they taught us in training. But this is not training; this is real. Every mistake could mean death—ours, or our people's. We scour the fields, the roads, and the villages for mines. Firearms, explosives, and ammo too. We track the bad guys and help our soldiers put them away. We're here to protect our soldiers, and we're essential. That's why the enemy wants us dead. They want us so bad that, if they had a choice, they'd rather kill one of us than a soldier. You've got to be paranoid to stay alive."

My hackles stand, and I don't know if I'm scared or angry, but I don't have time to wonder. My crate opens.

"Guinness, come."

I jump out and face-plant. My legs got numb from being locked in the cage. It's time for a little yoga. I raise my muzzle in an upward dog, then my rear in a downward dog, then I shake. That's not technically yoga, but it sets my blood pumping and helps rearrange my fur. That's my morning routine.

Butter's out too. We smell each other's butts, then she licks my nose, and I wag my tail. We're buddies now. I invite her for a play-fight when I hear a growl behind me.

"Wow! Two new chicks! Welcome, girls. Good to see you."

I turn around to stare into the brown eyes of the largest Malinois I've ever seen. He smiles from one dark, sharp ear to the other as his brown tail beats frenetically, agitating the dust.

"Viper! You're still here?"

"Butter! It's you! You're back! Good to see you, partner. Your tail looks younger than ever. Who's the new chick?"

"This is Guinness. Guinness, meet Viper. He and I worked together before."

Her voice is so bland that I know there's more to it than meets the eye. I glance at the Malinois. He looks friendly enough, but I know better. These Malinois, they're all a bunch of neurotics.

"Hello, Guinness. Welcome to Kandahar. Glad to have you. How do you like it here?"

I raise my nose, take a deep breath, and I sneeze.

"I'd like it better if you'd stop raising the dust with your tail."

His smile fades. Butter stares at me.

"Like really? What bug have you got up your butt? I was just trying to welcome you."

"Thanks. But no, thanks."

I lift my tail up high and go visit Silver, who's shaking hands with a bunch of uniforms. She pets me.

"So good to see that you've made friends already. We're all a band of brothers here. We can't survive unless we have each other's back."

I glance back at Viper, who stares at me like I've grown a second tail. Crap.

Good job, Guinness. You started your deployment with a bang.

CHAPTER 22

IT TURNS out that fighting a war is far less exciting than watching it in the movies. On a scale of bacon to kibble, it's behind taking a bath and ahead of getting my nails clipped. Every day is the same. We sleep in our crates, then we wake up to watch our handlers cooking breakfast. They squeeze some lumpy paste out of a bag, mix it into kibble, and add hot water to get a snotty, smelly slop.

"There's your stew," Silver says, placing it in front of me.

Stew! I wish. I glare at her, then sniff the dish as if it were an IED. I pick a piece or two, then sit and watch it cool.

"That's good for you. It has vitamins and minerals and supplements for strong tendons and joints."

"Yeah, yeah, yeah."

Next to me, Butter inhales her food.

"Lamb! I love lamb."

Butter is passionate about food. Whether it's lamb, chicken, or parsnip, Butter gulps it with abandon and looks for more.

"The heck lamb. That's mutton. You can smell it all the way from Helmand, for God's sake," Viper says, picking at his food after carefully studying every single bit. The Malligator's not a foodie, I recon, from his lack of enthusiasm and his lean muscles.

Unlike Butter, he's one of those K-9s who gets his reward from the ball, like me.

It's not that I don't like food. I love food—the right food. I crave popcorn, bacon, and cookies, but there's none of that here. Nothing but MREs, Meals Ready to Eat, for all the soldiers, with or without tails. Every once in a while, Silver slips me her cheese crackers, but they aren't bacon. Not even popcorn.

After breakfast, we take our handlers for a walk. We keep them on a leash, of course. That's when we do our business, as best we can, since there are no juniper bushes, no trees, not even mailboxes. Nothing but cracked earth and dust. Oh, how I miss the green, green grass of home.

Then we train. We run, jump, fight, and apprehend fake suspects. Most importantly, we search for IEDs inside the wire: under the trucks, inside the supply sheds, along the roads.

Whenever we get it right, we get rewarded. Butter, like all Labradors, loves food. Give her a little kibble, and she'll work forever. Not me, baby! I'd work my heart out for a burger. Even a hot dog, but there's none here, so I have to settle for the ball. Whenever I find the stuff she planted, Silver throws me the ball, and I squeeze and chew on it like it's a Malinois. When I do an outstanding job, she gives it a few tugs, so I feel like I'm fighting prey. That's way better than kibble.

Viper, who's a Malinois and therefore inferior, prefers the ball too. That irks me, but not enough to give up mine, so we keep tabs on who gets the ball more often. We pretend not to, but we watch each other closely. I hate to say it, but he's sharp.

Day after day after day, we look for IEDs inside the wire. They're fake, of course; everything here gets triple-checked before coming in. It's also way too easy. I can see the dust disturbance and sniff Silver's scent before detecting the IED, even though she wears gloves. Still, it eases the boredom.

After training, we chill in our crates until the evening walk. Butter mostly sleeps, but I have too much time on my paws, and chilling's not my bowl of kibble, so I spend my time remembering the days I clammed with Shorty and sang with Mom and Jones. Then I get so sad that I have to get moving, so I get up and chase my tail for a quick pick-me-up, but I wake up Butter.

"I'm sorry, Butter. I just couldn't be still anymore."

"No worries, Guinness. I know you're restless. We'll go outside soon."

"Outside where?"

"Outside the wire. We'll go looking for real IEDs and real perpetrators, and you'll get more excitement than you bargained for. Whenever we go out, we never know who comes back."

She falls asleep again. I sigh, and I lay my nose on my paws. I hope she's right 'cause I'm not loving it here. This is not like home. There, we spent all our time together. Not here. Gone are our movies and popcorn. Silver spends her evenings chatting, laughing, and playing cards with the other soldiers. She still feeds me and trains me, but she often has better things to do. I'm glad she's happy and content; I just wish something would happen someday.

Then it does.

The gunfire starts as we're having breakfast.

"What the heck's that?" Viper asks.

"Some diversion somewhere," Butter mumbles between bites of food. "They can't be serious. Before breakfast? It's way too early to fight."

The alarm goes off—like anyone needs it, really, on top of all that ruckus. The soldiers squeeze into their bulky bulletproof vests, slap on their helmets, and run to answer the gunfire. Well, they don't exactly run since their kit's so heavy it slows them to a crawl. Still, they rush to the camouflage net to shoot, even though there's no way they can see anything beyond ten feet—the dust around the camp is thicker than a mud wall.

We K-9s finish our breakfast as the gunfire keeps on, hurting our ears. We're behind the wire, so there's no immediate threat. I wonder if we'll train this morning, when the lieutenant calls off the fire. His mouth is tight, and his eyes red with dust stay glued to the surveillance blimp floating in the pale sky above us.

"This was a diversion. Our aerial surveillance shows three insurgents planting IEDs along the road while their friends kept us under fire to distract us. They've mined the roads again. K-9s!"

The handlers line up.

"We'll sweep the roads, the neighboring fields, and the villages. Silver?"

"Yes, sir."

"You and Guinness go first. Your K-9 is brand new, and she needs the experience. Go."

"Yes, sir."

Silver's face is gray and tight as she buckles my vest, then attaches her thirty-foot leash to my collar. I know she's thinking about the last time she was on a mission. That's when she lost her Malinois. I wish I could say something to give her confidence, but I can't. So I just head toward the gate, and she follows. The others line up behind us at a safe distance.

"Guinness?"

"Yes."

"This is not about being fast; it's about being smart. This is not a competition. Take your time and make sure every darn inch of that road is safe. Go slow. If you do well, I'll make it worth it to you."

"Like how?"

"What do you want?"

"Popcorn and a movie."

"I'll get your popcorn and your darn movie if we come back alive. Now go."

CHAPTER 23

THE METAL GATE creaks open to the desolate desert outside the wire. There is no living thing as far as the eye can see—just the never-ending dusty road cutting through the dusty fields and the village compound down the road. Everything is dusty, silent, and empty. There's no one here but me, dragging Silver behind me on her leash. The others are way behind, keeping a safe distance, in case I step on the mine instead of sitting next to it like I'm supposed to.

"You can find it, Guinness."

I sure can. I just hope I find it before it finds me. I step out gingerly, sniffing the air while trying to keep out the dust, and I'm not winning.

"Good luck, Guinness."

That's Butter's bark, somewhere behind. I'll thank her later. But for now, I step carefully through the soft beige dust, sniffing every small step. I've never moved this slowly, but slow is smooth, and smooth is fast, Silver says.

As empty as this desert is, it's full of smells. Gasoline. Smoke. Sweat. Fear. Where can they be coming from, since there's not a living soul for miles?

I feel Silver's heartbeat at the other end of the leash. Butter was right when she said that here in Afghanistan, feelings go up and down the leash. Silver follows every step I take, and that gives me confidence. She trusts me enough to go wherever I take her. That makes me trust myself more.

I take another step, then another. Oops! An acrid, sharp odor overcomes the dust that caked my nose. That's explosive; I'd bet my life on it. Actually, I am. But where is it? I step softly as the toxic odor burns my nose. I sniff again, trying to ignore the dust. Fat chance!

Butter was right. Accept the dust. I stop fighting it, even though the idea of breathing it in makes me sick to my stomach. I zero in on the scent. It's to my right, just feet away. I fill my nose with it—and dust, of course. I step to where the ugly sharp odor fills my nose, right by the camp back gate.

I sit, pointing to the scent.

"We have a signal."

Silver follows my tracks, kneels beside me, then leans over to brush away the dust with feather-light fingers. The silence is deafening. Rivulets of sweat pour down her brown face into her eyes, then down her chin, dripping to cake the dust, but she barely blinks. She gently sweeps the dust away until suddenly, her sweat changes odor. Before, it was heat and stress. Now it's fear.

She clears her throat.

"I feel the pressure plate. That's a positive ID. Good job, Guinness." She retraces her steps. I follow. Seconds later, we're both back.

"Destroy," the lieutenant says.

Gunfire rips the silence. A moment later, the IED blows up in an angry pyre of flames twisting around each other like a nest of angry snakes hissing at the sky. The smell of smoke and destruction scorches my nose and fills my lungs. There's nothing left of the place we were at just seconds ago. I'd be there, burning, if I stepped on the darn thing.

"Good work, Guinness."

Silver's voice cracks. I pretend I don't notice. It's the first time I really understand how she must have felt when Bear blew up, and I'm so sorry.

We file back inside the wire, where there's no bomb other than those planted by the handlers. Butter was right; this is our only safe place. For the first time, inside the wire feels like home.

"Not too bad for a first-timer."

Viper looks at me down his long black snout, wagging his tail in approval.

"Shut up, Viper. She did great. Awesome work, girl," Butter says, congratulating me with a nose lick. "I couldn't have done better myself."

CHAPTER 24

THAT FIRST MISSION was the end of the beginning. I was no longer a rookie; I was a real K-9. After that, the base felt like a home rather than a prison. Seeing the dangers lurking outside the wire made me appreciate the safety of being inside. I even learned to accept the dust. Its softness protected my paws, and I could detect the slightest movement for miles since a moving mouse would lift a plume of dust.

My brothers-in-arms, both K-9 and humans, looked at me with newfound respect. Silver was so proud of me she could burst. It was almost like she forgot her Malinois, though I knew better. But she had come into her own.

"See, Guinness, NORT was special. I'll never forget the joy of seeing you win. But competition is just that: a competition. This stuff here is real. Real life, real death. This is where you learn who to trust. I always knew I could trust you, but now, every person on the base feels safer when you lead them outside the wire. You've got your baptism by fire."

I don't know what baptism is, but I know fire. Silver was right. The soldiers would stop to say "Hi" as they went about their day. They'd slip me a tasty bit of their MRE when they thought nobody was watching. Even Viper started offering me his butt to smell first every morning. Now that's respect!

That's another strange thing about humans: they don't sniff each other's butts. You'd wonder how they even recognize each other. For us K-9s, sniffing butts is more than a handshake. Sniffing each other's butt is a combo of passport check, checking each other's resume, and peeking at each other's calendar.

Whenever I sniff Viper's butt, I first check that he's still a boy. You never know when he'll change his mind. By sniffing his butt, I can tell if he's healthy or ill, what he ate, and if he's in a good mood. I also find out if he feels like dating. For those who don't know: the dominant dog always sniffs first. When Viper offers me his butt to smell, it's like he bows to me. And I'm humbled. Well, sort of. We German shepherds aren't much into humble.

Regardless, those were the days. We gulped our breakfast glop, made trails in the dust, then played hide-and-sick with explosives. After dinner, we chilled telling stories—we K-9s, in our quarters, the bipeds in theirs.

One evening when Viper was sniffing somewhere else, Butter and I lay watching the soldiers play cards. She cleaned her tail real good, making it glow with the light, and it just struck me that Butter didn't look like a military dog. She was friendly and soft and kind, but there was nothing military about her. She loved food and never had a bad word for anyone—unlike Viper or me.

I had to ask.

"Butter, how did you get into the military?"

Her ears went down, and she glanced around to make sure nobody was listening.

"Guinness, can you keep a secret?"

"Of course."

"I'm... I'm not a purebred. I'm just a mutt, you see. My mother made a mistake, and she had an unexpected litter. Her owner couldn't sell us as purebreds, so he dropped us off at a dog shelter. That's where Brown found me when he came looking for a dog to train. So, here I am."

"What does being a mixed breed have to do with anything?"

"Oh, Guinness. There's your pure-bred privilege. Of course, you don't understand. People want purebreds, so they're worth a lot of money. That's why there are so many horrible puppy mills squeezing money and oppressing dogs. But nobody wants to pay for a mutt—unless they're one of those silly designer Labradoodles or Yorkipoos.

I struggle to understand, but I can't. I'm supposed to have a lengthy pedigree, but nobody wanted me either. I don't get it, but this isn't about me. This is about Butter.

"What mix are you?"

"That's the problem. I don't know. If I did, I could call myself a LabraPoo or a PitLab. I could do my best to look important. I could even pretend that's how I was meant to be and start a new fad. But I can't, so I just pretend I'm a Labrador and hope that nobody finds out."

"Oh, come on, get over it, Butter," Viper growls, dropping to the ground next to us. He's been on a long trip somewhere, and his tongue hangs to his knees from running in the heat.

Butter's eyes drop to the ground, and her tail hides between her legs. She's mortified.

"Leave her alone," I snarl.

Viper growls.

"Shut up, Guinness. Butter, nobody here cares about your breed. This isn't a pet store or a puppy mill; we're all K-9s here. I'm a Malinois, Guinness is a shepherd, you're a Labrador mix. None of that really matters. We're all in this together. It's the same with the soldiers: Silver's brown, Brown's black, and my handler, Sabrina, is Latina. So what? Nobody cares about your pedigree. The only thing people care about is how you do your job. And you're doing a fantastic job, Butter. I'm glad to work with you."

Butter sits up a little straighter.

"Thanks, Viper. That's kind of you."

I lick her nose.

"As he said."

"Thanks, guys. I'm so glad to have you as my brothers."

After that evening, I started looking differently at Viper. He wasn't just an ice-hole, after all. He was good at his job, and he could even be friendly. When he had nothing better to do.

CHAPTER 25

SADLY, the good days didn't last long. The insurgents got cockier and started pushing us harder, week after week. We got used to waking up under fire. A loaded truck struck the green gate and exploded, wounding two soldiers. A man in a suicide vest blew up the checkpoint down the road, killing an interpreter and wounding a soldier.

We went outside the wire most days, and Butter, Viper, and I took turns in the lead. I was shocked to find that being in the back was harder than being in front. The tension didn't ease, but there was little I could do but hope that the lead K9 would find the IEDs and stay alive.

That Tuesday was Butter's turn to lead. We went to the village down the road to look for the explosives that insurgents used to make IEDs. Butter and Brown took us to the compound. We divided into three teams and searched every house.

Silver and I got the two in the middle and made short work of them. Searching in the mud houses in Kandahar is easy, you see. They're not like American houses, with their garages, basements, and attics full of furniture, appliances, and stuff. These houses are tiny, just a room or two, and mostly empty but for maybe a chest, a rug, and the curtains that serve as doors. A well-trained

K9 will breeze through them in no time. It would be a piece of cake if it weren't for the people.

I don't think they like us.

People here are quiet and grim, and they smell like they're afraid of us. Even today. As I entered the house through the curtain, a woman in red kneeled on the ground, washing a half-naked kid. Another kid watched, exploring his nose. As soon as she saw me, the woman jumped back and the kids started screaming. They didn't try to pet me, let alone offer me a snack. I wouldn't take it since I'm on the job, but it would be nice! But that never happens. I wonder why.

We finished searching our part, and we joined the others. They hadn't found anything either. We filed behind Butter to return to the base. Silver and I were the tail that day, breathing everybody else's dust. I wish we were leading, I thought, when I heard the shots.

We dropped to the ground to take cover. That's when I heard Butter scream.

I leaped forward, but Silver pulled me back to the ground and kept me there.

"No! You can't help her, and you'll get yourself shot!"

She held me down as our soldiers returned fire, turning the world into a cloud of dust. Viper, Sabrina, and a few soldiers took off after the insurgents. I led the rest back inside the wire.

I wanted to stop to check on Butter, but Silver said no.

"The sooner we're back, the sooner we can take care of her. Her life depends on you leading us inside the wire."

I've never sniffed my way back faster. As soon as we got through the gate, I ran to Butter's stretcher and squeezed between the soldiers carrying her. Brown, her handler, was holding her paw.

"How are you doing, girlfriend?"

"I'm OK, Guinness. Thank you for bringing us back."

A weight lifted off my chest when I heard her speak, even

though I knew she was lying. She was anything but OK, a shivering mass covered in blood. Brown, his black face gray, kneeled to tighten the tourniquet around her paw. Silver opened her K-9 first-aid kit to get a needle and tubing. Butter didn't even flinch when Silver started an IV.

I licked her nose and sat by her head.

"You'll be all right, Butter. You'll be like new in a day or two."

"Thanks, Guinness. I need to rest now."

She closed her eyes. Oh boy, how I was burning to jump on her and shake her awake. But Silver and Brown were better at helping her, so I stayed put.

She just lay there as they listened to her lungs and checked her belly. I wanted to help, but I didn't know what to do, so I just sat there until Viper came, panting and covered in dust.

"How's she doing?"

"Not great. They called for a helicopter. It should be here any moment."

He sat by my shoulder as we watched the helicopter land inside the wire. It lifted so much dust that we could barely see the soldiers loading Butter's stretcher. Brown climbed in too, and they took off, raising more dust.

That evening, as Viper and I lay in our crates, Butter's empty cage between us burned a hole in our souls.

"You think she'll make it?"

Viper sighed.

"I don't know. But she won't be back."

CHAPTER 26

Life in Kandahar was not the same without Butter, As day after day went by without news from her, we walked around the base doing our jobs like a bunch of zombies. We were in mourning, even those who weren't close to Butter. We went on mission after mission to apprehend the insurgents but got nothing. One day we took four of them into custody, but none of them admitted to shooting Butter.

"Even if they didn't do it," Viper said, licking a scratch on his hind paw, "they know who did. I'd take care of it in an hour if they left them with me. They'd have no secrets after that, I promise you."

"I didn't know that was allowed. I've never participated in an interrogation. Have you?"

"Of course. I wasn't the one to ask the questions, but I was there. My handler said that my presence encouraged the subject to cooperate."

He licks his paw with a self-satisfied expression that makes me want to bite off his nose. But I remember that he's Butter's friend too, and I get over it.

"Did you bite them?"

"Not quite."

"What did you do, then?"

"I barked."

That sounds easy. I file that for later, in case I ever need to persuade somebody of something. Just bark at them. But I'm curious. Viper may be an ice-hole, but he's been places and has seen things. He knows a lot of things I don't.

"Did you ever bite a human?"

"Of course. Didn't you?"

"In training, of course. But I mean for real."

"A few times."

"Why?"

"They were bad people that I needed to apprehend. What did you want me to do? Ask them to stop?"

"Did they get hurt?"

"Of course. That's the whole idea. If you don't hurt the perps, they won't stop. Then you may have to do something more drastic."

"Like what?"

"Like kill them."

I stop to digest that. I did, once, kill a squirrel. Mom got upset. So did Jones. I promised I'd never do it again. I didn't really mean to kill him; I was just playing, but I shook him, and he died. That was bad enough. But killing a human?

"Did you kill any people?"

Viper's eyes are dark holes as he looks at me.

"I can't answer that, Guinness."

"So you did. How?"

"How what?"

"How do you kill a human?"

"Why do you want to know?"

Good question. I never considered killing anyone. But what if I found the guy who shot Butter?

"Just out of curiosity."

Viper doesn't believe me, but he answers anyhow.

"You bite deep and crush their throat. None of this nonsense with arms and legs. A good throat bite should do it."

I get a flashback to my first mission when I found the kidnapped little girl and the perpetrator, but I lost Shorty. I was desperate to go back for him, but there was no time. I had to go it alone. I did my best, but I almost lost that fight. Until I grabbed the perp's throat. That was the end of that fight, but I never realized that I could have killed him. That's scary.

"But…"

I don't get to finish since Silver comes to pet me. Her eyes are red and swollen, and I know she's got something awful to tell me.

"Guinness, I just spoke to Butter's handler."

"And?"

"The good news is that she's going to make it. The vest stopped the bullets from penetrating any of her internal organs."

I suddenly feel happier than I've ever been.

"But…"

"But?"

"But the bullets destroyed her leg. It was so bad that the surgeons couldn't save it. They had to amputate."

"To do what?"

"They had to cut off her leg. Butter will make it, but she can't come back."

CHAPTER 27

I LAY in my crate thinking about Butter: her luminous eyes; her silky golden ears; her warm, gentle tongue. I'll never see her again. Just like Mom, Jones, and Shorty, she disappeared from my life. I can't understand that. How can somebody you love just disappear? And, if even those you love just vanish from your life, who can you trust? How can you trust anyone? What if Silver vanishes next?

In the crate next to mine, Viper smells my distress.

"That's life, Guinness. People come, people go. There's nothing you can do."

"But then what's the point?"

"What's the point to what?"

"What's the point to life? If you can't trust anyone, ever, to always be there?"

He lays his nose on his paws and flattens his ears.

"I don't know, Guinness. I'm not smart enough. I just eat my breakfast, work through my training, and go on patrol trying to do my job and keep Sabrina and the others alive. Day after day after day. I don't want to think about the day when I'll step on a mine. Or even worse, miss it, and have Sabrina or one of the men step on it. If I did, I don't know that I could go on doing my job.

And doing my job is all I know. My job is who I am. So, I'll leave those questions to those smarter than me, and I'll just do my job the best I can."

I choked. Surely there should be more to life than doing your job every day. There should be fun, and friendship, and laughter. And love.

I looked at Viper, The Fur Missile, all eighty pounds of him lean muscle and iron will, and for the first time ever, I felt sorry for him. For all his macho bravado, he was nothing but a lonely, loveless old dog. That made me so sad. What's the point of life without love? I'm miserable, but at least I got to love Mom and Jones and Shorty and Butter. And I still have Silver. Viper only has his job.

Life went on like it always does. Breakfast and training and patrol and sleep, then repeat, day after day. Viper and I took turns leading the patrol, and it was like Butter never happened.

"When will Brown return?" I asked Viper one day. "He may have news about Butter."

"It's gonna be a while," Viper said. "He's got to train a new dog first."

That took my breath away like a stab in my heart.

"What do you think happened to Butter?"

He shrugged without answering, and that made me sick to my stomach. He knows something he doesn't want to tell me. That can't be good news.

But the good news wasn't far. One morning Silver let me out of my crate and hugged me, her eyes full of light.

"Guinness, guess what?"

"What?"

"We're going home."

"Home?"

"Yes. Our deployment is over. In less than a month, we're going home. We'll eat popcorn and bacon and cookies. We'll go hiking without sniffing for bombs. We'll walk through the snow instead of dust, we'll eat real food instead of MREs, and we'll be on our own for a change. Don't you love that?"

"I sure do."

The news that we're out of here gave me hope. And an idea.

"Can we visit Butter?"

"I don't see why not. I don't know where she's at, but I'll find out."

I was on a high after that. Every morning I asked Silver whether the day had come. It hadn't, but it was close. Until one day she said:

"Tomorrow, Guinness. Today is our last patrol. We're going home tomorrow."

I jumped around like a puppy. Viper looked at me like I was nuts. But I couldn't wait to go on patrol that morning. That was my last one. An informer had told us about a cache of weapons in a nearby field, and Silver and I were leading the patrol.

We got out of the wire as usual: me first, Silver following thirty feet behind me on her leash, then the others filing behind her at a safe distance.

I sniff my way down the road to the village. I've done it so many times, it's a piece of cake. Everything smells OK. I get to the eight-foot wall surrounding the compound, and I take the narrow path between the mud wall and the scraggly bushes. I'm extra meticulous along that path, stepping gingerly and sniffing every bush. I'm about to turn the corner to the fields when I hear something behind me.

I turn around and look back.

Something flew over the wall and fell on the path, twenty feet behind me. It hit the ground and rolled toward Silver. I turn around to catch it.

"No! Guinness, run!" Silver screams, letting go of the leash. "Run!"

Run? Run where?

"Run," she screams again, then drops to the ground.

I freeze.

What the heck do I do? I don't understand her command. Run?

Even worse, I feel alone without her on the leash. But she said run. Run after what?

I look ahead, looking for whatever she sent me after. There's nothing.

I turn around to go back. I take one step, and something punches me in the chest and throws me to the ground. I land on my head in a cloud of dust. What the heck happened? I wake up all alone in a world of silent orange dust.

Then I smell the explosive, and I remember.

The grenade blowing up. Silver, telling me to run.

I run back.

She's there, all alone, covered in dust, lying face down on the ground just where she took cover. I call her, but she doesn't move. I lick her hand. It's salty, and it smells like blood.

CHAPTER 28

I LAY on her and lick her ear to wake her up, but she won't move.

"Hey, Silver! Wake up! We need to go!"

I grab onto her uniform to drag her back, but the men push me away. They turn her over. Her mouth is open, and her dark open eyes stare at the sky. I call her again.

"Silver! Let's go!"

I jump on her, but someone drags me away.

They lay her on a stretcher like they did with Butter. Good. We're going back inside the wire to take care of her. I go to the lead to bring them back to camp since that's my job, but they won't let me. Maybe because she's not on the leash to follow me and give the warning? I walk behind the stretcher as Viper takes us back to camp.

We enter the green gates. I wait for them to start an IV and put on a tourniquet, but they don't. What the heck? Did they forget?

I pull her first-aid kit from her vest and drop it on her to remind them what they have to do. I bark my heart out to urge them, but they just stare at me with teary eyes. One even tries to pet me. I bare my teeth and growl.

"Are you crazy, people? Do something! Help her! Call the heli-copter! We're going home tomorrow! She needs to wake up."

She doesn't.

"I'm sorry, Guinness. She won't wake up."

I stare at Viper like he's lost his mind.

"She has to. We're leaving tomorrow."

He looks at me down his arrogant black nose, and if I didn't know any better, I'd think he's crying. But he isn't. Dogs don't cry, especially Viper, who doesn't love anyone or anything but his job.

I go back to Silver and shake her, but she doesn't wake up. They try to drag me away, but I won't let them touch me. I bare my teeth and growl until Sabrina, Viper's trainer, opens up her first-aid kit and takes out a syringe and a needle. I sigh with relief.

"Finally! I thought none of you was going to do anything. What took you so long?"

"Sorry, Guinness," she says, plunging the needle in my neck.

CHAPTER 29

I WAKE UP IN A KENNEL.

I don't often do kennels, but I know the smell: dog poop and pee, food, disinfectant. But this one's different. Besides all those, this one also smells like blood, fear, and death.

I look around: concrete floors, bare white walls, and kennels full of sick bandaged dogs wearing the cone of shame, so they can't clean up their wounds. Some sleep, some bark, some cry. Nobody looks at me.

I try to remember how I got here, but I can't. I went on a mission. The dust. The explosion. Silver, laying on the ground. The trip back, when they wouldn't let me lead. The men, staring at me instead of looking after Silver. Sabrina's needle.

The pain explodes in me like a grenade. Something chokes me, and I can't breathe. I pant, trying to get air through the tightness in my throat, but I can't. The room spins, then it turns dark. I lay down and close my eyes, waiting for it to go away. When I open them again, a dozen dogs stare at me.

"Where am I?"

"You're at the Holland Military Working Dog Hospital at Lackland Air Force Base, the best K-9 hospital in the country. What's wrong with you?"

I'll be darned if he doesn't look just like Butter. The same golden silky coat, the same ears. But he's not Butter. He has all his legs.

"I have no idea. How about you?"

"I got wounded in Iraq. I got some shrapnel in my hind leg, but they say I'll be better soon and I can go back. You?"

"I was on patrol in Afghanistan. We were looking for weapons."

"And?"

"And...my handler, Silver. She died."

"She stepped on a mine?"

That's a loaded question. If she did, that would technically be my fault since I failed to signal it. Or her fault if she missed my signal.

"No. Somebody threw a grenade."

"That sucks," a sable German shepherd says. He's all the way to the left, and his head is so bandaged he looks like a mummy. But he sniffs toward me, and I sniff back.

"Are you a German shepherd?" he asks.

"Yep."

"Me too. Name's Primus. You?"

"Guinness."

"Now that's a good name. You like beer?"

"I sure do."

He laughs, and chokes, and laughs again. He's old and arthritic, and he sounds like an old smoker, but he's one of my people.

"What happened to you, Primus?"

"It's a long story. But the bottom line is I got into a load of ammunition just as it blew up, and I lost my eyes."

The enormity of that strikes me. Losing your eyes! How can you live without them? The only thing worse than that would be losing your nose.

"I'm sorry, Primus."

"Yep. Not fun. But at least I still have my nose. What's up with you, girl? How are you hurt?"

"My handler died."

"That's too bad. But how are you hurt?"

I stop to think. I don't know the answer.

"I don't know yet."

"What hurts?"

"My soul?"

"Have you got PTSD?"

"What's that?"

"Post-Traumatic Stress Disorder. That's when the stress is too much, and we can no longer function."

"Of course not. That's got to be for sissies."

"That's what I thought until I saw my partner Ben," the Butter lookalike says. "It's real. I've never seen a braver dog. I don't even know how many lives he saved. Then one day, he just turned off. He was afraid of noises and growled at people. He could no longer do his job. That was hard to watch; I'd worshipped him since I was a pup. But he just lost his mojo."

"Why?" Primus asks.

He shrugs.

"I guess it got to be too much? The stress. The deaths. The losses. Either way, he couldn't go back to work."

"What did he do?"

"They tried to rehabilitate him, then they put him up for adoption. Dunno what happened next, but I sure hope they found him a family."

"How about his old trainers? I heard that retired dogs get to live with their old trainers and their families until they cross the rainbow bridge."

"Maybe he didn't have any? I don't know."

"Hey, Guinness?" Primus's old, whitened snout points to me as if he could see me, though I know he can't. He's got bandages all over his eyes.

"Yes, sir."

"We German shepherds need to stick together. Let me know if you need anything. I'll do my best to help you."

I stare at him. He's locked in his kennel, he can't see squat, and the curve of his spine tells me that his days of running and jumping are over. He's an old-timer, while I'm barely three years old, and he offers to take care of me. I'm ashamed.

"Thanks, Primus. I really appreciate it. Same here, you know. Let me know how I can help."

He nods toward me, and his shaky chin lands on his paws.

"I'd do anything for another set of eyes. Let me know if you'd like a companion."

CHAPTER 30

THE VET WAS slight and fast, with soft nimble fingers that smelled kind. She checked me from my muzzle to my tail, poking and prodding every inch of me. She X-rayed my hips and my chest and got enough blood out of me to build an extra dog. She took me to exercise and to training and tested me in every way.

I didn't do so good.

She didn't tell me, but I heard her speak to my lieutenant.

"I have bad news. Guinness won't be back."

"Why not?"

"She's got PTSD."

"I thought that only happened to people."

"Dogs are people too, you know."

She sounds irked. I like that, even though that's not how I'd put it. I'd say people are people, too, even if they aren't dogs.

"So what, then?"

"She'll have to go through rehab. We'll see how she does. If she does well, we may find her a civilian job. If not, I hope we can rehab her as a pet."

The lieutenant's hackles rise at the same time as mine.

"A pet? You've got to be kidding."

"Pets are people too. They make families happy, and they teach them the value of unconditional love."

The lieutenant bailed out. So did I.

Rehab was nice. They train you like you're a puppy, praising and rewarding you for every little thing. But the best was that Primus was there too, and we got to hang out.

I lent him my eyes, and he lent me his wisdom. We did everything together. And, since he could still smell, we could communicate without needing to see each other.

"They're a good pair," the vet said after watching us at rehab one day. "They help each other. Let's find them a home together."

The therapist shrugged.

"That would be nice, but it sounds unlikely. Who'd ever want two German shepherds, one blind, one with PTSD?"

"Let's spread the word and work on it."

That's how we found Tony. Or, more like, how Tony found us.

CHAPTER 31

I KNEW something was up when the tech came to take me out of my kennel one evening. In the hospital, stuff only happens in the morning: feeding, walking, training, doctor's visits. The evenings are for laying around and telling stories unless there's an emergency.

When the tech opened my door, the whole kennel woke up and stuck their noses to watch him put on my leash.

"Who's sick?" Primus asked.

"Guinness," Goldie said, his eyes dark with worry.

Primus groaned.

"Hey Guinness, you OK?"

"Yep."

"Where you going?"

"Dunno."

"Call if you need help."

"Thanks."

The tech took me to an exam room. I wondered what this was all about since I didn't feel any worse than usual, but I didn't have much time to worry. The vet came in, followed by a stocky, dark-haired man.

He smelled of cigar smoke and booze, which I hadn't smelled

in forever, but the strangest thing about him was that he was not in uniform.

"Hi, Guinness. This is Tony."

"Hi, kid. How ya doing?"

I look straight into his eyes. They're dark, unblinking, and warm.

"Fine, thanks," I say, slapping my tail to the floor. "You?"

"She's doing well. Guinness is healthy and very smart, but she went through some rough times."

"What happened to her?"

"I can't tell you that, but I can tell you that she got hurt while she was on a mission."

"She got shot, eh?"

"Sorry, Tony, her history is confidential."

"Where did she get shot?"

"Sorry, Tony. No can do. What do you think?"

"She's beautiful. Sleek, shiny, and almost black, but for those brown eyebrows. I bet you can't even see her in the dark. She's well trained, you said?"

"Best trained dog this side of the Atlantic."

Tony nodded and sat in the metal chair by the desk.

"Guinness, come."

I went and sat in front of him, as expected.

"Down."

I downed.

"Bark."

I barked.

The whole kennel erupted, barking up a storm. The walls shook with noise as they outdid each other.

"What's up?"

"You OK, girl?"

"You need us?"

I barked again.

"I'm good, thanks, guys. I'll call if I need you."

They went quiet.

"Wow. That was something else," Tony said.

"Yep. They all are buddies. Especially her old buddy Primus. He's blind. They go everywhere and do everything together. We'd like to find them a home together."

"I wasn't looking for two dogs. I only need one. Is that one trained too?"

"Of course. Primus is a K-9 vet. He lost his sight when he found a cache of explosives."

"German shepherd?"

"Yes."

Tony shrugs.

"I dunno. I wasn't planning on two dogs. That complicates things. Two dogs take a lot of room. Like how do you even fit them in the car?"

The vet crossed her arms, leaned against the wall, and said nothing. That's a negotiation tactic Shorty taught me when we went shopping for second-hand camping gear. "The one who speaks first takes the merchandise home," he said. He was right.

Tony sighs and stares at the vet.

"With two dogs, you need two of everything: Two dog beds. Two leashes. Twice the food."

He waits for her to say something. She doesn't.

"Can't you find another place for the other one? I'd be glad to chip in his adoption fee."

"Sorry, Tony. No can do. They're a team: She's his eyes; he's her strength. They're better together than they are apart. They come as a team."

"But I don't need a team. I just need a dog. A protection dog."

"I'm sure you can find one. Just google "protection dog." There are hundreds of them. European bloodlines, Schutzhund, champion parents, whatever."

"Yep. You buy them online, then it turns out you paid thousands of dollars for a dud."

"That's unfortunate, isn't it?

Tony glares at her, then turns to me.

"Hey, Guinness. Wanna come home with me? We'll live the good life—no dog food for you, girlfriend. You'll get spaghetti and meatballs, and lasagna every day. And bacon. You like bacon?"

I drool, trying to pretend it isn't me. But he sees it and thinks he's got me hooked.

"Hey, girl, I'll go all out for you. I'll even get you a cat to chase. What do you think?"

I can't help but laugh, and he sees it. His eyes shine brighter as he pats my head.

"Wanna come?"

I turn away.

"Not without Primus. Sorry."

The vet smiles.

"Tony, would you like to see Primus?"

Tony shrugs.

"What's there to see? A dog is a dog is a dog. Are you sure you won't let me have her?"

"Sure."

"Oh well. I guess I'll have to get a bigger car."

The tech goes back to bring Primus. He finds me by the smell, and I lick his nose to tell him that everything is OK. He sighs and sits by me, his shoulder touching mine, as usual.

Tony stares at us, and I'll be darned if I don't see tears in his eyes. But he turns away.

"I'll go get the car."

The vet hugs us.

"You'll be OK, guys. Tony's a little weird, but he's OK. He's my ex-sister-in-law's friend, and he vouched that he'll be good to you. Don't let him get away with anything, but do your best to keep him safe."

A horn blasts outside. We head out, walking shoulder to

shoulder, and jump in the back of Tony's black SUV. The leather seats smell like tobacco, hamburgers, fries, and something that I can't define.

Tony looks at us, curled next to each other in the back seat.

"I guess they fit in," Tony says. He slams the door, turns on the engine, and we're on our way.

"Hey, Guinness, you smell this?" Primus whispers.

"Yes. What is it?"

"Cocaine, baby. Life is about to become interesting."

CHAPTER 32

Primus was right. Our lives did become interesting.

Our new home was beautiful and big enough for twenty dogs, let alone some people. It stood alone, surrounded by acres and acres of birches, maples, and pines guarding a blue pool reflecting the sky. It was quiet and peaceful but for birds and squirrels since no one else lived there but for Tony, Primus, and me. People came to cook, clean, and tend the grounds, but they all left before dusk. In the evenings, it was just the three of us.

The vet was right. Tony grew on you. He was funny and kind when he wasn't an ice-hole, which happened often. And he talked to us like no other human ever did.

"You know, guys, I can talk to you since I know you won't go to the newspapers with any of it, but there's nobody else I can trust. My ex-wife, she can't wait to go and spill the beans. But we had a prenup, you know, so I told her:

"Evy, you're gonna be famous, or you're gonna be rich. Pick one. If you keep your mouth shut, like the prenup says, you'll be loaded. Sure, the media wants your story. What did he have for breakfast? How often did he shower? How was he in bed? They won't pay you much, but you think you'll go on TV, flash your mascara, and some big shot in Hollywood will be thunderstruck and make you the next movie star. I don't think so, baby, but it's your choice.

"She didn't go to the newspapers, but she started hating me even more. Even though she rolls in my money. She's not grateful, that one. Neither is my brother, Pig. You'll meet him soon, I bet. He can't stay away. He tries to be in my good graces, so he comes to visit and kisses my butt, but I bet he'd sell me for a burger if he could. He can't wait for someone to kill me, you know. That may happen, you know. In my line of business, few live to retire. And your family won't partake of the risks, but they feel entitled to what you earn, whether they're your wife, your kids, or your brother. Thank God I never had kids. I was always careful, you know? But I have Evy and Pig looking forward to my funeral. I'll be darned if I won't play one last trick on them. Just wait until Thursday."

On Thursday, Tony's lawyer came by. He was tall, unsmiling, and torn between holding on to his leather briefcase or to his combed-over white hair that looked about to fly away.

He let go of his hair just long enough to shake Tony's hand.

"Hi, Lance. Thanks for coming. I want you to redo my will."

"Your will? But you just changed it six months ago."

"I've changed my mind. There, meet my buddies, Guinness and Primus. I want you to write a will that leaves them everything I've got."

Lance turned purple and forgot his hair.

"But Tony, these are dogs."

"Observant, as usual. Thanks for pointing that out. That's why I pay you the big bucks."

"You're kidding, yes?"

"Not in the least. I want my dogs to be well cared for if something happens to me."

"Your brother and your ex-wife will get mad."

"That's the point, Lance. That's exactly why I'm doing this."

"But Tony, dogs don't need money. They don't buy houses or shoes or vacations. What would they need money for?"

"To stay alive and safe if something happens to me. I want Guinness and Primus to have a comfortable retirement. They're always here for me, and they do their best to keep me alive. There's no one else who doesn't want me dead. Not even you, Lance."

"Tony!"

"But we're about to fix that. You'll be my trustee, and you'll manage the funds for the dogs, should I croak. You'll pay for their upkeep and keep them comfortable, safe, and happy. Capisce?"

Lance stares from Primus to me, then back to Tony.

"Are you serious?"

"Totally. Draft the will, and I'll sign it next week."

Later that evening, when Tony was on the phone with a business associate discussing a new shipment, I asked Primus:

"What was that all about?"

"Tony loves us. Even more, he hates his family. He wants to see them squirm, so he makes sure they'll get nothing when he dies."

"But he's not old, Primus. And he's not walking into IEDs in Afghanistan either. Why would he die?"

"Land mines come in all sorts, Guinness. And Tony walks through them every day. That's why he got us. Kinda like insurance. His life is a nest of hate and worry."

"I can't imagine what I would do with money. Have you ever owned money?"

"Once. My handler gave me a dollar to take to the McDonald's drive-through to buy a burger."

"Was it good?"

"The best I ever had. I paid for a plain burger, but they gave me a bacon cheeseburger with all the trappings. It was phenomenal. Money is good, Guinness. It buys good things."

I like cheeseburgers, but I'd rather that Tony lives a long life. I'm getting really tired of death.

Primus looks at me with his blind eyes. He can't see me, but he can see straight into my soul.

"Death is part of life, kid. One of these days, I'll be gone. With the way Tony lives his life, he may be gone too. You can't anchor your life around someone else. It's between you and God."

"God?"

"He's up above, taking care of us all. He's always there when we need him, and he listens to our prayers."

Primus's empty eyes look up to the sky as if he's seeing God. I try to bite my tongue. I want to spare his feelings, even though he's clearly lost his mind, but I can't.

"If God is so good and powerful, how come he didn't save your eyes? How come he didn't spare Silver?"

"His ways are hard to understand. But he's all beauty and love."

I sigh and lay my nose on my paws. I hope God watches over Primus. And over Tony. I know he's not watching over me—I'm not worth it. But, if he takes care of those two, I'm all set.

CHAPTER 33

God must have been busy that day.

It was just a day like all the others. We got up and had bacon and pancakes while Tony drank three espressos and smoked his cigar; then we loaded in his car and drove to take care of business.

We had a routine. Primus walked with Tony wherever he went while I waited in the car by the open window, ready to join them if they called me. Primus looked really sharp since Tony got him a pair of dark doggles that covered his eyes, so nobody knew he was blind. He stayed glued to Tony's knee: walked with him, sat with him, and growled whenever Tony raised his voice. And, of course, he kept his nose open to warn him if anything smelled fishy.

My job was to sit in the car, waiting to be called. It never happened, and I was bored to death. Why should I always stay in the car when they had all the fun? I threw a hissy fit, but Tony explained that Primus was his deterrent while I was his weapon.

"When they see Primus, they'll think twice before they try anything. It would be just the same with you. But if there's any trouble, you can join us in a flash, while Primus would have trouble finding his way between all the crap."

That made sense since there was a lot of crap. Tony's business took place in warehouses and garages rather than offices. He walked in there in his fancy suit, talked to some mechanic in soiled overalls, exchanged his bag for another, then came back to the car, and off we went. It wasn't a strenuous job.

It was no different that morning. I watched Tony and Primus go to the warehouse, then I sat by the window, watching the street. It was a drizzly wet fall day in the wrong part of town. The warehouse wasn't pretty. Nor was the street: heavy trucks shook the road, cars fouled the air with their fumes, and people with umbrellas bumped into each other as they jumped over puddles. But I had a blast. I always loved the rain, almost as much as I love snow, but since my time up close and personal with the dust in Kandahar, I can't get enough of it. I also love the mud. It squishes between your toes when you step in it, and it soothes your feet. Primus loves it too. I'll take him for a nice long walk when we get home, I think. At home, we come and go as we please since there's no one there for miles. Except for the squirrels, of course.

As I imagine chasing the squirrels, I see a man in a black hoodie enter the garage, and my hair stands on my neck. Why? I wonder. Then I realize. He smells like explosives.

I fly out the window just as the metal door closes behind him. I need to find another way in. I sprint around the building, looking for an opening, but there's nothing.

I find an open window up high in the back. I sprint to gather momentum, but it still takes me three tries to grab onto the frame with my front paws. I push myself up with the back end and land on the concrete floor just as the first shot rings.

I roll, jump on my feet, and start tracking. I follow my nose around parked trucks, dismantled cars, leaking batteries, and piles of tires. I run like I never ran before, when I hear one more shot, then a scream. It's Primus, and my heart freezes in my chest. This is not the call for help; it's a scream of pain.

I leap over a pile of tires to see dust rising behind a metal container. The next shot rings as I jump on top of it. I find myself above the hoodie man with the gun.

Six feet away, Tony lays unmoving on the concrete floor, his fancy suit dripping red. Primus, his breath a spray of blood, holds a tight grip on the man's leg as the man points his gun to his head.

I leap at the man's throat, but I miss. I grab onto his arm and drag him to the ground. His head slams the ground with a hollow sound, just as I hear another shot. A sharp pain stabs my side and takes my breath away. I feel like I'm choking, but I don't let go until the man stops moving.

I finally take a breath, and it's like a grenade blew up in my chest. But I don't have time for it. I grab the gun and drop it a few feet away, then I check on Tony. His dark eyes are wide open, even the third one, a black hole in the middle of his forehead.

I move on to Primus, who lays panting on his side. His short, ragged breaths come out in red bubbles.

"Guinness?"

"Yes, partner."

"Thanks."

"What for?"

"For taking me with you. I know Tony didn't want me. He got used to me, but he didn't want me. If it weren't for you, I'd still be in that freaking kennel, eating kibble instead of dying on a mission."

"You aren't dead yet," I say, my voice breaking.

"I'll soon be. But thanks to you, I got to have the best time of my life, running free through the forest with my partner by my side, eating lasagna for dinner, and dying like a soldier should. Thanks, Guinness."

I choke, and I don't know if it's because of his words or the wound in my chest.

"Hang in there, Primus. Help's coming. I can hear the sirens."

"Not for me, baby, I'm done. But come here. I want to smell you one more time."

I lick his nose. It's cold and wet, and it tastes like blood. I rearrange his doggles, so he looks sharp as the sirens choke and the door slams open.

"Drop your weapons! Nike, search."

A K-9 in a bulletproof vest explodes through the door, followed by his handler. He sees Primus, then me, and stops dead in his tracks.

"What the heck? Who are you?"

" Sergeant Primus, Marine K-9, retired. This is Corporal Guinness, MPC K-9. You?"

"Corporal Nike K-9."

"Corporal Guinness disarmed your perpetrator. The gun's under the desk. But she needs medical help. Get your handler."

"Yes, sergeant."

By the time we get to the hospital, Primus is no longer with us. All that's left lying next to me is his thick, sable fur and his doggles. Everything that made Primus be Primus— his generous soul, his dauntless courage, his loyalty, and his wisdom - left to join Tony.

I hope they're together up above. God would better appreciate what a fantastic K-9 he got, because I can't believe that that beautiful, heroic canine soul vanished into nothing. The world deserves better than that.

CHAPTER 34

THIS HOSPITAL IS nothing like the K-9 hospital I was at before; it's small, dark, and weird. And it doesn't have my buddy, Primus.

The dogs here don't look like K-9s. They even have a few cats, for God's sake, and I'll be darned if I don't smell a ferret somewhere! But that breaks up the boredom. This is the first time I've gotten up close and personal with a cat, besides Jones's Whiskey. What evil creatures! They wait until you're half asleep, then start taunting you. There's a big orange one with a bandaged ear who's got a thing about Charlie, the small poodle mix across from her. She doesn't miss a chance to taunt him. I don't even know Charlie, but it's hard to watch.

She licks her paws with a pink tongue so raspy I can hear it from my cage.

"Hey, you rotten mutt. You think your human will come back to get you? A disgusting thing like you? Think again."

Charlie shivers, his weepy eyes scared.

"Who'd ever want a mangy mutt like you, huh?"

Charlie melts into the floor and looks away, pretending he can't hear her. He's not pretty, Charlie, nor terribly brave. But that's not a reason to be mean to him—just the opposite. One should be kind to those less lucky. That's what decency is.

"You stink. And you…"

I can't take it anymore. I bark like the mailman is coming, and the whole place goes quiet.

"Enough. Stop that right now, you useless evil feline, or I'll show you a thing or two. You hear me, Van Gogh?"

The orange fluffs up like a toilet brush and stares at me with his round yellow eyes. He hisses:

"How do you know my name, you K-9?"

"I'm with the CIA. I know everything. And I'm about to tell everybody what you did unless you stop that right now."

He hisses again, just to save face, then turns away and sticks his nose under his tail, pretending to fall asleep.

Ever since that, Charlie looks at me like I hung the moon, which is both funny and endearing. He asks me about the war, and I tell him stories. I tell him about Butter, how everyone loved her and what a heroic K-9 she was, even though she was a mutt. That gives him confidence. It also helps pass the time since I feel like I've been here forever. Being anywhere forever is not my thing, but it's not like I have a choice.

One day I get visitors. One's Lance, Tony's lawyer. The other one looks like a pig.

"There she is," Lance says, petting his white hair as usual.

Pig man looks at me with his porcine eyes buried in pink fat. He studies me from my nose to my toes.

"This?"

"Yes."

His fat lips tighten.

"You think she's going to make it?"

"That's what the vet said. She'll start rehab tomorrow. If everything goes well, she could go home in a few days."

"Home where?"

"That's why I brought you here. As Tony's executor, I have to arrange for Guinness's welfare. She's got money, you know.

Whoever takes her in will be well rewarded. Since she's your brother's dog, I thought I'd ask you first."

Pig spits to the side.

"Did he really leave her everything?"

"Yep."

"He was out of his mind. I'll contest the will."

"Up to you. But remember, I made the will, and I made it well. Getting it invalidated is less likely than getting Tony to come back and change it. But suit yourself."

Pig glares at me and then turns to Lance.

"How about we make a deal? You agree that he was cuckoo, we get the will invalidated, and I give you 10 percent of everything."

Lance turns red.

"There's something called professionalism, you know. I'm a lawyer. I'm here to represent my client's wishes. They'd take my union card if I did what you suggest."

"How about 20 percent?"

Lance's hair stands up.

"I don't think you're listening."

"Hold your high horses, Mr. Professional. Where was your professionalism when you agreed to be Tony's lawyer? You knew darn well what kind of business he was in!"

"That was his business. Everyone, even killers, has a right to legal representation. I did nothing illegal for your brother. I only helped him with his legal issues."

"So you say."

"Listen, man, I don't care what you think. You want the dog or not."

"No."

"OK. Thanks."

"What will you do?"

"I'll talk to Evy. She may want the dog and the money that comes with her."

"You've got to be kidding. That shrew?"

"Well, besides you, she's the closest thing Tony had to a relative. I think she may want the dog, not as much for the money but for emotional reasons."

Pig stares at Lance like he grew a second head, then bursts into thick, dirty laughter that makes my skin crawl.

"Emotional reasons? Evy?"

Lance shrugs.

"You never know. Either way, it's none of your business since you don't want the dog. Let's go."

Pig looks at me again but doesn't move.

"How much will you pay to whoever takes her?"

"I don't know yet. I'll have to evaluate Tony's estate, withdraw the taxes and expenses, and see what's left. But it will be a generous allowance. She, and whoever takes care of her, should be comfortable."

Pig shrugs.

"He's not that ugly, after all. Is he house trained?"

"It's a she. Her name's Guinness. And she's a retired K-9 officer and a highly trained protection dog."

"Well, I think I'll take it after all. My poor brother would certainly prefer that she, and the money, stay in the family. I always looked out for his interests. I'll take her. When do I get my first check?"

"I'll hand you the first check when she leaves the hospital, then another every month after that. But I'll come to check on her. She should be well cared for."

"Of course. What are you saying? I know how to care for a dog."

"Good. I'll let you know when they discharge her, so you can be ready."

"I'm ready already. Hey, Lance, what happens to the money if she dies?"

"I don't know. Unless Guinness makes a will, which is unlikely, a judge will decide what happens to her trust."

"But logically, the money should go to whoever takes care of her, no?"

"I don't know that logic has much to do with it. Logic and law don't always line up. But don't worry about that. The vet assured me that she's doing well, and she will live."

"What about if she gets sick? Gets hit by a car? Or eats rat poison?"

Lance's eyes narrow as he studies Pig.

"Listen, mister. If I were you, I'd make sure nothing bad happens to Guinness. Once she's gone, so are the monthly payments. She's worth more to you alive."

"Of course, of course. I just wondered."

CHAPTER 35

Life with Pig wasn't bad. Not good either. Life with Pig wasn't much of a life. He lived alone in a double-wide, and nobody ever came to visit. He took me for a walk in the morning, fed me, then left me alone until the evening walk.

I sat alone in my bedroom all day, day after day, listening to my thoughts and thinking about those I loved. I missed them all: Mom, Jones, Shorty, Butter, Silver, and Primus. Even Tony. I spent my time having imaginary conversations with them until I stopped caring about real things and real people.

When Lance came to see me, I laid in my room, and I wouldn't get up. He frowned.

"What's wrong with her?"

Pig shrugged.

"Nothing. That's what she does."

"Lay alone in the dark every day?"

"She's a dog. What do you want her to do? Play chess?"

Lance's face darkened.

"Listen, man. This is not what we agreed upon. You're supposed to take care of her and keep her happy."

"Sure. And you're supposed to pay me well."

"I did. You get a thousand dollars a month. The dog doesn't eat a tenth of that."

"I expected more."

"Too bad. It's not my fault that Tony's house was heavily mortgaged, the car was leased, and he didn't have much else. He liked to live well, and he blew his money."

"And how is that my fault?"

"That's not your fault, but you promised to care of Guinness."

"I do. I feed her, walk her, and keep her safe. What else do you want me to do, for God's sake? Marry her?"

Lance shook his head.

"This won't work. I'll find somebody else to take her."

"The sooner, the better."

It was déjà vu all over again. One family after another came and left. I don't know if it was me or whatever Pig told them, but nobody wanted me.

I was relieved. I was tired of loving people just to have them die. If Pig died tomorrow, I wouldn't give a damn. It was easier to not care.

People stopped coming.

I lay in my room, day after day, night after night, thinking about my people. I stopped eating. I no longer wanted to walk.

"This is no good," Lance said. "She looks worse every time I see her."

"Why don't you take her, then? The way she looks, I'll have to put her down before too long."

That gave me hope. If they put me down, maybe I can join Primus, Shorty, and Silver?

Lance shook his head.

"I'll see what I can do. But in the meantime, don't forget: no dog, no money."

Life went on, day after day of nothing but my memories. I was getting so feeble I dreamt awake. It was harder and harder to tell my dreams from reality, and I loved it. I was back with my people.

"How are you doing, Guinness?" Butter asked.

"I'm good. I'll come to join you soon."

"Join me? But I'm not dead."

"Not dead?"

"No. I just lost a leg, remember?"

"You did? Then who died?"

"Silver."

"Silver? Was he the Malinois?"

"That's Viper. Silver was your handler. Bridge Silver. Small, brown, and kind."

I wake up and try to remember Silver's face, but I can't. My brain is so fogged I don't recall much beyond the smells. The one that I remember best is Primus. He was my buddy, and he died.

They slowly come back to me: Primus, Silver, Tony, and Shorty. The pain is so excruciating that I wish I could die. If only I had another chance to find an IED, I wouldn't signal. I'd just step on it.

That fire would surely burn away this pain.

CHAPTER 36

But Kandahar is almost as far as the moon, and there are no IEDs here. There's nothing and nobody but Pig stopping by once a day to bring water and kibble. Day after day, he's less real to me than my friends. Because, wherever they are, they love me. Pig doesn't.

I spend all my time in my corner, but I'm not really here. I'm somewhere far away, clamming with Shorty, chatting with Butter, chasing squirrels with Primus, or singing with Mom under the red trees in Jones's yard. I finally understand what that song meant. And I think it's my time to die.

I lay my nose on my paws, and I close my eyes.

"Hey, girlfriend, how are you doing?"

"Silver?"

"Who else? I'm glad to see you. How are you?"

"I miss you. I miss you terribly. But I'm coming soon."

"Coming where?"

"Coming to join you."

"What are you talking about?"

"They're talking about putting me down. I can't wait for us to get together, watch movies and eat popcorn. Do they have popcorn there? How about bacon?"

Silver shakes her head.

"No, Guinness. We don't eat here. We left our bodies behind, remember? We're only as real as moving shadows."

"But..."

A dark Malinois sits next to her.

"This is Bear. I finally found him."

Bear slaps his tail to greet me, just like Viper, and all of a sudden, I feel sorry for hating him all this time.

"Hi, Guinness. Silver told me about you. Thanks for looking after her for me."

"For you?"

Anger fills me, and I'm about to blow up, but I'm too weak.

Then the door opens, and I realize it was just a dream. There's nobody here but me.

"Guinness?"

A woman stands in the door, waiting for her eyes to adjust. She's a mess: crumpled scrubs, a brown ponytail, tired eyes needing sleep. Then she steps in the light, and for a moment, she looks like she's on fire.

My heart skips a beat. It's Silver! She came to get me.

"Hi, Guinness. I'm Emma."

She's not Silver.

She doesn't look like Silver, and she doesn't smell like Silver, either. She smells like sadness and loneliness. And she needs a shower. But she also smells like magic.

She sits near the door.

"How're you doing?"

Her voice is low and tired. She's not a talker, but she tries.

"You don't feel like chatting, do you? Neither do I. Life sucks."

"Yep."

"I came to meet you. I know you need a friend. So do I. I thought maybe we could get along."

I remember all those I've lost. Mom. Jones. Shorty. Butter. Silver. Primus. I can't do it again.

"I don't think so."

"Are you sure?"

I look away.

"I see. I'm sorry. Well, then. I have a long drive home, and I need to find a toilet and some coffee first. I'd better get going."

"Yep."

She sighs.

"Life stinks. My daughter hates my guts. My ex-husband got bored with his pretty wife. And I think someone's killing my patients."

Her phone beeps.

"That's Taylor, my daughter. Did you ever have puppies, Guinness?"

"Are you kidding? I've done nothing but train and sniff for IEDs ever since I was a pup."

"You didn't miss much, trust me."

I blink.

"You're right. Why should you trust me? I'm just a stranger."

She crosses her legs like she has to pee.

"I have to go, Guinness. I'm sorry it didn't work out."

She picks up her bag.

"I forgot. I brought you something. You like Italian? This is Bolognese, loaded with basil and garlic. Garlic kills worms, you know. I'm not saying you have them; I'm just telling you what it's good for."

She sets the container near my water bowl. The aroma of garlic hits me like a bullet, bringing me back to the evenings when Tony taught us to cook pasta.

"Good luck, old girl. I'll root for you."

Nobody called me old before, but that hits the spot. I feel like I've lived a few lives. I feel old enough to die.

She'd like to pet me, but she knows I don't want to be touched.

"Bye, Guinness."

She heads to the door with her open bag, messy hair, and crumpled pants. The scent of her loneliness makes me choke. She needs someone to look after her.

Not me.

She leaves.

I sigh, and the garlic fills my nose and makes me drool. There's also basil, pepper, Parmigiano Reggiano, beef, San Marzano tomatoes. And oregano.

I check it out. It's barely defrosted, and it lacks the pasta. It needs spaghetti—not farfalle, linguini, or rotini. The only correct pasta for this Bolognese is spaghetti, cooked al dente. Eight minutes in a large pot of very salty water, then drained and coated in the sauce. Serve with aged Parmigiano grated at the table. None of that cheap stuff you buy already grated. That's real Italian cooking. None better on Earth.

Tony loved giving us cooking lessons. He wiped his forehead with a kitchen towel as he stirred the sauce and checked the pasta. Primus and I watched, sitting in pools of drool.

"The pasta has to have a little bite to it and resist chewing, you know. Overcook it, and it's dead—nothing but mush. Don't forget the crushed red peppers; that's where the magic is. The heat sets your tongue on fire and wakes it up to the flavor."

I sniff it again. I'll just taste it, I think, then I discover that I inhaled it. It's not as good as Tony's, but it ain't bad. It's the first decent meal I've had in months.

As I'm licking it clean, I hear a car start in the driveway. She's leaving.

Good. I don't need this woman. I have my people. It can't be long now.

My stomach growls.

I set my nose on my paws and close my eyes.

She's a stranger. Why should I care about her? I'll soon join my people.

But Shorty has his father; Primus has Tony; Silver has Bear.

Tomorrow, Pig will bring me water and kibble. Lance may stop by to check on me. I'll just lay here, daydreaming of my friends. The same the day after tomorrow and the day after that.

Unless I go with the shaman. She needs a shower, but she's got magic. And she can cook.

What would life with her be like? I don't know, but it can't be much worse than rotting in the dark.

I remember Shorty: "Someday, you'll save somebody's life." But I didn't. Not his, not Primus's, not even Silver's. I haven't yet fulfilled my mission.

I struggle to stand, but I'm so shaky I have to sit down again. It takes me forever to get to the door, then to drag myself down the hallway. Shaman's got to be gone by now; she was desperate to pee.

But no. She's still here, setting up her navigator.

I stare at her through the driver's window. She glances back and stares straight into my eyes. She lights up like a Christmas tree.

"Really?"

I wag my tail.

"Of course."

She opens the back door. I push aside a Red Cross bag to make some room, then curl up and thump my tail.

"What are we waiting for?"

Next in Series: **BIONIC BUTTER**

BIONIC BUTTER

A THREE-PAWED HERO

RADA JONES

BOOK 2 IN THE K-9 HEROES SERIES

CHAPTER 1

The lamb aroma hits my nose with a vengeance. I open one eye to see Brown stirring the magic lumps into my kibble and dousing them with boiling water and the scent makes me drool.

I lick my lips and wag my tail in appreciation.

"It's lamb! Guys, we got lamb."

I love lamb! It's my favorite, right there with beef, chicken, and fish. Especially the way my mom cooks it. She stuffs it with cloves of garlic, then rubs it with Dijon, rosemary, and thyme. And salt and pepper, of course. She cooks it on high heat, so it stays pink inside. But Diane is half a world away while we're at our base in Kandahar. And this isn't real lamb; it's the MRE, Meals Ready to Eat, version of it, and it stinks. But it still beats plain kibble.

"The heck lamb, that is ancient mutton, *quoi*," Viper growls, his French accent still thick with sleep. "I bet it died of old age. They must smell it from Helmand."

He crawls out of his crate and shakes, and just like that, he's ready for the day. His head held high, his sharp ears up, he wrinkles his dark nose at the fake lamb aroma. Viper's not a foodie. He'll turn up his nose at kibble, but give him a ball, and he'll work all day. But he has some redeeming features. Like he lets me finish his meals. I'm so grateful I'll even put up with his obnoxious Belgian Malinois attitude.

"Helmand? You've got to be kidding. They've got to smell it all the way back home."

Guinness crawls out of her crate to practice her morning yoga. She lifts her black snout in the air in an upward dog, then rears her rear in a downward dog, then shakes like she's been crawling through mud, and she's good for the day.

No wonder. Guinness looks slim in her sleek black coat. And she's young. She's only three and a German shepherd, while I'm six, and a bit on the chubby side. But that's just because I'm a yellow Lab. I bet I'd look thinner in black.

I'm still younger than Viper. He's got to be as old as the hills. He was here when I arrived for my first deployment, years ago, and I bet he'll still be here when I'm gone, since Viper lives for his job. Detecting explosives is all he knows and all he wants to know. Out of us all, K-9s and humans, he's the only one glad to be here. Everyone else can't wait to go home.

No wonder. With the humans' cots at one end and our crates at the other, this hangar is nobody's idea of home. It smells like BO, boots and gun cleaner, and other things that shall not be named. The soldiers plastered the plywood walls with pictures of their kids and dogs and green places where it sometimes rains, but that doesn't make it home. Oh well. At least we're safe here, inside the wire. And there's food.

"You guys are too picky. You'd complain if they fed you hot fries with ketchup."

I turn my tail to them and taste my food. The scent is potent, the taste not so much. It could use some garlic, real lamb, and a better chef than Brown.

Guinness sighs.

"I could go for some fries, especially if they came with a cheeseburger." She picks up a piece of kibble, sniffs it like she's looking for IEDs, then drops it to the side.

Viper shakes his head.

"Fries are nothing but salt and fat. You guys need to make better choices if you want to stay in shape."

He turns his pointed black nose away from his food and makes a show of cleaning his privates, like either Guinness or I give a poop. But that's Viper. He's an athlete, and he gets his highs from working out. He's one of those nuts you see on YouTube standing on top of a hydrant, jumping over a six-foot fence, or walking a tightrope. That's why he's nothing but muscle, iron will, and green bile.

Guinness ignores him like she usually does.

"Have you guys heard the plan for the day?"

"More of the same, I bet. We take our handlers for their walk, train them to look for explosives inside the wire, then dinner. Boring," Viper says.

"You don't think we'll go outside the wire?"

"I wish we would, but we've been out every day this week. The humans may need some time to recover."

"I do too," I say, licking my bowl clean. "I need my beauty sleep."

"You certainly do." Viper snickers, then leaps aside when I pretend to jump at his throat.

"You're wrong, Viper. There's no rest for the weary today," Guinness says, as Silver, her handler, slips her bulletproof vest over her head and buckles her in.

"Like really? What's wrong with these people, eh? Can't they take a day off?" I growl, eyeing Viper's bowl.

Viper nuzzles the bowl toward me.

"The insurgents must have different priorities."

Brown brings my bulletproof vest, slips me a cheese cracker, and rubs my ears with his large brown hands. He's my handler, and I've known him since I could fit in the palm of his hand. Six years later, he's still my favorite human other than Diane.

"It's our turn in the lead today, Butter. Are you ready?"

"Almost."

I grab a mouthful from Viper's food as Brown buckles my vest. I'm glad we're in front. When you're in the back, you swallow everyone else's dust, and you have no choice but to follow. In the lead, you breathe the cleanest air and get to set the pace. There's always a chance that you'll step on a mine and blow up, eh, but I'm not worried. I'm no longer a rookie; this is my fourth deployment, and I know how to take my time. Better slow than dead, Brown says, and I agree.

"Your turn again?" Viper mumbles as Sabrina kits him up like the rest of us. He's in the middle today, and he hates it. He'd rather lead, of course. We all do. Not today, Malligator.

The lieutenant, a short guy with sun-fried skin, briefs us.

"Today's mission is searching for explosives in the village compound. The insurgents stepped up their game. Almost every day, we find new IEDs. They must have explosives hidden somewhere. We need to find and destroy them. Brown and Butter, you're leading today. Good luck."

We file out in the yard. The massive green gate creaks open, and I step out. Brown follows, thirty feet behind me on his leash, to be safe in case I step on a mine. The others are even further back. Guinness and Silver come last.

I stop to take in the terrain. Tan dust covering the scorched earth as far as I can see. Nothing moves but a plume of smoke rising over the village, bruising the pale-blue sky. A few tortured bushes bake under the merciless sun. It's so hot that I'm grateful for the dust protecting my paws from the heat, as much as I hate breathing it.

Somewhere far behind, Viper barks.

"Do not rush, Butter, *ma chère*. After all, we have nothing better to do than watch the dust all day."

"Shut up, Viper. She knows what she's doing better than you do."

That's Guinness, of course. But Viper's right. There's a limit to how long we can stand this heat, we K-9s in our fur coats and the humans in their heavy armor and equipment. I step forward, trying to ignore the dust filling my nose as I sniff for IEDs. But this dust is so light it's everywhere. There's no fighting it, no avoiding it, no ignoring it. The one thing I can do is accept it and focus on the only thing that matters: keeping us all alive.

CHAPTER 2

I GET MOVING. Step after careful step, I sniff my way along the half-mile dusty path to the village. The others follow me far behind. I don't find much other than the dust: motor oil leaked from a truck, a cigarette butt, somebody's spent chewing gum, the spot where Viper peed yesterday.

Even more than the heat and the dust, the silence gets to you. There are no birds, no cars, no wind, no laughing children. Nothing but the soldiers' footsteps muffled by the dust and the occasional metal clanging against metal as they stumble under their heavy equipment.

We're all hot and tired when we reach the compound, but there's no time to rest. We divide into teams to check the dozen tiny homes. They aren't anything like American homes, with their basements, garages, sheds, and tons of stuff. These are just mud huts with curtains instead of doors and no furniture to speak of, but for a chest, a rug, and maybe a water jug. People here have even less than we have at our base. Our humans have cots, tables, and chairs, while we have our crates. These people have little more than what they wear. And they are not like our soldiers.

Males cover their faces with fur, while females cover their

hair with veils. They wear loose fluttering clothes to keep them cool. They're loose enough to hide suicide vests, so we, K-9s, have to sniff them close and personal to keep our humans safe.

The first hut is empty. There are two men and a kid in the next one, who watch me with wary eyes as I sniff every jug, every pot, and the painted chest in the corner. Brown waits outside to be safe if I blow up.

I find nothing, so I move on to the people, even though they aren't friendly. I sniff their robes, their feet, and their hands as they watch me with hard eyes. They all smell like anger and fear. I don't think they like me. Not even the kid who stares at me like I stare at cats: I ache to grab and shake them, but I know better.

I step out and wag my tail to tell Brown that I'm done.

"Nothing here."

We join the others. They didn't find anything either, so we file back into formation to head inside the wire. That's what we call our camp since the ten-foot mud wall that surrounds it is topped with rolls and rolls of razor wire to keep out the uninvited. It's not pretty, and it won't give you the warm fuzzies, but it keeps us safe.

We head back the same way: Me first, dragging Brown behind me, then the others. I sniff carefully every time I take a step, even though I just did it an hour ago. Why? You never know. What if some joker planted an IED when we weren't watching, hoping to get us on our way back? Because that's what they do.

I reach the end of the compound wall, and I'm about to step out in the open when I get a whiff of something funky. It's somewhere to my left, behind the wall. I lift my nose to catch the wind, but the dust makes me sneeze.

"Hey, Butter! No rush, *ma chère*. You do not want to mess up your pretty blonde tail."

Viper, of course. I turn around to tell the ice-hole where to put it when the earth explodes under my feet.

CHAPTER 3

IT'S NOT the earth that exploded. It's me.

A wave of pain rips through my body like a blasting grenade. I try to think, but the pain garbles my thoughts and scorches my brain. I'm nothing but a mass of pain.

Where am I? Who am I?

I hear someone scream, and it turns out it's me. I strain to breathe, but the dust clogs my throat and I shrivel as the burning pain squeezes the life out of me. Then the taste of dust reminds me.

I'm Corporal K-9 Butter, serving in Kandahar. I was on patrol, and I'm hurt. Did I step on an IED? Wouldn't that be stupid!

Brown kneels next to me and runs his hands all over my body, looking for injuries. I know he's careful, but everything hurts so bad that I cry.

Brown sniffs.

"I'm sorry, Butter. We'll take care of you."

He touches my leg. The pain explodes in me like an IED, and I scream again.

"Butter! How are you, Butter?"

That's Guinness, far away. I hear the panic in her voice, and I try to answer, but I can't. I'm too weak. I yell as the men lift me on a stretcher.

"Good luck, Butter, *chérie*" Viper barks as he leaves with Sabrina and a few men. "We are going to find the bandits who hurt you, and we will bring them to justice. I will see you at the base."

I smell Guinness coming, and she tries to stop by, but Silver won't let her.

"No time, Guinness. We need to rush Butter to the base where we can take care of her. Her life depends on how fast you can get her inside the wire."

Guinness runs to take the lead, and we get moving. The soldiers carry me on the stretcher as Brown holds my paw. A new stab of pain pierces my leg every time the men take a step, and they move so fast it feels like they're running, but they can't be. Guinness must sniff her every step; she can't go that fast. But she does.

Another burst of pain clouds my brain, and my world goes dark.

I wake up inside the wire. Brown holds pressure on my paw while Silver sticks a needle in my other leg and hangs a bag of fluid. Guinness squeezes between them to lick my nose. Her amber eyes are worried, and I know she's having an awful day even though I can't lift my head to sniff her butt.

"How're you doing, Butter?"

"I'm OK. Thanks for taking over and bringing us back to the base."

"Don't mention it. You're doing great. You'll be as good as new in no time."

I sigh. As sick as I am, I can still smell a lie. But it's coming from kindness, so I let it go.

"Thanks, Guinness. I need to close my eyes now."

I lay in a fog. Whatever Silver gave me dulled the pain but

muddled my brain even more. I'm too tired to open my eyes; I'm too tired to think; I'm too tired to live.

I hear them fussing around me. Brown tightens the tourniquet around my wounded leg while Silver gives me another shot. Someone calls for a helicopter; then the gate creaks open. The patrol is back.

I smell Viper. At least I think it's Viper, though he's never smelled like this before. He smells worried, anxious, and afraid, but that can't be. Viper doesn't know how to be afraid.

"How is she?"

Guinness growls.

"I don't know. They called the helicopter. It should be here any moment."

The helicopter rumbles closer and closer until it's so loud it covers everything else. The dust fills my nose as it lands, and I sneeze.

I feel the stretcher moving under me.

"Bye, Butter. I love you."

That's Guinness. I choke, and I don't know if it's because of the dust or because of Guinness's love.

"Love you too."

"Come back soon, Butter. I will save my lamb for you."

That's Viper. That promise is as close to mentioning love as I ever heard from him.

Then it gets dark.

CHAPTER 4

I DON'T REMEMBER who I am, but I see myself free-falling through a tunnel of swirling rainbows. I spin faster and faster, and the colors blend around me, pulling me in. I claw the air to slow down, but I find nothing to grasp on to. There's nothing here but the rainbows sucking me in. My stomach fills my throat, and I'm about to get sick when a voice breaks through the ringing in my ears.

"It's OK, Butter. You'll feel better soon. We'll take care of you."

I don't know who that is, and I'm too dizzy to open my eyes. I sniff a human female smelling like deodorant, disinfectant, and blood.

A hand pets my head, another one holds my shoulder. That anchors me enough to slow down the rainbows until they become the ordinary colors of ordinary things. A white ceiling, dark green walls, a gray concrete floor, a young female in blue scrubs petting my head. She bends over to wipe my muzzle with a wet cloth, and I smell Cheetos on her breath. My stomach twists, and I want to puke, but I drool instead.

"There now. See? You're better already."

I don't think so, lady. I'm dizzy, I'm sick to my stomach, and everything hurts, especially my left front paw. I'm lying down, but that darn paw feels like I'm walking on hot coals. I twist to reach over and lick it, but I can't. It turns out that I'm tied down. Where the heck am I? And how did I get here?

I cry for help.

"Guinness? Viper? Where are you?"

My throat is so parched that my tongue sticks to the roof of my mouth, and I can barely whimper.

"There now. Just a few more minutes to make sure you're OK; then I'll take you to your crate to take a nap."

"Where's Guinness? Where's Brown?"

"There's a good girl. You want some water?"

"I want Guinness. Where is she?"

The human brings a water bowl. I lap a little to wet my throat, but I'm so weak I have to lie back.

"See? Isn't that better already?"

"No. Where's Guinness?"

She pats my head.

"Good girl."

I'm so muddled it takes me a moment to figure out whether she's deaf or stupid. It turns out she's neither; she just doesn't speak Dog. Some humans do; some don't. Some are born with it. Some learn it as they live with dogs. Some never do. Most humans who work with dogs speak the language; otherwise, they couldn't function. Brown does, like all the handlers. But most of the soldiers, no matter how nice they are, don't get it. Speaking dog is kind of magic. It's not about rolling your tongue and making silly sounds. It's about watching, smelling, and feeling each other into your hearts. That's why dogs can't lie. How can you lie when you taste someone's tears, lean against their thigh, and listen to their heartbeat? There's no room for deception in dog like there is in human language.

But what's this girl doing here if she can't speak dog? Fortunately, I don't have much time to ponder.

"How's she doing?"

A pair of camo pants blocks my view. They contain a male smelling like iodine, soap, and stale coffee. He bends over to listen to my chest and push on my belly, and I'm about to upchuck on his silly paper booties when he steps back.

"She's doing great, Doc. She just had some water. I'm about to take her to the kennel."

"There's no hurry. Why don't we keep an eye on her a little longer, just to make sure she's OK? She's been through some rough times, and she's not quite out of the woods yet. Are you, girl?"

He leans over to shine a light into my eyes, then opens my lips to peek inside my mouth. His tired eyes are blood-red, and he's got fur around his mouth, unlike any human soldier I ever met.

"Where am I?"

"You're in the veterinary hospital. You got shot on a mission. Your bullet proof vest saved your life, but your paw didn't fare well. It must hurt."

It does.

"You've just had surgery. We worked for hours trying to save your paw, and it's still a little touch-and-go. We'll have to watch it closely for another day or two before we know where we stand."

I don't get what he says, and I don't care. But at least I can talk to him.

"Where are my people?"

"Your handler just went to get some rest, but I bet he'll be back tomorrow."

"Where's Guinness?"

"Where's what?"

"Guinness. My best friend."

He sighs.

"He must be in Afghanistan. You're in the best veterinary hospital in the USA, getting the best care a K-9 can get. But now you need to sleep; otherwise, you can't heal. Why don't I give you something to help you relax?"

He pushes something from a syringe into the tube in my leg. My pain dulls, then vanishes, and I get lighter and lighter, like a feather, until I melt into the sky.

CHAPTER 5

THE KENNEL SMELLS SICK. Dozens of dogs, some big, some small, some purebreds, some mutts, all reeking of pain and worry as they struggle to unwrap their bandages and shake off their cones of shame. And most of them are K-9s.

How do I know? By the smell. K-9s come in all sizes, shapes, and colors, but we all live for the job. We can smell that on each other like humans can smell perfume.

"How ya doing, girl?"

I struggle to lift my head. A white pit bull with one black eye sniffs at me across from my cell, wagging his hot-dog tail like crazy. He looks just like the dog in the Target commercial, and he grins from his black ear to the white one, despite his cone of shame and the bandages around his leg and chest.

I wag my tail—sort of.

"Fair to middling. You?"

"I'm good, thanks. So good to meet you! I can't wait for breakfast."

His short tail quivers with excitement as he dances on his feet, even the one that's in a cast. He's the happiest K-9 I've ever seen, so much so that I start to wonder if he is a K-9 at all. We, K-9s, are all sorts of wonderful, but happy is not at the top of the list.

He points his nose toward me and sniffs until the dust from the floor makes him sneeze. I know he'd love to get properly introduced and smell my butt, but we're too far apart.

"What's your name, lovely lady?"

"Butter. I'm K-9 Corporal Butter. You?"

"I'm Target."

No kidding.

"Are you a K-9?"

"Of course. I am a qualified customs agricultural agent. I work for the TSA, where I sniff for smuggled agrarian products. Say somebody tries to smuggle in lemons from Sicily or oranges from Costa Rica. Unless properly inspected, they may bring in diseases or aphids that could destroy our crops. My job is to find them and stop them. I also sniff for contraband animals. My sister Raisin works in the field too, but she specializes in Coconut Rhinoceros Beetle Larvae. They are the bane of palm trees."

"Wow. I didn't know such a job existed."

"Sure, it does. It's essential, and also lots of fun. I once found a suitcase full of pangolins."

"Penguins?"

"Not even close. Penguins are those fat birds dressed in tuxedoes. Pangolins are small animals wearing scaly armored vests instead of fur. They look funny, like miniature dinosaurs, but they're useful since they eat ants and termites. Sadly, Chinese traditional medicine practitioners believe their scales and meat have healing properties, so they pay big money to get them. Poachers bring them over from Sri Lanka and the Philippines. They pack them like oiled sardines, so most of them don't make it through the trip."

"That's terrible."

"Yes. Especially if you're a pangolin."

I try to imagine being locked in a suitcase with a dozen other dogs, but I can't. Good. I'm already miserable enough. Fortunately, the whole kennel starts barking, so I forget what I was worried about.

"What's going on?"

"They're bringing breakfast."

Breakfast! I try to stand, but my left front paw wants none of it, and I fall on my side as my leg explodes with pain.

Target cocks his blocky head, his nose wrinkled in worry.

"Are you OK?"

"Middling. You?"

"What happened to you?"

"I was on a mission. Then I got here."

"How?"

"I don't know. How about you?"

He looks down, his ears flat with embarrassment.

"I... I was stupid."

"What did you do?"

"My handler and I were going home after our shift."

"And?"

"I saw a cat."

"Yes?"

"I... I was a bad dog. I took off after it, and I got hit by a car."

"I'm so sorry, Target. That's terrible!"

"Terribly stupid. But enough about me. What happened to you?"

That's so unusual it makes me wonder if Target is really a male. He smells like one, but he's so caring you'd think he's female. Most males seldom remember to ask you how you're doing, and they never do it twice.

"I don't know."

I try to remember. We went on patrol. We were searching for explosives in the village near our base. I was leading the team inside the wire, then...

"I got shot."

"Where?"

"In Kandahar."

"No. Where in your body?"

"I don't know."

"What hurts?"

"Everything."

"What hurts the most?"

"My front paw."

"Do you still have it?"

What a silly question. Of course, I do. It's right there, bandaged, painful, and useless as it is. I can't stand on it or even lick it, but it's there.

"Sure."

"Good. Because some canines lose it, and that's the end of their K-9 career."

"Really?"

"Yep. Does it hurt?"

"Like a son of a gun."

"That's great. It's bad news if it stops hurting."

"Why?"

"Because it's like with us. When you stop hurting, you're dead."

CHAPTER 6

Eating breakfast while lying on your side is not for the weak, I tell you, but one's got to do what one's got to do. I'm a big fan of food—fast food, slow food, cat food, any food. Food is almost as important to me as my people and my job. Even more than my naps. But sadly, this breakfast is nothing to write home about. It's even worse than the MREs in Kandahar. Those at least pretended to smell like something, whether lamb, beef, or chicken, while this here is just a sloppy porridge. But it softens my throat and fills the void in my belly. I always feel better when I eat. Even the pain in my leg starts fading.

Since I'm lying down anyhow, I catch a nap. Technically, since I'm sitting still, I guess you could say that the nap caught me. Either way, my skin gets all prickly, and I wake up. You know, like when somebody stares at you? It's Brown, and he's beat. His uniform looks slept in, his eyes are red, and his mouth has thinned to a line, but his hands are gentle as he pets my ears.

"How're you doing, Butter?"

I slap my tail to the ground.

"Better now that you're here. Can we go?"

I struggle to stand, but I fall on my nose, and Brown's tired face crumples. He sniffs and wipes his eyes with his sleeve.

"Not yet, baby girl. Not yet. You've got to feel better first."

"I feel fine."

He clears his voice.

"I just spoke to Silver. Guinness and Viper send you their best wishes. They all miss you and can't wait to have you back."

I wag my tail. My best friend Guinness, AKA Corporal Guinness Van Jones, is all into combat, apprehension, and that sort of stuff. She's an MPC, Multi-Purpose K-9, just like Viper, but Viper is a Malinois, so we call him the Malligator. We work together on detecting IEDs, but I'm a Labrador and not much into fights. I'd rather eat or nap. We're all different, but they're my brothers in arms, and I miss them terribly.

"Tell them I miss them, eh? I can't wait to be back."

Brown blows his nose.

"Sure. But you need to get better first. Diane called too. She says she misses you. Her cooking hasn't been the same without your help. Aleta and BB send their love."

Diane, my mom, is Brown's wife, and Aleta and BB are my sister and brother, even though neither can sniff bombs or grow a tail. Aleta at least can tell when the bacon's burning and such, but BB can't talk yet, and he can't sniff either. They're my family, and I miss them. I love kids. They are fun to play with, and they always drop food, so I help clean. Some tasks are tastier than others, though. I could do without pumpkin and applesauce, but fries and peaches? Sign me up. As for cookies...

"Aleta started kindergarten. BB is walking now. He's not talking yet, but he should be soon. After all, he's almost three."

"I'm sorry, but the doctor wants to see her now."

It's the same female who doesn't speak dog. Today, she doesn't smell like Cheetos. She smells like bubblegum, and that's even worse. Speak about an evil thing! You chew it within an inch of its life, only to find your teeth glued together. The last time that happened, Brown had to pull my jaws apart to unglue me so I could eat and drink.

Brown picks me up gently and helps me to the stretcher.

"May I come along?"

"I'll ask the vet."

As we head out the door, Target barks.

"Hang in there, Butter. You've got this. You'll be like new in no time."

The door closes before I get to answer, but his words do me good. I can use some encouragement. As much as I love Brown, he acts like he's at a wake. Mine.

CHAPTER 7

BUT WE'RE NOT GOING to a wake just yet. We're back in the rainbow room that looks just the same, but for the rainbows. Brown helps the tech move me from the stretcher to a well-lit exam table. The lights above me are so bright that I have to squeeze my eyes shut for fear they will melt my brain.

The doctor is waiting for us, and today he smells fresh like coffee and soap, and his facial fur is gone. He smiles at me and nods to Brown.

"You must be her handler."

"I'm Brown. I trained Butter since she was a pup. She's my partner and my friend."

"Lovely dog."

Brown frowns.

"Butter is more than a dog. She's an explosive detecting K-9 who performed so many successful missions that nobody knows how many lives she saved. Mine, for sure, more than once. Throughout her career, she never made a mistake. And getting shot was not her fault. She's not only a hero, but she's great company. Always patient, happy, and loving."

My heart goes all warm and squishy when I hear Brown talking me up. Brown's a good man, but he's not much into PDA.

He'd rather feed me than praise me when I get it right, and that's fine with me. I'll take a cookie over two commendations any time. But right now, I can use a pep talk. I'm a little down on my luck, and between getting shot, leaving my friends, and being locked in this darn kennel, things are getting to me.

The vet comes over to check me out. He pets my head and scratches me behind the ears.

"Butter, you're a lucky girl to have such a loyal friend in your handler. Let's check your paw and see how your luck holds."

He holds up my paw, and the tech starts unwrapping the bandage. I brace for pain, but I can barely feel them touching me. Yesterday's agony has dulled into numbness, so much so that I can't even feel it when the vet pinches my toe.

"Does it hurt?"

"No."

He picks up a large needle and sticks it in my toe. I see it go in, but I feel nothing. It's like it's someone else's paw.

"How about this? Does this hurt?"

"No."

You'd think he'd be pleased, but no. His face darkens as he mumbles something to himself, then puts on a pair of thick lighted glasses that make him look like a giant bug. He touches, pulls, and prods every inch of my paw. Boy, am I glad it no longer hurts! He brings it to his nose and sniffs it like I've never seen a human do. He's got good technique, too, four short sniffs in, one out, then repeat. I'm impressed! But why my paw and not my butt?

I'm just about to ask him when he shoots his blue rubber gloves in the garbage, then turns around to speak to Brown.

"This is no good."

Brown stares at him like he's lost it.

"What do you mean it's no good? Didn't you hear her say that it didn't hurt?"

"Exactly. Sticking needles in your toes should hurt. If it

doesn't, that means the nerves are dead. I did my best to repair the ruptured blood vessels, but it doesn't look like it worked. There's not enough blood getting to her paw to keep it alive. And if the nerves are dead, I'm afraid the paw is dying too."

The paw? Dead? My paw? But I'm alive. How can my foot be dead?

Brown measures him with narrowed eyes.

"So what are you going to do about it?"

The vet sighs.

"I'm afraid we'll need to amputate her foot. Otherwise, the infection will spread through her body and kill her."

Brown's hands close into tight fists, and his head juts forward like he's about to punch the vet. He's got a short fuse, Brown, and his size alone is enough to scare most people. But the vet doesn't blink. His clear blue eyes look past Brown's rage into his soul.

"Wouldn't you rather have her live?"

Brown's anger melts. His shoulders drop as he shrinks into a sick shadow of himself. His eyes look everywhere but into mine, and he sighs.

"If you have to..."

Are you freaking kidding me? My blood boils, and I see red.

"Hey, humans! Are you speaking about me? How about speaking to me? What the heck's going on? What are you talking about? What's amputeete?"

The tech blows her nose in a corner, but nobody cares about her. I only have eyes for these two men who talk about me like I'm a defective fire hydrant.

I glare at the doctor and bare my teeth. He rolls his stool toward me and puts his hand on my shoulder.

"I'm sorry, Butter. I'm afraid we'll have to cut off your paw to save your life."

"What? Have you lost your mind, eh?"

That's not polite, I know, but he's got me frazzled. There's only so much that even a meek Canadian like me can take before she blows a gasket.

"Butter, your paw is dead. We need to cut it off; otherwise, it will poison your body, and you'll die too."

"Nonsense. My leg doesn't even hurt anymore."

Then I remember Target. "Legs are like us. When they stop hurting, they die."

Mine stopped hurting.

"What will she do without her leg?" Brown asks.

'She'll have to learn to walk on three limbs. Most dogs do, especially the young ones."

"She's no longer young. She's almost seven."

"And she's a big girl. We may be able to get her a prosthesis."

"Will she go back to work?"

"In Afghanistan? Definitely not. The war is over for her."

Brown wipes his eyes with his sleeve and looks away, and for the first time in my life, I'd love to bite him if I could.

"Are you crazy, man? The vet says I can't go back to my job and to Guinness and Viper? And what do you do? You just stand there and say nothing?"

I try to lunge, but I'm strapped to the darn table. So I bare my teeth, growl, and bark up a storm to make sure they get how I feel. Brown looks away.

"I'm sorry, Butter."

The vet plunges a needle in my neck, and it's all rainbows again.

CHAPTER 8

THE SEARING PAIN in my leg rips through the fog in my brain.
Where the heck am I? The sharp odors of chlorine, blood, and
fear fill my nose, and it all comes back to me. I got shot, and now
they want to cut off my paw. Seriously?

I lift my head to see Target's eyes, the white and the black,
glued to me.

"Hi, Butter."

"Hi."

"How ya doing?"

I don't know. I shake my head to get rid of the fog, but a stab
of pain pierces my leg, and I whimper.

"Sorry, buddy."

"Not your fault."

I glance at my leg, and my heart skips a beat. My paw's gone.
Like, gone. Vanished. All that's left of my leg is a stump encased
in a stiff white bandage. I stretch to lick it, but the cone of shame
won't let me get close. I pant in agony. I didn't know pain like this
existed. It's like someone nailed my paw to a board, crushed it,
and set it on fire. It hurts so bad I can barely breathe. But how can
that be? The paw's gone. So, if it's gone, how can it hurt?

My whole body, from my nose to my toes, throbs with waves

of pain. I brace myself to resist it, but that makes it worse. This is more terrible than the day I got shot. Then I didn't know what happened. Now I do, and this knowledge dwarfs the pain in my leg. My working days are over, and I'll never see my friends again. I'm so desperate that I can't help but whine.

Target's little tail quivers, and his whole butt shakes with it in encouragement. He dances on his paws, sending me good vibes, but I'm not in a place I can receive them.

"It's OK, Butter. It will soon get better, you'll see. They'll give you something to make you better in no time."

"How would you know, eh?"

I don't know where that came from, but I'm embarrassed. It's not Target's fault; he's just trying to make me feel better. But I'm too hurt and too desperate to apologize, so I turn my back to him and lie there, panting to soften the ordeal until the tech comes to check on me.

"You're hurting, aren't you? Let me give you something."

She slips me a pill, and the pain starts to fade. So does Target and the kennel, and all of a sudden, I'm no longer in the hospital. I'm back to that other kennel where, a lifetime ago, Brown came looking for a dog.

I was so small that I could barely see and hear, and I was too young to walk, so I crawled. My brothers and sisters snored, piled on top of each other, as I crawled around looking for food. I heard the door creak open like it did whenever we got fed, and I looked up.

Way above me, two humans stood looking, their heads close to the sky. I cranked up my head to see them better, but I lost my balance, and I fell.

The male laughed.

"They're so cute. How old are they?"

"Four weeks."

"Really? How come you got them so young?"

I recognized the female. She always brought the milk.

"It's a sad story. Some puppy-mill owner had his champion Labrador bitch escape. She came back pregnant, but they weren't purebred, so he couldn't charge an arm and a leg for them. He dropped them here instead of letting their mom look after them until they're old enough. In his business, time is money. The longer she has them, the longer it will take her to have another litter. But we were glad he didn't drop them in the dumpster."

"That's terrible."

"It is. You wouldn't believe the things humans do to dogs. We see them all here. You want a male or a female?"

"A male, maybe?"

"These two. The rest are females."

She pushed forward Brown and Black.

The man kneeled to see them, though there wasn't much to see. He petted Brown with one hand and Black with the other, but they didn't care. They burrowed further into the bedding, looking for milk. That's the thing with boys. They're slow. They hadn't figured out there was no milk in the bedding. Milk only came from the humans.

I was hungry, so I headed toward him, wobbling on my shaky legs, and I latched on to his finger.

He laughed.

"This one is something else. What's his name?"

"That one is a girl. She's Yellow."

"Yellow."

He picked me up and held me in his palm. He looked into my eyes and stroke my head. It felt good, so I sighed and settled in.

"Would you like to feed her?"

"Sure."

He fed me a syringe full of milk. I drank it, then the next and the next.

"She's hungry."

"She's always hungry, that one."

I was about to fall asleep in his hand when he stood up and cleared his throat.

"I'll take her."

The door slams, and I wake up to realize that it was just a dream. I'm no longer Yellow, the puppy Brown took home six years ago. That's just an old memory, so old that I never remembered it until now.

Brown adopted me and we trained for months before we deployed to Kandahar, where we went through mission after mission, detecting explosives and saving lives.

We were a team, Brown and I. Darn it, we were more than a team. We were a K-9 unit.

Then I got shot.

I lost my paw, and he abandoned me here.

CHAPTER 9

I LAY in my cell forever, torn between the wound in my leg and the agony in my soul, until I fell asleep. I woke up thinking it was all just a dream. One of those dreams like when you chase a cat and you're about to catch him, then he turns around, and you find he's a lion. This whole shooting thing must be just a nightmare. I can't wait to wake up and tell Guinness and Viper all about it after I gulp my mutton slop.

But the pain in my paw is real. The whimpering of sick dogs and the smell of disinfectant drag me back to reality and I open my eyes to Brown staring at me, his cheeks wet with tears.

"Hi, Butter."

He sits next to me on the floor and pets me through the kennel grates. That makes me so sad that I want to weep, even though dogs don't cry. Not even when our humans do.

"How are you?"

"I'm OK," I lie.

"Good."

We sit next to each other, the silence between us a chasm neither of us wants to cross. Brown clears his voice.

"The doctor said they had to amputate."

I say nothing.

"But he says you'll get better soon. The pain will go away, and you'll be able to eat and drink as usual."

For the first time in my life, the thought of food leaves me cold. There are things in one's life more important than food. Not many, mind you, but there are a few.

"Then what?"

Brown sighs.

"The doctor said they'll try to get you a prosthesis."

"What's that?"

"That's like a boot made to support your leg so you can walk again."

"What if they don't?"

Brown bites his lip and looks away, and I feel sorry. He's trying to make me feel better, and I'm not helping. But I can't. What will I do if I can't walk? How will I search for IEDs if I can't run and jump? How will I play with Guinness?

The enormity of my loss crushes me. I lay my nose to the ground and close my eyes. I don't want to make Brown feel bad, but it's like: Who am I if I'm not an explosive-detecting K-9? What am I here for?

"I don't know, Butter. I wish I did. I'll try to find out."

"OK."

He leaves, and I lie awake thinking. Will he go home? Will he tell Diane and the kids? Will they stop loving me now that I lost my leg and I'm useless? I choke with sorrow, and my heart bleeds as I miss my people. Especially Diane.

I'll never forget the first time I met Diane. The day Brown took me home from the shelter, he put me in the pocket of his jacket. I was warm, cozy, and full of milk, so I fell asleep at the sound of his heart beating, rocked by the rhythm of his steps.

A scream woke me up.

"Really? A puppy? My puppy?"

It was Diane. She picked me up from Brown's pocket and held me to her cheek. Her skin was warm and soft and smelled like food. Her black curls tickled my nose, and I sneezed. She laughed and kissed Brown.

"Our baby! Look at those lovely eyes and those silky golden ears! We'll call her Butter."

Brown taught her how to feed me, and I slept by their bed in a shoebox padded with Diane's old sweater, breathing her scent. Whenever I cried, she picked me up and fed me. I was loved, cared for, and happy.

Then they got Aleta. I don't know where they found her, but she was tiny and soft and smelled like milk. I got to be a big sister, look after her and teach her the ropes. Speak about a hard job! She's beautiful, but boy, was she slow! She took months to start crawling, and I'm still waiting for her tail to grow. But I love her anyhow.

By then, Brown and I had started training, and we spent our days in a vast hangar covered with cans. Some smelled like explosives: TNT, plastics, fertilizer, sulfur; others held all sorts of odors, from food to cats. I sniffed one can after another until I got them right every single time. Whenever I sat by the right can, Brown gave me one of Diane's chicken rosemary cookies.

In the evenings, I played with Aleta. I taught her how to sniff while Diane cooked us cinnamon chili and tiramisu.

The day Brown and I got deployed to Afghanistan, leaving Diane and Aleta behind, was the worst day of my life.

The grief of leaving them tore me apart. Who will look after Aleta? Who'll watch over her and lick her tears? Who'll teach her how to grow a tail?

Diane is a good mom, but she's only human. How will she cope on her own?

"Take good care of Aleta while I'm gone. Don't let her tumble down the stairs. Make sure she doesn't chew on Brown's shoes. You know how he gets."

"Sure thing. I'll look after her, and I'll send you pictures. But promise me you'll look after Brown."

"I will. I'll bring him back."

I did.

But who'll look after him now?

CHAPTER 10

I'M NOT BRAGGING if I say I'm a good napper. I'm the best napper I ever met, in fact. If anyone organized napping championships, I bet you a bowl of kibble against a three-mile run that I would win it no contest.

But sleep wouldn't come near me that night. It wasn't only the pain—the pill helped with that—but I was bewildered. The whole night I struggled to figure out how can I be a K-9 without my paw. And, if I'm not a K-9, then who am I? And what am I here for?

I must have fallen asleep by the morning since I wake up to Target wagging not only his tail but his whole butt to greet me. For a moment, I wonder what his blood tastes like. But it's not his fault, of course. He's just a happy dog, and nothing will change his cheerful disposition.

"How are you doing, Butter? You look lovely today."

I swallow my first two remarks, then my third.

"I'm good. How about you?"

"Excellent. It's going to be a great day. We'll get breakfast, and then we can chat, and then we'll have dinner. It doesn't get much better than this."

"Shut up, Target, you dumb pit bull."

The lugubrious voice comes from a dark corner. It's not loud, just a low, haunting howl, almost too soft to hear, but Target's happy grin melts like a snowman in the sun. He flattens his ears and shrivels, and I feel guilty because that's exactly what I wanted to say. But I didn't.

"Who's that?"

"That's Nora."

I strain my eyes to see her, but all I can see is a shadow. I can't even tell her breed.

"What's wrong with her?"

Target's voice lowers.

"She's dying."

"Why?"

His voice drops to a whisper.

"The old shrew used to be a drug-sniffing K-9 with the TSA. Some folks say she got addicted to drugs, and that's why she got sick. By the time they found out, it was too late to treat her, so she's on hospice care now."

"What's hospice?"

"It's when you're about to die, and they keep you comfortable."

That's an interesting thought. I'd like to be comfortable. But would I want to die?

Breakfast arrives, and it's no better than the last one, but I get it down anyhow. I always feel better when I eat.

"What did you eat in Afghanistan?" Target asks.

"Lamb. Chicken. Beef."

"Wow!"

"Well, not really. It was just kibble, but my handler would add some flavors from a bag, then douse it with hot water, and it wasn't too bad. How about you? What do you eat at home?"

"Just kibble. But then you know what it's like. You pick up after the kids and help clean the dishes, and it's not so bad."

"They never let us clean the dishes. Well, there were no

dishes other than our bowls. We only ate MREs."

"What are those?"

"Meals Ready to Eat. It's dried food that comes in a bag. You add hot water, and then it's food again."

"Good?"

"Some better than others. The meatloaf wasn't bad, especially smothered in ketchup, but the Chili and Macaroni Vegetable Lasagna...."

"What do you guys know about food?"

Nora's howl makes Target shrivel.

Not me. There aren't many subjects I consider myself an expert in, but food is my number one. I eat it all, from kibble to baby formula, marrow bones, and chocolate cake. Not at the camp, of course. There was nothing there but MREs. But Diane is a chef with a catering business. She does it all: barbecue, Mexican, Italian, fusion. Whenever she works on a new recipe, she tests it at home first. The kids aren't really into it, but Brown and I help her the best we can. I suggested sprinkling fried okra over her Tacos al Pastor and adding a touch of cinnamon to her smoky chipotle chili. I slobber just thinking about it. I'm an expert, and I won't have some drug-addicted mutt tell me that I don't know my food. So, with a voice sweeter than a well-soaked tiramisu, I ask:

"What sort of food would you like to talk about, Nora? Italian, Mexican, French? I'm from the south, so I'm partial to barbecue, but we can talk anything from béchamel to sushi if you want."

"Who are you?"

"I'm Corporal K-9 Butter, based in Kandahar, Afghanistan. I've been detecting explosives there for the last five years. How about you?"

The whole kennel holds their breath waiting to see what's going to happen. Chorizo stops chewing on the grates of his cell. Goldilocks forgets he was cleaning his tail. And Target? I think he forgot to breathe.

"I'm Nora."

CHAPTER 11

BELIEVE IT OR NOT, Nora isn't so bad when you get to really know her. It turns out she's a beagle, like Snoopy, Charlie Brown's famous dog. Her problem isn't her personality; it's her voice. Beagles are adorable. They look like stuffed toys, chunky and spotted, with silky pancake ears falling to their knees. They're cute as heck until they open their mouths. But then, beware! They have this low, haunting howl that makes them sound mournful even when they're having fun, and Nora is no exception.

I meet her in rehab as I struggle to walk on my three legs. And I'm not doing well. I'm good for three steps, but every fourth step, I fall on my face. So I get up and try again. And again.

"Hey, Three-Pawed. Just count to three, and skip the fourth step."

I thought I recognized the low howl from the treadmill, but I couldn't believe that this itsy-bitsy little thing could be the harpy who frightened a pit bull, like Target. I open my mouth to message her the nasties when I see her frail little body shake on her unsteady legs, and I close my mouth. But she persists.

"Seriously. It's like the waltz. 1-2-3, 1-2-3, 1-2-3. Just keep the rhythm and skip the missing paw."

"I don't dance," I growl, but I try to keep the count. 1-2-3, 1-2-3, and for the first time, I don't fall on my face.

"Good job, Three-Pawed."

"My name's Butter, not Three-Pawed."

"And mine's Nora, not Old Shrew."

My ears flatten in embarrassment. I didn't think she heard Target's whispers. It turns out I was wrong.

I go on waltzing as she struggles to keep up with that treadmill that's too slow for a mildly energetic turtle. I start to get the hang of it, and I barely face-plant anymore when all hell breaks loose in the gym. A fancy white poodle breaks a nail and goes into a total meltdown. The therapist rushes to console her as everyone else chuckles.

It feels like an excellent time to waltz toward Nora's treadmill and offer my butt in introduction. She sniffs it politely, then provides me hers. She smells old and sick but not sour, and I wonder what keeps her sparkle going. Once we complete the formalities, we get to chat.

"How does being a K-9 in Afghanistan prepare you to talk about food?" Nora howls.

"Afghanistan surely doesn't. But my mom is a chef."

"A dog? A chef?"

"My human mom, Diane. I never knew my real mom. She worked in a puppy mill."

"A puppy mill!" Nora cocks her head, and one of her pancake ears falls over her face, so she shakes her head to put it back in its place.

"Yes. One of those places that breed litter after litter to make money. They couldn't care less about the dogs."

"I know. I worked in one."

"You? I thought you were a drug sniffer."

"That was my second career. I started as a bitch in a puppy mill, but I stopped being productive when I was five, so my owner dumped me. The human who rescued me worked for the

TSA, so I ended up working with him. They didn't care about my puppy production; they only cared about my nose. And nobody has a nose like mine. We, beagles, have the best noses in the world."

I clear my voice, but I swallow my comment. She's not without confidence, Nora, even though she's just a scrawny little thing with ribs sticking out, ears hanging to the ground, and a howl that could wake up the dead. But she grows on you.

"Did you like detecting drugs?"

I bite my tongue, but it's too late. Target said she got addicted; that's why she's sick. What a stupid question! My ears flatten, and I look down in embarrassment, but Nora laughs.

"That stupid Target and his rumors again. That dog doesn't have the common sense of a squirrel crossing the road. Even worse, he couldn't keep his mouth closed if they wired his jaw shut."

I feel bad since Target is my friend.

"Come on, Nora, he's a nice, well-meaning dog."

"He is. He's also a stupid conspiracy theorist. It's not his fault, but boy, I wish he found a grain of common sense somewhere. I don't know if it's those citrus aphids he's been sniffing or if he was born that way. Either way, sniffing drugs didn't get me addicted, just like sniffing explosives didn't make you an insurgent. That's poppycock."

"Why are you sick, then?"

"I got breast cancer because of all those litters I had—eight in four years. And every single damn time, they took away my puppies before they were ready because they wanted me to have another litter. Then another. Every time was another heartbreak. I cried for days, looking for them everywhere. I couldn't believe they were gone. Then I'd have another litter, and I'd burst with joy. I cared for them and loved them, then they took them away again. It's not fun being a bitch in a puppy mill. Don't ever try it, Butter."

Her voice breaks into a heart-wrenching howl that shakes the walls, and every dog in rehab turns to stare at me like I bit her.

"I'm sorry, Nora."

"It's not your fault, girl. How are you doing?"

"I've been better."

"I know. Sorry about your leg."

"Thanks."

"But they make amazing prostheses these days. You may even get to do things you could never do with your own legs. Have you heard about Oscar Pistorius, the Blade Runner?"

"No."

"He's this guy who lost his legs when he was a pup, but he still got to win the Olympics. The other runners wanted him banned. They said that his blades were better than real legs and gave him an advantage."

"Really! Could he jump and sniff explosives?"

"I don't know about jumping, but as for sniffing, I'm pretty sure that's a no. He's human, and with or without legs, they can't smell worth a damn."

Talking to Nora gave me hope. If even a human, as clumsy and slow as they are, could win the Olympics on a prosthesis, maybe I could get one and go back to my work?

CHAPTER 12

Life's better in Butterland now that I have friends. Target brightens my mornings with some kind comment about my shiny coat or fluffy tail. I spend endless hours debating with Nora the importance of herbs and spices in Italian cooking before moving on to Mexican or French.

"Absolutely no garlic in fettucine Alfredo! That's blasphemy," Nora howls, and the kennel shivers.

I'm undaunted.

"You'll never know until you try. And you don't even have to mince it; you can just drop a couple of roasted cloves to hint at the aroma."

Nora shakes her head so hard that her ears slap her face. She's a purist and only goes for the classics, while, thanks to Diane, I'm more into fusion.

"That's ridiculous! What are you going to come up with next?"

"Chocolate in chili?"

"No way! Chocolate only goes in mole!"

"Absolutely not! Diane's Chocolate Cinnamon Chili was our best seller. We put it in a bowl of warm sourdough bread and sprinkled it with grated cheddar."

The banter helps us pass the days. It takes Nora's mind off her hospice and mine off my disability and unemployment. Now that my stump is almost healed, I spend day after day in rehab, learning to walk on three legs. But I really look forward to getting my prosthesis. I can't wait until I can run and jump again so I can go back to work. I'm so excited that I bend Target's ear about it every single day.

"With the prosthesis, I'll be better and faster than ever before. Paws are delicate, you know. They get burned when you step on hot metal—and every single freaking piece of metal is hot under the Afghan sun. Paws hurt when you step on sharp debris or thorny branches. The prosthesis will allow me to do things nobody else can."

"But will you know if you step on a mine?" Target asks.

I shake my head, but I keep my patience. It's not his fault he's naïve. After all, he's only an agricultural pit bull. How would he know?

"Prosthesis or not, once you step on an IED, you're history. They're designed to explode at the slightest pressure. Even a freaking cat could set them off. Someone said they trained rats to find IEDs. Rats don't blow up since they're light enough to step on a mine without triggering it. But I think that's poppycock. How would you train a rat to take that kind of responsibility? Rats are unreliable by definition, unlike us, K-9s. Either way, you should never step on an IED. To point them out to your handler, you sit next to them. Touching them is a recipe for disaster."

I lay down to lick my remaining front paw, wondering. Maybe I could get a prosthesis for that one too? From being Three-Pawed, I would become Bionic Butter. I'd love to show Viper and Guinness a thing or two!

"That's wonderful. I can't wait to see your prosthesis."

Target smiles from one ear to the other, his tail going a mile a minute, and his butt follows. He's been a great friend and an excellent companion, always listening and having something nice to say. He may be the friendliest dog I ever met, no disrespect to Guinness and Viper. They're my friends and heroes, but they're no cheerleaders. They're like: "Get off your assets and get going, will you?" Target is all about: "What a good job you're doing!" I'll miss him terribly when he goes back to his aphids and his pangolins tomorrow.

"I'll miss you, Target."

His wee tail shakes.

"I'll miss you too, Butter. I'd love to meet again. Any chance you'll get to California?"

I hope not. I need to get back to my work and my people, and they're half a world away from California, but I don't want to be rude.

"You never know. How would I find you?"

"The US Border and Customs Protection. Oh, Butter, I'd love to get together if we could."

"Me too, big boy. Me too."

And I'm not lying. When the tech puts a leash on Target to take him away, the whole kennel explodes in loving good-byes.

"Good luck, Target."

"Go get them, orange sniffer."

"There goes the pangolin hero."

Target's butt dances with excitement, and a goofy grin splits his face from his black ear to the white one. Even I sniff a little. After meeting Target, I'll never look at pit bulls the same way. I've heard people calling them cold-blooded mindless killers, but nothing could be further from the truth. There's a big kind heart beating in Target's broad chest. I hope he gets a beautiful life, and he looks both ways before chasing his next cat.

"I'll miss you guys. I hope you all make it home safely."

He's about to step out when a mourning howl makes the kennel shiver.

"Good luck, Target. You need it. You deserve it, too. Just hang off those rumors, will you?"

"Thanks, Nora. Be well."

The kennel feels hollow without him. He was the life of the party, and without him, we're all a little sadder. But it won't be long now. My prosthesis should come any day, and then I'm good to go. I can't wait to show it to Guinness and Viper.

When Brown visits that evening, his eyes are dark with worry, and he smells funny. I sniff again. Sadness, and...guilt? Why guilt? What did he do? He smells just like that time he forgot Diane's birthday. But I'm pretty sure it's not my birthday since I don't have one.

"How're you doing, Butter? What's new?"

"My friend Target went home today. He's going back to sniffing pangolins. I can't wait for my prosthesis to arrive, so I can leave too. I heard they're phenomenal, much better than paws. I'll get to be faster and stronger than I ever was. I'll be Bionic Butter, and I can't wait to show off to Viper and Guinness."

Brown's face melts like snow in the rain.

"What are you saying, Butter?"

Something bugs him, and he's not listening. I start over.

"My prosthesis. With it, I'll be a better K-9 than I ever was. I'll run faster and jump and work better than ever. I can't wait for it to arrive. What do you think? Tomorrow maybe?"

Brown clears his throat.

"Prosthetics are expensive, you know. And we don't have a lot of money."

Has he lost it?

"Money? What does money have to do with anything?"

He sighs.

"We'll see, sweetheart. We'll see what the army can do for you. I know they'll do their best to look after a K-9 hero like you. And I'll speak to Diane. We'll look into crowdfunding. But in the meantime...."

He looks away. That's terrible news. Something wrong with Diane? Or the kids?

"What is it, Brown? What's the matter?"

"In the meantime, I'll have to start training a new dog."

CHAPTER 13

I cock my head and stare at Brown, trying to understand what he said.

"A new dog? You want a new dog?"

Brown's face crumples like he's stepped on a nail, and the stench of guilt gets so intense it chokes me.

"See, Butter, I'm just a dog handler in the army. They need me back in Kandahar to keep our soldiers safe. I need to go back to work."

"Sure. Me too. We'll go back as soon as we get the prosthesis."

"There is no prosthesis, Butter."

"Not yet. But it's coming soon. We'll go back as soon as it arrives."

"Butter, the army can't wait. The soldiers are in danger now."

I sigh. Oh well. I guess I won't get to be Bionic Butter after all. It was nice while it lasted, imagining Viper's falling jaw and Guinness's delight. I'm a little sad, to be honest, since I really looked forward to, for once, stealing the show. Those two are so sharp and so competitive that I always feel like I'm last. It would be nice to be the best, just once. But it is what it is.

"Oh well. I hoped I'd show off to Guinness and Viper, but

what can you do? I know they love me just the way I am, three-pawed and all. Let's go then."

"Butter, you can't go. You can barely walk a few feet. You can't work as an explosive detecting K-9 on three paws."

"I'll train, and I'll get better. And then, when the prosthesis arrives, maybe they can send it over."

Brown's eyes are bright with tears.

"Oh, Butter, how I wish that were possible. But it's not."

"What do you mean?"

"You have to stay here and get better. I'll speak to Diane about how we can get some money for the prosthesis. Maybe crowd-funding? One way or another, we'll get you that prosthesis as soon as we can."

"And then we go back to our war?"

Brown shakes his head.

"No, Butter, I don't think you'll ever go back to war. But I have to."

"But Brown, you know you can't sniff drugs! You can't even find your own stinky socks, even though I showed you a thousand times!"

"Butter, I'll have to... I'll have to get another dog."

The enormity of it crushes me. Brown wants another dog? How can that be? I've been with him my whole life. I know no other life but with him. And now, just because I lost a paw, he's going to leave me and get another dog? I don't get it. If Brown lost a leg, would I go get myself another human? Not in forever and a day. So how can he? My brain is not big enough to take this in.

"You mean you'll get another dog and go back to war?"

"After I train him, yes."

"And you'll go on patrol with Guinness and Viper? And your other dog?"

Brown nods, and I choke. This new dog will not only take Brown. He'll take my job and my friends. Viper, and even Guinness. Then what? What's left?

Brown tries to pet me.

"You'll be all right, Butter. You'll go home to Diane and the kids as soon as you're better. They're looking forward to having you back. And I'll call when I can."

"You'll call? You'll call from Afghanistan where you'll take the other dog?"

I stare at Brown's face, which held nothing but love for as long as I can remember, and I only see betrayal. My world just got upended, and the love fell out of it. I'm left with nothing. I thought it was bad when I lost my leg. It turns out that I was living the good life. Then, I still had people who cared for me. Now, I'm on my own. I hoped to be Bionic Butter, but it turns out I'll be just Lonely Three-Pawed instead.

I turn my back to Brown, and I lay my nose on my paw. Oh, how I wish I didn't wear my bulletproof vest the day I got shot. I wouldn't be here to listen to Brown talking about the other dog who'll take over my life. He'll have four paws, and Brown, and Viper and Guinness, while I rot here in this crate.

I've never been so miserable, not even when I got shot. Then, I had Brown and Guinness and Viper.

I've never hated anyone yet. But this new dog, I hate him. He took everything from me. I've got nothing left.

CHAPTER 14

I DIDN'T EAT dinner that night. I couldn't sleep either. I just lay in my cell thinking about Guinness and Viper since I was too mad to even think about Brown.

I was flying to Afghanistan for my last deployment when I met Guinness. And I was bummed. Bad enough that I missed Diane and the kids already. But traveling as cargo? I was locked in a crate with nothing to do but listen to the engine noise and lick my paws. And I was desperate to pee.

I lay on one side; I rolled to the other; I crossed my legs. No good. I even tried to chase my tail to distract myself. Try that in a tight crate! Nothing helped. I couldn't stand it anymore, and I barked with frustration.

"What the fiddling funk!"

Far ahead, someone answered:

"Buddy?"

I was so relieved I almost peed myself.

"Who are you?"

"I'm Guinness. You?"

"I'm Butter. I need help!"

"What's up, Butter?"

"I'm hungry, I'm cold, and I need to pee."

"Same here. Just relax, buddy; we'll be there in no time."

"I can't relax. I need to pee."

"How about peeing in the crate?"

"I can't do that! I've never done it, not even when I was a pup."

I hear her mumble and fuss. Claws scratch the floor, then scrape metal. When I hear running water, I almost let go.

"Hey, Butter, are you a girl?"

"Of course."

"How about trying to pee like a boy? You know how they lift their leg and spray to the side? Try to pee through the grate. I just soaked a fancy golf bag smelling like cats, and it feels terrific."

I stare through my grate. Luckily, there's a pink Hello Kitty roll-on just ahead. Not as good as a real cat, but hey—beggars can't be choosers. Hello Kitty will have to do.

I turn sideways, balance on three legs, and let go, splashing the pink roll-on with the power of despair. Instant happiness courses through my body, and I can finally relax.

"That worked. Thanks, Guinness."

"Don't mention it."

That's Guinness. She's a rebel and a go-getter. And, despite her Teutonic pedigree, she's kind, funny, and sassy. I was ecstatic when we found out we were deployed at the same base in Kandahar.

My other best friend is Viper, and he's a different story. He's Belgian, a Malinois with a reputation to uphold. Have you ever met a Malinois? They're extreme athletes, intense, single-minded, and with a focus so sharp some call it neurosis. I once saw a Malinois jump on an IED and get himself killed just to prove a point. But that's not Viper. He isn't anything like that. Don't get me wrong now; he won't give you the warm fuzzies, and he won't tell you that you look thin when you're fat. But you can trust him to watch your back and tell you the truth whether you like it or not. He's strong, honest, and loyal, even though he's a little rough around the edges.

I wonder what they'll do when Brown shows up at the base with his new dog. Will they welcome and befriend him? Will they forget I ever existed? Or will they hold him at paw's length for the crime of stealing my life?

The thought of Guinness and Viper welcoming this imposter and sharing their lives with him makes me sick with loss and pain. The void in my heart hurts even worse than my missing paw, and I whimper.

"Butter?"

Nora's howl shakes the walls. Just one word, and every K-9 in the place is awake, wondering what's up. I'd love to pretend I'm asleep, but nobody would believe it. I sigh.

"Yes, Nora."

"I love you."

That came out of nowhere. We only met a few times in rehab. We barely know each other, and Nora's not into PDA. But her words find their way to my soul.

I sniff and mumble.

"Thank you, Nora."

Chorizo, the sausage dog to my left who never talks to anyone, sticks his long nose out through the grate.

"Love you, Butter."

My jaw falls. I occasionally spat some food toward his crate when I couldn't finish it, but we never talked. He never even thanked me.

"Love you, Butter."

That's Goldilocks, the Afghan hound in the crate kitty-corner from mine. He's an outcast. Target was the only one who ever spoke to him, but that's no wonder. Target would chat with a rock if he thought it needed a pick-me-up. That's the kind of dog Target is. Everyone else ignores Goldilocks. Not only because he's Afghan but also because of his long flowing hair, dark sultry eyes, and elegant silhouette. Goldie makes us all feel ugly and fat. I used to ignore him, too, until Target told me how heartbroken he is because his racing career is over. And, since he's Afghan and a hound, nobody wants him. I felt terrible, so I looked for something nice to say, but all that came to mind was the dust, the heat, and the IEDs. Then I remembered the Afghan food our translator once brought us.

"I love Kabuli palaw. Meaty rice, nutty pistachios, crunchy carrots, and especially the fried raisins topping. Mmm."

Goldie shook his head to uncover his eyes and looked at me.

"Really? My favorite is Qormah e Nadroo. Have you ever had it? Onions with yogurt, lotus roots, cilantro, and coriander. And lamb, of course."

After that, we exchanged recipes every once in a while. Now, as Goldie's smoldering eyes look at me with kindness and his mane floats around him like an aura, I'm so grateful I forget to be envious.

"Love you, Butter," someone says in the corner, and I don't even know who they are, but I love them too. I no longer feel lonely and useless. These are my people, and they care about me, even if Brown doesn't.

CHAPTER 15

Life was on the up and up after that, even though I didn't forget about Guinness and Viper. Nor did I forgive Brown. I still felt rejected, but I no longer felt alone. With my new friends rooting for me, I gave my all to rehab, and I got waltzing pretty good.

"Good job, Three-Pawed. One of these days, they'll recruit you to *Dancing with the Stars*. I'd better teach you the samba while I'm still around," Nora says.

"Shut up, Nora." I stick my tongue out at her as she struggles to keep up with that treadmill that's way too slow for a drunk snail, but I know she's kidding. We're friends now, and she helps fill the void Brown left behind.

"What's the samba?"

"It's this Brazilian dance where you wear skimpy clothes, sway your hips, and shake your stuff."

"I don't have any stuff to shake."

"Many don't, but they shake it anyhow. It's all in the attitude."

That was all good fun, but I still couldn't climb stairs. My remaining front paw wasn't strong enough to hold me, and my balance wasn't good enough to let me do it on my hind legs alone. But I didn't give up. Day after day, I kept trying. Some-where deep inside, I still hoped Brown was wrong, and if I worked hard enough, I could go back to work, even three-pawed as I was. But even I knew that to do that, I'd have to run, jump, and climb. Believe it or not, insurgents don't only place bombs where they're easy to reach. You need to look everywhere: under trucks, inside boxes, even on top of walls. And I couldn't even jump in a car.

The therapist watched me struggle with the stairs and sighed.

"It would help if you lost some weight, Butter."

My jaw dropped. I thought we were friends, and her words hit me right in the feels.

"Don't get me wrong now, pretty girl. I love you just the way you are. You're the best-looking three-pawed Labrador in the house. But, if you lost five pounds, you could do so much more."

"How do I do that?"

"You need to move more and eat less. But that's easier said than done."

She was right. I tried to leave some food in my bowl, but it kept calling my name until I licked the bowl clean. To help me out, they switched me to a low-calorie food that tasted healthy.

"Phew." Chorizo spat out the piece I'd sent him. "That's terrible. Is it vegan?"

"I dunno, but it's supposed to help me lose weight."

"It sure will. Don't send it to me anymore; it will ruin my appetite."

I kept trying, but I made little progress. Until one day, the therapist greeted me with a grin going from one ear to the other. She looked just like Target but for the black eye.

"Hey, Butter, I have a surprise for you."

My heart skipped a beat.

"I'm going back to work?"

"Not quite. But almost as good. Guess what?"

"What?"

"Your prosthesis arrived."

"My prosthesis?"

I'd been waiting for it for so long that I stopped hoping it would ever arrive. And now it had.

"Yep. Look!"

She opened a box full of bubbly plastic, the kind that sounds like a gunshot when you bite it. I totally love it, so I started bursting it until it sounded like a machine gun and half the gym dropped to take cover. She took it away.

"That's not what this is about, girl. Look."

She unwrapped a blue plastic contraption looking like a giant pizza wheel attached to a harness. I sniffed it, but I didn't smell any cheese—just chemicals.

"This is it?"

"Yep. Let's check it out."

She buckled the harness around my chest and adjusted it with the plastic wheel thing sticking out of my leg.

"Give it a try."

What the heck? I stood up and tried to waltz, but the wheel got in the way.

"Can you take out the wheel?"

"Nope. You've got to use it, Butter. Step on it. That's what it's for."

Use it? How do I use a pizza wheel when I don't have a pizza?

"Stop waltzing and try to tango. Instead of the 1-2-3, it's back to the old 1-2-3-4, my friend."

It's been so long, I forgot how to walk on four legs, but I tried. And go figure. Soon enough, I could walk and even run again! A little awkward at first, but I even got to climb a couple of steps by the end. Coming back down was another matter. I went helter-skelter and the thing twisted off.

The therapist gathered me off the floor and started unbuckling my new wheel.

"Wonderful job, Butter. I'm so proud of you! We'll do this again tomorrow."

"Can I please take it with me? Just for a moment? I want to

show it to Nora and the others. They've been looking forward to it coming!"

"OK. But just for a moment."

She takes me back to the kennel, and I explode through the door barking up a storm.

"Hey, Nora, Goldie, Chorizo, look at this, will you? I'll introduce you to Bionic Butter!"

Silence. Nobody says anything. They stare at me with long mourning faces, then look away.

"What's wrong with you people? You don't like it? Is it because it's blue? You don't think blue looks good on me?"

Goldie clears his voice.

"It's very nice, Butter. Blue looks great on you."

"Very nice? Very nice? This is more than very nice. It's tremendous. Exciting. Stupendous. Formidable!"

"Yep."

"What the heck's wrong with you, people?"

Chorizo sniffs and Goldie follows suit.

"Nora died."

CHAPTER 16

NORA, dead? I couldn't believe it, even though I knew Nora was dying even before I met her. Her spunk, her strength, her wisdom —where did they all go? Where do good dogs go when they die? And for that matter, where do people go?

I asked Chorizo and Goldie. They didn't know. I bet Nora did, but she wasn't saying.

The kennel wasn't the same without Nora. We all feared her howling and pointed words, but it turns out we all counted on her when things got rough. Whether we liked it or not, she nudged us to move forward instead of wallowing in self-pity. Just seeing that itsy-bitsy old dog stand at death's door with the strength of a hurricane made us ashamed to be weak.

Now that she was gone, we had to rely on ourselves. I worked hard on my rehab, and I got good at it. I could climb stairs almost as fast as I did when I had all my paws. I got so used to the funky-blue pizza cutter that I raced Goldie from one end of the gym to the other. He did three laps for each one of mine, and I still lost. How come, you ask? Well, why don't you try to keep up with an Afghan, for Dog's sake? They can run up to forty miles an hour. I could run maybe six for a minute or so, but that's just so I obey the speed limit. But at least I could run. Soon enough, I could go back to work, I thought.

I considered writing to Brown, even though I was still mad at him. He never came back to see me after the night he told me about The Other Dog. I thought I'd let him know that I was on the mend, and I'd soon be back to work, so he doesn't need The Other Dog. But I don't know how to write. And I didn't have his address. So I decided to wait until I was all better, then surprise him and Diane by walking home on my three paws and the pizza cutter.

"Where will you go? How do you know where your home is?" Goldie asked.

"I'll follow my nose, of course. How else? How do you know where to run?"

"I find things by sight. My nose isn't anywhere near my best feature," Goldie said, turning up his muzzle so we could all admire his elegant profile and silky ears.

Chorizo chuckled.

"Cut the crap, Goldie. We all know how pretty you are, and we're still your friends. Not because of it, but despite it."

Goldie's nose dove.

"I'm sorry; I just couldn't resist. You see, being pretty is all I've got—that, and my running. And I don't get much running these days. You all have something to be proud of. You, Butter, are a hero. You lost your leg while defending our country. You don't rub it in anyone's face, but we can all see you clawing your way through rehab just to go back to work. You, Chorizo, are a brave little soul, like all dachshunds. Your heart is larger than you are. Nora was our beacon of wisdom and honesty. Target has a heart of gold. He always has a good word for everyone, and he never failed to bring a smile to our faces. But me? I've got nothing but my speed and my looks. That's why I can't resist showing off every once in a while. It makes me feel like I'm worth something."

That made me sad. It's a sad day when you have to apologize

for being pretty. And I know how much Goldie misses his freedom. His ancestors hunted the endless Afghan desert, but he's locked in a kennel no bigger than mine.

"Don't listen to Chorizo. He's just envious. We all are," I said.

But Goldie's luck was about to turn. One evening as we sat telling our stories, the vet brought someone to see Goldie. The visitor was a fancy man smelling like a forest in the rain who must have borrowed his clothes from a parrot.

We all stuck our noses out of our crates to sniff him better. None of us had been out in the rain for ages, and we missed it terribly, but he only had eyes for Goldie.

"Isn't he beautiful! Look at that silky golden coat!"

Goldie was delighted, but he's shy with strangers, so he shook his head, and his mane covered his eyes.

"Can he see?" Fancy asked.

"Of course. When he wants to."

"Can I see him better?"

The vet let him out, and Goldie got into it. His head high, his eyes sultry, he strutted his stuff and ran from one end of the kennel to the other, his golden locks floating behind him like a train.

Fancy picked his jaw off the floor.

"I'll take him."

"Take him? Take him where?" Chorizo yapped.

The vet nodded.

"He's a beauty, but he needs a lot of work. He needs to run every day for at least an hour in an enclosed space, otherwise he'll be gone. Jogging doesn't count. He needs to gallop to loosen his limbs, and no human can keep up with him."

Fancy shrugged.

"I have a large fenced yard. He can run all he wants for hours every day."

"His coat needs a lot of care. An hour a day or more, otherwise, it gets so matted it may never recover."

Fancy laughed.

"Don't you worry about that, Doc. Goldie's coat will have the best care money can buy. I'm a fashion photographer, and I need him to look phenomenal. Hey, Goldie, what would you think about starring in *Vogue*, my man?"

Goldie slobbered.

"What's *Vogue*?" I asked.

"The fanciest fashion magazine there is. One picture in it, and you've got it made," Goldie whispered, his eyes glued on Fancy's peacock blue coat. Fancy didn't miss it.

"You'll just strike a pose, and we'll have humans mesmerized. They'll slobber at the high heels, eyeglasses, and bags. What do you think?"

"Really?"

"Absolutely. I'll take care of everything. Your only job is to look fantastic and sell accessories. Deal?"

"You betcha."

When Goldie strutted out with Fancy, his head held high and his flowing tail following him, we watched him, torn between sadness and envy.

"We'll miss you, pretty boy!" Chorizo barked.

I sighed.

"It won't be the same without him, but at least he found a good fit."

Chorizo laid his nose on his paws.

"I always knew it's better to be pretty than to be smart."

I sighed.

"Our turn will be coming soon, sausage boy. Just hang in there. "

I wasn't really lying. I do wish Chorizo the best, but I hope I leave first. I'm so tired of the kennel, I can't deal with being alone again.

CHAPTER 17

Days came and went; new dogs came and left, but Chorizo and I were going nowhere. We waited in the kennel for somebody to want us, but nobody did.

The hope that my prosthesis had revived faded away. I lost faith that I'd ever go back to work and be useful again. Nobody needed me.

My heart was no longer in rehab so I stopped pushing myself. My progress stalled, and it looked like I had reached my limit. Going back to work was just a pipe dream, so I resigned myself to being three-pawed forever.

Chorizo struggled too. Nobody wanted him either. We were like two inmates with no end in sight. So, since we had no future, we spent our time talking about the past. I told him about IEDs. He told me about badgers.

"That's what we, dachshunds, were bred for, hundreds of years ago in Germany. We were meant to dig into burrows and flush out badgers. That's why we're long, low, and stubborn. And brave, of course, but that goes without saying."

"Badgers? Why on earth would you want a badger? How do you cook them?"

Chorizo looked at me down his long nose, twitching his ears with impatience.

"For sport, of course. Badgers are fierce little creatures. Flushing them out of their burrows is not for the weak of heart; it takes courage and determination. Besides that, their hair is perfect for barber's brushes."

"Barber's brushes? Who uses them anymore?'

"Some purists still do. Badgers' hair is also good for paint-brushes. Anyhow, that's what we used to do, but that line of business is just about extinct. Nowadays, we're mostly pets."

I've heard of pets, but I've never been close to one. All my friends work for a living.

"What do pets do?"

"They wag their tails and eat snacks. They take their humans out for walks, then bring mud in the kitchen and eat the toilet paper."

"And then?"

"Then they nap and start over."

That didn't sound like fun.

"What work do they do?"

"That's just it: They don't work. Pets keep their humans company and make them happy."

"Sure, but I mean, what are they good for?"

Chorizo sighed.

"Oh, Butter. Once a K-9, always a K-9. How about trying to be just an ordinary dog for a change? Just chill, rest, and have fun?"

I didn't quite get it. But hey, to each their own. So when an elderly couple stopped by to see Chorizo and started babbling baby language to him, I bit my tongue instead of telling them off.

"What a cute little poopsy," the woman swooned.

"Yes. I'm cute. Really cute," Chorizo yapped, wagging his tail like crazy and laying on the charm.

"Poopsy!" I growled. They didn't hear me, but Chorizo did.

"Butter!"

"Yeah, yeah."

"That one's kinda noisy. How about this other one here?" the man said, bending over to stare at me.

The woman came to see me, and Chorizo's ears dropped.

"Poor doggy! He only has three legs. That's terrible! You're right; maybe we should take this one," she said, sticking her fingers in my crate to pet me.

Chorizo choked.

"Butter! You said you didn't want to be a pet!"

"What if I changed my mind?"

"But...but..."

"Just kidding, pal."

I bared my teeth and growled, and the woman pulled back faster than you could say pizza pie.

They left with Chorizo, of course. His short little legs moved a mile a minute, and his belly skirted the ground as he raced to the door.

He glanced back.

"Good luck, Butter. I love you."

"Love you too, pal. Have a good life."

And just like that, I was alone again. It wasn't new, but it was getting old. I had nothing left to fight for.

Some of the new dogs tried to be friendly, but I ignored them. You love them, and they leave, over and over again. I couldn't take any more heartbreak.

The therapist got worried.

"You've got to put your heart into your work, Butter; otherwise, nothing happens. You won't get better unless you try."

"Who cares? I'm doing nothing but lying in my crate all day anyhow."

"But Butter, you were doing so well. You made such progress. You can't stop now."

I did. I wanted nothing but to eat and sleep. My days of fighting were over.

The therapist told the vet.

"I think she's depressed. All her friends left, and she's still here."

The vet sighed.

"I'll see what I can do."

But nothing happened. I lay in my kennel, day after day, thinking about my friends. I wondered if Brown went back to Afghanistan with The Other Dog and if Guinness and Viper welcomed him. I thought about Target and his pangolins, about Goldie selling high heels on *Vogue*, about Chorizo bringing mud in his new kitchen. And about Nora, beyond the rainbow bridge.

That was the hardest. I missed Nora like crazy, but in a way, I was glad she wasn't there to see me. I knew she'd have a few choice words for me.

But one night she came to me in my dreams.

He ears hung close to the ground, but her fluttering wings kept her just high enough to ride that rainbow.

"Hey, you lazy Three-Pawed. Get off your butt and get moving, will you? You can't let yourself rot in that cage. You're a darn hero, remember? Act the part, for Dog's sake. Make me proud."

"But I don't have what it takes anymore. I spent it all."

"No, you didn't, you silly mutt. It's still right there, as long as you're willing to look for it."

"But Brown left me here. And all the others left. And nobody wants me."

"So what? Their loss. Get your rear in gear, you hear? Go do the work."

I did. Only because I was afraid that Nora would come back to berate me again. But I had no hope.

Then one day, the door opened.

"There she is!"

The voice sounded familiar, but I couldn't put my paw on it.

"Where?"

"There!"

I sniffed. The spicy aroma flooded my nostrils and lit up my brain. Cinnamon chili.

"Diane?"

"Butter!"

"Mom! Is it really you? And the kids!"

Diane and the kids hugged me and cried. I cried too, whimpering as I waltzed from one to the other. I licked their faces, I rolled on my back to let them scratch my belly, and then I hugged them again, trying to jump out of my skin.

"You're here! You came to see me!"

"Mom?"

"Yes, Aleta?"

"What happened to Butter's leg?"

"Butter worked with your dad in Kandahar. She got wounded as she took care of him."

Aleta kneels next to me, and her fingers trace the ugly scar below my shoulder.

"Will the leg ever grow back?"

Diane's voice cracks.

"No, it won't."

"But then, how will she walk?"

Diane blows her nose and looks away. I feel sorry for her.

"Oh, I can walk just fine. I can even run. Just wait until I show you my pizza cutter. I call her PC. "

Diane laughs and hugs me.

"So good to see you, Butter. We missed you terribly."

"I missed you too."

"OK, kids. It's time to go."

My heart skips a beat. They're leaving? Already?

"Go? Go where?"

"We're taking you home, Butter."

CHAPTER 18

Home? Taking me home?

I'm in such a rush to leave that I almost forgot my pizza cutter. I'm waltzing toward the door when the therapist catches me to buckle me in and show Diane how to adjust the harness.

"It has to fit just right to take her weight evenly. If it slips, it will chafe and give her blisters."

Aleta can't keep her hands off the buckles, struggling to fit it right, but BB cares more about the wheel-like foot. He tries to spin it and starts squeaking when it won't.

The therapist lets me go, and I dash to the door, dragging Diane and the kids in my wake, worried they'll change their minds and leave me here. I push through the door, but it's clogged. The vet, the techs, and every other human in the hospital stands there in my way. I try to squeeze between their feet, but Diane pulls me back as they clap and start singing.

"For Butter's a jolly good fellow,
For Butter's a jolly good fellow,
She's our own K-9 hero,
And nobody can deny."

They sound terrible, even though music is not my kind of art —I'll take a pork schnitzel over a piano sonata any day of the week. But what's wrong with them? Have they gone rabid? I check, but they aren't foaming at the mouth, so why did they all lose their minds?

The vet comes over. I figure he wants to listen to my lungs, but no. He hangs a shiny tag on a purple ribbon around my neck.

"Congratulations, Corporal K-9 Butter. I am proud to present you with a Purple Heart medal for your heroism in battle and selfless sacrifice. Thank you for your service. May God bless you, and may God bless the United States of America."

The whole kennel goes nuts. They all bark and howl, even dogs I've never met.

"Well done, Butter, you three-pawed hero you!"

"Good luck, Butter."

"Keep up the good work, Sunshine."

"Catch a cat for me, will you?"

"We'll miss you."

I'm flabbergasted. I cock my head, staring from the dogs to the humans and back, wondering what hit them all, while Diane laughs so hard she's crying.

"They're honoring you, Butter. They're giving you the send-off a K-9 hero deserves. They all love you and wish you well."

I choke a little. I don't deserve it since I've been lazy, morose, and even rude to many. But I appreciate it. I lick my therapists' tears, and I bark goodbye.

"Thank you all. I'm so honored I don't know what to say. I wish you well."

I turn to Diane.

"Let's get out of here before they change their minds and keep me."

Home smells like vanilla, cinnamon, and basil, and it's covered with toys, shoes, and clothes scattered everywhere. I sniff everything from the front door to the large white bowl in the bathroom, looking for IEDs, but there aren't any. So I clean the cookie crumbs under the table and make a short job of the applesauce on the carpet before settling in the kitchen to supervise Diane's cooking.

I'm lying by the stove in a puddle of drool when Aleta drags me to her room to show me her latest drawing. Like really? Now, while Diane is cooking? These humans and their inedible arts! But the kid insists on pushing her picture in my face, so I glance at it just to humor her.

It's a yellow three-legged milking stool. I saw one just like that in Kandahar, and I was not impressed. This one, with three buckling legs and a sloping seat, looks even worse for the wear.

"Very nice," I lie, since you've got to encourage young creators.

"I made it for school."

"Really. Do you have goats there?"

"But I promised I'll bring you as soon as I can. They can't wait to see you in person."

Me? I do a double-take, and it dawns on me. That's not a milking stool. That's me.

Well then. The legs aren't that bad, but...

"You forgot the ears. And the tail."

She grabs a pencil, which happens to be black, and draws two triangles on top of the stool. I'd be darned if it doesn't look like Viper, with his sharp upright ears. Mine are yellow and flat.

She puts the black pen down and picks a green one to draw my tail. I shudder.

"They can't wait to meet a K-9 hero. I told them all about how you fought in the war and killed people and...

"Not so fast, sparky. I didn't fight in the war, and I never killed anyone. I was just sniffing for IEDs, you know?"

"And I told them how you saved Daddy's life when you threw yourself between him and the bullet."

Where on earth is she coming from with this stuff?

"Now, wait a moment. Let's get it straight. I couldn't have jumped to take a bullet for Brown if I wanted to. And I didn't. I didn't even know a bullet was coming. If I'd known, I'd have run away."

"And they said they'll make you a cake and draw your picture."

The picture, I could do without. Between the milking stool and the green tail, my self-esteem hit rock bottom. But a cake?

"What sort of cake?"

"Strawberry cheesecake."

Well then.

"If you insist. But how about we skip the pictures?"

BB comes to lay on top of me and tickles my nose with his breath as he tries to spin my pizza wheel.

"You like it? Mom has one just like it, but smaller. I need this one, but you could take hers."

He ignores me and plays with PC until the harness buckles dig in my ribs and I have to stand. He shakes his finger at me.

"Doggy!"

"Mom! Mom!" Aleta shouts.

Diane rushes from the kitchen, her hands dripping with suds.

"What happened?"

"BB talked."

Diane's eyes widen.

"BB talked? Really? What did he say?"

"Doggy."

CHAPTER 19

BEING home with my family is everything I hoped for. That's what I dreamed about while I lay in my kennel, withering from the pain in my missing paw. That's what I looked forward to even when I was deployed with Guinness and Viper.

We lay in our crates waiting for dinner one evening. I was just chasing a nap when Guinness woke me up.

"What do you think will happen when this war is over?"

Now mind you, Guinness is as bright as a dog can be, and she's the best K-9 I ever met but for Viper. And even that's debatable. But she's still green. That was her first deployment, and she still hoped, like all youths do, to change the world and make it better.

But that one came out of left field. So much so that Viper forgot about cleaning his privates to stare at her.

"I would not worry about that. Once started, wars last forever. The one thing we have here, besides dust, is job security."

"I wasn't worried, just curious. What would we do if the war were over? What would you do, Butter?"

"I'd like to get home to Diane and the kids. I'd supervise her cooking, clean up the spills, and help her test new recipes. I'd play with the kids, take them out for long walks, and bark at the mailman. And clean up the house of food crumbles. Or something along those lines."

"How about you, Viper?"

"That is an entirely hypothetical question that I do not intend to entertain at this point, hein?"

Guinness cocked her head, then looked at me for a translation.

"He doesn't think that's gonna happen anytime soon, so he says you shouldn't worry about it. He thinks the war is here to stay."

"Common, Viper, work with me here for a moment. What about if they sent us home tomorrow. What would you do?"

Viper sighs.

"I would just do what they needed me to, which is most likely that I would go to fight the next war."

"But what if there was no war?"

"There will always be wars."

"But just for the sake of it, say there was no war for a year. What would you do?"

"That is a silly presumption, really. But I would sniff explosives for the TSA to curb terrorism, or I would work for the police, looking for firearms and perpetrators. But do not hold your breath, Guinness. The war is here to stay. But say you were right, and the war was suddenly over. What would you do if you had a choice, *hein*?"

Guinness shrugs like she's never thought about that, even though she kept harassing us.

"I'd go with Silver wherever she goes, and I'd look after her. She's got no one else, and she's my responsibility."

That got us all thinking. We were all so different, even though we all did the same job. Viper was obsessed with his work, I was committed to my family, and Guinness was devoted to her human.

"What if there was no Silver to look after?"

Guinness sat up straight, piercing Viper with narrowed eyes.

"What are you saying, Viper?"

"Say something happened to Silver, and she was no longer your problem. What would you do next?

"Nothing will happen to Silver as long as she's my responsibility. I'll take care of her."

Viper sighed.

"Guinness, I have been a K-9 for more years than you have been alive. Sabrina is my fourth handler. One quit, one retired, one died. Things happen in war. They happen to dogs and to people. You cannot build your whole life around a human, or you will get burned."

Guinness flattened her ears and laid her nose on her paws. When she finally answered, she woke me up from my nap.

"I don't know, Viper. I hate to see your point, but I do. Shorty, my first handler, was a great guy. He trained me and loved me. I was his partner and his family. I thought we'd be together forever until one night, he died in his sleep. Then the Army set me up with Silver. I was lucky that she's a good human and worth looking after. So, when it's all said and done, I guess I'd find another human to take care of."

Then dinner came. It was chicken, so I got busy eating, and I don't know what else those two talked about, but I'll never forget that night. Viper lives for his job, Guinness is devoted to her human, and I am committed to my family.

It's good to be home.

CHAPTER 20

DIANE, the kids, and I soon settled into a nice routine. I take them for a walk in the morning; then we drop the kids at school. I look after the house while Diane goes to work. After we get the kids from school, we take them to the park. I've been working on teaching them how to sniff the news at every mailbox, signpost, and the better bushes, but it's a slow go. Sniffing doesn't look like their thing. They're pretty good with the ball, though. They throw it, I catch it, and then they chase me to get it back. Great fun!

When we go home, Diane cooks dinner, and I supervise. She's lucky to have me taste her new recipes. She said nobody in the house has a palate like mine. Of course not. Flavor is all about the smell, and nobody has a nose like mine, certainly not the kids. BB still doesn't know when he pooped, even if I can smell it from the basement.

These kids, bless their hearts, aren't easy to feed. Diane composes these delicious creations with luscious sauces and crispy grilled vegetables—I'm particularly partial to asparagus with Hollandaise sauce. It's so good it doesn't even taste like a vegetable, but that's not the best part. The best part is the social interaction. Asparagus makes your pee smell amazing, and every dog in the neighborhood comes to check it out.

"You had asparagus again, didn't you?" the wiry terrier down the road asks, leaving his mark next to mine.

I sniff it.

"Small breed hypoallergenic? Really? That's the best you can do?"

But that's unfair. Wiry's human is not a chef, and I bet he does the best he can. But I digress.

My point is that Diane cooks all these yummy dishes, and the kids want nothing but pizza and PBJ sandwiches. Especially BB, who goes into a meltdown whenever Diane tries to feed him something new. He drifts into a world of his own that none of us can reach.

"You should try feeding them MREs. That would teach them," I said when he blew up because she'd undercooked his egg.

But she laughed and kept cooking, and I kept on eating. Life was good.

I wondered where Brown was, but I didn't want to ask. Truth be told, I didn't really want to know, just in case he was with The Other Dog. Until one day, Aleta spoke to him, then jumped up with excitement.

"Daddy's coming home!"

"Really? When?"

"Tomorrow."

Diane turned the whole house upside down. She vacuumed under the sofa and threw away every one of my old marrow bones; I had to recover them from the trash and hide them. There wasn't much left on them, but they still had emotional value, eh? She told the kids to clean up their rooms—that was worth watching—then cleaned up after them. She even brushed me.

I crawled under the bed, but crawling is the one thing Pizza Cutter doesn't excel at, so she caught me.

I tried to parlay my way out of it.

"You don't need to bother. Brown has seen me even worse.

After looking for IEDs in Kandahar, I was so dusty you couldn't tell me from the background."

You think she listened? Neh. She even cleaned the inside of my ears and trimmed my nails. She tried to brush my teeth, but that's where I drew the line. I hid under the table and growled until she gave up and went to take a shower.

I try to act cool, but I'm terribly excited. I'm half hopeful and half scared. I haven't seen Brown since he told me about The Other Dog, ages ago. Since then, I've made tremendous progress. I can walk, run, and even jump. I know he'll be surprised. But am I good enough?

I cleaned my privates really well, and I looked for something fragrant to roll in, but I didn't find much—just a smidge of duck poop in the park - but I made the most of it.

Diane gasped. Her eyes grew big as saucers.

"What are you doing, Butter! And I don't have time to give you a bath!"

"Good."

I kept away, so she couldn't smell me. Fortunately, she was so busy she forgot.

It was almost dark by the time we got ready. The house smelled of rosemary, garlic, and thyme; the kids were clean; and Diane had put on lipstick and perfume. I, for one, don't think much about perfume. I'd find her sexier if she rubbed herself with the roast, but hey. What do humans know about smells?

"How much longer, Mom?" Aleta asked.

"Any moment now."

The doorbell rang, and the kids ran to the door.

"Daddy, daddy!"

"Aleta. BB."

I hear them hug and kiss, but I can't see them since I was too chicken to join them. I hid in the bathroom instead.

"Joe! You're back!"

More hugging and kissing.

"Where's Butter?" Brown asks. "I have something for her."
For me? Something for me?
I dash out.
"I'm here."
Brown hugs me, and all is right with the world.
Then he says:
"Butter, meet your sister, Lovely."

CHAPTER 21

My sister, Lovely?

I cock my head to understand.

When I finally do, my heart blows up like I've stepped on an IED. Or is it my brain?

Lovely? Really?

My hackles go up as The Other Dog steps forward from behind Brown.

I should have sniffed her long ago, but I was so excited about seeing Brown that I lost my common sense. I stare at her in horror as she wags her tail and leaps toward me.

"Hey, Butter, old girl! I couldn't wait to meet you! Brown told me all about you, from when you guys used to work together. Remember when you stole a chicken bone, then puked it all over his best shirt?"

She puts on the charm, wagging her tail and acting playful. Then she proceeds to sniff my butt.

Are you kidding me? This interloper wants to sniff my butt FIRST? When she's not only an intruder in my home, but she's just a pup? I'm so outraged that I bare my teeth and growl as if I'm ready to rip her throat open. She whimpers, squeezes her tail between her legs, and hides behind Brown. I leap to get her.

"Butter! Stop it!"

Diane is horrified. Me too, just not for the same reasons. I stare at Brown.

"How could you?"

He looks away. Diane may be surprised, but he's not. Brown knew he was breaking my heart, but he still got The Other Dog and named her Lovely. He could at least call her Fatty, or Poopsy, or Blubber, but no. He had to call her Lovely. That takes the cake.

And what makes it worse is that she is lovely. She's a beautiful Springer Spaniel with long caramel ears and come-hither brown eyes. And she stinks.

"Look at her. Isn't she cute?" Diane asks, leaning over to pet her.

"Cute? Are you out of your mind? She's The Other Dog. She stole Brown, she stole my job, she stole my life. You call that cute?"

Brown eyes me wearily.

"Butter may need some time to adjust. She's used to being an only dog, you know, and she's gone through a lot. We may need to work on socializing her."

I blow up.

"Me? An only dog? How about Viper and Guinness? How about Nora and Chorizo and Target and the rest? I'm plenty socialized, thank you very much. You go socialize your Other Dog and leave me alone."

Brown sighs.

"I guess we'll have to give them time."

Believe it or not, dinner that evening wasn't fun. The Other Dog curled under Brown's chair. I watched her like a hawk, growling like a chainsaw whenever she moved. She dropped her ears and looked away, pretending she didn't notice me, but I made sure she knows whose home this is.

Later on, when she tried to explore the house, I made it clear that she should keep her nose to herself. Diane held me while

Brown showed her around. She sniffed everything, her little tail quivering as she moved from one room to the next while I watched, my blood boiling with anger. She even dared to smell Aleta's tripod drawing.

"Don't touch that, you stinky long-eared imposter," I growled. That's mine!"

"Come on, Butter. She's not hurting anything! Be nice! She's your sister!"

"My sister? Are you nuts? What would you say if Brown brought home another woman and told you to welcome her as a sister?"

Diane's face fell.

"If you put it that way...."

After dinner, we sat watching each other as if at a wake until Brown couldn't take it anymore.

"Let's take them for a walk. That helps shape a pack. Common purpose and all that."

We filed out, Brown and Other first, then the kids holding hands, then me, with PC and Diane. I had cooled down a little by then, so I tried to show Brown how well I was doing. I walked, I ran, I even jumped, but he didn't notice. He only had eyes for The Other. He talked to her, petted her, and rewarded her for every stupid little thing. He even called her a "Good Girl" for coming when he called her. Sickening!

Diane tried to help.

"That's OK, Butter. He needs to train her. Remember how he trained you when you were a just pup?"

"I remember. Does he?"

Diane sighed.

"He still loves you, Butter. He loves you just as much as he always did, but she's his work partner. He needs to teach her and train her."

"I'm his work partner."

Diane hugged me and wiped her eyes. We both know I'm no

longer Brown's partner. The Other is. I'm just useless Three-Pawed.

That night I slept with Aleta while Brown and The Other slept in Diane's bedroom. And I couldn't help but hear them talk.

OK, OK, I strained my ears to listen. So what? Wouldn't you?

"I don't like how this is going," Brown said. "I was afraid Butter wouldn't welcome Lovely, but I didn't think she'd try to kill her."

"Give them some time, Joe. Remember that Butter has been through a lot. She's just settled back home, and all of a sudden, there's this other dog who took her place and is about to take over her home. Of course, she's upset. Give them some time to work things out."

"What if they don't?"

"They will. We'll do our best to get them adjusted. We'll get a trainer, and...."

"I am a trainer."

Diane sighed.

"You're training them to detect explosives, not to get along. We'll find a K-9 behaviorist who specializes in that. Like Cesar and others. We'll get help."

"You know we don't have that kind of money. That prosthesis alone cost us an arm and a leg."

"Come on, Joe. It will be all right. Butter is nothing but love and loyalty. We'll find a way to make them get along. Just give them time."

"What if they don't?"

Diane sighed.

"I don't know, Joe. Do you?"

"If they don't learn to get along, Butter will have to go."

I have to go? Go where? This is my only home other than the base in Kandahar. And that war is over for me.

I have nowhere to go.

CHAPTER 22

Things didn't get any better. If anything, they got worse.

Brown acts like I don't exist. He only pays attention to Lovely. They go training every day while I stay home to look after the house. He doesn't speak to me, of course. But I can smell the TNT, the fertilizer, and the plastique on them when they come back home.

He only talks to Lovely, plays with her, and trains her. And I know he does it on purpose. So does Diane. I hear her speak to him one night.

"Listen, Joe, what you're doing is wrong. You can't treat Butter like she's useless. That's no good. You need to spend time with her too. Make her feel loved."

"There's only so much I can do. Lovely needs my attention. The pup has a great nose and excellent work ethic, but she's got a lot to learn before we get deployed. Plus, Butter needs to come back to her senses. She's been acting like a spoiled brat. She will get attention when she behaves like a good dog.

I don't want to be a good dog. I want to be a killer. Seeing this thief take over my life makes me boil inside. But there's nothing I can do but watch her win their hearts. BB spends hours combing his fingers through her long silky ears. Aleta plays with her while

I lie morose in a corner, watching them. Even Diane likes her and gives her tasty treats when she thinks I'm not watching.

The Other Dog stole not only my job; she stole my family, and I hate her guts. I'd love to kill her, but I'm not a killer. I'm just a peaceful Labrador who never killed anyone beyond a few flies. So, instead of killing, I just withdraw into myself as I watch her take over my life. There's a painful void in my soul, and the only thing that fills it is food. I eat more and more, even though I shouldn't, but nothing else helps me through this misery.

I'm in my corner with my tail covering my eyes, trying to sleep, when I hear Aleta ask Diane:

"Can I take Butter to school tomorrow for show and tell? My teacher said we can have a party for her."

"That may do her good. What do you think, Butter? Would you like a party?"

I turn away. I don't want a party. I just wish Lovely would disappear.

"Come on, Butter, you'll enjoy it."

"No."

Aleta's eyes fill with tears.

"Butter, you promised! Remember when I told you they can't wait to meet you? And they'll draw your picture?"

"You said cheesecake. Strawberry cheesecake."

"Of course."

What can a K-9 do, faced with a crying little girl and the promise of strawberry cheesecake? I sacrificed myself, and I agreed.

The following morning, Diane brushed me well, fitted my pizza cutter, and hung my purple tag around my neck. Aleta took me to her class, and that was something else.

If you thought going to war is terrible, just try going to kindergarten!

I'd never seen so many kids screaming, running, and jumping.

It's total chaos, and I'm about to run away when they see me and freeze in place.

Aleta walks me and PC to the front of the room. We sit while Aleta introduces us.

"This is Butter. Butter is a K-9 corporal hero. She got deployed in Afghanistan, where she detected explosives that can hurt people. Then she got wounded and received this purple medal. Her leg was destroyed, so they had to cut it off, but then she got a prosthesis and learned to walk again. Now she can walk and even run. Sometimes she even jumps."

"Very nice, Aleta," the teacher says. "Butter, thank you so much for coming. Kids, do you have any questions?"

A red-headed kid raises his hand.

"What sort of dog is Butter?"

"She's a Labrador."

"Can all Labradors find bombs?”

"Only if they are specially trained."

"Where is her leg now?"

"Her leg is gone, but the scientists made this replacement, and she's just as good as new."

"What does she eat?"

Now we're talking. Where's my cheesecake?

It took a while to get to the cheesecake. Every kid came to pet me, talk to me, and check out my pizza cutter. I sat for them to draw me, and they showed me their drawings. All I can say is WOW! I'd never have known that was me if they didn't tell me. But they meant well, and they were cute. And when we finally got to the cheesecake, I got two servings, plus the clean-up. All in all, I'd call it a success.

A little blonde girl comes to say goodbye as we're leaving. Aleta introduces her.

"This is Mia. She's my best friend."

Mia offers me a strawberry. I lick the frosting and try to avoid the red part without hurting her feelings. But she won't take no for an answer.

"It's good for you. It has vitamins and minerals that help you heal, my Mom says, and she's a doctor. I saved it especially for you."

Oh well. I do my best to swallow it without tasting it, but I still pucker from its tartness.

I lick Mia's fingers to say thanks, and she turns to Aleta.

"You're so lucky to have a friend like Butter. She's a hero, and she's beautiful. We only have cats. Would you like to switch?"

Aleta shakes her head but beams with pride. So do I. For the first time in a while, I don't feel worthless. What a good day!

Then we went home.

CHAPTER 23

I KNEW something was wrong the moment Diane picked us up from school. Her eyes were red and swollen, and she smelled damaged. Kind of like I did when I lost my leg. So, I checked her legs. They were there, just two of them, as usual. She didn't even limp, but I knew something was wrong.

She didn't even ask how the show-and-tell went. But then she didn't need to. Aleta didn't stop talking all the way home.

"My friend Mia said that Butter is not only beautiful, but also a hero, and how happy we must be to have a dog like her. They only have two cats who never do anything but sleep. She said she'd trade both cats for Butter. She'd throw in her bike and even the helmet, but I said no. I don't know how to ride a bike anyhow. We had cheesecake, and Kirk dropped his to the floor, but Butter cleaned it up."

Diane nodded. Once in a while, she'd glance at us through the rear-view mirror. Her blotched face looked sadder than I've ever seen it since Brown took me to war.

We got home, and the kids settled in the living room. Aleta undressed her doll while BB spun the wheels of his toy truck as usual. Diane started cooking dinner, but she was so distracted she forgot to put garlic in the tomato sauce, but she salted it twice.

She was just about to do it again when I stopped her, but it was too late. That sauce was terrible.

I was so worried about her that I got in her way at every step, sniffing for an explanation. She didn't smell sick, just upset and dejected, so I had a thought.

"Did Brown get you a sister wife?"

Diane covered her face with her hands, and I didn't know if she was laughing or crying.

But it didn't matter. I lay my head in her lap and licked her nose, and she wiped her eyes and stroked my ears.

"Oh, Butter, it's terrible."

"What happened?"

"I was..."

The front door creaked open. Brown and Lovely were back, so I slid under the table to avoid them.

Brown saw Diane and gasped.

"What happened?"

"BB."

"BB? What about him? I just saw him; he looks fine."

"He had his annual check-up today. His doctor is worried about him."

"Why?"

"At his age, he should be speaking, but he barely responds to his name. He also makes little eye contact and doesn't play with others, so she thinks he may be on the spectrum."

"What spectrum?"

"Autism spectrum. She wants BB to see a developmental specialist."

"What for?"

"To get him help. All kids with autism have trouble communicating. They start speaking late, if at all, and struggle with new situations. But they're all different. There's no telling how BB will progress, but the sooner he gets help, the better his chance to live a normal life."

I lie under the table, struggling to understand, but I can't. The one thing I get is that they're worried about BB. I can't imagine why. He's a sweetheart unless Diane pours his milk in the wrong glass or tries to brush his hair. But otherwise, he's so loving, he'd spend hours running his fingers through my tail.

Brown sobs.

"That can't be true. Not my boy! Not BB!"

I'm about to crawl out from under the table to lick him and make him feel better when I see Lovely put her pretty little paws on his knees and lick his face.

I lie back. Brown doesn't need me; Lovely has him covered.

But Diane and BB do.

CHAPTER 24

A FEW DAYS LATER, I watch Diane get ready to leave, and I crawl in my corner, feeling sorry for myself. But instead of saying goodbye, she harnesses my pizza cutter and clips my leash, then wipes off my boogers and scratches my ears.

"We're going on a visit today, so you need to look pretty."

"Who are we visiting?"

"A sick kid. His name's Tariq."

"Why?"

"His doctor is Mia's mother. Mia told her about you, and she thinks you could help him."

"With what? Does he need to look for explosives?"

"I don't think so, but we'll find out."

We drive to a small house at the other end of town. A tiny woman dressed in black opens the door, letting out a waft of exciting aromas: Cumin, cardamom, and coriander hit my nose and make me drool. I try to follow the scent to the kitchen to investigate the situation, but Diane holds me tight and we follow the woman to a crowded blue room.

A massive metal bed swallows the room, making the boy in it look small. He's pale, bald, and too busy with his tablet to look up.

"Tariq, this is Butter. She came to see you."

"Yep."

"Tariq!"

"Hi, Butter."

Tariq's eyes stay glued to his tablet while his narrow fingers tap on it like hail.

His mother sighs.

"Why don't we give them a moment? How about a cup of coffee?"

"Sure," Diane says.

They leave, and the door closes before I can follow, so I stand wondering what to do. Tariq has no use for me. His doctor was mistaken.

I watch him play on his tablet until I get bored. Then, since I've got nothing better to do, I start sniffing around for IEDs. You never know. There's no trace of explosives, but I find some cookie crumbs under the bed and I clean them up.

I try to crawl under the bed to look for more, but crawling is the one thing PC isn't great at, so I'm still struggling when Tariq calls.

"Butter?"

Oops. I flatten my ears.

"I was just checking, you know. Making sure there are no IEDs and such. I only found the cookies by mistake."

"What happened to your leg?"

"Oh, that? I got shot."

"You got shot?"

"Yep. In Afghanistan."

Tariq puts his tablet aside.

"What were you doing in Afghanistan?"

"I was a K-9, detecting explosives with my friends Guinness and Viper."

"Did you find any?"

"Explosives? Of course. There were plenty. More than anyone could want."

"What did you do with them?"

"Nothing. I just pointed them out to Brown. He told the team, and they defused them."

"Does your leg hurt?"

"Not anymore. It did when I got shot, but then they cut it off and gave me this pizza cutter instead."

"May I see it?"

"Of course."

He studies the harness, then the wheel.

"Does it work?"

"Like a charm. After they cut my leg, I had to waltz on my three legs, but now I can tango. I can even run and climb stairs."

"Don't people stare at you when they see you?”

"Sure, they do. So what?"

"You don't mind being stared at?"

"Not in the least. I see it as a compliment. If people didn't like me, they'd look elsewhere."

Tariq leans back.

"Really! I never thought about it that way."

I cock my head.

"What other way is there?"

"Like, you are not like the others. You're less than the others."

"I'm not less than the others. I am more. I am me, and also PC.”

Tariq laughs like he forgot how it's done.

“PC?”

"Yep. Pizza Cutter. That's what I call my prosthesis."

"You like it?"

"Are you kidding? I love it. With it, I get to be Bionic Butter. Without it, I'm just Three-Pawed."

Tariq stares at PC for a long time. Then he glances at me.

"You know, Butter, I also lost my leg."

"Really? How could you lose it? Wasn't it attached?"

He laughs again, easier this time.

"I mean, they had to cut it off."

"I see. Just like mine. You got shot?"

"No."

"What happened to you?"

"I got osteosarcoma. That's a sort of cancer."

My tail hides between my legs. Cancer is terrible. That's what Nora died from, but she got it from having all those litters. Tariq doesn't look like breeding stock, but who knows?

"What happened? You had puppies?"

"No. I had cancer. It's like a disease."

"I know. How did you get it?"

"I don't know. But they had to cut my leg to stop it from spreading to the rest of my body and killing me."

"Oh, good. So it's gone now?"

"Yes. But so is my leg."

"That's OK. You can get a new one. Maybe they can make you a pizza cutter like mine."

"I don't want a pizza cutter."

"Why not?"

He looks at PC, and I know he's about to say something nasty, but he refrains.

"I just want my leg back."

I don't know what to say. Fortunately, I don't have to say anything since the door opens and Diane comes in.

"Time to go, Butter. We need to get the kids from school. Nice meeting you, Tariq."

"Thanks for stopping by," Tariq's mother says. "Please come back soon."

"Bye," Tariq says, his eyes back to his tablet.

CHAPTER 25

Diane cried all the way back. She's still upset after we pick up the kids, and she sets them to play in the living room.

She sniffs as she starts on a coconut curry, and I lie by the stove to support and supervise her. And clean up the spills, of course.

"Like learning that your kid has cancer wasn't bad enough! They had to amputate his leg. And after all that, to watch him wither. That poor woman, I don't know how she does it."

I cock my head.

"What does she do?"

"Oh, Butter, you don't understand. There's nothing harder for a mother than to watch her child suffer and be unable to help. It's terrible."

She stirs the coconut milk in the frying aromatic spices, and I start drooling. It's not that I don't care; I care very much. But the food smells terrific, I'm starving, and there's nothing I can do for Tariq. The kid will have to work his way through this mess by himself like I did.

"That poor kid! He won't go out, he won't see his friends, he won't try his prosthesis. He hides in his room, since he doesn't want anyone to see he's disabled."

I swallow my slobber while looking out for any drips from her spoon, ready to catch them on the fly. With these things, you can never be too careful. But I feel her pain.

"That's what I thought too. But it makes no sense whatsoever. Why would you be embarrassed by something that's not your fault? I understand being ashamed of doing something wrong, like pooping inside, chewing the tips of Brown's shoes, or stealing someone's life. But why would you be ashamed of something that's not your fault? You, humans, are weird."

"That's why I thought meeting you could help him. You have such a healthy way of dealing with your disability, Butter. I hoped some of it would rub off on Tariq. You aren't embarrassed to be missing your leg, are you?"

"Are you kidding? I'm proud of PC, and I'm happy to show it off. It's not quite like having a real leg, especially when you crawl. But if I had my leg, I'd be in Kandahar sniffing for IEDs instead of being home supervising dinner. Anyhow, it is what it is. I might prefer things to be different, but they are what they are. And I have nothing to be ashamed of."

Diane stops stirring to stare at me.

"You miss Afghanistan, Butter?"

"I don't miss the dust, the MREs, and the heat."

"But?"

"I miss my friends, Guinness and Viper. I miss being part of a team working to protect our people. I miss being useful."

"But you're useful here. We love you."

I sigh.

"I love you too."

A drop of curry falls to the floor, and I clean it up.

"How is it?"

"Not enough to tell."

She pours some in my bowl. I sniff it carefully. The rich aroma of curry, coconut, cilantro, and cinnamon bathes my nostrils, sending me into a drooling frenzy. I taste it.

"A bit more salt, maybe. And a touch of shrimp paste."

Diane tastes it too.

"I'd be darned if you aren't right. You should be a professional taster, Butter."

"Now that's a job I'd do for love."

It felt good to chat, just the two of us like we used to when I had all my legs and there were no intruders in the house. But it didn't last long. That evening, over dinner, Diane told Brown about Tariq.

"The poor kid's so distraught he won't even look at his prosthesis, let alone use it. And his mom is at the end of her rope. That's why Mia's mom sent us there. She thought that if Tariq sees how well Butter does with her prosthesis, he may give his a try."

"Did it help?"

"I don't know. He didn't seem interested."

"Maybe he just needs time."

"Maybe."

"How about talking to his mother about giving them Butter?"

Diane's spoon clangs as it drops on her plate. Curled under Brown's chair, Lovely wags her tail. My jaw drops.

"How about doing what?"

"Well, it sounds like they could use Butter. We have no use for her. Wouldn't it be great to have some peace if she weren't here to harass Lovely all the time?"

"Are you kidding?"

"Not in the least."

Diane raises her voice.

"How can you say that, Joe? Butter lost her leg to keep you safe. And you want to discard her like a used napkin? I hope you're a better man than that."

"But Diane, it would be for her own good. She's not happy here. She may be happier as an only dog."

Lovely wags her tail and snickers at me. I bare my teeth and growl, but she won't back down. She does the "Nah-Nah-Nah-Nah-Nah-Nah" victory dance, and I lose it. I leap from my spot under Aleta's chair, grab Lovely by the scruff of her neck, and shake her like a ripe fruit tree. She squeals bloody murder, but I won't let go. I've had enough.

"Let her go! Let her go!"

Let her go? Are you kidding me? I bite even deeper, filling my mouth with her fur like Guinness taught me, until I taste her blood.

The kids scream. Brown tries to pull me away, but I won't let go. I growl like a lawnmower. Lovely squeals. Diane cries.

Brown kicks me in the face.

I'm so mad that I can't see straight. A red veil covers my eyes, and I can't see anything but the rage consuming me. And Brown's angry eyes.

I let go of Lovely, and I bite him.

CHAPTER 26

I WAS A BAD DOG. I deserve to be in jail.

I'm locked in my crate. I've been here for days now, waiting for my sentence. And one thing is sure: It won't be pretty.

Biting Lovely was bad enough. But biting Brown? There's no worse sin other than biting one of the kids. Everything else—pooping indoors, eating shoes, even stealing someone's life—pales by comparison. My name is Butter, and I'm a criminal. I lie in my crate with my ears so flat they're like gone, my tail tucked between my legs and my heart full of remorse. I was a bad dog.

Lovely cherishes every moment, and she stops by my crate every once in a while to snicker at me. She's got a tidy row of stitches. As far as she's concerned, it was all worth it. A few stitches and she's got the whole family on her side. Brown hasn't even glanced at me since he locked me up. The kids aren't allowed to talk to me. The only one who still speaks to me is Diane, but she's not happy with me either. Whenever she brings me food or takes me out, her eyes are dark with worry.

"You shouldn't have done that, Butter. It's not Lovely's fault you lost your leg and can no longer go to war, and it's not Brown's fault that he has a job to do. He must train her. He could be more sensitive, but that doesn't excuse what you did. You're in BIG trouble."

"I know."

"Will you do it again if he lets you out?"

I wish I could say no, never, but I'm not so sure. I don't know what I'll do if Lovely provokes me again or if Brown kicks me.

"I don't know."

She locks me back in my crate, but that evening I hear her talk to Brown.

"We need to let Butter out. She's been locked up for days."

"So? You know what she did. You can't let her out since you can't trust her. Not only with Lovely but even with us. Especially with the kids."

"That's silly, Joe. Butter loves the kids. She's looked after them since they were born, and she's never hurt them. Aleta loves her, and BB is so much easier to handle when he's with Butter. You know that as well as I do."

"I know nothing except that she bit Lovely so ferociously that it cost us three hundred dollars that we don't have to get her stitched. And she bit me. What's she going to do next time she's in a rage?"

"Joe, she can't live in that crate forever."

"She won't have to. I'm working on it."

"What are you working on?"

"On rehoming her."

"You're still thinking about giving her to Tariq's mom?"

Brown shrugs.

"I wish. You can't place an aggressive animal in a home with a disabled kid. I'm looking for a home with no pets and no kids, willing to take on an old, disabled, dangerous dog. It's not easy, believe me."

"What will happen if you can't find it?"

"We'll talk about it when the time comes."

"Let's talk about it now."

"I'll work harder."

"And if you still don't?"

"If I don't, we'll have to put her down."

CHAPTER 27

"PUT HER DOWN," Brown said.Me? Put me down? Down where?

I struggle to understand what he means, but I can't. Brown's words turn over and over in my mind. They make no sense. Where will they put me? Then I remember Viper's twin.

It was hot that evening, like every other evening in Kandahar. Guinness, Viper, and I lay panting in our crates, talking about the days of our youth. The soldiers played cards at the other end of the hangar. Then somebody turned up the music, and Gotye's "Somebody that I Used to Know" blasted from the radio.

"Now and then, I think of when we were together.

I told myself that you were right for me

But felt so lonely in your company

But that was love, and it's an ache I still remember."

Viper's ears went up like the music stirred something in him. He sighed and lay his nose on his paws.

"That used to be his favorite song. My brother Jinx and I were twins, you know. We both enrolled in the military. We trained together and passed every test with flying colors. Looking at him was like looking in a mirror. We always tried to outdo each other, but it was darn hard since we were both so good."

His amber eyes shone as he looked somewhere in the past.

Guinness and I sat up to listen since Viper rarely talked about himself.

"Who was better?" I asked.

"Sometimes me, sometimes him. Jinx was fast, sharp, and tireless."

"You sound like you're talking about yourself," Guinness said.

"He was all that and more. Our handlers could not tell us apart. We were microchipped, of course, so there was a way to tell who was who, but not by watching us work, *hein*?"

"Did you guys ever switch trainers just for laughs?" Guinness asked.

Viper's jaw dropped.

"How did you know?"

"I didn't. But I would have if I had a chance."

"We did. One day we switched trainers. I went to his home, and he went to mine. We pretended we knew everyone and acted as if we belonged there. It was fun to sneak like that in the home of a stranger, acting like I knew everyone, even though I had never seen them. I did not know where to find the water dish or where pooping happened, but I managed. No one noticed, but...."

"But who?"

"Jinx's cat, Turbo. He was a stray tabby Jinx had found in the street. They called him Turbo because he purred like an over-charged engine. That is probably because he was deaf, and he could not hear himself. Turbo and Jinx grew up together, played together, and ate together. They were inseparable."

"Really? A Belgian Malinois and a cat?"

"Yep. Weird, I know. Jinx was fond of Turbo, and Turbo loved Jinx. They slept together in the same bed and shared a language their humans did not know. So, that evening when I went to Jinx's, Turbo immediately knew I was not him."

"What did he do?"

"He fluffed himself all over like a toilet brush and hissed at me. He spat, making the fire-engine noises cats do when they are angry, and he lunged at me to claw my eyes out. Jinx's trainer thought Turbo had lost his mind."

"What did you do?"

"I told him to shut up. 'I am Jinx's brother. He is all right; he will come back tomorrow,' I said, but Turbo was too mad to listen. Or maybe because he was deaf. He drove me nuts. The only reason I let him live is that I had promised Jinx I would not hurt his cat, no matter what. So, I bit my tongue but never touched the darn thing."

"And then?"

"The humans locked him away for the night. The following day at training, Jinx and I switched back. I surely hope he gave Turbo a good talking to when he went home. I, for one, was glad to be back in a catless home. Bad enough, they had kids, *quoi*? I do not understand why people do not just keep fish. Or even better, plants."

Guinness and I laughed, but Viper wasn't kidding. He couldn't understand why anyone would bother to take care of useless creatures that don't pull their weight. Viper is the kind of guy who'll die working and feel sorry for every day off he ever took.

Guinness shook her head.

"Malligator Newsflash: There are things beyond work, Viper. Like love and friendship and fun. Someday you may find out. So, where's Jinx now?"

Viper looked away.

"He is gone."

"Gone where?"

"He died."

I gasped.

"Oh, Viper, I'm so sorry! What happened to him? Did he hit an IED?"

"No. Jinx was too good for that. They put him down."

"They put him down? Why?" Guinness asked.

"One day, when they were on a mission to apprehend a suspect, Jinx attacked his trainer. He bit him, over and over, and would not let go until his handler shot him. His handler wounded him so badly that they had to put him down."

Guinness and I stared at each other. What do you say to your friend whose twin brother got shot by his own handler?

We smelled the sorrow and the anger in his heart, and we felt them too. People call that empathy, but we call it friendship. I licked his nose. Guinness followed.

Viper sighed.

"Sometimes, I wonder if it was him or me who died."

Viper's raw pain burned our souls.

"But...but why?" Guinness asked.

"That is what I always wondered. Why did Jinx attack his trainer? And if he did, why did he not kill him? I plan to find out someday."

The menace in his voice made us shudder. I still do, even though it was like a lifetime ago.

But I remembered what putting down means. Putting down means killing.

Brown is planning to kill me.

CHAPTER 28

IF I HADN'T HEARD it with my own ears, I couldn't believe that my own human, the person I loved all my life, wants me dead. I had a hard time wrapping my head around that. Maybe he was kidding, I thought. But, as time went by and I stayed in jail, it became evident that Brown wasn't kidding.

Thank Dog for Diane. No matter how stressed out and tired she smells, she still pets me, takes me out, and never fails to slip me a taste of whatever deliciousness she has concocted in the kitchen. Diane is my only hope. Sooner or later, she'll talk Brown into his senses, I thought.

Until the day Diane didn't come home.

She took me out in the morning, gave me a taste of the green beans casserole with French onions she had in the oven, and then left to get the kids from school. I waited and waited for them to return. Dinnertime came and went, dusk became dark, and I was still alone. I crossed my legs, waiting for someone to bring me some water, or at least let me out, but nobody came.

The sun was up by the time Brown came home. He clipped on my leash but not my pizza cutter, and he loaded me in the car where Lovely was waiting.

I feel naked without PC. Especially with Lovely staring at me while pretending she isn't. It's bad enough to lose a leg, but lose your prosthesis too? That's negligence.

Nobody says anything, but the tension is so thick you could chew on it like a marrow bone.

I decide to act cool. I turn my back to Lovely and stare out the window like I'm busy driving. I'm worried about Diane, and I'm burning to ask about her, but I don't want to give Brown the satisfaction of ignoring me. I try to think about something else. Like, where are we going?

And it just dawns on me. Diane's gone, so Brown decided to put me down.

I stare at the trees rushing by, sporting a shy shade of green, and I wonder what being put down feels like. And what will happen next? Will I join Nora? Who will look after Diane and taste her food? Who'll ever teach Aleta how to grow a tail? Who'll help BB out of his meltdowns? Will Tariq ever try his prosthesis and walk again? Will Guinness and Viper miss me?

Oh, boy, how I miss them.

My heart heavy, I lay my nose on my paw and close my eyes.

"Hey, Butter?"

I open one eye. Lovely cocks her caramel-colored head and stares at me, her ears hanging low. She looks guilty and stinks of remorse.

"I'm so sorry."

That does it. If I wasn't sure before, now I know. I'm history.

I close my eyes.

"No, really. I'm sorry."

"What for?"

"For being snarky to you the other night. And for all your troubles. You know, Butter, I never meant to take your place. But I didn't have a choice, you know. When Brown got me and told me about you, I couldn't wait to meet you. I knew you're a hero and all that. I looked up to you and couldn't wait to learn from you. I have no idea how things went so wrong."

I can smell that's true. And Lovely really didn't do anything wrong. I did. I hated her because she was whole and young and pretty, and I treated her like crap.

"I don't know either. You'd think one paw out of four shouldn't be a big deal. After all, I had three left, plus the pizza cutter. But it looks like it was."

"Oh, Butter, how I wish we had this conversation weeks ago."

"Me too. But what can you do? It's too late now."

"You really think he'll put you down?"

I glance at Brown's strained dark face in the mirror. His knuckles are white as he clutches the wheel.

"Yep."

"Can I come with you?"

I eyeball her to see if she's kidding. Common, sister. You brought me here, and now you want to come with me? Really?

"I don't think Brown will let you. You're his partner, after all."

Lovely opens her mouth to say something, but the car pulls into a driveway and stops. Brown gets out and clips my leash. We're facing a long building smelling like dogs and cats. That must be where they put them down.

I tumble out of the car and waltz away on my three paws.

"Good luck, Butter."

"Thanks. Hey, Lovely. Can you do me one last favor?"

"Yep?"

"Tell Diane I love her and the kids. And tell her I know BB will be OK."

You wouldn't think Lovely's ears could get any lower, but they do. She looks like she's crying, even though we all know that dogs don't cry.

But then, she's not the one about to die.

CHAPTER 29

BROWN DRAGS me inside before I can answer. I check the execution place: gray concrete floors and drab tan walls smelling of disinfectant and grief. The blonde girl at the desk doesn't look like a killer, but then how would I know? I haven't met many killers. She smiles at me as she takes the leash from Brown.

"Thank you for taking her on such short notice. My wife got in a car accident last night. She's in the hospital, and there's no one to look after the dog."

Diane? In the hospital? How about the kids? My heart skips a beat.

"I'm sorry to hear that. I hope your wife does alright."

"Me too."

Brown leans over to pat my head.

"Bye, Butter. Be a good girl."

Seriously?

The girl leads me down a dark corridor that stinks like disinfectant. I follow her into a vast room packed with kennels holding every possible kind of dog. I step in, and they all bark like the mailman is coming.

I'm in shock. Seriously? Are the humans really going to kill all of them? But why?

The girl puts me in the only empty cell and gives me food and water. It looks like it will be a long wait.

The inmate to my left, a Great Dane, sniffs my way.

"Who are you?"

"I'm Butter. You?"

"I'm Thor. How long are you here for?"

"I dunno. As long as it takes them to get to me, I guess. You?"

"Until tomorrow. My family had to go to a wedding, and I couldn't fit in the car."

My jaw drops. They'll put you down for that? I thought I had it bad, but at least I bit Brown. This horse of a dog will die just because he couldn't fit in the car? That's ridiculous!

The scrawny mutt across from me stares at me like he knows me from somewhere. I sniff him. Nope. Never met him before. I know it since I never forget someone's smell. But he won't quit staring.

"What's up, dude? Who are you, and what's your problem?"

He wags his itty-bitty tail and dances on his paws.

"I'm Charlie. My folks dropped me here to go visit a relative."

Now that's downright weird. Putting down your dog for a social commitment? That makes my respect for the human race plummet. And I thought Brown was bad.

"Eh, ma'am?"

"Yes, Charlie?"

"You said your name was Butter?"

"Yep."

"Would you happen to know a K-9 named Guinness?"

I jump to my feet.

"Guinness? A black German Shepherd with brown eyebrows, a wicked sense of humor, and a lousy attitude?"

"Yes, ma'am."

"Where is she?"

"I don't know, ma'am, but I met her a few months ago at the veterinary hospital."

"Guinness? Really? What was she doing there? Was she sick?"

"She got shot, ma'am, but she was on the mend."

"Wow! Did she go back to Afghanistan?"

"I don't know, ma'am, but I don't think so. So you are that Butter? Corporal K-9 hero Butter?"

I'd blush if I knew how. But I don't, and that's good since Charlie is on a roll.

"Corporal Guinness told me all about you. She told me how you found all those bombs, saved hundreds of lives, and then got shot on a mission. She told me about your medal too. She's terribly proud of you, ma'am."

"Call me Butter," I mumble. I'm choked with a smorgasbord of emotions: longing, pride, and love for my friend Guinness. Her old words to some random mutt came back to remind me that I'm actually worth something. I'm not a useless three-pawed; I'm a freaking damn decorated hero.

Charlie clearly agrees.

"I wouldn't dare, Corporal Butter. I'm so honored to meet you. Thank you for your service and for your sacrifice."

I struggle to find words, but I don't need to. The whole kennel erupts into barking, so they couldn't hear me anyhow.

"Thank you for your service and for your sacrifice, Corporal Butter."

CHAPTER 30

And just like that, I'm the star of the kennel. From the Saint Bernard to the Pekingese, they all want to know about Kandahar and about my service.

"What is it like up there?" Thor asks.

"Hot and dry. More dust than around a cement factory. And I never found a single place to swim."

"Do they have snow?"

"Not where I was at. I heard they have snow up North, in the mountains, but I never saw it. And there's like no rain."

"No rain? So there's no mud?" Charlie asks.

The kennel gasps. If there's one thing we, dogs, all agree upon, it's mud. Mud is comforting, healing, and delightful. Mud soothes your toes, cools your skin, and makes you smell sexy. That's why we all love mud baths. Sadly, few humans know that, so they avoid it like we avoid shampoo.

"No mud. But there are no baths either. Water is too precious to waste on a K-9 who'll get just as dirty in an hour."

"Have you met the local dogs?"

"I saw a few. Those dogs are not like us. Other than the Afghan hounds, they don't have breeds like we have here. They're all scrawny and so hungry, they'd eat anything, even their own humans.

From Thor to Charlie, they all stare at me like I've lost it. But that's true. Dogs there are more like hyenas. You wouldn't want to meet them on your own. They hunt in packs, and Dog bless you if they happen to meet you before dinner. That happened to Viper once, and he barely lived to tell the tale.

I was on my first deployment when Viper caught a whiff of a hot, willing local lady of the night. She was off base somewhere, but Viper being Viper, he managed to escape outside the wire to look for the love of his life, and he found her. Unfortunately, she was surrounded by a pack of local dogs competing for her favors who decided to have Viper for dinner.

"They came at me like ten on one," Viper said, licking a fresh wound on his leg. "They ambushed me, and I had to run away."

I stare at him, and I can't believe it.

"You? Ran away? That can't be."

Viper flattens his ears.

"Yep. I've never done it before, but there was no other way to get out of there alive."

"How did you get back inside the wire?"

Viper looks away.

"I have my ways."

"Didn't they follow you?"

"Sure they did. But after I killed the first two, the others had enough to eat."

That's not the kind of story I should share with these folks here. It's so ugly that I can barely believe it, even though I know Viper never lies. So I figure I'll change the subject.

"You guys wanna learn how to sniff for IEDs?"

They howl with excitement, so I teach them how to sniff for IEDs and sit next to them rather than dig them out, and they all start practicing in their cells.

Sometime that night, it dawns on me that I'm not here to die.

They can't really put down all these dogs, even though some of them smell bad enough to deserve it. Brown brought me here to stay while Diane isn't home.

What happened to her, I wonder? And the kids? I wish there were someone I could ask, but there isn't. So, to distract myself, I chat with Charlie and ask him about Guinness.

"When did you last see her?"

"In the fall, Corporal Butter. She left the hospital the day before I did."

It's spring now, so it's been a while.

"How did she get shot?"

"She didn't say. She seldom spoke about herself. She mostly spoke about you. That must be because of her work for the CIA."

The CIA? Guinness never worked for the CIA! She trained in the North Country and came to Kandahar as a rookie! That's got to be another one of her tricks. What was that girl up to?

"What did she tell you about the CIA?"

"Nothing, really. But there was this one-eared orange cat who taunted me all the time. He told me that I was useless and ugly, and no one would ever want me. He harped on and on until Corporal Guinness got mad, even though she didn't know me. She raised her heckles, stared the orange in the eye, and growled:

"Shut up, Van Gogh, you useless feline, if you don't want me to tell everyone what you did. You and I both know it. You'll be the laughingstock of the kennel."

"How do you know my name?" the cat hissed.

"I know everything. I work for the CIA," Corporal Guinness said, and the cat went silent.

"Did he leave you alone?"

"Of course. Immediately."

Yep. That's my girl Guinness, bluffing her way out of disasters, as usual. What a dog!

"Corporal Butter?"

"Yes."

"Would you please tell me about Corporal Guinness? I admire her greatly."

So I did. I told Charlie about the day we met when Guinness peed out of her crate on a golf bag smelling like cats. I told him how she found her first IED, how she chased her tail in her crate out of boredom, and how she was the best friend I ever had.

"There's something about Guinness. She's sparky, she's funny, and she can be a pain in the butt. But whenever she's around, you know you'll never be alone."

I choke and look away.

"You miss her," Thor said.

I nod, and I lay my nose on my paw, wishing I could sniff Guinness's butt and lick her nose one more time. But it wasn't meant to be. There's no way I can get back to Kandahar.

The little mutt smells my thoughts.

"I don't think Corporal Guinness went back to war. I think she went into civilian life. She left the hospital with a man she called Pig. You may be able to find her."

"I wish."

"Me too. I'll be glad to help spread the word. How can Corporal Guinness find you?"

How can she find me? I don't know. Who knows where I'll be next?

Then it dawns on me.

"Tell her to look for a one-legged kid named Tariq."

CHAPTER 31

Days came and went, and dogs came and left while I stayed put.

So much so that I started wondering if Brown's new plan was to let me rot here instead of ever taking me home. Better than putting me down, I guess.

But little Charlie's words had rekindled my spark. After I got shot, I got so caught up in self-pity for losing my paw, my job, my family, and with it, my whole reason for being that I forgot who I was.

My heart broke when Brown got Lovely and rejected me. And for a good reason, but I forgot that Brown doesn't owe me any more than I owe him. He brought me up and trained me, but I saved his life over and over.

Yes, he needed to get another dog to go back to the freaking war, but he didn't need to be a jerk about it. He could include me and ask me to help train Lovely instead of ignoring me and making me feel useless. But he didn't. He rejected me, and I got so upset that I forgot that I'm no longer Brown's dog.

I'm Bionic Butter, a freaking decorated K-9 hero. I won't let myself go to pieces just because Brown says I'm useless. Thanks to Charlie and Guinness's praise from afar, I remembered that I deserve better.

So, when the girl at the desk brought a visitor, I wasn't desperate to see them. I was curious, of course. I hoped it was Diane, but I couldn't care less if it were Brown riding Lovely.

It wasn't Brown, and it wasn't Diane. It was a small woman dressed in black who looked familiar, but I couldn't put my paw on where I met her until I sniffed cardamom on her clothes.

"Hi, Butter. I'm Tariq's mom."

Of course. Tariq. The kid with one leg and a tablet.

"I came to invite you to stay with us."

That's weird. Nobody ever invites me anywhere. They either take me somewhere, or they don't. But invite me?

"I spoke to Mr. Brown, and he said it was fine with him if you wanted to stay with us for a while."

That's humbug. Brown said no such thing. He said something like, "Go ahead and take her if you want; just make sure you watch your kid. She's a killer."

"Really. How kind of Mr. Brown."

The woman has the grace to blush.

"I believe that Tariq has a lot he can learn from you. He has no friends, you know. He refuses to go anywhere or meet anyone. He spends all his time on his tablet, and he is so lonely. In the beginning, I was glad that it took his mind away from his pain, but now I worry that it is no longer helping him. My son needs to accept his condition before he can move on. I hope you can help."

Really.

"What exactly would you want me to do?"

She shrugs.

"I am not sure. Just be there and spend time with Tariq, I guess? Your grace and poise in using your prosthesis would go a long way in having him try his before he outgrows it."

I'm not sure what grace and poise are; they must have something to do with PC. But I don't even have my pizza cutter. Brown dropped me off without it, so all I can do is waltz.

The woman clears her throat.

"I must also mention that before I talked to Mr. Brown, I took the liberty to contact Ms. Diane and ask for her advice."

"Really? What did Diane say?"

"Ms. Diane informed me that you retired from active duty due to your disability and that you are interested in employment opportunities. She suggested that I offer you a job. So, I came to enlist your help in mobilizing my son. Ms. Diane said that you are not interested in money. We do not have much money anyhow. But she mentioned that you are a discriminating gourmet with a taste for exotic cuisine, so I brought a few samples of my cooking for you to test."

She takes out a few plastic containers and places them in front of me.

The scents of allspice, nutmeg, and cumin fill my nose and make me drool. I haven't had anything but kibble in ages, but right here, there's creamy white labneh with za'atar, juicy lamb kebab, green shiny dolmas wrapped in grape leaves, and fragrant biryani chock-full of carrots and nuts.

I drool so hard it hurts as I devour one dish after the other. This is better than any Middle-Eastern food I've seen on this side of the Tigris. Even better than Diane's.

When the food's gone, I stop to breathe. There are a few crumbs on the floor, so I clean them too, then look at the woman with new respect.

"Wow! That's incredible. Where did you learn to cook like this?"

"At home, in Iraq. My son and I are refugees. We came to the US after Tariq's father, who worked as a translator for the US Army, got killed in a suicide bomb attack."

CHAPTER 32

THAT'S SO SAD. I'll never forget Abdul, our Afghan translator. He was a lovely man who hoped to make Afghanistan a better place for his daughters. He used to bring us home-cooked meals to make us feel welcome. We loved him.

The Taliban didn't. If there's anyone the Taliban hates more than us, K-9s, it's the Afghan translators. They call them traitors and attack them, their homes, and their families to discourage anyone who'd want to help us. Even I, a bomb-sniffing dog, can't think of a more dangerous job than being a war translator.

Tariq's father must have been a brave man. What a terrible loss for Tariq and his mom! They had to leave their home to immigrate; then Tariq got cancer and had his leg cut off. Compared to theirs, my problems feel small.

There's no freaking way I could say no to helping them, even if this woman cooked like a donkey. But her food is so good that it makes me feel guilty. I almost wish that it were lousy, so I could feel virtuous. But not quite.

"I accept your job offer. When should I start?"

Her face lights up like a Christmas tree.

"As soon as it is convenient. Maybe..."

"Today?"

"Yes, please. Let me work through the details."

She gathers the empty dishes and she's about to leave when I realize that I don't even know her name. To me, she's Tariq's mom. But that's not right. She deserves to be her own person.

"What's your name, ma'am?"

She beams.

"I am Amira."

I wag my tail.

"Glad to meet you, Amira. I'm Butter."

She laughs.

"I know."

Minutes later, she's back with a leash.

"Mr. Brown said he will drop off your prosthesis. Can you walk at all without it?"

"Of course."

I waltz out of the kennel, and we drive to Tariq's house.

"Hey, Tariq. You have a visitor," Amira says.

Tariq watches me waltz in, and his eyebrows join in worry.

"What happened to you?"

"Nothing. Anything happened to you?"

"Where's your prosthesis?"

"It should be coming any moment. How about you? Any news?"

He shakes his head and goes back to his game.

I hope I didn't come all this way for nothing.

Amira leaves us, and I lie by the bed, thinking. I'm out of death row, I'm out of the kennel, and I even landed a job paid in good food. Advantage me.

But to keep my job, I'll have to get this kid moving, and I have no freaking clue how to do it.

I panic. My skin tingles and my heart starts racing. What on earth am I doing here? I'm about to go back to feeling crippled and useless, when I remember Charlie's words. I'm a darn war hero, while Tariq is just a sick child with too much on his plate.

He's had enough to deal with. Time to relieve him of his responsibilities. That's what I'm here for.

"Tariq?"

"What?"

"Tomorrow, we're going for a walk."

He stares at me.

"What?"

"I'm here to get you moving, and I plan to do exactly that. Tomorrow we're going for a walk."

He laughs.

"I don't think so, Buster."

"I'm not Buster. I'm Butter. Corporal K-9 Butter, Purple Heart decorated hero to be precise. And I'm telling you that tomorrow we're going for a walk. Get ready."

He's not sure how to take this, so he just looks away and mumbles:

"Get lost."

That night I stole his tablet.

CHAPTER 33

Now let me be clear. You may think that we, K-9s, are subordinate to our human handlers. Not exactly. While we obey their orders, we OUTRANK OUR HANDLERS. I didn't mean to scream here, but I think it's essential. When Guinness came for her first deployment, she was as green as a K-9 gets, but she still got promoted over her handler's grade. Why, you ask?

Some say it's to prevent our handlers from abusing us since that would mean assaulting a superior. But that's poppycock. We're in better shape than they are, we're better trained, and we have better teeth. Even now, on my three paws, I could take down Brown before he could say Marrow Bone. Unless he used his gun.

I think the reason we outrank them is to remind us, K-9s, that we aren't there to blindly obey orders. We must use our judgment and ignore any order that could get our handlers in trouble, whether they like it or not.

That's why I felt no shame stealing Tariq's tablet. I'm not here to listen to his orders. I'm here to get him moving, and I get paid for it in delicious food better than what I got in any of my deployments. I have a job, and I'm going to do it whether Tariq likes it or not. I just hope the pizza cutter arrives in time, but if it doesn't, I'm going to waltz my way alongside him.

That morning, Tariq wakes up and reaches for his tablet. It's not there, of course, and he can't believe it. He looks under his blanket, under his pillow, under his bed. Nothing.

Then he looks at me.

"Where's my tablet?"

"How would I know?" I ask, munching on a hot, crunchy falafel just off the fire.

He stares at me.

"Are you lying to me?"

"I never lie. In fact, most dogs never do." I move on to my hummus. It's creamy, salty, garlicky, and just downright delicious.

"Did you take it?"

"Yes."

His eyes would wilt you if you were that kind of person. But I no longer am.

"Give it back."

"After our walk."

"I'm not walking anywhere."

I move on to my tabouleh. I know it's not really a K-9 thing, but I love parsley. Especially in chicken piccata, even though it gets stuck between your teeth. It has this freshness...

"Give me my tablet."

"Of course. After our walk."

"You damn dog!" He jumps out of his bed and falls on his face. Because, unlike me, he hasn't practiced.

"Mom. MOM!"

I start on my dessert. It's fudgy daheen sweetened with date syrup, crunchy with dried coconut, and loaded with enough clarified butter to give you a heart attack.

Amira rushes in.

"What happened?"

"That damn dog stole my tablet. Give it to me."

Amira stares at me. I stare back, and she looks away.

"Sorry. I do not know where it is."

"Well, look for it, damn it!"

Amira is about to kneel and look under the bed when I growl.

"You hired me to do a job. I'm doing it. Don't get in my way."

She clears her voice.

"I am sorry, Tariq. I cannot help you. Butter is in charge. She will get it for you when she thinks you are ready."

"Butter? A dog? You let a dog be in charge?"

"Better than a silly kid," I say, and Amira makes herself scarce.

Tariq crawls back to his bed. He's so angry that his ears are fire-engine red. They look good on him, I think. I lay my nose on my paw and catch a nap.

The shadows have grown short by the time I wake up. I need to go out, so Amira brings my leash and fastens my pizza cutter, and I can smell her worry.

"Tariq is not happy."

"Of course not. If he were happy, he wouldn't do a darn thing. He's got to get unhappy enough to get moving."

Amira nods. "You are right. Is the food OK?"

"Excellent. Keep it going."

The evening goes pretty much the same: Tariq stares at the ceiling; I lie with my nose on my paw, thinking about my people.

The sun is down when he asks, "When are you going to give me my darn tablet?"

"After we go for a walk."

"I don't want to go for a walk."

I ignore him to inhale my masgouf. It's crispy golden carp skewered and grilled. I wasn't much into fish—I thought of it as cat food—but this dish changed my mind.

Tariq balks.

"That's not dog food."

"I know. I'm not a dog. I'm Butter, a decorated K-9 officer. I don't do dog food."

He looks like he'd like to kill me. I wag my tail.

"I understand. But to kill me, you'll have to catch me first. And that means walking."

I slept like a baby that night. Not because I enjoyed frustrating him—I really didn't. But because I felt that I finally had a job and a purpose. I'll get this kid walking if I die trying. It felt good to be in charge again.

When he woke up the following day, Tariq looked for his tablet, then glared at me.

"How long, the walk?"

CHAPTER 34

THE WALK WASN'T LONG, but getting ready took forever. Adjusting Tariq's prosthesis was harder than fixing mine. His fake leg was not a plastic pizza cutter like mine. It was like a real leg, with knee and all, made of shiny metal with a plastic foot at the end.

Amira stuffed Tariq's stump inside the artificial leg, put a sneaker on his plastic foot, and got him his crutches.

Tariq's mouth tightened into a narrow line as he struggled to stand, looking anywhere but at me. I didn't mind. I knew where he came from. He felt comfortable lying in his bed playing on his tablet the whole day. Learning to walk again wasn't much fun, and he resented having to do it.

Even worse, he loathed being told what to do. Throughout his illness, he got used to telling his mother what to do, and she did it. But that didn't work with me.

We filed out of the house, PC and I first, then Tariq, then Amira, ready to help him. That reminded me of my Kandahar missions when I was the first to walk outside the wire. I looked for explosives while everyone else stayed safely behind. But this wasn't Kandahar, and there were no IEDs. The only thing ready to blow up was Tariq's temper. And boy, did he have a short fuse!

Between balancing on his crutches and moving his metal leg,

Tariq's every step was a challenge. His face got strained and his knuckles went white around his crutches as he wobbled, struggling to keep his balance. Right behind him, her eyes dark with worry, Amira stood ready to catch him.

Between his anger and her worry, I was exhausted by the time we reached the gate. As we started along the sidewalk, a cool breeze smelling like spring hit my nose, but nobody else seemed to notice. Tariq's whole energy was focused on hobbling down the sidewalk, and Amira only had eyes for her son.

I stopped when we reached the first corner.

"That's good enough for today, don't you think?"

Tariq glared at me and turned the corner. I followed him, filing that for later. Rather than listen to me, he'll do the opposite even if it hurts. So that's the way I'll have to play it.

He turned the next corner, then the next. By the time he hobbled back inside and plopped on his bed, I felt like we'd been gone for a week.

"My tablet?"

I pointed my nose to his side table, where I'd dropped his tablet as we left.

He no longer looked at me that day.

CHAPTER 35

Tariq hid his tablet under his pillow that night. What an amateur! You have a lot to learn, my friend, if you want to outsmart an old bomb-sniffer whose job is to find things that don't want to be found.

I stole it, hid it, and got ready for a fight.

"Damn you!"

His eyes pierced me with impotent anger.

"You stole it again!"

"Of course. What did you expect?"

He punched his pillow, then clutched it and hid under his cover to cry.

I felt bad. The last thing I want to do is to add to Tariq's burden, but I can't let him sit and rot in that bed. He has to get up and live, and that requires a good kick in the butt. But he's entitled to his privacy and dignity, whatever is left of them, so I lay my nose on my paw, pretending to sleep, until he calls his mom.

"Let's go. Bring me that stupid prosthesis."

We file out again.

"We don't have to go as far as we did yesterday if you're feeling tired," I say innocently. "That was too much for you."

I watch him push himself even further. He's getting good at it, too. He gets steadier with every step, and he's no longer exhausted by the time we get back.

Just as we reach the gate, it starts snowing. Fluffy snowflakes twirl in the air like feathers, then settle on the ground, the trees, and the tired little house, covering everything with a dazzling white blanket. I open my mouth and stick my tongue out to catch them, but they vanish before I get to taste them.

Tariq lifts his face to the sky and closes his eyes. The soft flakes melt as they touch his burning cheeks, leaving behind clear water drops and, for a moment, he seems to smile.

Back in his room, he glances at his tablet.

"Where did you hide it?"

I wag my tail.

"You're funny."

He shakes his head and goes back to his tablet, but seconds later he puts it down.

"Are you going to do that every day?"

"Yes."

"Until when?"

"Until you're ready to be on your own."

"I'm ready."

"I don't think so."

"What do you want me to do?"

"You need to do the right thing without being forced to, just because it's the right thing. You owe your mom to get better. You owe it to yourself. And we both know you won't get any better by lying in that bed."

His hands clench into fists.

"Do you realize what it feels like to lose a leg?"

"As a matter of fact, I do."

He glances at the pizza cutter and blushes. He was so incensed he forgot all about it. He sighs and goes back to his tablet.

The following day, he doesn't even look for his tablet. He gets up, we get ready, and we file out.

But today, we're in wonderland. Yesterday's snow has covered the drab world in brilliant white. The trees, the mailboxes, the roofs, even the ugly concrete sidewalks—they all sparkle.

"This is so beautiful. In my country, we seldom get snow," Amira says.

Tariq shrugs.

"It's cold," he says, but his eyes sparkle.

The snow doesn't help with the walking, but it's good for the soul. We do our tour and, as we get back to the gate, Tariq starts over. Amira's eyes shine with tears.

"Thanks, Butter," she whispers.

"Don't mention it."

We get back, and Tariq glances at the tablet for a moment, then looks at me.

"You don't have to hide it anymore."

"Good," I say. But I'm going to hide it anyhow.

"What's next?"

"Next?"

"Yes. How much further do I have to walk?"

"I don't know. It's not just the walking. It's about getting your life back. Doing things. Meeting people. Whatever matters to you. There's more to one's life than a leg."

"How did you get to be so wise, Butter?"

"By being stupid."

Tariq's face lights up as he laughs, and he's suddenly back to what he should have been all along: a happy kid.

CHAPTER 36

WE SETTLED INTO A ROUTINE. We took longer and longer walks every day. Before long, Tariq ditched a crutch, then the other; he used a cane until he learned to walk on his own.

He wore long pants, of course, and boots, so nobody could tell he had a fake leg, unlike me, with my bright blue pizza wheel that drew every eye. People often asked about it, especially the kids, and Tariq couldn't wait to answer.

"She's a war hero. She lost her leg in Afghanistan, and then she learned to use a prosthesis."

"Wow! What courage! What determination!" people said, and Tariq beamed with pride. I wondered how much of it was for me and how much for himself.

Life was pretty good until Tariq got invited to an old friend's birthday party.

"I'm not going."

"Why not? We will buy her a nice gift and...."

"I'M NOT GOING."

He turned around and slammed the door. That was one problem with getting him walking: He could walk out on you whenever he felt like it.

"He's going. Just buy that gift."

I followed him. He glared at me.

"I'm not going, no matter what you say."

"Why not?"

"They all know I've lost my leg. They'll stare at me and maybe even ask about it."

"So?"

"I don't like that."

"Why?"

"I'm uncomfortable."

"Tariq, you have to be uncomfortable to grow. You were uncomfortable walking, and you were uncomfortable leaving the house not long ago. And look at you now!"

"I'm not going!"

We went.

I don't think they expected him. Faces grew long as he walked in the room, steady but flushed with emotion. Tentative smiles and awkward greetings followed. It would have been a total cluster, but for my pizza cutter. PC was the life of the party.

The kids' faces lit up when they saw me, and they gathered around me, bombarding Tariq with questions.

"What's her name?" our host, a cute redhead, asked.

"She's Corporal K-9 Butter."

"What happened to her leg?"

"She got shot in Afghanistan."

"Can she do any tricks?" a chunky little kid asked.

Tariq's face darkened.

"She's not that kind of dog. But yes, she can detect bombs."

Eyes widened as everyone looked at me with new respect.

"Where did you get her?" a sour-faced teenager asked.

"As a matter of fact, she got me. She came to help with my recuperation."

"Isn't that cool."

I wondered if he was so sour because Tariq stole his show. Before we arrived, Sour-face must have been the life of the party.

"I wish I had a cool dog like that," Chunky said. "Mine has four legs, not something cool like this."

Tariq laughed, and the others did too. I ate too much cake, and I had so many hands petting me that I almost longed for a bath. But Tariq was happy, and that was all that mattered.

They saw us to the door when Amira came to take us home.

"Hey, Tariq," Sour-face called.

"Yes."

"I'm having a few friends over for pizza and a movie on Friday. Wanna come? With Butter, of course."

"Sure."

I went to bed feeling accomplished. My work here was done. From now on it's just the fun.

CHAPTER 37

I KNEW something was up as soon as I heard the doorbell. We, dogs, smell these things. It's like the universe sends us messages. The doorbell sounded the same, but I just knew it wasn't the mailman.

I was right. I was chatting with Tariq in his room when I heard Diane's voice. I ran out to meet her, but I stopped dead in my tracks when I saw her leaning on a cane.

"Diane! You're back! How I missed you! How are you?"

She laughed and cried and hugged me.

"I'm good."

"The kids?"

"They're fine too. How are you?"

I wagged my tail.

"Great. Even better now that you're here."

Amira offered her a seat, then coffee, and we sat looking at each other in silence. I don't know why, but the air suddenly got so thick with tension you could chew on it.

Amira cleared her voice.

"What happened to you, Diane?"

"I got in a car accident. I broke my leg, and I had surgery. But I'm much better now that I ditched my crutches."

"How are the kids?"

"They're great. They keep asking about Butter."

About me? I don't know. They didn't seem to care much when I was in jail. But I let that pass.

"How are you guys doing?" Diane asks. "How is Tariq?"

"He is doing great. Butter did a fantastic job. She got him walking. He got so good on his prosthesis that he no longer needs a cane. She also helped him reconnect with his old friends, so he is no longer lonely. Our Butter is a miracle worker."

"She totally is. We miss her terribly at home."

Who's "we"? I wonder.

"Aleta keeps asking: 'When is Butter coming home? I miss her!'"

The room's so quiet you could hear a fly sneeze. Amira pours some red juice into glasses and the noise breaks the silence like a hammer.

"This is homemade pomegranate juice. It helps with healing," Amira says.

Diane takes a sip and sets the glass down.

"It's delicious. Thank you."

We sit staring at each other, pretending there's no elephant in the room.

Amira clears her throat.

"Tariq is very fond of Butter. He looks up to her in every way. She is the only person he obeys. I am so glad that she is here to set him straight."

Diane nods.

"I can see that. Butter is amazing. I knew that from the day Joe brought her home. She was so tiny she fit in the palm of my hand, and I had to wake up every night to feed her milk from a syringe. Butter is my first baby, before Aleta and BB, and I couldn't love her more. To me, Butter is not a dog. She's family. We all miss her terribly."

Amira takes a tiny sip of juice.

"A bit tart, no? Please correct me if I am wrong, but Butter seemed to have some rough times in your home. She did not get the love and respect she deserves. Here, we cherish her. Nothing is too good for our Butter."

Diane's mouth tightens.

"Every family has problems and needs time to work them out. Things change. New situations and new family members may throw things out of whack for a while, but one must work on them and find a new balance."

Amira's smile doesn't reach her eyes.

"Of course. Situations change. People do too. I know I did. I must make a confession: In my culture, people do not think much about dogs. They see them as dirty animals. Where I come from, being called a dog is an insult. I am sorry, Butter, but I have to be honest with you."

She clears her throat.

"I had a hard time asking for Butter's help. I only did it because I was desperate. My son Tariq had a hard life, harder than any child should. He was only eight when his father died, leaving him to be the man of the house. That was already too much responsibility for him. Then we came to the US. He left behind his home, his friends, and everything he knew. He had to learn a new language and adjust to a new culture. Then he got cancer and went through countless painful procedures. With his leg, he lost his hope and his desire to live. I watched him get deeper and deeper into depression, and there was nothing I could do to help him. When his doctor told us about Butter, I had no choice but to give it a try. She was my last resort."

Amira's voice breaks.

"We were fortunate that Butter agreed to help us. Please forgive me, Diane, but she would not have come to us if she got the respect she deserved in your home, and you know it."

Diane nods, her eyes cast down.

"This hero dog came to my son's rescue. She put up with his

disrespect and his ugly moods. She somehow managed to get him out of his shell and got him to enjoy life again. Nobody, ever, in my life, did more for me. I worship the ground Butter steps on, and our home is her home, now and forever."

Diane opens her mouth to say something as the door slams open, and Tariq barges in.

"What's going on?"

His mother smiles.

"My friend Diane and I are chatting."

"About what?"

"About Butter. Diane wants to take her home."

Tariq's face falls.

"What?"

Amira shrugs.

"You tell him, Diane."

"Tariq, I'm so glad to see the progress you've made. I'm very proud of you. I'm sure you're very fond of Butter, and I'm glad she helped you through your journey, but now that you've gone so far, her place is at home with us. The kids miss her, and so do I."

Tariq stares at Diane, trying to understand.

"You want to take my Butter?"

Diane's eyes move from his troubled face to his prosthesis. She clears her throat.

"I'd like to take Butter home."

"But this is her home. We love her here."

"I can see that. Butter is a lucky girl to have you and your mom care so much about her. I'm glad to see her happy and content."

She leans on her cane to stand up.

"I have to go now. I'll tell the kids that Butter is doing great. I'll be back."

She hugs me and slips me a strip of smoky homemade beef jerky.

"I'll be back soon."

I feel guilty as I watch her hobble out, leaning on her cane. She's my mom, and she's always been there for me when I was in trouble. And she needs me.

Tariq leans over me, wobbling on the prosthesis he poorly adjusted himself.

"Butter?"

"Yes?"

"I love you."

CHAPTER 38

THAT NIGHT, I lay awake watching Tariq's steady breathing as he slept, and wondered what to do.

I'll have to choose between going back home and staying here to help Tariq become the man he needs to grow into. I know what life with Tariq would be like. But home? I don't know. More of the same? Brown, flaunting Lovely in my face to make me feel old and useless? Diane, sneaking me snacks and trying to protect me from his wrath? The kids, who don't know what it's all about, torn between the old doggie and the pretty doggie? I don't know.

What would Guinness do?

I remember the night when Guinness, Viper, and I lay in our crates talking about the meaning of life.

It had been a bad day. That morning, Carlos one of our soldiers, just twenty-three, shot himself in the head before dawn. That was the beginning of our saddest day in camp.

We woke up thinking we were under attack. The men jumped out of their cots, grabbed their kits, and ran into position. They looked long and hard for the intruders, but there was nothing. It took us a while to find Carlos lying on the dusty ground behind the trucks. That was the only place he'd found some privacy. The men tried to revive him, but it was too late. The thirsty Afghan desert had sucked his blood and his life.

It was a terrible time for all of us. The patrol was canceled, and the men spent the day talking about Carlos, trying to understand what happened. All but Carlos' best friend, Leo. His face ashen, his shoulders slumped, Leo sat staring into space smelling like guilt. The lieutenant tried to give us a pep talk, but he had no pep left either.

"What the heck is this all about, *hein?*" Viper asked, his long black snout up in the air like this whole grizzly affair was beneath him.

Guinness shrugged.

"I guess he didn't want to live any more."

"But why?"

Guinness cocked her head to stare at him.

"How about turning this question on its head. What was he living for?"

"Are you serious? He had a job to do!" Viper spat.

"Viper, did it ever occur to you that not everyone lives for their job?"

Viper stared at her like she'd gone nuts.

"What else is there?"

"Lots of things. Friendship, love, and justice, and food, and the good of the planet, and the polar bears, and...."

"Have you lost your mind? The polar bears? Who cares about the polar bears?"

"I do. I once saw a documentary showing how baby polar bears starve to death because of climate change. Their moms can't find food anymore, and...."

Viper shook his head with impatience.

"Common, Guinness. Carlos did not kill himself for the polar bears."

"Probably not. But my point is that there are things in life even more important than doing a job."

"You're wrong. There's nothing more important, I assure you."

"Maybe not to you. But others may think otherwise. Butter?"

"What?"

"What's the most important thing in life for you?"

I hate to be put on the spot between these two. They could argue day and night and then forever, but there I was.

"I don't know. A few things. Friendship? Love? Loyalty? Feeling that you make a difference in people's lives?"

Guinness wags her tail in agreement.

"Atta girl, Butter. There, Viper. I rest my case. There's more to life than work."

Viper glares at her and opens his muzzle to say something nasty when Sabrina, his handler, comes and hugs him.

Viper's ears go down, and his tail hides between his legs. He's mortified. Viper hates hugs, and he'd love to get away, but he doesn't want to hurt Sabrina's feelings, so he sits there as she sobs, hanging onto his neck. He tries to ignore her until he can't take it anymore.

"There, there. Everything will be alright. Just wait and see. It's going to be OK."

He licks her tears, and she finally relents.

"Thank you, Viper. This is so terrible! Poor Carlos couldn't take it anymore. You know, I could never do this without you. Your love and support make all the difference in the world. I'm so happy I have you."

Guinness and I exchange glances but say nothing. Like really, what is there to say? Viper sees us and seethes.

"That was nothing."

"Of course."

"She just needed some moral support. She was upset that her buddy died."

We cock our heads. Viper growls.

"OK, OK, go ahead and tell me. What's the most important thing in life? What do we live for?"

"Love? Friendship? Feeling like our lives weren't wasted?" Guinness says.

I can't disagree.

"I think we live to make a difference. We want to leave behind something good that wouldn't have been there if it wasn't for us. Whatever that is."

"I get you. We live to make a difference on earth. To leave the world better than we found it. That's a tall order."

That was the one, and only, time I heard Viper admit that he was wrong.

Now, as I watch Tariq sleep, I wonder what to do. How can I leave the world better than I found it? I fought in Afghanistan for most of my life. Day after day, I put my life in danger, choking on the dust, suffering through the heat, and living on MREs. That war took my youth, my leg, and my friends, and I don't know that I made any difference.

And I was young and whole. Now, that I'm old and crippled, and running out of time, can I still make a difference?

Or is it too late?

CHAPTER 39

Day after day, I struggled to figure out what I should do to make my life matter and I got nowhere.

Tariq needs me. He's not ready to be left by himself. He's about to start school, and he'll need a kick in the butt and a shoulder to cry on when things don't go his way.

Diane needs me too. I've never seen her so exhausted. No wonder. She's got to hobble on that cane and look after Aleta, BB, and the house by herself. And she's got no one to listen to her worries, taste her food, supervise her cooking, and lick her nose to make her feel better.

The day Diane returns, still leaning on her cane, I still don't know what to do.

Amira pulls her a chair and pours her sweet mint tea. They sit, and we stare at each other.

Diane clears her throat.

"What a nice day."

I glance outside. It's only noon, but it looks like dusk. A howling wind whips the rain into the windows as the sky grows darker by the minute.

"Very nice," Amira says.

I cock my head, staring from one to the other, trying to figure out if they lost their minds or if they're speaking in code, but they go quiet.

That's when I figure it out. It's just "throat-clearing"—the human equivalent of sniffing each other's butt to establish common ground before getting to the real deal.

"How have you been?" Amira asks.

"Much better, thanks. I should ditch the cane in a few days."

So maybe Diane doesn't need me anymore. I don't know if that makes me happy or sad.

"How about you guys? What's new with you?"

"We are doing good. Tariq looks forward to starting school next week. He can hardly wait to be with his friends every day."

There now. It looks like Tariq doesn't need me either. My ears drop. A few days ago, I was so hot they fought over me. Now I'm last week's news.

"How are the kids?"

"Great. Growing like weeds and asking about Butter all the time."

So, do they still want me? I want to ask, but I don't want to sound needy.

Diane sets down her tea.

"Listen, Amira, what will you do with all your extra time when Tariq goes back to school?"

Amira shrugs.

"I have not thought about that. I will get a job, maybe? We could surely use the money."

"I have an idea," Diane says.

"Yes?"

"Tariq's doctor asked me if I could take Butter to visit other kids who lost their limbs, like Tariq did. Most of them have trouble adjusting to living without a limb and struggle with their body image. That makes it hard for them to reclaim their lives. She thinks that Butter may help those kids like she helped Tariq."

"I see."

"But, as you know, I have my work and the kids. I don't have much spare time. I thought maybe we could share the work? You know so much more about this than I do. You could tell them about Tariq and maybe even show them pictures. That may help."

Amira cocks her head in question like I've never seen a human do.

"Diane, are you saying we should share Butter?"

"Pretty much. I'm saying let's help Butter do what she does best: Help people. To feel accomplished, she needs to have a purpose and feel useful. She could help those children who struggle like Tariq did."

Amira sighs.

"What do you think, Butter?"

What do I think? I'm not sure what I think, but feeling useful is what I need. If I could help those kids like I helped Tariq, I might still make the world a better place.

"I'd love to be useful. I live for that. But where are these kids? And what do I do with them?"

Diane smiles.

"Some are in the hospital, waiting for their surgery or recovering from it. Some are at home, learning how to walk and struggling to reclaim their lives. You'd visit them, like we did with Tariq, and help them see that losing a leg is not the end of the world."

"And I'd sometimes go with you, and sometimes with Amira?"

"Yes. Maybe even with Tariq, if he's willing."

"Where would I live?"

"Where would you like to live, Butter?"

"I want to go home."

CHAPTER 40

But that's a lie. I don't want to go home. I have to go home.

Not because of Diane, as much as I love her. Not even because of the kids. Because of Brown.

I can't let Brown have the last word. He abandoned me, shunned me, locked me in my crate, then ditched me in that kennel and left me there. I can't let that pass. I couldn't respect myself if I did.

I won't bite him again, no matter what. I no longer am the bewildered, insecure Butter that he used to bully. I'm Corporal Butter, a Purple Heart–decorated K-9 hero and a working support dog. I'm not ashamed of my missing leg; I'm proud of my pizza cutter and everything I've accomplished with it. I'm proud of who I am.

That's what I tell myself as Diane drives me home, and I pump myself up to meet Brown and Lovely. I just wish I could believe it.

I felt so lost that I couldn't figure out what to do. So I wondered: What would Guinness do?

And I know she'd do precisely what I'm doing. I can almost hear her: "Butter, you can't let the bastages get you down. Go and show them who's boss."

But I'm not Guinness. And, to be honest, I don't so feel good about this.

I'm worried about what's coming. I'm concerned about Brown and Lovely. I'm also worried about Tariq and Amira, and I feel guilty about leaving them.

When I left, Tariq was so angry he didn't even say goodbye. He went back to his bed and his tablet and didn't even glance at me when I said goodbye.

Amira sobbed. "That's terrible! What will I do if he goes back to where he was before you came, and you're not here to deal with him?"

I licked her hand. It tasted like butter and honey. And tears.

That made me realize that if there's only one person—one person here that I should help, that's Amira. Not because of her fabulous cooking. Not even because she pried me out of the kennel that Brown left me in. But because Amira has the most growing to do. Not Tariq. He'll figure it out eventually. Not even Diane. She'll ditch her cane and go back to being her competent self. The most challenging path is Amira's. That girl needs to grow into her potential, and I know she can, but she doesn't.

I lick her tears, and she doesn't pull away. It's been a while since she avoided touching me. But we've never been this close.

"Amira, you'll do exactly what I did. You'll take away his tablet, and you won't give it back until he does what he needs to do."

"But he'll ask for it!"

"Of course he will. And you'll say no."

Amira shrivels, and I choke with guilt. But she needs to grow like Tariq did.

"Amira, Tariq is not the man of the house. He's just a little kid who needs help, boundaries, and guidance. You are his mom. You have to guide him whether he likes it or not. You can't let a kid take control of your lives. That's unfair to you both. It's your job to make decisions."

Amira sighs.

"I guess you're right, but I just wasn't brought up that way."

"But you can learn. If you love Tariq, you have to set him straight. And I'll be back, remember?"

She hugs me and gives me a brown bag smelling like cardamom and roses.

"There's a little something I made for you with love. Enjoy!"

"Thank you, Amira. I will."

The scents from the brown bag make me slobber as I sit in Diane's car, watching the roads I know so well. But I can't touch food now. My stomach is in turmoil, and my heart is too. I'm afraid to go home. I'm terrified to see Brown, and I dread seeing Lovely, but I have to. So I keep telling myself:

"Don't let the bastages get you down. Go show them who's boss."

CHAPTER 41

THE CAR TURNS RIGHT, and I recognize every mailbox, every yard, and every bush, even though they're now all dressed in green. The old lady's calico cat sits in her usual window, cleaning her paws. She pretends she doesn't see me, but I know better. She's still mad at me for chasing her so far up a tree they had to bring a ladder to get her down. But Wiry, the terrier across the street, sees me and yaps like crazy.

"Butter! You're back! Good to see you, partner! I missed you!"

I wag my tail to say hi, but I'm busy. My heart pounds as the car stops in the driveway, and Diane lets me out. I sniff the mailbox and check-in as the door opens, and the kids run out screaming.

"Butter! Butter! You're back."

Aleta hugs me. She got so big that she's taller than me. I lick her face, and she laughs.

"Doggy! Doggy!"

BB is next. His black curls tickle my nose, and I sneeze. They all laugh but Diane. She wipes her tears as I lick the chocolate off BB's face.

"Butter? Butter?! Butter!!!"

Lovely explodes through the door barking like crazy. She runs so fast that her caramel-colored ears float behind her. She salutes with a downward dog, then turns around to offer me her butt to sniff. I oblige. She's had chicken kibble for breakfast, she's healthy, and she's totally thrilled to see me.

I turn around to let her sniff my butt. She does it respectfully, then comes around and licks my nose. My heart melts. Nobody's licked my nose since Guinness, and that's the most fantastic feeling in the world. Try it sometime. It will give you warm fuzzies.

I lick her nose, and we start jumping and playing like puppies. The humans laugh, even Brown. He stands in the doorway, looking smaller than I remembered.

"Butter?"

I stare at him.

"How are you, Butter?"

I wag my tail.

"Fine, thanks. You?"

"Come!"

He slaps his hip.

I sit.

"I don't think so. I'm fine right here, thanks."

His face darkens.

"I said..."

Diane interrupts, "You said you were sorry, didn't you, Joe? You said you were sorry you were mean to Butter. You said you wish you didn't humiliate her and mistreat her, didn't you, Joe?"

"But..."

"No, but. That's what you told me only last night. Otherwise, I wouldn't have brought Butter back. You said you were stupid and mean, and you promised to make it up to her. Remember?"

Diane's gaze pierces Brown, and he sighs.

"Yes."

"So?"

He takes a deep breath like he's about to jump in cold water.

"I'm sorry, Butter. I'm sorry for being harsh to you. I wish I was smarter and kinder. But I was scared, you see. When you got shot, I was devastated. I tried my best to keep you alive. But when it became obvious that you couldn't go back to work, I still had to. That's my job and our livelihood, so I had to take another partner. That's why I got Lovely. I didn't really have a choice."

He sighs.

"But Diane is right. I should have treated you better. But I was a coward. I couldn't bring myself to come back and tell you that I got another dog. It was easier to just leave you there until Diane brought you home. And then I felt even more guilty.

"When I brought Lovely home, that made it worse. I felt embarrassed and guilty, even though it wasn't really my fault. I should have tried to include you, but it was easier to feel angry than guilty. So I shut you out and ignored you. You responded with anger, so I felt justified to shut you out even more. I'm sorry."

I smell that's true. Brown was too weak to support me and too weak to admit to his guilt.

"I understand."

He smiles and opens his arms.

I stay put.

"I don't think so, my friend. I know all about unconditional love. I tried it, and we both know how that worked for me. If you want love, you'll have to earn it."

I walk inside with Lovely, and the kids follow. Diane brings in the brown bag.

"This yours, Butter?"

"Oh, yeah."

My heavenly smelling cardamom cookies. BB and Aleta grab them and start chewing. Lovely looks at them and drools.

"Help yourself."

"What are these?" Diane asks.

"Hadji Badah, Amira's unique Iraqi cookies. That girl could

teach you a thing or two about Middle-Eastern cuisine, you know."

Diane gives me a side glance.

"Just check them out."

The cookie crunches as Diane bites into it.

"They are good! I'll have to ask her for the recipe."

I wag my tail.

"Are you kidding? Ask me! Flour, eggs, cardamom, rose water, sugar, almonds...."

CHAPTER 42

BEING BACK HAS BEEN BITTERSWEET. Everything is the same and still so different. The kids are still a lovely full-time job. Diane ditched her cane and got back to work, and she's glad I'm back to help with her cooking. Our latest creation, Grandma's Spitting Cake, was a hit. My idea, of course.

"Come on, Butter! That's silly. I can't put the whole plums in!"

"Why not?"

"What if someone bites into them and breaks a tooth?"

"Like really? How come they don't break their teeth while eating plums?"

"But they know the stones are there!"

"So, tell them. It's a swell idea. You get to have a spitting contest with dessert. Whoever spits further gets to win. It's more fun than watching TV."

Diane shrugs.

"I don't know, Butter. If I keep the plums whole, the batter will rise better, but who'd want to do a spitting contest over dinner?"

"Come on, give it a try."

"If you insist. But I still think it's a bad idea. And you don't even know how to spit."

"Says who?"

Diane proceeds to wash and dry the plums. She flavors the batter with lemon peel and cinnamon, pours it over the plums, and sighs.

"I don't know, Butter...."

"How bad can it be? There's always ice cream."

"Yeah. But I hoped to do better for their last supper...."

Brown and Lovely are heading to Afghanistan tomorrow. This is Lovely's first deployment, so I did my best to teach her everything I know. I hope they send them to our old base in Kandahar to work with Viper and Guinness. I know Charlie said Guinness retired, but you never know.

I did my best to prepare Lovely.

"You can always trust Guinness. Always. Whether you like what she tells you or not, she's probably right. She always is."

"How about Viper?"

"He's usually right too, but he's got this snotty Malinois attitude that makes it hard to listen to him. But you can trust him with your life. He's the kind of guy who'll tell you if you have parsley in your teeth, though you won't find much parsley there. They're more into MREs. Regardless, never fail to ask for advice. Nobody will laugh at you. And if they do, so what? That might just keep you alive."

Lovely licks my nose, and I lick hers. I'm terribly worried. I wish I could be there to help her.

"Thanks, Butter. Thank you for your friendship, and your teaching, and all the kindness I know I don't deserve. Is there anything..."

"Dinner, everyone," Diane calls.

We gather into the dining room for supper. The kids are in their high chairs; I sit next to Diane, and Lovely sits next to Brown, as usual, but it's been a long time since I seethed with hate. Now Lovely is my friend, and I'll miss her terribly.

The bacon-wrapped sweet potatoes with spicy chili dip are perfect. The bacon's crispy, the potatoes smooth and sweet, and the chili dip gives them that extra kick that makes your mouth water. Even the kids, who'd rather eat their boogers than people's food, polish them off.

Juicy meatloaf with mashed potatoes and horseradish sauce comes next. The horseradish makes you cry in a good way. I sniff my way through it, hoping it won't settle on my hips.

And now to the pièce de résistance! Our cake is golden, fragrant, and smothered in whipped cream. Diane should be proud, but it's Grandma's Spitting Cake, and she's anxious.

"Today's dessert is presented by Butter, who wanted to make dessert into a game. The plums have stones, so please be careful. Once you find a stone, you're ready to play."

The house smells like sweet vanilla, tangy plums, and lemon zest, and I choke on my drool. Brown smiles.

"You outdid yourself, Diane." He takes a bite, and he puckers.

"I got a stone. What do I do?"

"Spit it as far as you can."

Brown spits, and the stone hits the ground two feet from his toes. Not looking like a winner.

"Maybe next time."

I work my way through the cake and save my two stones.

"My turn!"

Aleta spits her stone beyond Brown's.

"Like really?" he huffs.

"Me too! Me too!"

BB doesn't talk much, and he seldom engages with others. He inhabits a world of his own, spinning the wheels of his truck or staring at lights. But this silly game drew him in. He spits his stone, but not far enough, rand he sits back looking forlorn. He's got no stones left.

I lick his hand. He opens it, and I drop a stone in his hand.

Aleta's next try is better than her last. Diane drops her stone on her best skirt. Brown makes no progress. But BB does better, and he claps his hands.

"I have one left," Diane says and proceeds to drop it between her toes.

BB stands up, holding my last stone.

"Me. Me."

He puts the stone in his mouth and spits it. It hits the side of the table and ricochets, falling far away. BB straightens up, smiles, and looks at his mom.

"I won."

Diane hugs him with tears in her eyes.

"You sure did, sweetheart."

I've never seen her so proud.

The following morning is our last. The kids say goodbye to Brown, then hug Lovely as I watch from the kitchen. Brown comes to say goodbye.

"Goodbye, Butter. I'll give your regards to your friends."

"Thanks. But more importantly, look after Lovely. She needs all the help she can get."

He frowns.

"You think I need reminding?"

I stare at him until he lowers his eyes, then I wag my tail and go say goodbye to Lovely.

"Be careful, Lovely, and you'll be all right."

"Thanks, Butter."

"Tell Guinness I love her, but don't say that to Viper. He doesn't do love. Just tell him I'd be glad to eat his mutton anytime."

My throat tightens as I watch them file out the door. I wonder if I'll ever see them again. War is a harsh place to be, and tomorrow is not guaranteed. But I know that Lovely will do her best. She's a bright girl with an excellent nose. And Brown will look after her and teach her like he taught me.

I'll keep my toes crossed for them.

Bᴛᴛ...

BUT IN THE MEANTIME, I need to get ready. I have a big day today. Amira and I are visiting a one-legged kid named Peter.

Next in Series: **K-9 VIPER**

K-9 VIPER

THE VETERAN'S STORY

RADA JONES

BOOK 3 IN THE K-9 HEROES SERIES

CHAPTER 1

The day Butter got shot, I lost a piece of my soul.

We, dogs, often feel things before they happen, but I didn't see that one coming. That day looked just like any other day at our base in Kandahar.

I woke to the smell of fake mutton. So did Butter, and she started drooling. That Lab thinks she's a gourmet, but she's fooling herself. No foodie would lust over these stinky MREs. Even their name is fake. They call them Meals Ready to Eat, but they aren't. They need hot water, time, and an undiscerning palate to be edible. I only eat them to maintain my nutrient intake, but I wish Sabrina would stop doctoring them with those bogus aromas; I just don't have the heart to tell her. She does her best to deal with this war, the heat, and the men, and she has no one to look after her but me. I try to protect her while pretending I don't care because I don't want to ruin my reputation. Here, they all think I only care about my job, and that's fine with me. I'd rather look like a manic Malinois than a softie.

The low sun's horizontal rays hit the windows, and for a moment, this drab place looks magical. The dirty wooden floors, the plywood walls, the tired soldiers putting on their boots, even the dust speckles look dipped in gold. But it's all over by the time the handlers bring our food. Two dozen men get kitted for mission, coughing their thick morning cough; the floors creak; the smell of boots covers that of cleaning oil; and the cool morning becomes another scorching day.

I crawl out of my crate to stretch as Butter devours her food. She's getting chubby, the old girl, and that's no good for her joints. In K-9 business, the lighter, the better, but, like all unwanted pups, Butter's always hungry. That's why I let her have my food. And because it keeps me slim.

Sabrina brings my bowl. Her brown eyes are still heavy with sleep, and her hands smell like coffee as she scratches my ears.

"How're you doing, Viper? I hope we stay in today."

Brown, Butter's handler, nods.

"Me too."

His uniform is crumpled and his dark face tired; but then they all are. Our humans have been struggling since the Taliban went crazy with the IEDs. In the last few weeks, the insurgents buried hundreds of improvised explosive devices around the base. That's why we patrol outside the wire every day to find them. But the danger, the dust, and the heat are getting to our soldiers, and they smell pooped. All but Silver, Guinness's handler, who's on a roll.

Oops. I forgot to mention Guinness, my other partner. She's a gorgeous German shepherd, all black but for her brown eyebrows, and she has a wicked sense of humor for a German.

Butter finishes her food and eyes mine, so I nudge my bowl toward her. She wags her tail in thanks.

"Me too. I could do with a day off for a change," she mumbles as she sniffs my food.

Guinness ups her black muzzle in an upward dog, raises her rear in a downward dog, and finishes her yoga practice with a shake. She glances at Silver, who's bringing her bulletproof vest.

"No rest for the weary today, boys and girls."

Silver buckles her in. Brown does the same with Butter as Sabrina fits mine, and we file toward the heavy green gates where the soldiers are waiting.

Butter and Brown are leading today, and Guinness and Silver bring up the rear. That leaves Sabrina and I in the middle, breathing everyone's dust. Oh well. It still beats lying in the crate counting your toes.

The metal hinges scream as the gates crack open. Butter wags her golden tail like it's a flag as she steps out, leading Brown on his thirty-foot leash. She takes a few steps, raises her nose to sniff the wind, and stays put.

I don't know if she's working on her tan or figuring out what leash to wear, but she keeps us baking under the brutal sun until I can't take it anymore.

"No rush, Butter, *chérie*. Please, take your time."

Somewhere behind me, Guinness growls.

"Shut up, Viper. Butter knows what she's doing better than you."

I can't argue with that, so I bite my tongue and dance on my feet until Butter gets moving. Today's mission is to comb the village compound, searching for explosives. It's a hot mile in the sun since the scraggly bushes scattered through the desert couldn't shade a malnourished mouse, and, other than them and the mud wall surrounding the compound, there's nothing but scorching orange desert.

My paws burn as we shuffle forward breathing the dust risen by two dozen boots. I'm not loving it, but a job is a job, and the sooner we're done, the sooner we'll be back inside the wire.

The village is nothing but a handful of mud huts surrounded by a tall wall. As usual, we divide into teams. We K-9s search inside the houses while our soldiers wait outside, their arms ready, in case we find trouble.

I'm glad to be in the shade. Bombs I can deal with, but there's only so much heat I can take. And the job's easy. I whiz through the first hut, all empty but for a rug and a jug. The narrow slits in the walls kept it cool, but the heat swallows me once I step out. I pant and wag my tail to Sabrina.

"Anything?"

"Nope."

She wipes the sweat off her face and follows me to our last hut. The other two teams will take care of the rest, and we'll head back to base in no time.

There's no door, so I push in through the curtain. This hut is just like the other — baked earth floor, a rug, and a water jug — but for a painted chest and the two men glaring at me. They smell like hate. That's nothing new — after six years of service, I have yet to meet a native who likes me — but something about them rubs me wrong.

Their baggy shalwar kameez flutter in the breeze as they stand near each other, doing nothing. They ogle me like I'm a snake, not a trained K-9 on a mission, and I wonder what they're up to.

I sniff their feet, their fists, their clothes. There's no hint of explosives, but their sweat smells like they're scheming something. I don't trust them. I bet they're planning something treacherous.

But I'm a trained explosive detecting K-9. I didn't come here to look for hate and revenge. There's no shortage of either here in Kandahar. My mission is to find explosives, and they don't have any. Time to move on.

But I can't.

I stare at them and they glare back. Their eyes say they'd love to kill me. But they can't. What can they be up to? I don't know what to do.

"You OK, Viper?"

That's Sabrina. She's getting antsy. I need to make up my

mind, but I can't. My training says that my work here is done, but my instinct tells me otherwise.

"Hey, Viper. Nice quarters you moved into."

That's Guinness. She's pissed. They all are, standing under the killer sun waiting for me to be done. But I don't know what to do. My hackles are up, my skin prickles, and something stirs in my gut. I feel something's wrong, but I don't know what. If I found any trace of explosives, I'd give the signal and the soldiers would take them away. But I have nothing but a hunch, and I'm a professional. My mission is finding explosives, not haters.

I follow my training and step out to find our soldiers waiting, their arms ready. Sabrina sighs with relief.

"Anything?"

I sort of wag my tail.

"Not really."

We file back into formation to return to camp. I can't wait to be back inside the wire, but I'm terrified that I made a mistake. I bet I missed something. What were those two up to? I'd love to go back if I could.

Somewhere behind me, Guinness barks.

"What the heck took you so long?"

I'm tired and annoyed, and I know she is too. But this isn't a conversation I'll bark across the desert, even though most soldiers don't speak dog, so they wouldn't understand us. I ignore Guinness and drag myself forward with my dust-coated tongue hanging to my knees as we crawl back. Butter takes her sweet time sniffing every speckle of dust like she didn't just do it on the way over.

Then she stops.

She raises her muzzle to sniff something by the corner of the wall. The sun beats on us, but she freezes with her golden head held high and ears pricked like she's posing. I sniff that way too, but I get nothing, and I lose it.

"Do not rush, Butter, *chérie*. We have nothing better to do than to enjoy this dust all day."

Butter cocks her head. She opens her mouth to tell me where to put it when the earth explodes, and she rolls to the ground in a cloud of dust.

CHAPTER 2

DID I FEEL GUILTY? I had no time.

By the time our soldiers dropped to the ground and opened fire, the orange dust had cut our vision to a couple of feet. The gunfire stopped as fast as it started, and we gathered ourselves from the ground. Sabrina spat out the dust, wiped her mouth with her sleeve, and pulled me back with both hands when I sprung to check on Butter.

Just a few leaps away, my old friend lay motionless in a puddle of blood, looking dead. But Brown kneeled by her side, tightening a tourniquet around her paw, so I knew she must be alive. I pulled forward to see how she was doing, but Sabrina dragged me back.

"Not now, Viper. We don't have time. Half the men will go after the insurgents who shot Butter, and we must show them the way."

That I can do. I glance back, where Guinness leaps forward, dragging Silver. I know they'll look after Butter, so I bark my goodbye as I follow Sabrina.

"Good luck, Butter. We're going to get the ice-holes who shot you. Hang in there, my friend. I'll see you inside the wire."

I sniff the gunpowder, track the scent, sprint uphill behind some scruffy bushes, then canter downhill into a dry riverbed where the smell grows stronger. I follow it, inhaling dust with every breath until I fall upon the gun tucked in the elbow of a twisted tree.

I sit next to it. Sabrina gives the signal, and the men rush over.

"It's still hot from the shot," Emil says. "This must be it."

"Of course. But that doesn't tell us who shot it. Sabrina? Can Viper track them down?"

Sabrina lets me sniff the weapon. Not for explosives, this time, but for the scent of whoever held it close. The sharp odor of gunpowder overpowers every other smell, so I struggle. I sniff and sniff until I catch a musky odor. And mint, which counts for nothing, since here everyone drinks mint tea.

"Viper, track," Sabrina says.

No kidding.

I ramble at first, struggling to find my stride. But I soon find my groove and follow the track that takes us back to the village in a roundabout way. The scent gets stronger and stronger, and I drag Sabrina back to the hut that puzzled me this morning.

The two men are still here, reeking of hate and glaring at me, but there are half a dozen more surrounding them, all wearing shalwar kameez that hide their skinny bodies and possibly suicide vests. Their brothers, sons, and grandsons, some just toddlers, came to protect them, and they all smell like hate.

The stench of stress sweat overpowers the gunpowder on their clothes, but I didn't train all these years for nothing. I sniff every inch of every man like it's going out of style, and I sit by the elder to point him out. The soldiers handcuff him and take him away as I move to the next man, then the next.

A crooked man with eyes the color of storm wants to kick me so badly he bites his lip to stop. I know he's the one who shot Butter, and I fight the urge to open his throat right here and now.

I point him out and move on to the last one. He's just a kid, not old enough to sprout a beard, but he stinks of guilt just like the others, and his clenched fists betray his hate.

I wag my tail to Sabrina.

"That's it."

"Are you sure?"

"Yep. The others don't smell like gunpowder. I bet they all knew, but nobody else touched that weapon."

We file back to the base, and I sniff every step, like Butter did, wishing I wasn't such an ass. I hope the last words Butter ever heard from me weren't a snarl. We both deserve better than that.

The green gates open, and we file inside to safety, but that's the last thing on my mind. The air is thick with grief, and I wonder if Butter's still alive.

She lies motionless in the middle of the yard, her stretcher surrounded by grief-stricken men. Brown and Silver work on wrapping her paw. Guinness hunches by her head, her ears flat with worry, smelling like sorrow.

I sit by her shoulder, and she leans on me.

"How is she?"

"Not well. They called for a helicopter. Should be here any moment."

Just heartbeats later, the growling of the engines deafens us while the blades raise a sea of dust. We're just two feet away, but I struggle to discern Butter's face as the soldiers lift the stretcher.

She doesn't move as they race to load her in. The last thing I see is her mangled paw wrapped in a white bandage; then she's gone.

"I love you, Butter. You'll be OK," Guinness barks.

I wish I could say it, but I can't. I've never said, "I love you." So I do my best:

"Take care, Butter. I can't wait to have you back. I'll save my mutton just for you."

Brown climbs in the helicopter, and they're off.

I choke with sorrow as I watch the flying monster take my friend. I know I'll never see Butter again, and it's all my fault.

CHAPTER 3

AFTER THAT, our nights became lonely and sad. Guinness and I lie in our crates with Butter's empty bed between us, reminding us of our loss. Like we needed reminding.

But, as day after day went by without news from Butter, I felt relieved. That meant she was alive. I'd seen her paw, so I knew she'd never return. But Guinness didn't, so she spends her days waiting for her. Whenever the trucks come to bring mail, supplies, or new recruits, Guinness sprints to the gate, hoping they brought Butter. But they never do, so she comes back with her head hanging low, smelling like grief. It hurts to watch her, but I don't have the heart to crush her hope.

One evening when two trucks came and left without Butter, Guinness set her nose on her paws and whined.

"Oh, how I miss her. You know, Viper, there's something about these Canadians. They're just nice. Not like us."

I cocked my head.

"I beg your pardon?"

"No offense, Viper, but nobody would call us nice. We may be loyal, reliable, and hard-working, but nice?"

"You forgot attractive and modest, *hein*?"

Guinness slapped her tail to the floor in a weak dog smile.

"Common, Viper, you're not offended, are you? Would you really compare yourself to Butter in the nice department?"

"I would not, but that's not so bad. Some folks are just too nice. You and I would never let someone walk all over us. Nor would we fall apart because some ice-hole doesn't like us. Butter might. In our line of business, that's a liability. There's always someone whose paws you must step on. They won't like you, but so what? We aren't here to be popular; we're here to do our job."

Guinness agreed, though she hates thinking that Butter isn't perfect. But she's not. She's delightful, but perfect? Nobody is.

Now that Butter's gone, Guinness and I take turns in the lead, and I discover that I hate being in the rear even more than being in the middle. I dislike the dust, of course, but even more, I dread the thought of Guinness missing an IED. How silly is that? Guinness is a well-trained professional and a K-9, and she's got her own job to do. But I got so attached to her that just the thought of seeing her hurt gives me the heebie-jeebies.

At first, I thought it was because of Butter getting shot. If Guinness gets hurt, I'll be the only K-9 left. Terrible, *quoi*? I have to keep her safe. But then she got that letter.

The mail truck came and left without Butter, as usual. Guinness returned from the gate and lay her nose on her paws when Silver brought her a brown package.

"This came in for you."

Guinness pricked her ears.

"For me?"

We K-9s seldom get mail. I, for one, never get any. No wonder since we can't read. We can smell it, of course, but the scent has already faded by the time it arrives. And who even remembers us? I've had no one since Jinx died. And he couldn't write worth a damn.

"Yep. For you. K-9 Corporal Guinness Van Jones. Should I open it for you?" Silver asked.

Guinness glared.

"Hell no. Thanks."

Silver shrugged and left. Guinness sniffed every inch of the box as if she were looking for IEDs, then dispatched it with a quick bite and shook out its insides. She checked them one by one, and her ears flattened.

Bad news? I wondered. But it was none of my business, so I turned around to clean my privates, pretending I wasn't watching.

"Viper?"

"Yep."

"I got a package from home."

"Home?"

"Upstate New York. My mom's place."

"Oh."

"She lives with Jones. He taught me how to swear."

Wow. This Jones must be a talented guy. I've never met a lady with a more colorful vocabulary.

"Good news?"

"Sort of. Mom's alive and well, and she sends her best wishes."

Guinness shows me the picture of the best-looking K-9 I've ever seen, and that's a tall order since I'm a Malinois. German shepherds are our rivals, and it's not a lighthearted competition — it goes to the core of who we are. We're more driven — they're more balanced. They're stronger — we're leaner. And they think they're smarter, but they're wrong. But Guinness's mom would turn the head of any male who walks on four paws and fans himself with a tail.

"She's beautiful."

"That's just the beginning. Mom is wise, patient, and funny. I wish I grew up to be like her, but I took after my father."

"He couldn't be that bad."

I cock my head and take in Guinness's elegant muzzle, her fluffy tail, and those golden eyebrows that get my heart pumping. I'd never been into eyebrows before I met Guinness.

"Thanks, Viper. You care for some popcorn?"

"Don't mind if I do."

I love popcorn. It's nothing but air with a touch of butter flavor, but it makes you feel full, and that's good. I've gained a few pounds since Butter left, and there's no one to save my food for.

"Anything else?"

Guinness looks puzzled. She cocks her head to stare at a picture, then scratches her right ear with her hind paw to help herself think.

"I guess so."

"What's up?"

"There."

She points to the picture of a dog like I've never seen before. He's orange, but he'd look just like Guinness if he wasn't the wrong color.

"Who's that?"

"Beats me."

She grabs the letter and goes to find Silver. I'm half asleep by the time she returns with the answer.

"He seems to be my brother Fuzzy. Apparently, Mom had another litter, and they turned out orange."

"Orange shepherds? How can that be?"

Guinness glares at me.

"What do you think, Viper? Their father was a free dog, a golden retriever named Ranger. That's why the kids turned out weird."

"Oh."

I don't know if this is good news or bad news. Guinness's mom going interbreed may open Guinness's mind, but she doesn't look excited about her new brother.

"Jones says the kid takes after me and went into the military. Keep an eye on the new recruits, he says, just in case he ends up there."

I look for something to say, and nothing intelligent comes to mind. But I'm not the sort of guy who'd let that detail stop me.

"Well. With that color, he'll be hard to tell from the dust, so the Taliban are less likely to shoot him."

Guinness's eyebrows join as she frowns at me.

I flatten my ears and close my eyes, pretending I'm asleep. What a freaking charmer!

CHAPTER 4

FORTUNATELY, thanks to the Taliban, I didn't have much time to make a fool of myself. Guinness and I spent our days searching for IEDs, weapons, and suspects. We rarely had time for ourselves other than the evenings when we chatted in our side of the hangar while the humans played cards with the most wanted men on the other side.

"I'll raise you Chemical Ali against the Anthrax Lady," Ben said.

Fred shook his head in disbelief.

"Seriously? How about some swamp land somewhere?"

The others laughed, but they weren't kidding. To help them recognize the wanted men, the army had issued playing cards with their pictures. Instead of kings and queens, our soldiers played poker with angry mustached men.

Guinness watched them deep in thought.

"Do you think that works?" she asked.

"Dunno. To me, they all look alike. I couldn't tell them apart but for the smell."

That reminded me of the day Butter got shot. I never had the guts to tell Guinness, but I know that the men who shot Butter are the same two I let go. I'd bet my tail against an empty bowl of kibble that I'm right. I recognized their rancid stench of revenge and the fire in their hooded eyes.

The memory of that day weighs on me. I think of it every night and every day and tell myself that it's my fault that Butter got shot. Butter would be here today if I wasn't such a stickler for the rules and had listened to my instinct. But I let them go just because they didn't smell like explosives, like you need explosives to destroy someone. Butter's gone, and we don't even know if she's alive. And it's all my fault.

I'd love to tell Guinness and lift this weight off my soul, but I don't dare. What will she say? What if she holds me responsible and hates me forever?

Guinness pricks her ears.

"I just had an idea! They should make something like smelling cards for us. That way, we'd learn them, and we'd recognize them for sure."

"And what would we do?"

"Bring them to justice, of course. What else?"

"But that's not what we do. We are explosive-detecting K-9s. We're here to detect explosives, not to play the Avengers."

"Says who?"

She glares at me, and I shrink.

"Guinness, we are both K-9 officers, and we must play by the rules. You know that as well as I do."

Her hackles raise.

"I know no such thing. I know right from wrong, and I don't give a hoot about the rules. I have a nose to follow and a heart to listen to. And so do you."

I'm so anxious I get all prickly, and I start scratching. How do I know what's right and what's wrong? Would it be correct to detain people before they did anything? Or would that be wrong? Darned if I know.

"Guinness, you know we must obey the rules."

I wag my tail to mollify her, but it's not working.

"Seriously? You know as well as I do that the humans who make the rules don't have the commonsense Dog gave a squirrel crossing the road. And you want to abide by them? Come on, Viper!"

I shrivel. Thank Dog, she doesn't know. But she sniffs my guilt like it's painted on my forehead. She cocks her head and stares at me, then comes over to smell my butt and find out more, so I curl my tail between my legs to cover it.

"Viper, what did you do?"

"Nothing."

She yawns.

"So, what did you not do?"

This girl is too smart for her own good. And for mine. But there's no point in lying; she'll know it. I may as well come clean.

"I'm afraid I let Butter's attackers go."

Guinness doesn't raise her hackles. She doesn't even growl.

"Tell me about it."

I tell her how I found those men and how I agonized about what to do. Then I let them go, and Butter got shot. Guinness listens, her amber eyes so calm it's scary.

"You think it was them?"

"I do."

"Why?"

"They smelled like hate and revenge, just like those we picked up that smelled like gunpowder."

"Everyone here smells like hate and revenge. Even us."

I breathe.

"So, you think I was OK to let them go?"

She looks at me with pity.

"Of course not. You should have brought them over and had the humans check them. If you had, Butter might be here now."

I'm befuddled. Why isn't she mad, then?

"So, I did the wrong thing."

"Of course. But you did the Viper thing. You always play by

the rules. You don't know how to do anything else. It's not your fault — you do you. But it's high time you grew up."

She turns away to lay her nose on her paws and closes her eyes, and I feel more chastised than I've ever been. And I get angry. Very angry. Who does she think she is to tell me what to do? I'm twice her age, and I have more experience than she'll ever have. My whole life, I've done my job the best I could and played by the rules. And this green K-9 thinks she knows better? I'm so furious I fathom tasting her blood, and she smells it.

"Go ahead if you think you'll feel better," she says, without opening her eyes.

My rage melts, and guilt takes over. I crawl into my crate to lay my nose on my paws. In my mind, I see Butter's sad eyes.

"There's more to one's life than a job, Viper," she says.

I wish I had a hole to crawl in.

CHAPTER 5

MY ANGER against Guinness didn't last long. She just raised her eyebrows and wagged her fluffy tail, and I got hooked again.

It took me a while to understand that my feelings for her went beyond friendship. I couldn't believe that an old dog — I'm seven and a half, that's like more than 50 human years — could fall for a female less than half his age. But my heart flips when I hear her bark, and my insides turn squishy every time she sniffs my butt, so even an old curmudgeon like me has to admit that I've found The One.

So I started courting her the best I knew how: I left her the best place by the fan, I saved Sabrina's special treats just for her, and I did my best to not be an ice-hole, but she didn't even notice. And that's OK. Being ignored is no fun, but being laughed at? That's worse.

I didn't lose hope. I offered her my butt to sniff every morning — there isn't much to learn since we're together all the time — but that's how dogs communicate. Sniffing each other tells us what the other had for dinner, the mood they're in, and if they feel like dating.

That's how I knew that Guinness had the runs last week after she snitched a bar of Dove soap from the showers. She's a big fan, and she finished it in one sitting, as witnessed by her bubbly pink, sweet-smelling diarrhea. I didn't mention it, of course, but I filed that info in case I happen upon a bar of Dove. Wouldn't that make a lovely gift? We dogs have no money, so we can't buy flowers, wine, or chocolate. That makes it hard to woo someone — other than letting them smell you.

But Guinness didn't notice, even though she sniffs my butt every day. Isn't that odd? Even Sabrina noticed, and she never smells me. But she's a girly girl, Sabrina, all into lipstick and fake eyelashes, even though she doesn't need them. Any human at the camp would love to date her, but she's not interested.

"Then why tart yourself up?" I asked.

She shrugged.

"Just to remember that I'm still a girl."

That made no sense. How could you forget? Even if I did, I'd remember every time I clean my privates. Maybe humans don't clean their privates? Weird creatures. Either way, Sabrina knows I've got my eye on Guinness, and she's worried.

"Viper, are you sure this isn't your midlife crisis?"

"What's that?"

"It's when mature men mourn losing their youth, so they drive fast cars and date young girls."

"Sabrina, I don't drive. And, no offense, but I never met a girl I wanted to date. Even the pretty ones lack in the tail department."

Sabrina laughed and brushed me until I got all shiny, then got me a new collar. She always compliments me when Guinness is around, but Guinness doesn't seem to notice. So, to get her attention, I started bragging.

"If they left those prisoners with me, I'd get the truth out of them in no time."

"Really? I didn't think we were allowed to interrogate prisoners. Have you done it before?"

I cock my head.

"Sure. Haven't you?"

"No. How did you get them to cooperate?"

"I barked."

"Really? That's all it took?"

"It depends. But for me, that's all it took."

I watch her file that, and I wonder what she's thinking. That's the thing with Guinness. You never know what she's got in mind until she comes out of left field with some weird idea.

"Have you ever killed anyone?"

As I said.

"I thought we were talking interrogation. Why do you ask?"

She looks away, and I know she's about to lie. That's the thing about dogs. Unlike people, we don't lie staring into each other's faces. We couldn't get away with it anyhow because lies stink.

"Just curious."

I wonder who she plans to kill. I hope it's not me.

I run our roster, but I can't come up with anyone she hates, so I tell her.

"Go for the throat. All this stuff humans teach you in apprehension, like grab onto the arm and such? That's for when you have plenty of time and good backup. But when it gets real, go for the throat."

Guinness's eyes glaze over in thought, and I'd love to sniff her butt and find out what she's thinking, but that's against the protocol.

I try to think about something to say, but nothing comes to mind. Except...

"Would you like some popcorn?"

Guinness cocks her head. Popcorn is her weakness. That, and bacon. But I couldn't get bacon in Kandahar if I sold my tail. The Afghans are Muslims, so they don't eat pork. They think pigs are dirty and useless. That alone explains why I could never be a Muslim. But Sabrina had gotten me some popcorn, and I hid it, waiting for the perfect time. Popcorn for dogs is like champagne for humans: it sets the mood.

Guinness wags her tail.

"I'd love it."

I pull the popcorn bag from under my bed and spread it on the floor. Guinness and I pick one kernel after another, staring into each other's eyes, and I've never felt closer to her. She raises her eyebrows, and my insides turn hot and squishy. We're finally getting somewhere.

I crawl and lick her nose. She wiggles her eyebrows, and I'm ready to jump out of my skin when I hear boots.

It's Silver. Her eyes bright with tears, she kneels to hug Guinness.

"What happened?"

"Butter. She made it."

Like seriously? You interrupted us for that? I knew that a month ago!

"But they had to cut off her leg. She'll never come back."

CHAPTER 6

GUINNESS WILTED like a snowman in the sun. Her ears flattened, her head drooped, and her sexy, confident scent turned into the stench of dejection. Her sad puppy eyes tore at my heart.

"What are we going to do, Viper?"

Oh, how young she is! Our Guinness is so wise and confident that I forgot she's only three. She hasn't lived through years of this war that sucks you dry and steals your youth, your friends, and your hope, leaving you hollow inside. You learn to expect nothing but misery and rejoice if you get something better.

I sighed and licked her nose.

"We'll do what we always do, Guinness. We'll do our job. We'll patrol, we'll look for IEDs, we'll have each other's back, and we'll protect our humans, so they don't end up like Butter."

Her grief chokes me. I wish I could help, but Guinness wants Butter, and I can't bring her back. Nor do I want to. The old girl deserves better. I hope she has found peace and comfort wherever she is and gets real mutton every day. I hope she doesn't miss us one bit, no matter how much we miss her.

"I'm sorry, Guinness. I wish I could help."

She lays her nose on her paws and closes her eyes, and the scent of her anguish reminds me of losing Jinx.

Jinx was my twin. Not my littermate — we had seven of those — but looking at Jinx was like seeing myself in a mirror. We were inseparable, and no one could tell us apart.

When we got imported from Belgium, we were assigned different handlers, so we lived in separate homes. But we still trained together every day, we could read each other's thoughts, and we loved playing tricks on our handlers.

My human was Andrew. He had two kids and a large wife he called Mom. She lived to clean. She went nuts chasing every hair I shed and went berserk every time Andrew and I came home covered in mud. She drove me crazy, but at least I had Jinx to vent to.

"She vacuums the house and then weighs the hair. Who'd do that? And why? I don't know where Andrew found her, but I sure hope he takes her back."

Jinx spat the ball we were chasing.

"I don't know, brother. But at least you don't have a cat."

"A cat? Are you crazy? Where did you get a cat?"

Jinx flattened his ears and looked away, so I knew he'd brought that upon himself.

"I found him in the gutter. He must have washed in with the rain. It's just a little tabby, but he's a pain in the butt. He follows me everywhere and sniffs my stuff when I go to the bathroom. Imagine that! A cat! And he's deaf. He doesn't wake up when I bark."

"Why on earth did you pick him up, *hein*?"

"I don't know! He was all soaked and muddy, crying and smelling dejected. I couldn't leave him there to drown. I picked him by the scruff of his neck, shook him to get rid of the mud, and brought him home. The kids love him, but he likes me more, so he follows me like a shadow. He's only as big as an onion, and he stinks even worse, but I don't have the heart to tell him no. He wouldn't hear anyhow; he's just a cat and deaf too, for Dog's sake. But he's the bane of my existence."

I stare at Jinx, and he looks away, so I know he's lying. He loves that cat, but he's ashamed to admit it. I would be, too, if I loved a cat.

Life went on. I dealt with Mom, and he dealt with his cat until the day we decided to play a switch on our trainers. I went to his home, and he went to mine. We knew the humans wouldn't notice if we played it right.

I briefed Jinx.

"Shake before you step in the house, and ignore the vacuum cleaner. It's on all the time. Avoid the female and ignore the kids unless they feed you treats. Don't let her catch you on the sofa, or she'll have a conniption."

"That doesn't sound like much fun."

"Who said anything about fun? We're doing it for the experience, to see how good we've got it and feel better about our plot in life. So, what are my instructions?"

"The potty place is by the tall hedge. Don't drink from the toilets; the water smells like chlorine. And be nice to Turbo."

"Turbo?"

"The cat. He purrs like a broken engine, so we call him Turbo. He's my... my friend."

"I thought you hated him."

Jinks looks away.

"That was long ago. Now he's my friend. So, be nice to Turbo. Everything else is fair game."

I went home with Jinx's trainer, and he went home with mine.

Tricking the humans into thinking you're their dog was a piece of cake. Fun too! Jinx's car was littered with kids' toys, fast food wrappers, and all sorts of bits and bobs, not clean like ours. It was awesome! I had to refrain from checking everything out, and I reminded myself to not go sniffing around Jinx's house like I was new there.

I did well until I stepped through the door and heard this terrible siren noise. Then this tabby cat attacked me and tried to claw my eyes out. It took all my self-control to not tear him to pieces. I told him:

"Relax, Turbo. I'm Viper, Jinx's twin. We switched places for the night. He'll be back tomorrow."

Turbo didn't listen. He hissed, spat, and tried to kill me. The audacity! It was easy to dispatch him, but I knew Jinx would get mad, so I endured Turbo's foolish antics, hissing and roaring like a fire engine until Jinx's trainer grabbed him by the scruff of his neck and locked him up.

"You had to get that useless cat from the gutter, and now he's lost his mind."

He cleaned my scratches with plenty of hydrogen peroxide and very little patience. Boy, was I glad to switch back the next day.

"Your Turbo is out of his mind. I had a hard time keeping my eyes safe."

Jinx glared at me.

"If you touched one hair of his back..."

"Then what?"

He sighed and got himself together.

"Sorry, Viper, I just love that kitten. Other than you, he's my best friend."

He sure did. He loved him enough to die for him, not much later.

CHAPTER 7

THE DAY BUTTER got shot had been atrocious for us all, but finding out that she lost her leg and won't return destroyed the camp morale. Guinness was dejected. So was I, and so were the humans, even those who didn't work with her, since Butter's friendly tail wag never failed to bring a smile to people's faces.

Guinness and I couldn't replace her even if we tried. There's something special about Labradors; like puppies, they touch a soft spot in people's hearts, and everyone loves them. Guinness and I are loyal and reliable, and we work hard to keep everyone safe. But nobody ever comes to pet us or bring us treats other than our handlers. And that's fine with me since I'm not into PDA. And neither is Guinness.

That's why, when Silver came to hug her, Guinness shrank. She wanted to bolt, but she didn't since she didn't want to hurt Silver's feelings.

"What happened?"

"I have fantastic news! We're going home!"

"Home?"

"Yes. We're going back home, you and I! We'll take long hikes in the forest without looking for IEDs, we'll play in the snow, we'll eat bacon and watch TV! What do you think of that?"

Guinness cocked her head.

"Really?"

"Yes. We were due to go back a while ago, but we lost Butter and Brown, and we were short one team. But they have a new K-9 unit coming, so they'll let us go."

"When?"

"Soon."

Guinness jumped up to lick Silver's face, licked my nose, then started chasing her tail like a silly pup. She caught it and fell into a panting heap, smiling from one black ear to the other.

I wagged my tail to show her I was happy for her, but I was devastated. What will I do without her? How can I be without her? And I'm not even talking work, though it's terrible to have no partner.

"I'm so happy for you, Guinness. I know you can't wait to be home."

She sniffed my sadness, so she came to lick my nose.

"Thanks, Viper. I'll miss you."

"I'll miss you even more."

In her heart, she's already gone. She can't wait to be home, away from this miserable war. I can't blame her, but boy, how I'll miss her. I try to not be a party pooper.

"What's the first thing you'll do when you go back?"

"I'll find the biggest pile of snow, and I'll roll in it, eat it, and bury myself in it. Then I'll come out and start over."

"What if it isn't winter?"

That's another thing about being here. Every day is just like the others: hot and dusty. Since I don't have a calendar, I don't even know if it's summer or winter. And it doesn't matter, since here they're just the same. I miss watching the seasons change. I love winter's snow, spring's mud, summer's swims, and chasing leaves in the fall.

Guinness wags her tail.

"If there's no snow, I'll roll in the mud. That's even better."

Every morning and every night, she asks Silver if it's time, and every time she breaks my heart again. She can't wait to be gone, and she doesn't even know she's hurting me.

Sabrina does.

"I'm so sorry, Viper. I know you'll miss her, but remember we're getting a new team. You'll make a new friend."

See, that's the thing about humans. Even the smart ones can't put themselves in your paws. Just because this new K-9, whoever it is, has four legs and a tail doesn't mean we'll be friends. We may even hate each other. That happens to humans too — you'd think she'd understand.

But it is what it is. I'd better make the most of every moment left with Guinness. I'll have plenty of time to be sad when she's gone. So, Sabrina and I decide to have a party, and she's in charge of the details.

"We'll make two cakes: One for Silver, one for Guinness. Silver's will be sweet. I saved my MRE desserts to build it. But I don't know what to do for Guinness. What would she like?"

"Bacon."

"Wouldn't we all? But I can't get bacon. What else?"

"A cheeseburger? With a nice candle?"

"Let me see what I can do."

When the last day came, Guinness was so excited that Silver had to chase her all over the hangar to buckle on her bulletproof vest.

"This is our last day! Our last patrol! We're going home tomorrow!"

"I know. But we still have this last job, and we must do it well. Be careful, OK?"

"Of course," Guinness barked, running around the hangar to chase the zoomies. It was her turn to lead that day, but she was so wild I worried she'd get distracted.

"Hey, Guinness? How about you take the rear and let me lead today?"

You'd think she'd be grateful, but no! She growled at me.

"Are you out of your mind? Just because you're male, you think you can lead better? I've done this a hundred times. I can do it just as well as you can. Even better."

I flattened my ears and went to look for Sabrina. These darn feminists! Can't appreciate a chivalrous gesture!

Sabrina buckled me in.

"We're all set for the party. Emil donated a meatloaf MRE, and Ben gave us two tortillas to make Guinness's cake. It's not exactly a burger, but it will have to do."

"And we'll light a match for a candle."

"Good thought."

She clipped her leash to my collar, and we filed to the gate for Guinness's last patrol.

CHAPTER 8

THE GREEN GATES CREAK OPEN, and Guinness dances out like she's late for a party, dragging Silver behind on her thirty-foot-long leash. The soldiers file behind them, and Sabrina and I close the rear. It's just another hot and dusty day outside the wire, but the deep silence of the desert unsettles me. The memory of Butter getting shot hits me like a ton of bricks, and I wish Guinness would let me lead the patrol, but there's no point in asking again; she's stubborn as a mule. So, I bark.

"Guinness?"

"Yes."

"Be careful."

She glances at me like I've lost it, then pushes forward without answering. But what is there to say? "Thanks for telling me, Viper; without you, I was going to be careless as usual."

Guinness sniffs her way step by step, and nothing happens. We cross the open field without even a mouse bothering us, and we reach the compound. Everything's still and quiet, just as it should be.

I start thinking I'm just paranoid because Guinness is leaving tomorrow. One after the other, the soldiers round the corner and file along the eight-foot-tall wall, and I follow. It's all good until something flies over and lands between Guinness and Silver.

It looks like a baseball, but I've never seen them play baseball here. The thing rolls slowly toward Silver, then stops a few feet from her boots. She stares at it, then drops the leash and screams:

"Run, Guinness. Run."

That makes no sense. What is she saying? Guinness doesn't get it either, and she turns her head to stare at Silver.

"Run? Run where?"

Guinness screens the desert, looking for a perpetrator, but nothing moves as far as the eye can see. Silver drops to the ground, and Guinness rushes to help her just as the earth shudders under our feet.

The ball bursts in flames, and a wall of noise crashes into me as the explosion blasts Guinness high in the air. She twists and twirls before crashing in a motionless heap as I bite the dust.

Our fire is fast and furious, but our soldiers can't see anything beyond the orange dust that drowns us. The shooting stops, and we run to help Guinness and Silver, who were nearest the blast.

I can tell Silver's dead as soon as I get near her. It's not just the pool of blood or her unblinking eyes. It's that funny smell dead people get when life flies out of them. We all learned it after so much war. All but Guinness.

She lays her paws on Silver's chest and licks her face.

"Come on, Silver, get up. We're leaving tomorrow, remember?"

Silver's frozen eyes stare at the sky. She doesn't answer.

Guinness grabs her vest to pull her up.

"Come on, Silver. We have no time. Let's finish this patrol and go home!"

The soldiers try to pull her away, but she'll have none of it.

"Let me be! Help Silver! She needs to get up! We're leaving tomorrow!"

"She can't get up, Guinness."

She looks at me like I'm crazy.

"Sure, she can. She has to. Don't you remember? We're leaving tomorrow!"

The men lift Silver on a stretcher. Guinness dashes to the head of the file to lead us back inside the wire, but they won't let her, so she follows Silver's stretcher as I lead us back.

As soon as the green gates close behind us, Guinness starts barking.

"Come on, people! Do something! We're back inside now; we're safe! Put on a tourniquet! Call the helicopter. Do something! Remember, like you did with Butter?"

The soldiers stand frozen, watching her with teary eyes. Guinness runs from one to the other, nudges them and barks. No one moves.

She thinks they don't understand, so she pulls out Silver's first-aid kit from her equipment and drops it on her chest.

"There. Her first-aid kit. Come on, everyone! What's wrong with you? Start an IV! Give her something! Call the helicopter! She needs help!"

A soldier tries to pet her, but she leaps aside. Another one wants to pull her away, but Guinness bares her teeth and growls. She's about to sink them in his flesh when Sabrina takes out her first-aid kit.

Guinness relents.

"Finally! I thought nobody was going to do anything. What took you all so long?"

Sabrina fills her syringe. The long needle gleams as it catches the sun.

"Sorry, Guinness."

The needle sinks deep into Guinness's neck, and she falls to the ground.

CHAPTER 9

WHAT? My jaw falls. I turn to Sabrina, bare my teeth, and growl.

"What the heck did you do that for?"

Sabrina drops the syringe to check Guinness's pulse.

"Sorry, Viper. I had to calm her down before she hurt someone. You saw she was out of control, and you know what happens when K-9s attack people."

That I do.

After graduating from our training, Jinx and I started work. Andrew and I got deployed to Iraq, but Jinx and his handler landed a cushy stateside job, watching paint dry someplace or other. I got news from him through the grapevine every now and then, and I knew he was well.

I was envious. Jinx stayed home to enjoy good food, take mud baths, and watch the leaves turn while I listened to the call to prayer five times a day. What strings did he pull? How did he get to stay home while I breathed dust and ate MREs?

When I stopped hearing about him, I didn't worry. Jinx was more likely to get hit by a car than step on a mine wherever he was. I just hoped he'd get fat from living the good life, so I could laugh at him when we met.

Then Andrew and I went home. It was nice to walk without

searching for IEDs, soak in the rain, and take mud baths. But Mom drove me nuts. She wiped my feet every time I came in and had me wear booties when it rained. A Belgian Malinois with red booties! Humiliating!

Andrew didn't like it much either, so one morning he went to buy cigarettes and didn't return. A few days later, the army assigned me a new handler.

George checked my papers.

"You had a brother Jinx?"

My heart froze.

"Jinx is my twin."

He looked into my eyes and I smelled pity.

"Sorry, Viper. Jinx died."

"Jinx died? How?"

"He got injured, and the vet had to put him to sleep."

"Injured? How did he get injured? On the job?"

"Yes, but not the way you'd think. It says here that Jinx's handler shot him."

My throat tightens, and my hackles rise. That's got to be a lie. I know this man. I know his home, his family, even his cat. How could he shoot Jinx? And why?

"Why?"

"Jinx attacked him, and the man had to shoot him to stay alive."

That day was the worst of my life, but today came close. Silver died, Guinness went berserk, and the insurgents got away with it. I hope I never see a day like this again.

The soldiers covered Silver with the American flag and stood guard around her, their faces contorted with grief. They all knew they could be under that flag. Unlike missing an IED, which could be someone's mistake, that grenade was nobody's fault. Just Silver's bad luck.

The helicopter lands to take Silver and Guinness. Silver won't be back. But Guinness?

She lies on her side smelling like no other dog I ever sniffed. I wonder what she's dreaming about. Is she running in the fields, chasing squirrels? Eating bacon? Rolling in the snow? I hope she gets to do all that again, even if that means she won't return. Grief chokes me as I lick her nose one last time.

Sabrina pats her shoulder.

"What a great K-9."

"You think she'll ever come back?"

Sabrina shrugs.

"I don't know. She's in shock, but she may recover. Some do, some don't. You want her back?"

I don't know. I'd love to see her again, but I know she hates it here. This war stole everyone dear to her: First Butter, then Silver. I don't think she'd be happy here.

The engines growl, and the helicopter lifts off in a cloud of orange dust, taking her away. I watch the monster grow smaller and smaller as the noise dies down, and I wish I told Guinness how I loved her instead of listening to my pride. What an awful waste!

"Until we meet again, my love."

CHAPTER 10

SINCE SABRINA and I are the only K-9 unit left, we're so busy with patrol, training, and searches that we never have a dull moment from dusk to dawn.

But at night I lie in my crate with nothing to do but listen to the men snore. Once in a while, someone screams, and I wonder what horrors they dream about. I hope they wake up soon to escape their fears. I wish I did too, but my demons won't quit because they're real. I remember Guinness, Butter, and Silver and what this darn war did to them and to the rest of us. And I'm wary.

War is my job. It's what I'm trained to do, so it's what I do, whether I like it or not. Being a K-9 is my career, and it gives my life meaning. But, as the war took my friends one by one, I grew leery.

Sabrina struggles too. Silver was her friend, and seeing her die crushed her soul. Then the extra work, the loneliness, and the stress got to her. She doesn't eat, and she barely sleeps, so she withered like the desert bushes. I'd love to help her, but I don't know how. She needs rest, but with us two doing the work of three K-9 units, she's got no hope of getting it.

That's why I was mighty pleased when the new K-9s arrived.

It took them so long that I started thinking they were slackers. They were supposed to arrive weeks ago, but we heard nothing and I started losing hope. But one afternoon when the truck arrived I sniffed a dog.

"Hey, Sabrina! They're here! The new K-9s arrived."

"Really?"

She ran her fingers through her hair and smoothed her uniform. I could tell she wanted to take a shower and maybe even brush me to impress them, but I didn't give a hoot about what they thought. They'd taken their sweet time to arrive, and I was pissed.

"Come on. Who cares what they think? I only care about what they do! Let's go meet them."

I dashed to the truck, and she followed. A tall long-chinned man climbed out, then an orange dog that looked familiar.

The man shook Sabrina's hand and flashed a white smile.

"I'm Dick."

Sabrina's brown eyes softened as she studied him. She forgot to take back her hand.

"I'm Sabrina. We're glad to have you aboard."

"Good to be here. I think."

Dick's clear blue eyes took in the dusty trucks, the razor-wire topping the wall and the ramshackle buildings and his mouth thinned to a line. I could tell he was disappointed without even sniffing his butt.

Sabrina unglued her eyes from his to glance at the dog who dashed to bless a scraggly bush.

"And who's he?"

"That's my dog, Fury."

That settled it. I knew right then that Dick was going to be trouble. I didn't like how he looked at Sabrina; I didn't like how he held himself. And calling his partner, a trained K-9 officer, a dog? What sort of jerk would do that?

But there's something about Fury that bothers me even more.

Looking at him makes my skin prickle, like when you get brushed the wrong way. I can't put my paw on it, but something about him feels weird.

Oh well. I may as well find out. I approach Fury, and he turns around politely to offer his butt. I sniff every inch of him, performing a complete evaluation. He had chicken and rice kibble for breakfast, but it's been a while. He's thirsty, and a bit stressed after his long travels, but he smells like a decent guy, even though he's just a pup. But something about him still irks me.

I turn around, and Fury sniffs my butt respectfully, wagging his fluffy tail. When he's done, we sniff each other's noses. I want to be friendly, but I notice Sabrina staring at Dick like he hung the moon, and that pisses me off. So I blurt:

"You sure took your sweet time coming over."

Fury cocks his head in surprise, and the wind fluffs his ears. How on earth can he hear with those orange things hanging like pancakes?

"I beg your pardon?"

"You were supposed to be here weeks ago. Where were you? What did you do? Did you walk all the way here?"

Fury shakes his head so hard that his ears slap his muzzle.

"And a good day to you too."

He leaves me standing there and follows Dick.

CHAPTER 11

After Guinness left, I didn't think I could get any lonelier, but it turns out I was wrong. When Fury arrived, I learned that being lonely is not the same as being alone.

He hasn't come near me since that first day when I was rude to him. I know why, but I can't bring myself to apologize. He's just a pup, and he's new. He should be asking for my friendship. There's so much I could teach him. He may be trained to sniff explosives, but he knows nothing about camp life, about the desert, about the enemy, and even about life. It would do him good to be humble and make an overture. But he doesn't.

Night after night, we lie in our crates, pretending we don't know the other one's there, though we can smell each other's thoughts. I know Fury misses his family and wishes he wasn't here. He knows I often feel the same. But nobody says anything, so it's lonelier than being alone.

He's good at his job, I'll give him that. Whenever he leads, I watch him like a hawk, and he makes no mistakes. I can't say the same about Dick, who's so full of himself you'd think he's the bomb sniffer. Even worse, he's got Sabrina wrapped around his little finger. She's so enchanted with him that she rarely has time for me.

Even now. Sabrina's fixing my breakfast, but her cheeks are all flushed, and her eyes are full of light as she smiles at him. That hurts. I know, deep in my bones, that he's no good for her, and I wish I could tell her, but she can't see anything beyond Dick's blue eyes.

I'm crawling out of my crate to get my breakfast when the earth shudders. My ears ring from the blast as I drop to the ground, choking in a cloud of dust. The soldiers grab their weapons and start shooting blindly, so I take cover, waiting for the chaos to settle.

When it finally does, we discover that a truck loaded with explosives crashed into the green gate, warping the solid green metal into a smoking mess. Its twisted remnants hang loosely between the damaged walls.

Our impregnable camp is invulnerable no more, so there's no more safety inside the wire. That's earth-shattering.

I glance at Fury. He lays in his crate with his nose on his paws like nothing happened. He acts cool, but I can smell his anguish, and I bet he smells mine.

Poor pup. I look for something comforting to say, but I don't get to find it since Sabrina brings my bulletproof vest.

"Let's go, Viper. It's our turn to lead."

"Are you serious? We're going out on patrol after this?"

"We have to. We can't sit here waiting for the enemy to attack now that we're vulnerable. We have to go on the offensive."

We file at whatever's left of the gate as the soldiers struggle to open it. When they finally do, my heart skips a beat. The orange desert is littered with smoldering debris, for as far as I can see. Shredded tires, twisted scraps of blackened metal, bloody rags that used to be clothes, unrecognizable bits and bobs. They're all smoking, and every single one may hide an unexploded IED.

I've never had a job like this. I'll be darned if I know what I'm looking for in this field of charred remains. I glance at Sabrina.

"What are we looking for?"

She shrugs.

"The enemy, I guess."

I walk warily, sniffing the acrid fumes as my nose burns with the smell of explosives. I feel Sabrina's heart racing at the other end of the leash, and I know she's as worried as I am. It's impossible to find something here. It's like looking for a needle, not in a haystack but in a pile of needles, since everything smells like explosives.

I trudge through the debris to the open desert beyond where the fumes fade, and my smell starts to return. I take my time heading toward the village since there's no point getting there nose-blind.

I catch a whiff of human to my right. I follow my nose and the scent gets stronger, so I know I'm up to something. There we go! I leap forward, dragging Sabrina when someone behind me barks.

"Get down, Viper!"

My mind tells me that I don't take orders from dogs, but my feet are wiser, so I roll to the ground as a shot raises the dust where I was just a second ago. Another bullet grazes my vest as our men open fire.

It's hell on earth. A hail of bullets whistles over my head as I melt into the dust. I lie there, thinking it's no fun to be me when the fire stops as fast as it started. I jump up and leap forward to the shelter beyond a tiny hill where we find the insurgents. One's dead and one's wounded, and they're both just kids. I almost feel sorry for them, but I remember Butter, Silver, and Guinness, and I get over it.

That evening I lie in my crate pretending to sleep, keenly aware of Fury in the crate next to mine. I should thank him for saving my life, but I can't make myself do it.

"Hey, Viper?"

"Yes."

"I'm glad you're not dead."

"Me too, brother. Thank you."

CHAPTER 12

BEFRIENDING Fury was like lapping cold water after patrolling the desert. After weeks of loneliness, I finally had someone who understood, since he walked in my paws.

When I was just a pup, I used to think of myself as a loner whose whole life was his job. Sure, I cared about my humans, but they changed so often they weren't worth the emotional investment.

I had to grow old to understand that my pack is my life. That's why, when Butter got shot, I lost part of my soul. Butter and I worked together for three deployments, and she knows me better than anyone else. Sometimes I wonder if she knows me better than I know myself, and that's scary.

Then Silver got killed and Guinness had her breakdown, and it got even worse. I felt lonely and hollow. I got wondering if the war was the right place for me. Was I in the wrong place, doing the wrong thing? Was my life's work worthless? Sure, I found some bombs, and I saved a few lives. But did I make the world a better place? And if I didn't, what did I do with my life?

That got me into some dark places, and I started losing it. My mentals were going downhill fast.

But then Fury came. Having him here is like fresh air to my nose and soft mud to my paws. Buddies are good for the soul.

Day after hot stinking day, we patrol this hateful land, looking for IEDs, chasing the enemy, and hoping to make it back inside the wire. But the evenings are ours to lick our charred paws and tell each other stories as the humans chat and play cards at the other end of the hangar.

I glance over to check on Sabrina, but she's missing. So is Dick. Where is she? I'm about to go looking for her when Fury asks:

"Tell me about your first mission, Viper. When was it?"

"Oh, boy. That's so long ago, I can barely remember. Let me see, *hein*? Jinx and I were twelve months old when they brought us from Belgium. We trained for months before I got deployed, six years ago, in Iraq. My first handler, Andrew, was a good man, but his female was awful. She rode him like a rented mule, so going to Iraq was like going on vacation. The army had fewer rules than his home."

"How was Iraq?"

"It was a blast. Everything was new: the heat, the smells, the food, the people. Those humans weren't used to K-9s. Everyone — the kids, the women, the elderly — stood in the sun for hours to watch us work. They had never seen dogs at work, and they couldn't believe it. There, if a dog touches a dish, they scrub it with sand and set it in the sun for 40 days to purify it before they can use it again. If they touch a dog after washing for prayer, they must scrub themselves all over again. They think that dogs are useless, filthy, and disgusting, so imagine their shock when we found a whole pod of artillery rounds and grenades under a house in Ramadi. They couldn't believe it. Andrew and I saved hundreds of lives on that mission alone.

Fury wags his tail in appreciation.

"What a great mission! What else did you do?"

"We accompanied military convoys. We always rode in the

first vehicle, then popped out to check the bridges, the crossings, or anything that looked fishy. We got to stretch our legs without sniffing everyone's dust. And speak about appreciation!"

"And then?"

"When our deployment was over, we went back home. That stank since we'd gotten used to living without Mom's rules. So, one day, Andrew left, and I never heard from him again. I hope he's somewhere by the ocean, loving life."

Fury cocks his head.

"But...how about his wife? And the kids? And you?"

I sort of wag my tail. The kid's right.

"I see your point. But I can see Andrew's too. He was like a kid who loved life, and that woman sucked the joy out of him like a vacuum cleaner. That's one reason I'm wary of relationships. Not like I got many offers, but still."

"Then what?"

"The army assigned me to George, and we deployed to Afghanistan. That's when I met Butter."

"Who's Butter?"

"Butter is the nicest bomb sniffer you'll ever meet. She's Canadian since she's a yellow Lab. We worked as a team until the day she got shot. She's my best friend other than Guinness."

"Guinness?"

"Yep. Guinness is a K-9 too, but she's a German shepherd. She's an MPC, a Multi-Purpose Canine, and a darned good-looking dog.

Fury cocks his head.

"Sleek, shiny, almost black? Fluffy tail and brown eyebrows?"

"And a rebel with tons of attitude. You know Guinness?"

"I know of her. Guinness is my big sister."

CHAPTER 13

WHAT?

I stare at Fury, and I finally see what bothered me all along: the long slick muzzle, the amber eyes, the way he carries his head — all Guinness. All but his frilly golden coat and silly floppy ears.

"Seriously? Are you Fuzzy?"

"I used to be, but Dick didn't think that was an impressive enough K-9 name, so he changed it to Fury."

I shake my head like I'm wet. I can't believe it! He's just like Guinness, but he's not. Guinness is a quintessential German shepherd, while Fury is...I don't know what Fury is.

"I hope you don't mind my asking, but... what breed are you?"

"I'm a golden shepherd."

"Never heard of it."

"It's a new breed, you know, like the cockapoos and the Labradoodles, except we're working dogs. My mom is a German shepherd from champion bloodlines, but my dad's a golden retriever. He's a free dog named Ranger. So, I'm a golden shepherd. Some call us German retrievers, but I don't like that. I'm neither German nor much of a retriever. I'm a shepherd at heart."

I wag my tail. Fury is even less German than Guinness, who's the least Teutonic shepherd I've ever met. He's not much of a retriever either, but he's a damn good-looking dog and quite the K-9 if you ask me.

He cocks his head.

"Would you tell me about Guinness? I so hoped to meet her. Mom and Jones are so proud of her; they never tire of telling stories about her puppyhood. They called her Red, and she was a riot. Jones still has the red sweater she ate a hole in when he left her in the library. He can't bring himself to throw it away."

"Guinness is a character. She always has a unique angle on everything. When she tells you a story, it's like she turns on a flashlight in the dark. Things make sense differently. Guinness is compassionate, hard-working, and funny, but you don't want to get on her wrong side. One time, when she thought I disparaged our friend Butter, she almost ripped open my throat."

Fury's eyes sparkle and his head lifts high.

"Guinness loves popcorn, bacon, and playing with the ball. She's a champion at staring. When we got bored, we held staring contests. Guinness and I stared at each other without blinking until Butter fell asleep. Guinness usually won. Oh, did you know she won NORT?"

"What's NORT?"

"NORT, the National Odor Recognition Test, is like the K-9 sniffing Olympics. The best K-9s compete in finding explosives, firearms, and such. Guinness is the only K-9 I know who even competed in it, let alone win it. Your big sister is an exceptional K-9."

"Oh, how I wish I met her! Where is she?"

"She went home a few months ago."

"Will she come back?"

"I don't think so. When we were on patrol, an insurgent threw a grenade that killed Silver, her handler. Guinness took it badly. This was just weeks after Butter got shot and lost her leg. Guinness had a breakdown, and they sent her home for treatment.

Last I knew, she was in rehab, and they were looking to get her a job stateside."

Fury lays his nose on his paws just like Guinness used to do and looks away. He doesn't say anything, but I smell his disappointment.

"I'm sorry, Fury."

He sighs.

"You know, my whole life, I hoped to grow up and be like Guinness. She was my hero. She could do no wrong. So finding out that she lost it and got sent home is a bummer."

My hackles rise, and I bare my teeth to growl and give him a piece of my mind, but I manage to keep my cool. It's not the kid's fault. He just doesn't know any better. He thinks that having a breakdown is something to be ashamed of. But he's wrong.

"Listen, Fury, Guinness is a hero. She's the smartest, strongest, and bravest K-9 I ever worked with, and I'm proud to be her friend. Getting PTSD from this darn war is not her fault, and it's not a sign of weakness. She's nothing to be ashamed of. She's brave, loyal, and resilient. I just hope you grow up to fill her paws someday."

Fury cocks his head.

"You think so?"

"I don't think so. I know so. Guinness is..."

All of a sudden, Sabrina kneels over and hugs me, her eyes full of tears. I don't know what this is about, but I bet it has to do with Dick, and I don't like it one bit. And I HATE being hugged! But I don't want to hurt her feelings, so I hunch there, waiting for her to let go, but she won't.

I break down and lick her face to make her feel better. I'm embarrassed to do this in front of Fury, but he doesn't seem surprised. Isn't that odd? Dick doesn't strike me as the touchy-feely type. Oh well.

I do my best to comfort Sabrina.

"There, there. Take it easy. Everything is going to be OK; you'll see."

She sobs.

"No, it won't. It can't. Viper, I just found out that I'm expecting."

CHAPTER 14

EXPECTING? What is she expecting? Whatever it is, it can't be good. I wonder if it's that MRE we had yesterday. It was even more disgusting than usual. I only had half of it, and I wanted to barf.

I sniff her bottom. She smells a little funky, but she doesn't smell like she pooped recently, which gives me an idea.

"How about pooping? That always helps me feel better. Or at least drink lots of water. That may help you barf."

Sabrina gasps, and I don't know if she's crying or laughing.

"Oh, Viper. That was precious. You almost made me laugh. Thanks for that, I needed it. But this is really serious, you know. I think they'll send me home."

Home? Now that's a thought! I could look for Guinness and Butter. Wouldn't that be a riot if I could track them? As long as Sabrina gets better, I won't miss this dang war one bit. I'll miss Fury, of course. But we won't be gone long, I bet. And I can't wait to have some actual weather for a change, whatever it is, as long as it's not summer in the desert.

"What season is it at home now?"

"It's winter."

"That's totally awesome. I love snow. Do you know how to

make snowballs? I love to leap and catch them and then chomp on them. Or we could make Snow Boogeymen we could wrestle into the ground!"

Sabrina's mouth corners turn down, and she starts crying again. I can't imagine why. I was sure she had enough of the heat and the desert.

"Oh, Viper. How I wish we could go back together."

She blows her nose, hugs me once more, and leaves. I stare behind her, wondering what this is all about. She makes no sense whatsoever.

I glance at Fury, who's lying in his crate with his nose on his paws pretending to be asleep, but I see his ears twitching. I bet he didn't miss a single word.

"What the heck was all that? Did she make any sense to you?"

Fury cracks open one eye.

"Viper, you understand what she's expecting?"

"No."

"I thought so. Sabrina's pregnant. She's going to have puppies."

My jaw falls.

"What? Are you out of your mind? How do you know that?"

"I learned it at home, just before I left for training. The neighbor asked Jones why Mom got so big, and he told her she was expecting. She was going to have a new litter."

"But Sabrina can't have puppies!"

"Why not?"

"Well, first of all, she's not a dog. If she had anything, she'd have babies."

"Wow! I didn't think about that. That's even worse."

"You aren't kidding."

I crawl back in my crate to think. I remember Andrew's wife and her vacuum cleaner. I wonder if Sabrina will turn out like that after having babies, harping at everyone about everything. I hope not. But at least we'll get to play in the snow, eat real food, and get rid of the dust. All in all, it sounds worth it.

"I can't wait to play in the snow. I haven't seen snow in years.

Fury glances at me.

"You think you'll go back with her?"

"Why not?"

"You aren't pregnant. And the army is short of explosive detecting K-9s."

"Sabrina won't leave me here. I know she'll take me back with her."

"If she can. But they may not let her."

"But I have nobody to work with."

"They'll get you a new handler."

CHAPTER 15

WHAT? My hackles go up. Fury must be wrong! They can't get me a new handler! I belong with Sabrina, and she belongs with me. I can't let her go. Who'd look after her?

But then I remember my other handlers. In the army, handlers are interchangeable, just like K-9s.

Andrew and I trained together and deployed together. I thought we'd be together forever, but he disappeared.

The army gave me George. He was wise, patient, and wifeless, and he taught me most of what I know. But George was old, and he'd already paid his dues to the country, so he retired.

The army passed me on to PJ, who was on his first deployment and thought he knew everything. He reminded me of myself as a pup. I thought I knew it all and hated being told what to do. But by the time I met PJ, I'd learned that staying alive beats looking cool. PJ hadn't.

He strutted down the desert, veering off the track I'd sniffed just to show he was unafraid. The lieutenant talked to him, and PJ nodded, staring at his boots, then did it again. But not for long.

We were looking for explosives in a nearby compound; as usual, I went inside one hut after another, as PJ waited outside to stay safe. I found a box smelling funky, and I called PJ, but he didn't answer. I waited and waited until the locals got restless. So I opened the box, even though that was against the rules. The iffy smell turned out to be just a box of matches, so I went to tell PJ, but he was gone.

I started tracking him when the earth shuddered, and the place went up in flames.

The power of the blast threw me to the ground, and it took me a while to get up, deaf and dazed. I wobbled on shaky legs to look for PJ.

But all I found was his helmet and a damaged boot. The rest was spread over the desert. PJ managed to find the cache of arms protected by the mother of all IEDs, but he didn't get to brag about it.

I was once again without a handler, so the army gave me Sabrina. She had a voice like melted chocolate and magic hands that always found my itchy spots. She brushed me, threw me the ball, and saved the best bits of her MREs just for me.

"You don't have to do that," I said.

"I know. I do it because I love you."

That, right there, was a choker. Nobody had ever told me they loved me. Not my trainers, not Jinx, not even my mother. That's how Sabrina won my heart.

I promised her that nothing bad would come to her while I was around, and I did my best to keep my promise.

But now I'm out of my depth. I'd die for Sabrina if that helped, but I can't fix the trouble she's in. So, I do what I can: I try to be the best friend I can be, I follow her orders, and I struggle to stay awake when she tells me stories. But the danger is looming. I don't know what it is, but it's here. Our time together is almost over. I can smell that like I can smell storms, fear, and explosives, so I do my best to comfort her while I'm here.

CHAPTER 16

But nothing happened. Camp life stayed the same: breakfast, patrol, long chats with Fury in the evening, sleep, repeat. I'd have stopped worrying if it weren't for Sabrina fading every day. She woke up tired, fell asleep over breakfast, and puked all the time.

We were walking one morning when she turned white, leaned against a truck, and puked her heart out. I sniffed it carefully. There was no food. No wonder, since she never eats. But there wasn't even grass, wood splinters, or peach pits like I puke when I eat things I shouldn't. Sabrina's barf was nothing but bile.

She dropped on a box, hiding her face in her hands, as Fury and Dick passed by.

Dick's face fell. He came over and touched her shoulder.

"You OK, sweetheart?"

Sabrina shook her head.

"What's going on, baby? Did you eat something that didn't agree with you?"

Sabrina sighed.

"No, Dick. It's not what I ate. I'm pregnant."

"You're what?"

His hand pulled away like she was hot.

"You heard me. I'm pregnant."

Dick blanched. He glanced around at the parked trucks to make sure nobody listened, then cleared his throat.

"Are you saying it's mine?"

Sabrina's cheeks caught fire.

"What do you think?"

He looked away.

"How would I know?"

Her voice stayed low, but I could smell her anger.

"Yes, Dick, it's yours. I haven't dated anyone else since I left home. So, what are you going to do about it?"

"Me? There's nothing I can do. The question is, what are you going to do about it? Did you report it yet?"

"Not yet."

"You should. You want to have enough time to...deal with it."

"Deal with it?"

"Of course. Get rid of it. You aren't thinking of keeping it, are you?"

She jumped to her feet, and he stepped back.

"Dick, do you understand it's a baby we're talking about? Our baby?"

"Sorry, Sabrina, but you have to leave me out of this. You know as well as I do that we aren't supposed to have sex while deployed. We broke the rules. I don't want to get in trouble with the army. And my wife must never find out."

Sabrina stepped back.

"Your wife?"

"Yes. What did you think? I have a wife and three kids. If she finds out, she'll make my life a living hell."

Sabrina wavered and steadied herself against the truck.

"You forgot to mention your wife before."

Dick shrugged.

"You didn't ask."

"I didn't ask. Really. That's all you have to say?"

She turned to leave.

"Let's go, Viper."

Dick grabbed her arm.

"Listen, honey. You've got to be reasonable. The only sensible thing to do is get rid of it. The army will send you back home, where you can get a termination. Quick, safe, and clean. You'll be back in no time. It's so much easier than dealing with a kid for eighteen years. They're a pain in the butt, all of them. And you have no idea how much they cost! The diapers alone...."

Sabrina shook him off, but he didn't let go.

"Come on, Sabrina. You're still young! You have all the time in the world to have kids. And think about what people will say if you keep it! They'll think you got yourself pregnant just to get out of the army, and they'll hate you. But I know that's not true. Or is it? Did you do it to get out of the army? Or did you imagine I was going to propose?"

Sabrina's fists tightened.

"What a loser you are, Dick. Get lost."

"Sorry, Sabrina, I didn't really mean that. You know how much I love you! I'm just in shock. And I'm worried about you. Let's sleep on it, and I'm sure we'll come up with a plan."

Sabrina tried to leave, but he wouldn't let her. His knuckles blanched as he held on to her arm, and she whimpered.

I couldn't take it anymore. I rose my hackles, bared my teeth, and growled, ready to rip off Dick's throat.

"Sabrina told you to get lost. Get lost."

Dick frowned.

"Down, Viper."

I growled louder.

"Are you kidding me? I don't take orders from you, not now nor ever. Get lost, I said."

I was ready to leap when Sabrina pulled me away.

"Let's go, Viper. He's not worth it. Forget it!"

I followed her. But I won't forget.

CHAPTER 17

Things got worse after that. Sabrina shrank until you could barely see her from the side, and her brain seemed to drown in a fog. She forgot her vest, she forgot her weapon, she'd even forget me if I didn't keep my eye on her. Sabrina's heart was no longer in her job, and I hated to agree with Dick, but she needed to go home. She knew it too, but she couldn't bring herself to do it.

One evening when Fury and Dick were away, Sabrina brought me her dinner. I refused it since she needed it more than I did, but she insisted. I didn't want to be rude, so I started picking at her so-called meatloaf as she got talking.

"You know, Viper, I'd love to go home. I'm so tired of this war, of the enemy always looking for new ways to kill us, of the blistering heat and the freaking dust choking us. I'm tired of lukewarm water and rehydrated food, and I'd give anything for a bath. But more than anything, I'm worried about what this does to my baby. It can't be good. None of it is good. But I can't bring myself to report and get sent home."

I cocked my head.

"But why? I'd love to go home. You said it's winter."

She sobs, and I shrink. I hate it when she does that. I don't know what to do other than licking her tears, which only makes it worse.

"Oh, Viper. I'd go home in a heartbeat if I could take you with me. But I don't think I can. You're just a few months shy of eight, so you're close to retirement, but you're not there yet. I hope I can last a couple more months, so they let you retire with me. Wouldn't that be wonderful? We could be home together, just you, me, and the baby.

Oops. I forgot about the baby. I'd better keep it in mind since Sabrina seems to have her heart set on it.

I wag my tail in agreement.

"That sounds great. Where would we live?"

I've never lived with Sabrina anywhere but here. I don't know anything about her home. I just hope she doesn't live in Florida. My buddy Rigatoni, a retriever I worked with in Iraq, came from Florida. He said life there revolves around oranges, and I hate oranges. They're almost as rude as lemons if you bite into them. And that's not the worst part. He said that lawns in Florida crawl with alligators; you'd better watch out where you poop if you want to hang on to your assets. They don't have snow, just dust, and I've had enough of that.

"We live in Vermont. Have you been to Vermont?"

"Not yet. Do they have snow?"

Sabrina laughs for the first time in ages.

"Sure, we do. More snow than anywhere but Maine. And New York."

"That sounds good. How about the food?"

"We make the best maple syrup."

Phew.

"That goes on everything, from popcorn to bacon."

Now you're talking. I could live with that, even if it's not healthy food.

"How about organic? Do they do organic?"

"More than anywhere else but California. And they have green mountains and rivers and lakes."

"Sign me up," I say, just to cheer her up. "I'm in. Let's go."

Sabrina sighs, and I smell there's more.

"Viper, you're the main reason I can't bring myself to leave, but not the only one."

I cock my head.

"What else can there be? You said you wanted out of here."

Her eyes avoid mine, and she smells embarrassed.

"It's Dick. I hope...I still hope he'll change his mind."

"About what?"

"About the baby. I hope he comes to want him as much as I do."

Like really? He told you he doesn't want your baby. He already has three of them. And a wife.

"And about me. I know it's not likely. But one can hope, can't we?"

I yawn like we dogs often do when we're stressed. I don't know, girl. Hope is one thing, and reality is another. I'd go with the facts, but what do I know? I've never been pregnant.

I'm still pondering this when Fury crawls in his crate and lays his nose on his paws, smelling troubled.

"What's up, buddy?"

"It's Dick. He's in a state. Ever since he talked to Sabrina, he's been a pain in the butt. You'd think he's the pregnant one."

"I'm sorry."

"Me too. It's a mess. I wonder why humans don't neuter their females before sending them to combat like they do with K-9s. It would be so much easier."

I gasp.

"Like, really? How about the males?"

"Males don't get pregnant."

"Neither do females, without a willing male. It takes two."

Fury glares at me.

"Are you nuts? You're saying they should cut our balls before they send us here?"

"Of course not. But what about the females? What if they feel the same?"

"They can't. Females have no balls."

I don't know what to say. He's technically correct. I've sniffed many butts, and I can't remember a single female having balls. But...

"They must have something, whatever that is. Look at Guinness. And Butter. They're just as ballsy as I am."

"So there. Whatever they take out, females don't miss it. So why not do that to humans too?"

That pisses me off. Fury acts like this is all Sabrina's fault. But I can see where he's coming from. Fury is loyal to Dick, just like I'm devoted to Sabrina, so I try to keep cool.

"Listen, Fury, it's not Sabrina's fault that Dick ignored the rules, forgot his family, and gave in to his instincts."

"But how could he resist? He's just a male."

That makes my blood boil.

"You and I are just males. When was the last time you got anyone pregnant?"

He stares at me like I'm crazy.

"But we're not humans. We're K-9s. That's different."

I've had it.

"Why don't you leave my Sabrina alone and worry about your Dick instead?"

CHAPTER 18

FURY TURNS AWAY WITHOUT A GROWL, and I feel terrible. I wish I bit my tongue instead of being rude, but it's too late to unsay it. And it's true. I once almost died chasing love, even though I should have known better. But blood ran hot through my Gallic heart, and I wasn't too old to be stupid.

That was before Guinness when Butter and I were the only K-9s at the base. One night I lay in my crate minding my own business when a burst of wind tickled my nose with the scent of a willing lady of K-9 persuasion.

I thought I was dreaming at first. I was in Kandahar, and I knew damn well there was nothing but desert for hundreds of miles and no dog other than Butter and me. And, as lovely as she is, Butter doesn't give a hoot about sex.

I sniff again. This is no dream. The scent is real. Remote, but clear as a bell. Somewhere in the desert, a lady needs romance, and I have no choice but to go. One can't argue with nature.

I crawl out of my crate, silent as a ghost, and glance around. Butter snores in her crate, and Sabrina plays cards with the men. Nobody sees me as I slip out and run. I reach the fence, and for the first time ever, I wish it was lower, instead of ten feet tall and topped with rolls of razor wire. There's no way I can scale it without getting shredded.

But I can't let this keep me away from my love. I know a tunnel in the back where a couple of insurgents tried to break in last week. We caught them before they finished, so the hole is less than a foot wide, and it's filled with rocks. For the first time ever, I wish I had opposable thumbs rather than my splendid teeth. But it is what it is, so I get digging, and before you can say, "What a good dog!" I squeeze out from the safety of the wire into the desert night to look for love.

I know that's stupid, but my insides burn so hot I don't care. I've done many silly things in my life, and I hope this is not the last.

I rip through the moonlit desert like a silent shadow, following my nose toward my object of desire. And there she is!

My eyes say she's dirty, mangy, and flea-ridden, but my heart tells me she's beautiful. And I'm about to follow my heart when I notice the dozen filthy mutts surrounding the love of my life.

They're mesmerized. Their glowing eyes glued to her, their tongues hanging to their knees, they're too busy to notice me, thank Dog. I step back, ready to flee when the wind changes and they smell me. They turn to me like one, bare their long yellow teeth, and growl.

What happened to love? As soon as they see me, they lose interest in the lady, and I must admit I feel the same. I raise my hackles and growl back, but I know I'm in trouble. I'm alone in the desert with a dozen starved strays who slobber just looking at me.

A big one-eyed mutt licks his lips.

"Hello, Dinner. I've always wondered what infidels taste like. You hungry, boys?"

A tall skinny mutt with his left ear missing drools so hard he chokes when he barks.

"Starved."

"Let's get him," another one calls.

They move to surround me. Their teeth gleam in the moonlight, and their red eyes glare as they leap toward me like a pack of hungry werewolves. For the first time in my life, I'm terrified.

"Stay back, you ugly mutts!" I growl, but they laugh like hyenas and tighten their circle, pushing closer and closer until I give up my pride, turn my tail, and run.

I've never been so humiliated, but I don't have time to worry about my honor. That can wait. What I need now is shelter, and there's none but the base, miles away.

That's not far for a K-9 with my training. I can run like the wind, but I've never fought another dog, let alone a whole pack. I only learned to apprehend humans, whose canines aren't worth mentioning. But these hungry, red-eyed beasts? I've never been in so much trouble.

I might outrun them, but I can't crawl back through that tunnel with them on my tail. They'd rip me apart as I scrambled to squeeze through.

"Take the left, and I'll take the right," One-Eye growls.

"He's ours, boys. The best dinner we've had in weeks," Missin' Ear barks.

I fly across the dark desert with the pack on my tail as I struggle to find a plan before I reach the tunnel. But nothing comes to mind. My heart racing, my brain on fire, I catch the smell of the base. I'm getting close, and I'm running out of time.

I make a right U-turn and leap, landing on One-Eye, who smells even worse than he looks. His one eye widens, showing the white all around it as my teeth tear his throat. I bite deep, like I'm trained to, and taste the salt of his blood as it splashes my face. I drop him and dart forward, hoping his partners will stop to look after him. And they do. The scent of blood excites them to a howling frenzy, and I hear them ripping him as I fly to the base.

Oh boy, that was close. But I'm almost there. I sigh with relief until I see Missin' Ear waiting for me by the tunnel. How the heck did he get here?

His teeth glimmer in the moonlight as he snarls.

"Come on, lover boy. Let's see you crawl in."

His partners' barking gets louder behind me. They're on their way. I only have moments, so I do what I have to do.

I pull my tail between my legs and roll on my back, presenting my belly in submission.

Missin' Ear comes to sniff me like he's supposed to. I wait until he's right above me before I spring to open his throat.

His tortured cries follow me as I squeeze back inside the wire. I stop right behind the tunnel, waiting to kill the first one coming through, but there's no need. They're too busy fighting each other. It feels like forever until Missin' Ear's agonizing screams fade as his friends tear him apart. But for the grace of Dog, that would have been me.

I wait until the silence tells me they're done; then I hobble back to my crate. I'm exhausted, damaged, and humiliated, all in the name of love.

Butter hears me whimper and opens her eyes.

"You OK, Viper?"

"I'm not OK. I'm stupid."

I told her.

She licked my nose, and I felt better.

But I'll never do that again.

CHAPTER 19

STILL, I shouldn't have been rude to Fury. He turned away, pretending to sleep, but I feel his sadness, and I know he smells mine. Too bad that his loyalty to Dick conflicts with my duty to Sabrina. It's not Fury's fault that Dick is Dick, but Sabrina deserves better.

The following day we both pretended nothing happened, but we knew better. Our devotion to our humans pulled us apart, and our friendship became another casualty of this darn war. We went about our jobs, took turns leading patrol, and watched each other's back, but the unease never vanished. It got even worse when Dick and I got close. I couldn't forgive how he treated Sabrina, and he didn't forget that I threatened him. He couldn't wait to get even.

It was like navigating land mines inside the wire. Sabrina hid her pregnancy, hoping that Dick would change his mind. Dick lived in fear that Sabrina would expose him. Fury was torn between his duty to Dick and our friendship while I struggled to protect Sabrina. We were all stuck with no end in sight.

Until Sabrina fell.

It was a hot morning like they all are in Kandahar. The aerial surveillance blimp had detected unusual activity in a nearby field, so we went to check it out. We filed out as usual: me first, dragging Sabrina on her leash followed by the soldiers, with Fury and Dick in the rear.

I was sniffing underneath a crooked bush when the leash pulled me to a stop. I glanced back to see Sabrina fall in a cloud of dust. My heart skipped a beat when I remembered Silver's death.

But there was no noise. No shots, no grenades, not even a scream. Nothing moved across the desert but a lazy plume of smoke bruising the faded blue sky over the village, far away.

I retraced my steps and sniffed Sabrina. She didn't smell dead. I licked her face, and she opened her eyes.

The men who came to her help looked as confused as I felt. They took her back on a stretcher, and I followed. Fury and Dick led us back.

Sabrina tried to laugh it off.

"It's just the heat. It gets to you. And I didn't drink enough water. I'll be fine by tomorrow."

The lieutenant didn't listen. He shipped her out to get her checked, and I knew her secret was over. That night I lay awake in my crate, wondering if I'd ever see her again.

"Hey, Viper?"

"Yes."

"I hope she's all right. She's a good human. I know you care about her."

"Thanks, Fury."

"What will you do if they send her back?"

"I don't know. I guess the army will assign me another handler."

"Are you worried?"

"About what?"

"About getting another handler. What if you don't like him? What if you don't get along?"

I yawned.

"It doesn't work that way, Fury. Work is work. I'll do my best to get along, and I bet he will too. We're all brothers in arms here. We need to have each other's back."

Fury wagged his tail, but he wagged it left, so I knew he was worried.

What I didn't know, is how right he was.

CHAPTER 20

THAT NIGHT and the next day, then another night and another day, I did nothing but waited for Sabrina. I watched the gates, I listened for trucks, I sniffed the wind for her scent.

She didn't come.

I followed her with my mind's eye, willing her to return.

She still didn't.

When my heart felt so empty that I wanted to howl, I stole her socks, and I lay on them to breathe her scent. I was still chewing on them when the lieutenant came to see me.

His eyes avoided mine, so I knew he had bad news.

"Hey, Viper. How're you doing, pal?"

I waved my tail left.

"Fine, thanks. And you?"

"Great. Great. I have a message from Sabrina."

I took a deep breath to slow down my heart.

"Yes."

"Sabrina... she's fine, but she's not coming back. She'll have a baby."

At least she's not dead.

"Viper, Sabrina made a request for you to retire with her, but our rules don't allow for that. You're still healthy, strong, and productive. We can't let you go. And we all know how important your work is to you. You're nowhere near ready to retire. So I put in a request for a new handler. I'm sure you'll work with him just as well as you did with Sabrina."

That's bull, and he knows it. I know it, Fury knows it, even my kibble bowl knows it. But he's got to say something.

"In the meantime, Dick agreed to look after you and train you alongside Fury. Isn't that great?"

Seriously? How thick can you be? How about using your eyes if your nose is blind?

But there's nothing I can do. It is what it is. I can do a few days. Not like I have a choice anyhow. I'll do my best to work with Dick, even though he's the only human I ever hated — besides Jinx's killer, of course. But I never had to work with that one — I only had to bring him to justice. But I digress.

Dick's smirk is hard to take. Now that Sabrina left without spilling the beans, Dick is back to his cocky self, and he can't wait to pay me back for challenging him.

He's good about it, too. He doesn't hit me or scream at me since he knows people would notice. He's a small man, so he does small things: He "forgets" to fill my water bowl, skips adding supplements to my kibble, and fails to let me have my evening walk, so I spend my nights crossing my legs to hold on to my bladder. He watches me squirm, and he smiles.

It drives me nuts, but I tell myself that the new trainer should arrive anytime. I'll be out of Dick's reach before you can say Grass-Fed-Beef-Kibble. I can take a few days. Anyone can take a few days.

Fury sees this, and he's distraught. Like a pal, he shares his water and food with me, but he can't share his bathroom break.

"I'm sorry, Viper. Dick must be troubled by everything that happened, but I'm sure he'll get over it soon. I love you, brother. I'm here for you."

His friendship is the only thing that keeps me sane. I don't know what I'd do without him, and I hope I never find out. With Fury's help, I can take a few days and refrain from tearing Dick's throat. Because I know what happens if I do.

CHAPTER 21

I FIRST SAW George as I waited for Andrew by the dining room window. He'd been gone for days, but I knew my human wouldn't abandon me like a second-hand bone. He'll be back to get me any moment, I thought.

I was still a pup.

I'd already learned how to deal with explosives and perpetrators, but what I knew about humans could fit in my water bowl with room left over. So, day after day, I sat by the window awaiting Andrew's return.

An old jeep parked in the driveway, and a man in uniform rang the doorbell. I knew he wasn't Andrew or the mailman, but I barked just in case. His gray eyes crinkled in a smile as he took off his cap and ran his fingers through his mop of white hair, waiting for the door to open. He looked up at Mom as she filled the doorway.

"Yes?"

"Good morning, Ma'am. I'm sergeant Whitby. I was sent to collect Viper."

"To collect Viper? What are you talking about? Viper belongs to my husband. Andrew will need him when he returns."

"I'm sorry, ma'am, but my superiors sent me to collect him.

Here are the papers. Viper is a working K-9, and he belongs to the army. I'm sure your husband will clarify things when he returns, but for now, Viper belongs with the military."

Mom's eyes glimmered with tears. I wondered why. Not like she liked me — to her, I was just a dirty nuisance. Maybe she also thought that Andrew would come back for me someday?

She brought my leash and handed it to George.

"There."

"Thank you, Ma'am."

Mom slammed the door.

George offered me his hands to sniff. He smelled like hot dogs, sweat, and gunpowder, and I instantly knew I could trust him. I wagged my tail, and he scratched my ears.

"Good to meet you, Viper. You and I will make a good team."

He drove us to a tidy little trailer sitting between dogwood and maple trees, where he let me out to do my business.

I sniffed everything first, of course, but there wasn't much besides George. Squirrels, a couple of stray cats, and some faded dog smells, so old I couldn't tell the breed. What happened to that dog, I wondered? I started exploring, but George called me in.

I checked every inch, of course, but there wasn't much there either. No IEDs, no females, no kids, and no cats, thank goodness. Nothing exciting other than the peppered jerky in the left kitchen drawer.

George laughed and offered me a strip, then put on his glasses to read my papers.

"This is your record, Viper. Good job on your first deployment! You apprehended two suspects, uncovered three IEDs, and found a cache of weapons. No misses that we know of. Not a bad record for a green K-9 with a rookie handler. You miss Andrew?"

I growled.

"Sure, I do. I still can't believe he ran away and left me with

Mom. Andrew was my human, the most important person in my world other than Jinx."

George glanced at me above his glasses.

"I'm sorry, Viper, I know it's hard. I know exactly how you feel. I was there too, and I was devastated. But I was too busy to dwell on it, and you will be too."

He shuffled the papers.

"It says here that you and your late brother Jinx were imported from Belgium."

My heart froze.

"My late brother Jinx?"

George sighed.

"You didn't know, did you, Viper? Darn. I'm so sorry. Jinx was put down six months ago."

My stomach turned.

"You're saying Jinx is dead?"

"Yes."

"How?"

George's face darkens as he reads on.

"It says here that Jinx attacked his handler. The man had to shoot him to stay alive."

"What?"

I knew Jinx's trainer. I knew his whole family since that night Jinx and I swapped. They were OK, all but that darn Turbo. How could Jinx attack his human? And why?

"I don't understand."

"Neither do I. The records say that Jinx was an excellent K-9 with no history of aggression. Why would he attack his handler? It makes no sense."

George clears his voice.

"You know Viper, the reason this is in your records is to warn people that someday, for no good reason, you may turn out to be a liability. They're afraid that you're not trustworthy."

Me, not trustworthy? Me? I've always done my job the best I

could, ever since I was just a pup. I live for my job. And I'm not trustworthy? My human abandoned me. His wife made my life a pain. Jinx, my twin, died shot by his own handler. And I'm not trustworthy?

This is the worst day of my life. I flatten my ears and lay my nose on my paws, drowning in my misery.

George comes to pet me.

"I'm sorry, Viper. This is terrible. I don't understand it either, but I promise I'll do my best to find out what happened."

I yawn.

"Whatever."

That won't bring back Jinx. Nor my trust in humans.

CHAPTER 22

George was right. After we started training, I got too busy to feel sorry for myself. Then we learned we were getting deployed, so finding out about Jinx would have to wait.

But the day before we left, George came home flushed with excitement.

"I've got Jinx's trainer's address. Wanna pay him a visit?"

My heart froze. Jinx's trainer? Could I trust myself to see my brother's killer without tearing his throat?

George felt me.

"Can I trust you, Viper? Will you stay calm and listen?"

"Yes."

"Are you sure? If you attack him, we won't find out anything. And we'll both get in trouble."

"I'll listen," I growled, hoping it was true.

George drove us to Jinx's old home, and my throat tightened. The last time I was here, Jinx and I were just pups. We had our whole lives ahead of us, and everything was fun. Now, Jinx is dead, and I'm here to find out why.

The woman who opens the door looks nothing like the one I remember. Her bright eyes were blue, and she smelled happy.

Now they're red, and she reeks of pain. She glances from George to me and steps back.

"Jinx?"

"No, ma'am. I'm not Jinx. I'm his twin, Viper."

She stares at me like she's seen a ghost. George clears his voice.

"Could we speak to you for a moment?"

She lets us in. Everything looks the same but smells different. This house no longer smells like Jinx or his human. I can't even sense the darned cat.

"Thank you for speaking to us, ma'am. We're trying to find out what happened to Jinx. We know he attacked your husband and got shot, but we couldn't find out why. Can you help us?"

The woman shakes her head.

"I don't know. Jinx was the best K-9 we ever had. He was good with the kids, good with me, he was even good with Turbo. He never did anything wrong.

"The day it happened, they went to work as usual. That evening someone called to tell me that Jim and Jinx were on a mission, apprehending a perpetrator, and something went wrong; Jim was in the hospital, and Jinx was dead.

"I thought the perpetrator had shot them both until I found out that my husband was being treated for dog bites, not gunshot wounds. When I asked him, he said that Jinx attacked him, and he had to shoot him. I couldn't believe it.

"Jinx bit you? But why? What did you do?

"Jim told me to leave him alone. I insisted, but he wouldn't answer. He didn't tell the kids either. He just told them that Jinx got shot on a mission. They were heartbroken."

The woman sobs. I know George feels sorry for her. I would, too, if it weren't for Jinx, but we're here to get answers, so I push George to insist.

He sighs.

"I see. Could we speak to your husband to find out?"

The woman looks away.

"I'm afraid you can't. My husband is not here."

"Tomorrow, maybe?"

She sighs.

"I may as well tell you. My husband is dead. He got shot last month on patrol. It looked like an ordinary traffic stop, but the man had a gun and killed him on the spot. Jim didn't even get to draw his weapon."

She wipes her eyes.

"And you know the worst part? I know it in my bones that he'd still be alive if Jinx was with him."

"I'm sorry, Ma'am, I didn't know."

"It's not your fault. It's nobody's fault. But it's hard. I stay awake at night, wondering how to tell the kids. I couldn't bring myself to tell them he's dead; I told them he's on a mission. I looked for some way to tell them that doesn't hurt, but I can't find it. I guess I'll have to tell them anyhow."

"I'm sorry, Ma'am."

George stands to leave. I follow him with a heavy heart. All this, and I still don't know what happened.

I try the woman one more time.

"Is there anyone else who could know? Anyone we could ask? I really need to understand why my brother died."

The woman shakes her head.

"I can't think of anyone."

As I step out the door, I remember:

"What happened to Turbo? Jinx's cat? Where is he?"

The woman bursts into tears.

"He died the same day Jinx did. The evening before, Turbo was chasing squirrels in the driveway when my husband came home. The cat was deaf, so he didn't hear Jim's truck, and my husband ran him over.

"The vet did her best. She watched him overnight, but Turbo got worse, and they had to put him down. I called Jim to tell him, and he flipped. He was terrified to tell Jinx he'd killed Turbo."

CHAPTER 23

THAT'S how I know what would happen if I tore out Dick's throat. So, I suck it up, one nasty trick after another, waiting for my new handler. No matter what, he can't be as bad as Dick. Nobody can be as bad as Dick, can they?

Fury and I take turns leading patrol with Dick. Whoever isn't leading brings up the rear with one of the soldiers. But the real work is always in front: sniffing for IEDs, watching for any scent or movement that could mean an ambush, or chasing insurgents.

Today is Fury's turn to lead, and I'm glad to let him have Dick all to himself. Being last is no fun, but I'd rather be as far from Dick as I can.

We file out through the gate. I watch Fury clear the way, and I can barely tell him from the background. His coat blends so well into the orange desert that all I can see is his bulletproof vest and the trail of dust he leaves behind.

He advances smoothly, sniffing his every step. He crosses the open field and reaches the tall mud wall surrounding the village, then follows it along the dry riverbed lined by a bunch of scraggly bushes. That, to me, is the danger zone: That's where Butter got shot, and Silver got killed. There's always some danger lurking behind that cursed wall. Boy, how I hate it. I wish we crushed it into desert dust.

But Fury pushes on, heading toward the open land behind the village where an informant told us the Taliban hid a cache of weapons. That may be true, or it may be just another lie meant to bring us out in the open, where we're vulnerable. We never know.

A few more steps and Fury is out in the open again. Dick follows, then the other soldiers. It's all quiet, and I breathe a sigh of relief. I'm the last to reach the corner when the gunfire blasts, shattering the earth.

I drop to the ground as our soldiers return fire. The hail of bullets raises a cloud of dust so thick I can't even see my paws. My nose burns with the stench of gunpowder, and my ears ring with the clamor of shots. It's like I'm deaf, blind, and nose-blind as I wait with bated breath for the chaos to settle. I don't know what happened to Dick, but more important, I don't know what happened to Fury, and I'm sick with worry.

The gunfire stops, but the ruckus continues. Weapons clang; people scream, groan, and swear; and I still can't see anything but dust. But I smell blood; I just don't know whose it is. I bark.

"Fury! Are you OK?"

"Yep. Waiting for the dust to settle."

I sigh with relief. I'm so glad Fury's OK that I don't even care if Dick is dead or not. But he's not. We have one dead and three wounded, and we still don't know where the fire came from. As far as the eye can see, there's nothing around us but the desert. But the enemy is still here. If they had run away, we'd see the cloud of dust following them. There's nothing, so we know they're sheltered somewhere, waiting for us to move. We're trapped.

The lieutenant shouts.

"Everyone stay put. Let the K-9s go."

CHAPTER 24

Now, THIS is what I live for. Apprehending suspects is my thing, even more than finding IEDs. Bombs don't fight back — unless you step on them. But finding and capturing suspects, that's what I love. I love the chase and the fight and the danger. But for all I know, Fury's never done this before. So I bark.

"Fury, wait for me. Don't get going until I'm next to you. Two targets are harder to hit than one. If they divide their fire, we both have a better chance."

"Yep. Thanks, buddy."

"Move as fast as you can, and don't stop. A standing dog is a dead dog."

"Got it."

I slow down my breath as Dan unhooks my leash.

"Go!"

I explode forward, fueled by rage. I fly over the orange field, ignoring the IEDs. Now is the time to take my chances. I hopefully won't find any mines. But if I'm slow, I'm dead. I'd rather risk the IEDs than the bullets.

I hear Fury take off to my left, but I have no time to look back. The gunfire started, and bullets hit the ground behind me like hail. Fortunately, they're shooting at wherever I was a second ago, and I'm no longer there. A cloud of dust follows me, but everything ahead is clear, and I see where the fire comes from. Not far ahead, there's a divot in the desert. It looks just like a shadow, but there's nothing here to throw a shadow, so I fly to it like the wind. Am I afraid? No time for that.

Just heartbeats later, I see the hole hidden by a dust-covered tarp. It's camouflaged, but the weapon barrels staring at me give it away. I'm flying to it when a burning pain stabs my hip, and I know I've been hit, but I have no time to worry. One last glorious leap, and I land on the tarp. It sinks with me, covering everyone inside. Their weapons fire at the sky, then fall silent as I go do my work, and it's not pretty.

There's three of them under that tarp, all white with fear and unarmed since they crouched to the ground leaving their weapons behind. They scream, call for Allah, and cover their faces while I show them what good behavior looks like. I've never fought three before, so there's some learning, but it turns out you only have to bite one at a time. The other two would love to run and hide, but that's a no-no. There'll be no running and no hiding today.

The joy of victory fills my heart. I'm proud of myself, and I'm happier than I've been in ages as I wait for our soldiers to come and take over. Then a thought crosses my mind, and my heart freezes.

Where's Fury?

Last I knew, he was right behind me. But that was ages ago. Where is he?

I wish I could leave these men and go look for my buddy, but I can't. Every moment I wait for our men to relieve me burns my soul. The insurgents whimper in their corners, covering their bellies and their faces, as I fight the urge to open their throats here and now. I so want to believe that Fury got mislaid and went somewhere else, but I know better.

Our men jump in the hole one after the other and grab the prisoners. I leap out to look for Fury.

I find him halfway back to where we started. He lies on his side, and his breath sprays red into the thirsty dust.

"Fury? Buddy? Are you OK?"

I know that's stupid as soon as I say it, but what else can I ask?

"Yep," he lies.

"What happened?"

He coughs a glob of blood.

"I guess I just wasn't fast enough. I always knew you were faster, but I didn't know you were that fast. Nobody could keep up with you. Next time you should give me a handicap."

He coughs up another blob of blood, and we both know there is no next time. This is it. I should have been a better friend when he was here. I should have been nicer, wiser, and more patient. But I wasn't since I was too busy being a jerk.

My throat tightens, and I struggle to breathe.

"I will. But how about you just run faster?"

His lovely rich tail, so much like Guinness's, slaps the ground, lifting a cloud of dust.

"I'll try, Viper. But there are things one can't do. No matter how good I am, I'll always be a golden shepherd. And no matter how bad you are, you'll always be the Malligator."

I choke, and I hurt. I lick his nose, and it tastes like blood and sorrow.

"Viper?"

"Yes, Fury."

"I need you to do one thing for me."

"What's that?"

"I need you to find Guinness."

"And?"

"Tell her I did my best to be like her. I'm sorry I couldn't. But I tried. And tell her I'm so proud of her. We all are — Mom, Jones, even the freaking neighbors whose cats she chased. I love her, and I so wish we got to meet. But tell her that Mom has another litter, will you? There's got to be a puppy there who hopes to grow up to be like her."

The grief chokes me. I somehow manage to wag my tail.

"Sure. I will. But why don't you do it yourself? You'll get better in no time."

Fury's glazed eyes look at me, and his tail slaps the ground.

"Oh, Viper. You've grown soft in your old age. You've never lied to me before. We both know this is the end for me. Thank you for everything, my friend."

I struggle to say something, but I can't. My throat is too tight. I lick Fury's nose and watch his eyes lose focus as he dies.

"No, Fury. Thank you for being my friend."

CHAPTER 25

MY HEART BLEEDS as our soldiers lift Fury on a stretcher to take him back to camp. This mission was the deadliest ever. Two dead soldiers, Fury and Josh, and three wounded. We took three prisoners, but we found no weapons. I bet they don't even exist.

The medevac lifts with the wounded, and we file back to camp in mourning silence. I'm first, then Dick, followed by Josh's stretcher and the prisoners. For the last time ever, Fury brings up the rear.

The soldiers drag themselves back, their hearts heavy with loss, but I don't have time to mourn. I must get them back to safety first. The men who ambushed us have pals who can't wait to strike us when we're weak. What holds them back is the fear of killing their own.

My heart races as I skirt the wall, waiting for death to strike. It may be a grenade blowing us up or a hail of bullets mowing us down — you never know. I smell no explosives, but the stench of hate chokes me.

I take step after weary step, but nothing happens as we leave the wall behind and crawl through the desert to the green gates. When they close behind Fury, I finally have time to mourn.

The soldiers cover the bodies with American flags. One after another, we all share thoughts as tears run down dusty cheeks and loyal hearts bleed.

The lieutenant's voice breaks.

"Fury was a brave and loyal K-9. It will be my honor to nominate him for a Purple Heart."

Pimply Dan, a kid who dreams of becoming a K-9 handler someday, sobs.

"Fury gave his life to keep us safe."

"Fury was my loyal partner and my friend," Dick says, and, for a moment, I forget to hate him.

"He saved my life," I say. "I wish I could save his."

Someone carved Fury's name and number on a wooden plate. The lieutenant lays it in our memorial garden, next to Lobo's, Mika's, and other K-9 soldiers who'll never return to serve. Dick kneels to lay Fury's ball and his collar next to it, and that's that.

Fury is gone.

I crawl in my crate to lick my wounds. A bullet grazed my hip, and it burns like the dickens, but that's nothing compared to the grief of Fury's empty crate. His place still smells like him, and the sorrow chokes me. A piece of me died with Fury. I can never be the same again — this war has robbed me of too much. How I hate it! Still, I'll be here until the day I die or until the army lets me go. But where would I go, anyhow?

It's not the first time I've lost a partner and a friend, but what makes it worse is that it's my fault. I told Fury to wait for me to divide the fire, then I flew by him and left him behind since my speed is my strength. The bullet that hit him was meant for me. If he had gone first, would he still be alive? Would the cold body under his flag be mine?

I don't know, but the guilt crushes me. I was Fury's mentor and his friend; it was my job to keep him safe. And I failed.

I lay my nose on my paws, thinking about all the friends I've lost, K-9 and human, and I choke with sorrow. This can't get any worse, I think, when the lieutenant comes to see me.

"You did good work out there, Viper. Thanks to you, we were able to neutralize this enemy unit. Your bravery saved our soldiers' lives. Thank you for your service. I will be honored to nominate you for the Dickin Medal of Valor."

I know he means well, but I couldn't care less about any Dickin' medal. The only thing I care about is Fury, and he's dead. If only....

"But I do have some good news for you. Remember I asked the army for a handler?"

I cock my head. Now that's something. Will I finally get rid of Dick?

"Well, since Fury is no longer with us, Dick needs a K-9 partner. We don't need another handler; we need another whole K-9 team. I already put in a request, but you and Dick will team together from now on. Isn't that great?"

I stare at him in disbelief.

"Are you kidding? You're assigning me to Dick full time?"

"Yes. Isn't that good?"

I fight the urge to puke. This man's so thick he couldn't find his own ice-hole without a funnel.

"Unbelievable."

And I thought it couldn't get any worse.

CHAPTER 26

I always thought that depression, like most feelings, only happens to the weak. For a K-9 and a Malinois like me, the only thing that matters is doing your job. Nothing else counts.

But working with Dick changed my mind. Doing my job brings me no pride and no joy.

Though I must admit, he got better. He allows me my evening break and fixes my food like he's supposed to. He even tried an apology of sorts.

"Listen, Viper. I know you love Sabrina. She's a great girl. I'm sorry you thought I was rude to her. That wasn't my intent. I was just trying to make her listen, but I never wanted to hurt her. Or you, for that matter. Let's start over, shall we? We're both stuck here, and it would be better for us both. After all, we share the same purpose: putting the bad guys away to keep the good guys safe."

I look at him like he's dirt because that's what he is. He's a miserable partner, a lousy soldier, and a jerk. He's a sorry excuse for a human: He betrayed his wife, failed the army, and deserted Sabrina. I can't think of a single way he's faithful and worthy. He doesn't even deserve a fight.

"Sure."

I don't trust him. But the fact that Dick is a jerk doesn't preclude me from doing my job, even though it frees me from caring about him. I feel free to ignore his orders, I don't care if he ever gets letters from home, and I have no need to protect him.

The one thing I refuse to do is chase the ball. That used to be my reward for a job well done. The handler throws it, I catch it, and I tug on it a few times to make me feel like I got a live one. That's as fake as tofu burgers, but so what?

So I do my job, but I ignore Dick whenever I can. I watch him throw the ball when we train, and I love seeing his face fall when I look the other way. That feels good, but it's awful. In enemy territory, you need to trust your partners and know they have your back. Dick and I don't, and that's scary. And there's no end in sight.

But one day, the lieutenant comes with good news.

"I have great news, folks. Excellent news, in fact. Our old buddy, Brown, is coming back."

Dick doesn't know Brown, so he couldn't care less, but my heart skips a beat. I jump to my feet.

"Brown? The same Brown?"

The lieutenant nods.

"Yep. The same Brown. I can't wait to see him."

"How about Butter? Is Butter coming?"

I should know better. I knew Butter wouldn't come back since the day I saw her mangled paw. But one can only hope.

"I don't think so. He's bringing a K-9 named Lovely."

Lovely? What sort of name is that for a K-9?

Oh well. At least I'll get some relief. And news of Butter.

CHAPTER 27

I WAKE up every morning hoping today's the day and Brown is coming. I listen for the truck every evening, then I rush to meet it, but there's been no Brown and no dog, Lovely, Ugly, Homely, or other.

But two of our wounded men returned, and we celebrated with MRE desserts. The third one lost a leg and went home.

Many humans wish they were in his shoes. This war has no end, and they'd give a limb to go home.

Dick and I still butt heads. I want nothing to do with him, and he doesn't like me either. But to him, I'm essential equipment, like his gun, his helmet, and his bulletproof vest, so he isn't keen to destroy me. That's why he leaves me alone.

But I miss my friends. I miss Fury, Guinness, Butter, and Sabrina, and my nights are terribly lonely.

I think about them all the time. I remember that night, long ago, when Guinness, Butter, and I talked about the meaning of life.

It had been a terrible day. Carlos, one of our soldiers, shot himself with his gun before dawn.

We woke up thinking we were being attacked. The men jumped from their cots, grabbed their weapons, and ran into position. We searched long and hard. We found no enemy, but we finally found Carlos.

He lay under a truck in a pool of blood, his face a gaping wound. The men tried to revive him, but the thirsty desert had already sucked his blood and his life.

Patrol got canceled, and the men spent the day inside the wire, talking about Carlos and trying to get to terms with what happened.

Matt, Carlos's best friend, stared in the void, smelling guilty. The other men dragged their feet like zombies, their hearts filled with misery. The lieutenant tried to give a pep talk, but he had no pep left either.

Butter and Guinness felt sorry for them, but I didn't. I wasn't sad. I was too angry.

"Why would a healthy soldier kill himself? He had a responsibility and a job to do. He should have gone and killed some Taliban instead of doing their job for them," I growled.

Guinness sighed.

"I guess he didn't want to live anymore."

"But why?"

Guinness cocked her head.

"I dunno. But how about turning this question on its head. What was he living for?"

"Are you kidding me? He had a job to do!"

Guinness's amber eyes gazed inside me.

"Viper, did it ever occur to you that not everyone lives for their job?"

I stared at her.

"What else is there?"

"Lots of things. Friendship, love, and justice, and food, and the good of the planet, and the polar bears, and...."

"Have you lost your mind? The good of the planet? The polar bears? Who cares about the polar bears?"

"I do. I saw a documentary showing how baby polar bears

starve to death because the ice melted and their moms can't find food anymore...."

"Come on, Guinness. Carlos didn't kill himself for the polar bears."

"Probably not. But some things in life are more important than doing your job."

I yawned with frustration. I just couldn't listen to that nonsense anymore.

"You're wrong. There's nothing more important than doing your job, I assure you."

"Maybe not to you. But others may think otherwise. Butter?"

"What?"

"What's the most important thing in life for you?"

Butter sighed. She hated to be put on the spot between Guinness and me. The two of us could fight all day and still have some fight left over for tomorrow, but Butter is a Canadian pacifist, and she hates arguing.

"I don't know. Friendship? Love? Loyalty? Feeling that you made a difference?"

Guinness wagged her tail.

"Atta girl, Butter. There, Viper. I rest my case. There's more to life than work."

I'm about to set them straight when Sabrina comes to hug me, and I'm petrified. I hate hugs, especially in public. I'd love to pull away, but I don't want to hurt her feelings, so I hang my head, hoping she'll go away.

But she doesn't.

She hangs onto my neck, sobbing like it's the end of the world, and I ignore her until I can't take it anymore.

"There, there. Everything will be alright. Just wait and see. It's going to be OK."

I lick her tears, and she finally relents.

"Thank you, Viper. I couldn't do this without you. Being with you makes all the difference in the world. I'm so lucky to have you."

She finally leaves as Guinness and Butter exchange glances. They say nothing, but what is there to say?

"That was nothing," I growl.

"Of course."

"She just needed support. She was upset that her buddy died."

They nod, but I know that inside, they're laughing at me. I sigh.

"OK, OK, go ahead. Tell me. What's the most important thing in life? What do we live for?"

"Love? Friendship? Feeling like our lives weren't wasted?" Guinness says.

I can't disagree.

"We live to make a difference. To leave something good that wouldn't be there if it weren't for us," Butter says.

I can't believe I agree with these snowflakes, but there it is. And it's all Sabrina's fault.

"I get it. We live to make a difference and leave the world better than we found it. That's a tall order."

Guinness wags her tail in a dog smile.

"You know, Viper? That's the first time I heard you admit you're wrong."

"Of course it is. I've never been wrong before."

Butter wags her tail and licks my nose. It's been many months, but I can still feel her loving pink tongue, and the grief of my loss explodes in me like a grenade.

I had her, and Guinness, and Sabrina, and Fury. Now all I've got is Dick.

CHAPTER 28

BY THE TIME I finally caught a whiff of a dog inside the wire, I had lost all hope. I can't tell time, so it feels like forever. We dogs don't have calendars, iPhones, or watches, so we can only tell time by our bellies growling, the days turning into nights, and the change of seasons. That's why whenever you humans return from the bathroom, we act like you've been gone forever.

Anyhow. I'm lying in my crate thinking about Sabrina when the gates screech open and a heavy truck motors in. The sun's down, and the day's almost over. I turn on my other side, trying to sleep. But, just out of habit, I catch a quick sniff. The usual odors tickle my nose: gasoline fumes, engine oil, seriously stale stress sweat. That's got to be the new men. They traveled for days to get here. Then a tantalizing scent drifts by, and my feet hit the ground before I know it. I smelled a dog.

I sniff again. Yep. It's real.

I squeeze between the soldier's legs and dash to the gate. As always, the men rushed to meet the truck because every truck brings hope: An old friend coming back; a letter from Grandma who never learned the internet; a Christmas package from Aunt Rose, who knitted you a pair of gloves, God bless her heart, and sent you her famous fudge. That makes you drool just thinking of it.

Numb after their long travels, the new men shuffle out on stiff legs. Then comes the mail, and then...

She stumbles out of her crate and falls on her face and my heart sings. I just know my life will never be the same. I've never seen anyone so beautiful. I take a moment to catch my breath and get myself together before I introduce myself.

She's compact and furry, with a long, slim muzzle and come-hither eyes that make my knees go soft. She's got cinnamon-colored pancake ears that hang down to her shoulders and shadow her eyes. She blinks, and I'm hooked. I remember having a crush on Guinness, even though she was too busy to notice, but it wasn't like this. Never like this. I'm in love.

"Welcome to Kandahar," I mumble, offering my butt for sniffing, though I know I shouldn't. I'm older, I'm her superior, and I should sniff her butt first. But she's so pretty...

Her little tail quivers a mile a minute as she learns everything about me: what I had for dinner, how I feel about life, and if I'm interested in dating. Oh, boy, am I!

She turns around to let me sniff her, and, right then and there, she breaks my heart. She's spayed. Just like Butter, Guinness, and every other K-9 lady I worked with. Like really? How unfair is that?

I struggle to get myself together and pretend that her being spayed is not my concern.

"Name's Viper. So glad to meet you, Ma'am."

She shakes her head, and her sexy ears float around her head like an aura.

"Call me Lovely, please. I'm no Ma'am, and I expect we're going to be great friends. Are you the real Viper?"

That throws me off. I didn't know there were any fake ones. Oh well.

"I hope so. Why?"

"Would you happen to be acquainted with a Labrador named Butter?"

"Of course. Butter is my dear friend. You know her?"

"Are you kidding? She's my best friend and my mentor. She told me all about you."

I don't like how this sounds. All about me? But why? And especially what?

"Would you care to elaborate?"

"Butter said you're the bravest, most driven, and best K-9 she's ever met. Other than Guinness, of course. She said she never met a K-9 like you. She sends her best regards."

Guinness? Really? Oh well.

"Thank you. I miss Butter terribly. How is she? And where is she?"

Lovely's ears flatten, and she hangs her head, embarrassed to tell me.

"Butter and I had a rocky start. It took us a long time to get close to each other, but I'm glad we did. You know she lost a paw?"

"I do."

"Did you hear about PC? Her Pizza Cutter?"

"No, I didn't."

Nor do I understand what that has to do with Butter. Though she's always been obsessed with food.

"Did she get into cooking?"

Lovely's tail twitches with glee.

"Not really. Butter's more into eating, but that's not what PC is about. That's what she calls her prosthetic paw. She can walk, run, and even jump with it. She became a local hero. Many folks back home look up to her as a role model."

I'm not sure what a Pizza Cutter has to do with being a role model, but I let that pass.

"It sounds great. Let's talk about that sometime. But in the meantime, what if I showed you around?"

She wags her tail, and her little butt wiggles with it. Be still, my heart. I've found the love of my life.

CHAPTER 29

I TAKE her around wishing our camp was something exciting like a muddy swamp, a chicken coop, or at least a forest in the fall so we could play in the leaves. But it's not. So I make the most of what I've got and show it to her like it's my kingdom.

"We're inside the wire. That ten-foot wall topped with razor wire keeps us safe from the enemy. In all the years I've been here, nobody got killed inside the wire. Just once, a truck loaded with explosives blew up the gate, but nobody died but the driver."

Lovely raises her pretty muzzle and sniffs toward the wall, but she's unimpressed. So I move on.

"This here is our training area. This is where our handlers hide fake IEDs. They could be anywhere — inside the trucks, under the gravel, or hidden by a piece of debris — and it's our job to find them."

Lovely crinkles her pretty nose and asks:

"Is it always this dusty?"

I gawk at her. Today is as clear a day as I've ever seen here. There are no bullets, no helicopters, not even a dozen people and dogs walking ahead of you to raise dust. But I guess this air takes some getting used to. After all my years here, I don't even notice the dust until it gets obnoxious. This pretty girl will have to learn.

"Of course not." It's usually way worse, I want to say, but I bite my tongue. "It depends. Some days are better than others." But most are way worse.

She wags her tail politely as I struggle to find something else to show her. I can't think of anything pretty, lovely, or even pleasant. This is a remote camp in enemy territory, and the best we can do is survive.

She clears her voice prettily.

"Errm. Where's the grass?"

I cock my head and stare at her.

"The grass?"

"Yes. You know. Where we... empty."

I'm so thick it's not funny. I forgot I used to need grass. That was the cue. But that's like forever ago. And I haven't seen a blade of grass since I arrived in Kandahar.

"We don't do grass here. There isn't much of it. We just let go in the dust."

Her ears perk up, and she stares at me like I'm nuts. Something tells me she's not into dust.

"Are you sure about that?"

Am I sure? You've got to be kidding me. I'm beyond certain. I've been here for most of my life, and I haven't seen a single blade of grass inside the wire. If she were male, I'd tell her to go find out for himself. But she's not. She's the cinnamon-colored lover I never had, and I bite my tongue till it hurts.

"I'm quite sure. But feel free to check and see if you find something better. I'd be delighted if you found a lawn."

She nods and takes off with a new urgency. She's been closed in that crate forever, so she must be looking forward to that grass. She starts sniffing, and I follow her closely. Not because I think there's any chance on earth she'll find grass, but because she's beautiful.

She sprints from the massive trucks to the tall mud fence covered in Concertina wire and back. I follow, watching her sniff her way. She's pretty good, even though she's stressed by the urgency. But there isn't a single blade of grass in this darn compound, and she grows more disturbed as time goes on.

I'd love to get her grass, but I can't. So, I do my next best.

"I'm sorry, Lovely, but I can't wait anymore. Would you mind if I took a moment behind those tires?"

"Of course not."

"I'll be back in no time."

I run behind the tires and lift my leg like I need to go, but I don't. I haven't had a drink in hours, and this desert sucks the water out of you. But that's not the point. The point is giving Lovely some privacy and a chance to relieve herself.

I try to squeeze something out, watching her with the corner of my eye. She's hiding behind a dusty truck, where she thinks she's safe, but I can still see her squatting in the rearview mirror. I wait until she's done, then I step back like nothing happened.

"I'm sorry it took me so long. Now, do you want to go back to look for grass?"

"I'm good for now, thanks, Viper. How about showing me the living quarters?"

CHAPTER 30

I take her inside the massive hangar where the soldiers are celebrating Brown's return. The day Butter got shot was terrible for us all, and they're all delighted to have him back.

Brown's dark face lights up when he sees me.

"Good to see you, Viper. How ya doing, pal?"

"Good, thanks. How about you?"

"Fair to middling. Where's Guinness?"

The lieutenant fills him in.

"She's gone, unfortunately. You didn't hear about Silver?"

"No."

Brown's face falls as he hears the story.

"What a loss. So terrible to hear about Silver. She was a great soldier, and so was Guinness. I never imagined they wouldn't be here when I returned. Where's Sabrina?"

"She's gone too."

Brown pales.

"She got shot too?"

"Nope. She got pregnant."

"Sabrina? She got pregnant here?"

The lieutenant nods.

"But she's OK. She went back home."

"So, who's Viper's handler?"

The lieutenant points to Dick, who reaches his hand to grip Brown's. His knuckles turn white as he tries to show Brown who's tougher.

"Good to have you here. Me and Viper have been the only K-9 team for a while, and it's getting old. It'll be good to have some backup. Would you like me to show you around?"

"No need, thanks. This is my third deployment here, and I don't think much has changed."

"Really? Your third deployment? With this?"

Dick points to Lovely, and my hackles go up. "This?"

Brown's heckles go up, too, though he's got no hair on his neck.

"No. This is Lovely's first deployment."

"Lovely, eh? What a name! But it fits her well. She surely doesn't look like a military K-9."

"Lovely has a great nose, as good as any K-9. She's a springer. They're well known for their tracking ability."

"If you say so. But surely not for their fighting."

Brown smiles.

"Lovely is not here to fight. She's an explosive detecting K-9. That's her assignment, and that's what she'll do. I'll do whatever fighting is needed."

Brown's hard eyes look Dick up and down. He's already taken his measure, and I can smell he likes him just as much as I do.

Isn't life interesting!

CHAPTER 31

TODAY IS Lovely's first mission outside the wire, and it's a scorcher.

Patrolling around the base isn't hard once you learn the ropes. I'm not saying it's easy, but if you take your time and pay attention, you'll be all right more often than not. And if something's fishy, you can abort and return to base. Mishaps may happen, but if you're vigilant, you retain some control.

But that's not today's mission. We're driving to man a highway checkpoint miles away.

Our informers told us that the Taliban expects a massive load of explosives coming over the Kabul-Kandahar highway. We don't know when, we don't know what, we don't know how. We just know that this load means hundreds of IEDs to kill our men if we miss it.

If that's true, of course. Half of our informers work for the Taliban, and they feed us loads of poppycock to bring us out in the open where they can hurt us.

At the checkpoint, you're a sitting duck, miles away from the base, out in the open where everyone can see you. You're stuck there for hours to check whatever's coming, and every truck, car, or bike could be a bomb aimed at you. And by the time you sniff it, you're up with the angels.

I don't like it one bit, but nobody asked for my opinion. And what I like the least is that this is Lovely's first mission. She hasn't been outside the wire yet, and she wouldn't be here today, but Dick made a fuss.

"I've been outside the wire every freaking day for weeks. And now you've got this suicide mission, and you want me to go alone? How about the other K-9s? They've been here for weeks, sitting on their assets. It's high time they did something besides trimming their nails."

The lieutenant was torn. Dick was right, but this wasn't a mission for a rookie. Lovely should have been out patrolling, but like everyone else, the lieutenant succumbed to her charm. He tried to give her time to adjust and kept her safe for as long as he could.

"But they've never been outside the wire, and this is not a mission for a rookie."

Dick snickered.

"And whose fault is that?"

The lieutenant shrugged.

"OK then. You all go. Stay safe."

Fat chance.

The rising sun drips blood over the desert as we load into the massive army trucks to ride to the checkpoint. A wailing song cries through the air from the nearby compound. I've heard it so many times I don't notice it anymore, but Lovely jumps to her feet, and I remember how my insides used to twist in knots every time I heard it.

"What's that?"

"It's the Muslim call to prayer. It happens five times a day. Nothing to worry about."

Lovely shivers, even though the desert wind is hot, and sniffs the air like she wants to smell the song.

I lick her nose.

"Listen, baby. There are plenty of things to worry about down here, but that ain't one of them. Wipe it off your radar. Listen for firearms, detonators, steps, voices, even for the silence. But the call to prayer is not your problem. It's just a distraction you need to ignore."

She slows down her breath and forces herself to calm down.

"Thanks, Viper. Anything else I should know?"

Oh, boy. Where should I start? I wish I didn't have to start today, but here we are.

"That checkpoint? It's a trap. We'll be like sitting ducks there, waiting for someone to take us out. This whole thing about the explosives transport is likely a hoax to get us away from the safety of the base and blow us to high heaven. The enemy hates K-9s even more than they hate our soldiers. They'd give anything to see us dead because we are so good at what we do."

"Who does?"

"Everyone."

"So, what can I do?"

Good question. I've done it for so long I don't remember. It's like swimming. It's easy to do but hard to explain.

"The first thing you should do today is to sniff for people rather than explosives."

Lovely cocks her pretty head.

"What do you mean? I was trained to sniff for explosives, not people!"

"That's exactly what you'll do when we're on patrol. You'll check every inch of the desert for IEDs, and that's going to keep us all alive. But this mission is different. The would-be suicidal bombers, whether they walk, ride a motorcycle, or drive a truck, they're so amped up they stink like stress. They sweat bullets, hoping to get close enough to destroy us when they kill themselves. That's why you need to keep away."

"But then, how can I detect explosives and point them out?"

"That's just the point. When the air reeks of hate, dread, and fear, point that to your handler, whether you smell explosives or not. It's their job to sort it out. Don't get near anyone who smells like they're ready to take off to heaven and want you with them."

Lovely's brown eyes look at me like I'm God, and my heart melts. I wish I could keep her out of danger, but I can't. Dick can't wait to get Brown in trouble, and there's nothing I can do.

"Thanks, Viper. I'll do the best I can."

"I know you'll do great."

My heart sinks. I wish I wasn't lying.

CHAPTER 32

Lovely and I sit shoulder to shoulder as the truck rattles our brains all the way to the checkpoint. The darn thing is just a massive cube of filthy concrete by the roadside, broken by wide openings letting the wind through. As well as the dust, the heat, and the bullets.

Lovely yawns. I smell her worry, and I know she senses mine. This no man's land in the middle of the desert is tricky, and we all know it. The soldiers' faces shine with sweat as they raise their hands to stop the vehicles. They're all kitted in bulletproof vests and helmets, and they buckle under the weight of equipment, weapons, and ammo. I can't see their eyes since they all wear dark glasses, but I can smell their fear as they wonder where death's coming from.

Their job is to stop the cars; Lovely's and mine is to find the danger. We divide into teams, and we each take one direction of Afghanistan's deadliest road.

I sniff under cars, check people, and keep track of everyone's sweat. I watch the desert for any movement that might mean badness coming our way. I also watch Lovely and everything that heads her way, so I'm plenty busy without worrying about Dick's rage.

I thought he'd be glad to have Brown and Lovely here for this dangerous mission, but it turns out he's not. He watches them with a nasty frown. Deep inside, he wants them to fail.

Oh well. Dick will be Dick.

I wriggle under a rusty car to check the chassis, struggling to ignore the dust. There's nothing here. I crawl out and stick my head in the window to sniff inside. There are two men and a goat, and they smell OK other than needing a shower.

Dick glares at them.

"Where are you going?"

"Suq. Market."

The goat bleats in agreement.

Dick glares at her, and she stares back. He lets them go and moves to the scooter behind them. Two men and two little kids squeeze together on a tiny scooter, their shalwars swelling in the wind, their sunburned faces split by white grins.

"Where are you going?"

"Al'usra."

"To visit family," Abdul says. Our translator is a slight man in combat fatigues with a soft voice and weary eyes glancing back often. And for good reasons: The translators are the only targets the Taliban hate more than they hate K-9s. To them, they're traitors. They'll stop at nothing to make an example of them and their families.

I sniff the scooter. The four smell alright. Better than that, in fact: they smell like mantu — steamed dumplings with yogurt, mint, and garlic.

I swallow my drool and glance across the road.

Lovely crawls under a massive truck. Sniff-sniff-sniff. Sniff-sniff-sniff. She moves slowly but smoothly, checking every inch, and I'm proud of her.

Dick isn't. He spits to the side and mumbles.

"Just take all day, will you? After all, you only have two more vehicles waiting."

Usually, we'd help them clear the load, but not today. Dick watches Brown lift Lovely in the massive truck and frowns:

"Like, really? You call that a working K-9?"

I'm about to add that to my list of grievances against Dick when I sense something funky.

It's just a plume of dust heading down the road toward us, but it moves too fast. My hackles go up. I signal Dick, but he's too busy hating on Brown to notice. I have to bark twice before he turns to me.

"What?"

The blue car heads toward us at full speed, and I know my instinct was right. I bark to draw Brown's attention as Dick takes out his weapon.

"Stop!"

The car shoots forward as if it wants to meet the hail of bullets flying toward it. The quiet dusty road explodes into a cacophony of gunfire, groaning engines, and screams. Just heartbeats later, the car plows into the massive truck Lovely was checking and bursts into a fireball spitting shrapnel. The world disappears in a cloud of dust, stinking like death. The air's too thick to breathe, so the soldiers cough, scream, and choke. And so do I. There's so much noise my ears hurt, but I don't hear Lovely.

I have to find her.

The smoke's so dense I can hardly see, but I leap into the burning truck to look for her. There are three dead bodies, none of them hers. I jump out as the truck blows up. The blast throws me to the ground, and the world goes dark.

I open my eyes, wobbly and dazed. I shake my head to clear it and look around for Lovely, but I can't see her. Down the road, our soldiers brave the dust struggling to regroup, but she's not there either. I call her, but she doesn't answer.

My heart freezes. Lovely can't be gone. Not the love of my life! That can't be!

I check behind the truck. I sniff inside the concrete cube. I race up and down the road, calling her. Nothing.

That can't be. I can't lose her. I just can't.

My voice breaks as I bark for her one more time.

"Lovely? Where are you?"

"Viper?"

Thank Dog, she's here, right behind me. She's a bit dusty, but she's just as petite, soft, and lovely as ever. And she looks unscathed. My heart melts.

"Lovely!"

"Viper? Are you hurt?"

Hurt? I taste the blood in my mouth, and I feel my paws burning. I guess I am, but I didn't notice.

"Just a scratch. How are you, Lovely?"

"I'm good. Let's look for Brown."

We head back to the burning mess of tangled metal, burning tires, and body parts scattered between the screaming wounded. There are debris, blood, and guts, but there's no Brown.

"He isn't here."

"He was here a moment ago. He pulled me out of the truck when you warned us, and we took cover. Then the world exploded, and I lost him."

We keep looking, though we can barely see or smell anything but the burning mess.

"Sorry, Lovely. I'm afraid...."

"Absolutely not. I know Brown's alive. He was just here."

I feel sorry for her and for Brown. He was a good man.

"Lovely, I'm..."

She won't even listen. She rushes to sniff one body after another, then makes a beeline to the ditch behind the truck. I follow her.

"Brown!"

Sure enough, it's him.

CHAPTER 33

Bloodied and covered in dust, Brown kneels over Dick, struggling to breathe life into him. He compresses his chest again and again, then starts over.

But Dick is beyond this. Even if you can't smell he's dead, his frozen blue eyes and the gaping wound in his neck tell the story.

"Come on, Brown. He's dead. And we will be too if we don't get out of here," I bark.

Brown sighs.

"You're right. They must have heard this explosion from Helmand. Any loser with a Kalashnikov within a hundred miles will rush here to finish what his friends have started. Let's go."

We join the rest of the soldiers, and I'm glad to see they're all alive. But Abdul is in trouble. His left hand hangs by the skin, so Brown helps Dan tie a tourniquet to stop the bleeding, as the soldiers burn a purple flare to get the medevac. We're all scratched, bruised, and shaken, but we're lucky to be alive. That car must be scattered over half of Kandahar. The men in the truck didn't make it. Nor did the grinning kids on the scooter.

We wait until the helicopter takes Abdul before we load back in the truck and suffer through the long trip back in mourning silence.

I managed to stay alive through another bloody mission. So did Lovely and Brown. But Dick didn't make it, which makes me sad, even though he wasn't my friend.

The sky is blood-red as we reach the base at dusk. We drag ourselves back inside, all too tired to talk. But the army says we must have a debriefing, so the lieutenant tries to engage the men and give them hope. He'd fare better if he didn't smell hopeless too.

Brown checks Lovely all over, then cleans up my wounds and covers my blistered paws with soothing ointment.

"Not bad, Viper. The wound on the hip is just a scratch, and the paws will heal in no time. Let me see your mouth."

My mouth's still bleeding since I pulled the truck door open with my teeth when looking for Lovely. I loosened a tooth and bit my tongue.

Brown cleans me up and pushes the tooth back in place. It hurts like heck and it still feels loose, but he does his best to anchor it to its neighbors with wire and glue.

"If I were you, Viper, I wouldn't try for any beauty contests right now. But you should be all right if you keep your mouth shut."

I cock my head.

"Are you nuts? I can't keep my mouth shut."

"There's that."

He pats my back and brings our dinner before attending his debriefing. I'm hungry, but my mouth hurts, and I don't feel like eating, so I lay my nose on my paws to think.

Dick died. It was his own fault, even though I won't tell anyone. We, brothers in arms, stick together even if we hate each other. If you rat on someone, you're a snitch, and people no longer trust you, even when you tell the truth. But Dick is dead, and he won't come back to torment me. I should feel happy, but I'm not.

I feel sad, tired, and old. Today's ordeal aged me, and its

memory will stay with me forever. I'll never forget those two grin-ning kids on the scooter who smelled like mint and garlic. Their family must be waiting for them. I'm glad I won't be there when they get the news.

I'll never forget Abdul's ashen face nor his hand hanging by its skin, nor Dick's frozen blue eyes. His wife and his kids don't know yet, but they will soon. What a terrible waste.

I try to think about something happy, but nothing comes to mind. All I can think about is death, loss, and disaster.

"Viper?"

"Yes, Lovely?"

"To me, you are the most handsome K-9 ever, broken tooth or not."

Really? I gaze into her chocolate eyes, I see her tail quivering, and my heart melts. Maybe I'm not so old after all?

"I was so scared, and you were so brave. I lay in that ditch paralyzed with fear. Then I saw you jump in the burning truck to look for me. That gave me courage. Thank you for saving me."

Well then. I didn't really do anything. But I'd be a fool to throw away the credit. So I sigh like I'm about to expire, and I do my best to look exhausted, brave, and heroic.

"I'd die for you," I say. And, as corny as that sounds, it's true.

Lovely crawls in my crate. I move aside to make room for her. I've never shared a cage before, but it's not bad. She lays her pretty head next to mine, and my insides melt.

She licks my nose and says:

"Let's hope that won't be necessary."

I lick her nose, and I forget about everything else. For the first time in forever, I don't feel alone.

Hope blooms as I lie next to my Lovely and listen to her heartbeat.

CHAPTER 34

FALLING IN LOVE IS MAGIC. It's like all these years of muddling through, striving to stay alive, washed off my back. My scars, my aches, even my nightmares vanished. I feel young, strong, and hopeful, and I've got a new spring in my step. Even the dust tastes better when I share it with my love.

I know it's not real, of course. I'm not an idiot. I'm almost eight, and I've seen more death and loss than most soldiers, K-9 or human, but it's terrific to dream. It's like watching a movie or listening to a story. I haven't done much of either, but Guinness told me about it.

After Butter got shot, we were so broken that we lay in our crates, talking about anything but Butter. I told Guinness about Jinx and his cat; she told me about the movies she loved to watch.

"You know it's not real because you can still smell the stinky library carpet as you watch border collies herd sheep over green meadows, but it still does your heart good. You escape your surroundings to live in your brain. It's like dreaming, but you're awake. They call it suspension of disbelief."

"Where did you learn all that?"

"At home, watching movies with Jones. Then with Silver. You've never watched a movie?"

I shake my head.

"In Belgium, we lived in the kennel. Then, when Jinx and I came over, we got assigned to the army kennels, and we had no movie night. We barely had bathroom privileges."

Guinness cocks her head.

"But you lived in your handler's home, didn't you? Didn't your family watch movies?"

"I don't know. Mom didn't like me in the living room. She said I shed like an animal, so she kept my crate in the mudroom. I stayed there unless Andrew took me out. He often did, just to get away from her."

"That explains a lot."

I wonder if I should feel insulted.

"What do you mean by that?"

"Have you ever been in a loving home, Viper? A place where you can relax and feel safe? Where you don't have to sniff for bombs, don't have to talk unless you want to, and you feel comfortable and loved?"

I shake my head.

"Never. You mean just lie there without worrying about orders, or shedding, or bombs?"

"Yep. You stretch out to sleep. You can even lie on your back if you feel like it because no one will ever hurt you."

"Nope."

Guinness sighed.

"You know, Viper, I never realized how lucky I was. I've had not one but three loving homes where I never had to worry. I was always loved with Mom and Jones, even when I ate Jones's boots and puked them all over the kitchen. Mom cleaned up after me, so I never had to face the music. Then I moved with Shorty, who taught me to dig for clams, listen to country music, and drink beer. He also taught me about unconditional love. I was heartbroken when he died, but then Silver opened her heart to me. I'm one lucky dog."

I don't get it. My life has always been my job. Guinness is only half my age but has so much to teach me.

"I can't wait to go home. Silver and I will go for long hikes in the woods, we'll eat popcorn, and we'll watch our favorite movies: *Homeward Bound*, *Old Yeller*, and *Babe*. Even *The Art of Racing in the Rain*, though that's nonsense. No self-respecting K-9 would want to drive a car rather than run. That movie is weak on the specifics, but it hits you in the feels. I almost cried when I watched it."

I cocked my head.

"You didn't. You couldn't have. Dogs don't cry."

Guinness shook her head.

"Oh, Viper. You have so much to learn."

I remember her voice, her scent, and the sadness in her golden eyes, and my heart tightens. Oh, how I miss her! That was just days before Silver got shot and Guinness...

Lovely lifts her pretty head.

"What's up, Viper? Everything OK?"

Her voice brings me back to here and now. I'm a lucky dog. I'm happier than I've ever been. With Lovely by my side, I'm ready to take on the world. So why the heck are my eyes watering? Dogs don't cry.

"I'm great, Lovely. How about you?"

"I'm wonderful. Just wonderful."

She lies back, and I rest my muzzle on her shoulder, remembering Guinness.

"Oh, Viper, you have so much to learn."

Damn you, Guinness.

Why do you always have to be right?

CHAPTER 35

THOSE WERE THE DAYS! Lovely and I were always together. Brown trained us both, and we challenged each other to find the fake IEDs he hid for us. Whoever found them first got a treat. Lovely loves food, but my favorite treat, as always, is the ball. Brown throws it, I fetch it, he gives it a few tugs, and it's all worth it.

At night, Lovely and I lie next to each other, talking about everything under the stars. I tell her about Belgium, but it's not much since I was too young to remember. She tells me about Butter.

"We didn't get along at the beginning since she was so bitter."

My jaw drops.

"Butter, bitter? You've got to be kidding! Butter is a Labrador! She's the sweetest K-9 I ever met."

"Really? There, see this? Butter did it."

Lovely shows me a three-inch-long jagged scar along her neck, and I'm flabbergasted.

"Butter? But why? I've never even seen her mad."

"Lucky you. But to be honest, I deserved it."

"What did you do?"

"I took away something important to Butter."

"What?"

"Her self-respect."

I cock my head, trying to understand, but Lovely is done.

"Enough about that. Just remember that when you take away somebody's treasure, even the meekest person can become a killer."

I don't see how that's news, but OK. I'm about to fall asleep when I hear boot steps around me, and my hackles go up in a panic. The last time that happened, they tried to give me a bath. I had to fight for dear life. I thought they'd learned their lesson, but there they are again. I jump to my feet, looking to escape when they start singing.

"Happy birthday to you,

Happy birthday to you,

Happy birthday, dear Viper,

Happy birthday to you."

It's my birthday? Really? Why didn't anyone tell me?

The lieutenant sets an MRE birthday cake in front of me, and it's the ugliest thing I've ever seen, but the aroma makes me slobber. It's a slice of rehydrated meatloaf frosted with ketchup and sprinkled with cheese cracker crumbs with a burning match instead of a candle.

The lieutenant blows off the match, and I inhale the cake and the match before I remember to leave some for Lovely. Oh well.

"Happy Birthday to Viper, our veteran. Thank you for your hard work and all the lives you saved."

I wish I had something to say, but I don't. So, I wag my tail in thanks.

"Good cake. Thanks."

They clap their hands, Brown scratches my ears, and Lovely licks my nose. Life is good.

Then I hear the gates screech open.

"They finally arrived," the lieutenant says, and they all rush to the truck. Lovely and I follow.

"Who?" I ask.

"The new K-9s."

CHAPTER 36

My heart skips a beat.

The new K-9s? What new K-9s? Why did no one tell me?

I dash through the door and run to the truck, and Lovely follows. I sniff so hard that I sneeze, but other than the dust, I only smell a hot engine, gasoline fumes, and men in dire need of a shower.

"Lovely, do you get anything?"

She sniffs her heart out.

"It's a male. But I can't tell the breed."

Seriously? Lovely smelled him before me? My male pride gets seriously wrinkled, but I manage to act like I knew it all along.

I keep sniffing until I catch a whiff, and I'll be darned if she's not right. That makes me look at her with new respect. She may be female, small, and cute, but her nose is excellent. Even better than mine.

We sit shoulder to shoulder, waiting for the new K-9, and watch the newcomers scramble out on stiff legs, numb after long hours of travel.

"Did you know anything about this?" I ask.

"No. But I felt something. There was like a stir in the air."

She's right. I feel it too. It's like when you sense a storm brewing, even if you don't know how. Your skin tingles, your ears get itchy, and your stomach stirs. I feel this new dog will change everything, and I'm sick with worry. We're usually excited to get new K-9s because they share the work and bring color to our social life. But not today.

The crate door creaks open, and the ugliest dog I've ever seen jumps off the truck to faceplant in the dust. The poor guy's so ugly that I can't tell his breed or even color. I only know what he's not. He's not a Malinois, nor a Labrador or a German shepherd. Not even a springer. He's sturdy and compact, with sharp ears and a coat the color of burned toast and crummy weather.

Lovely cocks her head in wonder.

"What is that? Is it a hyena?" she whispers.

"I don't think so. It's got to be the new K-9," I reply, observant as usual.

"He's different."

"Yep. Interesting."

That was Andrew's rescue word. He never said he hated something, whether it was the food, the weather, or Mom's new haircut. Whenever he disliked something, he called it interesting.

But, interesting or not, this is our new buddy, so we step forward to introduce ourselves.

"Hi, buddy. I'm Viper. This is Lovely."

"Glad to meet you, guys. I'm Rambo."

He wags his tail and perks his black ears. His hazel eyes are kinda glazed, and that's no wonder since he's been traveling forever and he just landed on his head. But he seems friendly enough as he turns politely to offer us his butt. He's tired and thirsty, and he could do with some food, but other than that, he's OK.

We offer our butts to reciprocate. Rambo sniffs Lovely with more interest than I care for, then gives me a cursory check and wags his tail. We turn around to chat.

"Where are you from, Rambo?"

"Iowa."

"Originally?"

"Oh. I'm Dutch."

"Really. I'm Belgian."

"I know."

He wags his tail left, and I know exactly what he's thinking. Our countries are neighbors, but the Dutch believe they are superior. There's this old joke: Whenever a Southern Dutch moves to Belgium, the average IQ of both countries goes up. That's nonsense, of course, but there's your Dutch mentality. I'll have to nip that in the bud.

Lovely seems mesmerized.

"Are you a Dutch shepherd?"

"Of course."

"Wow! I never met one before."

She stares at him like he's unique, and I wish she weren't meeting one now.

"We're quite rare," he says modestly.

I refrain from baring my teeth.

"What color are you, if you don't mind my asking?"

"I'm brindle. We all are."

"Brindle!" Lovely steps closer to check his coat like she's looking to buy it.

"I'm a golden brindle. Some of us are silver. But we all have to be striped. It's a breed requirement."

"What a stupid thing. Like the color makes any difference. We Malinois can be any color we want. It's what's inside that matters."

Rambo gives me a side glance but keeps his mouth shut.

Lovely doesn't. She glares at me.

"Viper, you always have something interesting to say."

I think she just called me stupid.

CHAPTER 37

I SPENT that night alone in my crate. Gone are the nights when Lovely and I lay with our bodies touching. Now, she doesn't even look at me, and I'm heartbroken.

I thought we had something real, something different, something unbreakable. And all it took to break us apart was this ugly stranger. I don't get it.

I listen to her breath and sniff to read her feelings. But there are no feelings. She's snoring like a chainsaw while I toss and turn. On Lovely's other side, Rambo's crate is quiet. He traveled for days, and now he sleeps like he'll never wake up. If only.

The morning finds me raw and restless. I'm so ready to show this intruder what's what that I shake with excitement. I've been here for years while he just arrived, so I hold the home advantage. I look forward to showing Lovely who's the best K-9, even though the sleepless night and the worry didn't do much for me.

We head out for our morning walk with Brown and Ashley, Rambo's handler. She's a slight blonde girl with a narrow face and bright blue eyes who looks too young to be here. This has to be their first assignment, so I decide to show off.

"This is where we train, and our handlers hide fake IEDs for us to find."

Rambo wags his tail like he doesn't care, so I proceed with my lecture.

"They're not active, of course. It's just about perceiving the smell and signaling it to the handler. We do that by sitting next to it. We don't paw at it, we don't bite it, we don't try to dig it out."

"Yep."

"I'll show you."

I take off like an arrow, looking for the decoy I know Brown hid somewhere. I saunter down the field, doing my best to look sleek, macho and *vaillant*..

I watch for Lovely's eyes to stay glued to me, but they aren't. She's fascinated with this ugly Dutch, even though he doesn't do much to entice her.

I swallow my bile and push on until I hear Rambo clear his throat.

"Hey, Viper?"

"Yes?"

"If I were you, I'd check the left rear wheel of the truck you just passed. It might hold something interesting."

I take a deep breath to slow down my heart. I have never, ever, in my entire career missed an IED. That I know of. That can't be true. But I have to check if only to dismiss it, so I retrace my steps.

Sure enough, there's a decoy just where he said it was, even though he never went near it. My heart plummets, and my head is about to blow up in smoke. But he's right, and you can't argue with right.

"You're right. Thanks, Rambo."

"No worries."

I keep myself from glancing at Lovely. I used to be her hero, and now I'm what? I don't want to know. The bile in my throat flows thick and bitter as I sit back, letting the others have a go. To say that I'm embarrassed doesn't start to cover it.

I watch Lovely go through her turn flawlessly, albeit a bit slow. Her legs are half the length of mine, so she's got to hustle, but she finds the fake IED hidden in the back of the rusty truck and sits next to it, her tail quivering with joy.

"Good job, Lovely."

Brown rewards her with a treat, then we fall back to watch the newcomers. This is our home. I've gone through it a thousand times, and I know every inch of this place. I've smelled the dust; I know the shadows on the ground; I've sniffed every rusty screw in those trucks. But Rambo and Ash haven't been here before, and they have to learn.

"Go."

Rambo heads out, sniffing his steps like a smelling machine. "Sniff-sniff-sniff. Sniff-sniff-sniff." He moves slowly, but he never stops. I remember Guinness: "Slow is smooth, and smooth is fast." Rambo is smoother than any K-9 I've worked with. His sturdy brindle body moves like the energizer bunny clearing up the yard.

He seems ready to jump in the next truck, but he doesn't. He gives it a couple good sniffs and goes down his way to the next one. He stops and sits next to nothing.

Has he lost it?

Apparently not. Ash throws him his Kong, and he catches it in mid-air, then he gets a good tug while I still wonder what this is all about.

Ash digs out a few matches buried half a foot into the ground, and Rambo goes crazy licking her face.

"Good job, boy. Good job, Rambo."

She pets his ears and kisses his black muzzle, and he doesn't seem to mind. I'm horrified. What kind of relationship is that?

He wags his tail.

"You guys ready for lunch?"

Lovely stares at him like he hung the moon.

"That was fantastic. Totally amazing. Where did you learn to work the terrain like that?"

"Here and there. It's no big deal. It's all about paying attention and not getting distracted."

That's a jab in my ribs, and I deserve it. I screwed up. I'm lucky it was just a decoy. If it were real, we could all be dead.

"No, seriously. Is this your first deployment?"

Rambo's tail wags as he tries to pacify me.

"Not exactly. I've been in minefields before."

"How so? And where?"

"Have you heard about Princess Di's work on land mines?"

"Who's Princess Di?"

"Never mind. I spent some time demining in Angola a while back. Then I went to Cambodia for a stint. I loved it there. Asian food beats MREs every time. And a few other places. So, even though this is technically my first deployment, I've been around a little, and it helps."

I hung my head. What's most humbling is that he's not even trying to humiliate me. He's just matter-of-fact as my liver smolders.

"Nice job, Rambo," Lovely says, squeezing close to him.

Females!

CHAPTER 38

THAT WAS JUST THE BEGINNING. This ugly stranger's arrival turned my life upside down. I used to think I was the best K-9 ever, but for Jinx. And I was right.

Now, watching this hyena-like intruder showing me what's what burns my guts. He's young, strong, and fast. His hips don't ache, his eyes don't tear, and he doesn't have seven years' worth of desert dust lining his lungs. He's smooth and unflappable, and he's not even a jerk so I can hate him openly. Lovely looks at him like she used to look at me, and he doesn't mind one bit.

Never mind. I'll just have to work harder. Soon enough, she'll get bored with him and remember who saved her life.

A few days later, when we go on a mission, I'm glad I'm leading. The aerial surveillance recorded someone hiding something in a hole a few miles down the road. We don't know what, but whether it's weapons or explosives, we need to find them.

It's my time to shine. Brown fits my bulletproof vest and clips my leash.

"Be careful, Viper," Lovely barks.

I wag my tail and head to the gate, followed by Brown and the others. Lovely and Dan are in the middle, and Rambo closes the file with Ash.

The gates open, and I step out. It's still early morning, and the glowing red sun has painted the desert into a sea of blood. It's just like when Dick died, and my heart skips a beat. Is this an omen?

I wonder if that's how Butter felt the day she got shot; or Guinness, the day she lost her mind; or Fury, the day he died. It's hard to explain how we dogs feel things. The foreboding engulfs you like smoke. It's not just in your nose; it's everywhere. Your skin crawls, your throat tightens, your stomach roils, and your heart freezes. You sense danger with all your body, and I've never felt it stronger than today.

Oh well. It is what it is.

I sniff my way to the field, and the others follow. The earth is already hot under my paws, and I'd love me some shade, but there's nothing here to give shade but us.

Once in the field, we're out in the open. Nothing stirs the dust as far as the eye can see. Nothing moves, but the smoke marring the pale sky far away, over the village. The soldiers hold their arms ready as we spread to comb the field.

I sniff something to my right. I track it, and sure enough, I find the place where the earth was disturbed. It smells funny, so I sit next to it.

Brown kneels to finger-sweep the sand, looking for the pressure plate but doesn't find it. He calls back.

"There's something here, but it doesn't look like an IED. The earth was disturbed, but they covered it with dust."

We step back to let the defusing team do their magic. But there's no bomb. Just a canvas bag full of American uniforms that gets us all scratching our heads.

"What the heck is this about?"

"Whatever it is, it can't be good. We need to get whoever hid them to find out. Bring the K-9s."

We sniff the uniforms, then Rambo and I start tracking, shoulder to shoulder. Lovely follows, her short legs moving at double speed.

"Wait for me!"

Are you kidding? We ignore her as we try to outrun each other, but we're still shoulder to shoulder when we reach the village.

The locals stare at us with dread as soldiers line them up for me to sniff them. I move from one to the other, looking for the scent I tracked, while Rambo keeps an eye on the lot to make sure they behave.

They all reek like hate and fear, but that's not what I'm looking for. I look for those who left their scent on the uniforms. Like this dude whose fists are so tight, his knuckles turned white. If eyes could kill, I'd be a dead Malinois. But they can't, so I point him out. Next is a white-haired elder with an unkempt beard, then a kid barely taller than me.

My job here is done. I watch the soldiers take them away.

"Mind if I take a sniff?" Rambo asks.

My hackles rise.

"Suit yourself," I growl.

He sniffs one man after another and points out a short skinny kid whose shalwars drag on the ground.

Seriously? I sniff him, and I'd bet my tail against a second-hand bone that he didn't touch those uniforms. Rambo lost it, I think, when I notice the kid's American combat boots.

I'm mortified. My ears go flat, and my tail hides between my legs as we head to base. Technically, I was correct. The kid's scent was not on those uniforms. But practically, I ignored an essential clue and missed a suspect. If it weren't for Rambo, that kid would be free.

That night I lie in my crate with my nose on my paws, wondering if I'm too old for my job.

CHAPTER 39

THE FOLLOWING day I act like those boots never happened. And, thank Dog, they're all too excited to pay attention to me.

"The new K-9s arrive today," the lieutenant says.

My jaw drops.

Really? New K-9s again? We just got Rambo and Ash, and now we get another team? We've never had four K-9s at the base. I wonder if that means they're getting rid of me. I'd love to know, but I'm too proud to ask. And what on earth would I say? "Did you get them because I'm a loser?"

So I spend the day shaking on my paws as everyone looks forward to meeting the newcomers.

"Who are they?" Lovely asks.

Brown shrugs.

"Dunno. I think they're new. Never heard those names before. Like Chantix or something. But we're about to find out, aren't we? And what difference does it make, anyhow?"

Good question. What difference does it make? I don't know many active K-9s. All those I knew — Jinx, Butter, Guinness, Fury — they'll never return. I'm the last one left. And not for long, I bet.

"I hope it's a Labrador," Lovely says. "They are the nicest dogs on earth."

I give her the stink eye. I saved her life, and that counts for nothing? Rambo wags his tail left.

"What does that say about Viper and me?"

Lovely is so embarrassed she yawns.

"Sorry, guys. You're both wonderful. I was just thinking about Butter. I hope whoever comes will be as nice as her, that's all."

We go about our day, as usual, and by the time we hear the gates open to let in the growling truck, I'm too exhausted to care. Between yesterday's SNAFU, my unslept night, and the incoming team, I'm spent.

They all file to the gates to meet the newcomers. I stay behind and consider a nap, but that would be rude, so I drag myself to follow.

By the time I reach the truck, Lovely and Rambo are already speaking to a shaggy yellow dog with droopy ears who's got to be a retriever. I may as well be done with this, so I force myself to meet him.

He's too busy bonding with Lovely and Rambo to notice me. But when he does, he jumps back, and his eyes pop out.

"Jinx? Is that you?"

Lovely and Rambo stare at him like he's lost it. I'm stunned. Meeting someone who knew Jinx turns my heart inside out.

I manage to wag my tail.

"Name's Viper. And you?"

"Sorry, Viper. For a moment, I thought I saw a ghost. I'm Prozac, your new mate."

He turns around to offer his butt, and I take my time checking him out. He's not as young as he looks. He's been places and done things, and this long trip took a lot out of him.

I let him sniff my butt, and he takes forever. Nobody has checked me that thoroughly since the Army procurers who selected Jinx and me to join the Army. They didn't sniff our butts, of course, since they were humans. The military isn't bright enough to employ K-9s for that job. But they poked, prodded, and checked every inch of me, even those that aren't on display.

Prozac comes to sniff my nose, and I smell his sorrow.

"You're Jinx's twin."

It's not a question; it's a statement. My heart burns raw with losing Jinx like it happened yesterday.

"I am. And you?"

"I was his best friend. We worked together, trained together, and shared things we couldn't share with anyone else. He told me all about you. He was so proud of you for finding IEDs in the Middle East, but he missed you terribly. He told me so much about you that I feel like I've known you forever."

"What did he tell you?"

"He told me you're brave, sharp, and relentless. He told me you can't quit, and you'll push yourself to the end, no matter what. He hoped to be as good as you someday."

I choke. I always thought Jinx was better than me, and I still do. Oh, how I miss him!

"Do you know what happened to him?"

"Don't you?"

"I know the official line, but not the details. They said Jinx attacked his handler, but I never understood why."

"The man killed Turbo, Jinx's cat. He ran over him with his truck."

"Yep. But..."

"But what?"

"It was an accident. The man didn't mean to hurt that cat."

"Maybe not. But he was drunk. He had no business driving."

CHAPTER 40

WHEN THE LIEUTENANT comes to see me the next day, his eyes avoid mine.

"Good job on finding those uniforms, Viper. We all know that we can always rely on you."

He doesn't mention the boots, and I'm grateful. Everyone knows it anyhow.

"I have great news for you."

He looks away, and I know he's lying.

"After seven years of service, you are finally ready to retire."

"I am what?"

"You're going home, Viper. Thank you for your lifetime of service. We are proud to have served with you."

I cock my head to understand as the men gather around us, clapping.

"Thank you for your service, Viper."

"You so do deserve to retire."

"Our old Viper's going home."

I'm going home? What home? I have no home other than the base. My tattered gray crate has been my only home ever since George retired, and that's too long ago to count.

The lieutenant leans over to hang a dark tag with a brown

and blue ribbon around my neck. There seems to be something written on it, but I can't read.

"I am honored to present you with the PDSA Dickin Medal for Gallantry and Devotion to Duty for your extraordinary service. The Dickin Medal, also known as "The Animal Victoria Cross," was inaugurated in 1943 to honor the work of animals in war. It's been awarded to thirty-four dogs, thirty-two messenger pigeons, four horses, and a cat."

My ears flatten.

"A cat? You're going to give me a medal they gave a cat and a bunch of pigeons?"

"Simon was no ordinary cat. He served on *HMS Amethyst*, and he disposed of many rats, even after being wounded by a blast. His behavior was of the highest order. And the pigeon GI Joe flew twenty miles in twenty minutes to save a hundred Allied Soldiers from being bombed by their own planes. As for Warrior, a horse in World War I...."

My hackles go up. Like really? I need a pigeon medal like I need a catnip refill.

"Where am I going?"

The lieutenant sighs.

"Good question. You know, Viper, we do our best to retire our K-9s with their old trainers. When that's not possible, we look for volunteers to adopt them. But that's not easy. Our K-9 veterans are not pets. After fighting the war, many have trouble adjusting to family life, especially in homes with young children or cats. That's why all the families who adopt K-9s have to be thoroughly vetted. Still, some K-9s can't adjust to living in a civilian home. But you're lucky."

"I am?"

"Dick's family wants to adopt you. His wife hopes you'll bring them comfort."

WHAT? Dick's family? You've got to be kidding! I don't know

those humans, and I don't want to. Dick was the worst human I ever knew, and I want nothing to do with his family.

"How about Sabrina? Or George?"

The lieutenant shakes his head.

"Sorry, I don't know where they are. But I'm sure you'll be happy in Dick's home."

I'm not so sure, and I'd rather not find out. But nobody asked me.

I've served in the army since I was a pup. Seven years of breathing dust, braving the heat, eating MREs, and following orders. Seven years of getting shot at and dodging bombs. Seven years of living to serve. And now they're ditching me like I'm a second-hand bone. That's what my service was worth. That, and a cat medal.

That night I lie with my nose on my paws, remembering Guinness.

"There's more to life than work, Viper. Someday you'll find out."

CHAPTER 41

As they load me in the truck, I catch a last glimpse of Lovely's tail waving goodbye, and I've never felt more hopeless. Not even when I found out about Jinx's death. Then, I was too angry to be sad. Now I'm spent.

Lovely tried hard to give me hope.

"You'll be all right, Viper. Just because Dick was Dick doesn't mean his family is the same. They may be lovely humans. They must be if they asked to adopt you, though they never met you. And it's great to have kids in the house."

I cock my head, wondering if she's lost her mind.

"Kids? Great? Are you nuts?"

"Not at all. Brown's kids, Aleta and BB, are lots of fun. And, wherever there are kids, there's food. Lots of food. I don't mean kibble. I mean fries, and ice cream and hot dogs and cookies. Real junk food. And the kids? Even Butter loves them!"

I snort.

"Butter! Butter loves everybody! She doesn't know how not to love! She doesn't have a hateful bone in her body."

"Viper baby, you don't know Butter as well as you think you do. She's way more discerning than that. Go ask Brown if you don't believe me. Either way, she loves the kids and wouldn't trade them for the world. You'll love yours too."

No self-respecting K-9 could ever love kids. She's just trying to make me feel better. I just wish it worked.

Lovely licks my nose one last time and steps aside to let Rambo say goodbye.

"Good luck, Viper. I was honored to work with you. I hope your retirement is everything you hope for and more."

He doesn't know it, of course, but I hoped to never retire. I don't know what to do with myself without work. But I don't have a choice.

"Thanks, Rambo. I'm glad I met you. Do me a favor, please? Look after Lovely. She's young and vulnerable, and she has a lot to learn."

Rambo glances at Lovely, who's chatting with Prozac, and wags his tail.

"Of course. I'll always have my partners' back. But you don't need to worry about her. She may be young and cute, but she's got the best nose on the base, and she's as crafty as a honey badger. That K-9 is anything but vulnerable."

He steps aside to make room for Prozac. He hunches with his ears hanging low, and his eyes show he's hurting. But why? We only just met. Why would he care? But he does. I smell it, and I see it in his eyes.

"Goodbye, Viper. I'm so sorry we didn't have more time together. I miss Jinx like he was my brother, and I know you do too. When I met you, I felt like I got him back. But it wasn't meant to be. I'm sorry we didn't get to share our memories and be friends."

He wags his tail goodbye, and I drown in sadness. Yet another joy the army stole from me. Prozac and I could have talked about Jinx, about life, and grown to be friends and fill each other's void. But they'll ship me out today, and I'll never be back.

"Thanks, Prozac. And thank you for telling me about Jinx. All these years, I tried to understand what happened. Now I do, and I'm grateful. Take care of yourself, will you? We aren't young anymore. Don't be stupid like me."

Prozac shakes his head.

"Jinx would be so proud of you, Viper. I hope he sees you from wherever he's at and gets to brag to his friends about his hero brother. Until we meet again, my friend."

I don't feel like a hero. I feel like a useless old dog. I'm leaving my home, my work, and my friends to live with the family of the only human I ever hated. I'd rather be with Jinx and with Fury, wherever they are. But this isn't Prozac's fault.

"Thanks, my friend. See you on the other side."

The truck takes off, and I catch the last glimpse of my buddies' sad eyes and droopy ears before the dust drowns them and leaves me alone with my thoughts.

I remember what Guinness said about home.

"Home is where you let your guard down. You can fall asleep on your back if you want. You don't have to worry because everyone loves you, and you're safe."

Wherever I'm going, it won't be like that. I'll never, ever sleep on my back. And I know better than to trust those humans.

CHAPTER 42

When the engines stop, my ears start ringing. It's been so long that I can't remember what silence sounds like. I feel like I was born in this crate. But I'm back on the ground, and someone better let me out before I explode.

I've been locked in since the truck in Kandahar rattled my brains through miles and miles of dusty roads. Still locked as I shivered in the dark on the plane, trying to chew my way out of jail. But I couldn't, so I chewed my ball into smithereens. That's the one thing that kept me sane, and I'm grateful to Rambo for dropping it in my crate as I left.

"You'll be all right, Viper. You're the Malligator. If anyone can do it, you can. I can't wait to meet you again."

He dropped his red Kong in my crate as a gift. It couldn't be easy since our balls are precious to us. They keep us going through our training.

The kid's all right, but for being uglier than a jackal. But he grows on you.

I lie in my crate at the special luggage counter, waiting for someone to come, but nobody does. Did they forget? My bladder's ready to pop, and everything inside me hurts. I'm about to embarrass myself when a large woman with dark greasy hair kneels by the grate and stares at me. She smells of meatloaf, detergent, and worry.

"Viper?"

"Who else?"

"I'm Charity, Dick's wife. I'm glad you made it. I'm sorry I'm late, but I had trouble finding someone to look after the kids. Let's go."

Two men load me in a pick-up truck, and off we go. There goes my bladder, I think. But I forget about it as I stick my nose through the bars to breathe the scent of mowed grass and moist earth. It's raining, so I hold out my parched tongue to catch a few drops. It's the first rain I've seen in years, and I love it. There's nothing better than rain — except mud and snow — but there won't be any snow here. Everything's green — the trees, the bushes, the grass. It smells like summer, and this lawn would get a piss out of an old guy with a swollen prostate, I think, as the truck stops by a blue doublewide with black shutters.

Charity opens the crate, and I tumble out. I let go of my bladder, and it's heaven. It takes me forever, but Charity looks away to give me privacy. Like I care!

When I'm done, I sniff the mailbox, then the bushes, and the fence. What a useless little thing! This is nothing like our base fence with its razor-wire topping. This is just a silly white fence with no excuse to exist. I could leap over it with a paw tied behind my back, and I bet even Lovely could clear it. And it doesn't even have a gate.

That throws me off. Seriously? What's the point of a fence without a gate?

"Why do you have a fence without a gate?"

Charity smiles.

"It's nice, isn't it? I always wanted a white picket fence."

"But what's the point if you don't have a gate?"

"Dick painted it only last year."

She doesn't understand me. She's clearly one of the humans

who don't speak dog. Some do, some don't. That doesn't make them bad people, but it makes it hard to communicate.

"Let's go meet the kids, shall we?"

"Do I have to?"

She opens the door to let me in. Dick's home smells just like her: meatloaf and detergent. And kids. Lots of kids.

I step in, and they ambush me. I struggle to keep my teeth to myself.

"There they are: Dick, Carl, and Harry."

Dick, the oldest, is his father's spitting image: blue eyes, straight back, cocky attitude. The other two are dark, sturdy, and submissive.

"Kids, this is Viper, Father's partner. Viper fought alongside your father until the day he died. He got wounded as he tried to save your father's life. We are so lucky that the army allowed us to adopt him, aren't we, kids?"

The young ones nod, but Dick stares at me.

"What happened to my dad?"

Unlike his mother, he speaks dog. I'd rather he didn't, but I do my best to answer.

"Your father got killed on a mission. He was a brave man and did his best, but he had a bad day."

The kid's eyes fill with tears. He's old enough to hurt, but the other two are too young. They hug me, mount me, and touch me everywhere. I hate it. I'd rather be in the desert sniffing bombs or even manning the freaking checkpoint. But I'm not.

Thanks to the army, I'm here. So I lie there as they comb their fingers through my tail and taste my toes, telling myself that killing them is not an option.

It feels like forever before Charity puts them to bed. I curl in a corner, hoping for a peaceful night, but it's not over yet.

"Oh, how I wish I could speak to you, Viper. I'd love to hear about Dick, his last days, and his sacrifice to our country," Charity says.

"No, you wouldn't," I growl.

Fortunately, she doesn't get it. But young Dick does.

"What do you mean?"

Boy, do I wish I'd kept my mouth shut.

"Your mother doesn't want to know what happened to your father. It wouldn't bring her any joy."

"How about me?"

"You neither. You want to remember the man you knew."

Dick's hard eyes look into my soul. He doesn't like me and doesn't trust me. I wonder why.

I wag my tail.

"I never lie."

He stares at me, trying to read my thoughts, then turns to his mother:

"Mother, why don't we let Viper rest? He had a long trip. You go to bed. I'll take him out, then tuck him in for the night."

CHAPTER 43

THE RAIN'S soft touch softens my heart. I can't remember the last time I was outside without sniffing for IEDs. I breathe in the moist wind, delight in the soft lawn cuddling my paws, and study the memos on the mailbox post.

It's incredible. There's a whole bunch of dogs I never met who live their entire lives without going to war. They eat food that needs no rehydrating, and they have homes and humans that belong to them instead of getting shuffled from one handler to the next. I bet some of them don't even have jobs.

That, to me, is unthinkable since all I know is my job. I sniff and sniff, reading one message after another, and I can't get enough.

Young Dick can't wait any longer.

"What did Father do?"

He's just a kid, barely taller than me. He deserves better than finding out what a small man his father was. He "forgot" to feed me, "forgot" to let me out, "forgot" he had a family when he got Sabrina pregnant, and then "forgot" it was his fault. Even his death was his fault. He was so obsessed with hating Brown that he ignored my warnings until it was too late. There may be worse soldiers out there, but I don't want to meet them.

But this isn't the kid's fault. Thinking his father was a hero will help him cope with his loss. I wish I could tell him that Dick was a wonderful man, but I can't. I never lie, and I'm not about to start now. So I look him in the eye and wag my tail.

"You don't want to know."

"I do."

I yawn.

"You don't. Your dad was your dad when he was here. He loved you and your brothers, and he cared about your mom. War is hell. It does bad things to dogs and to humans. Whatever happened in Kandahar has nothing to do with you. It won't help you, and you don't want to know."

But Dick doesn't believe me. I wish I could help him, but I'm exhausted.

"I'm sorry, Dick. I've had a long day. I have to go."

My bed is an old sweater that smells like Dick, but I'm too tired to care. He's been dead long enough that I've stopped hating him, so I sleep like a log.

The air is clean and crisp, and the grass soft and fragrant as I take my morning walk. Just out of habit, I sniff for IEDs, but there aren't any. Just moist earth, grass, and a few silly squirrels. Cold raindrops fall on me, and I love them.

But I hate being caught in a lie. Dick is a hero to his family. That brings them solace and helps them through their loss. Every day, they ask me about him, and I do my best not to hurt them.

"He was wonderful, wasn't he? He was big and strong and brave," Carl says.

"And handsome," his mother adds.

"He had blue eyes and a straight back," I say.

That's good enough for all of them but Dick. He's torn between wanting to know more and being afraid of it. He's as wary of me as I was of the Afghans.

We continue this terrible truce that makes me feel like an imposter until the day the doorbell rings.

"Open the door," Charity shouts from the kitchen.

Something stirs in the air. My skin tingles, my throat tightens, and I just know my life is about to change.

Dick opens the door to a blimp of a woman who leans back to balance the weight of her belly. I catch a whiff of her, and my heart skips a beat.

This is not a woman — this is Sabrina! I bark with joy and jump to lick her face. She cries and hugs me.

"Viper!"

"Sabrina!"

"I found you! I really found you!"

She hugs me again, and her hair makes me sneeze. She laughs and cries, and I lick off her tears, then I smell her butt to see how she's doing.

Wow! She smells like no other human I've ever sniffed, and she looks like she swallowed a refrigerator. Something's terribly wrong, and I'm worried about her.

"Are you OK?"

"Yep, Viper. Much better now that I found you. How're you doing, my friend?"

"Fair to middling. How did you get so fat?"

I bite my tongue, but it's too late. I flatten my ears in embarrassment, but Sabrina laughs.

"I'm not fat; I'm pregnant. But you wouldn't know the difference, would you?"

"Sorry. Never been pregnant."

She hugs me again, then turns to young Dick, who watches us like a hawk. Her breath catches in her throat as she sees how much he resembles his father.

"Hi. I'm Sabrina. I used to be Viper's handler, and I worked with your father. I'm sorry about your loss."

He nods.

"Let me get my mother."

CHAPTER 44

Sabrina keeps her arms around me as we wait for Charity, and I don't mind her being so close. She's always been touchy-feely. I used to find that embarrassing in camp, but now I love her closeness.

"How did you know I was here?"

"Brown emailed me. Lovely harassed him into breaking the rules."

I spare a moment of gratitude to Brown's breaking the rules and to Lovely.

"I heard you had a thing for her. Is she pretty?"

I'd blush if I knew how.

"She's Lovely," I say, as Charity comes to meet us.

She's had a rough night with the baby. Her eyes are red, and she's sweaty and tired, but she smiles as she shakes Sabrina's hand. I bet she wouldn't if she knew where Sabrina's belly comes from.

"Good to see you. We're happy to welcome Viper's friends. And Dick's. I understand you worked together?"

Sabrina's eyes move from Charity's messy hair to her cracked hands.

"Yes. I worked with Viper when Dick worked with Fury. Then

I...had a medical issue and returned home. Dick was kind enough to take on Viper and work with him, even though he already had Fury."

Sabrina bites her lip. It's hard to pretend that Dick was anything but an ice-hole, but she does her best.

"Thanks for coming. We all cherish Dick's memory, and we'd love to learn more. Is there anything you could share with us?"

Sabrina stares at the kids, and they stare back. She sighs.

"Fury was a lovely K-9. He was smart, handsome, and dedicated, just like his older sister Guinness. I worked with her too. What a great K-9 she was. After she left, it was wonderful to work with Fury. You couldn't hope for a better K-9."

Young Dick's face twists with pain. For the first time, I realize that Fury was his puppy. How thick I am! Young Dick and Fury grew up together. The kid must have loved Fury and mourned his loss. Oh, how I wish I'd thought about this before. I could talk about Fury for weeks and have nothing but good things to say!

Sabrina wipes her eyes.

"Dick was a remarkable man. He was good-looking, smart, and such a charmer. I've never met anyone like him."

So far, she's stuck to the truth, but I can see her struggling to say something nice about Dick.

"There was this one time. We were on a mission. Viper and I were in the lead while Dick and Fury brought up the rear. Viper sniffed for IEDs, and I watched his back. We were close to our target when Viper smelled the enemy. We took off after them, and we were both so busy that we overlooked the sharpshooters who waited for us. Fury and Dick saw them and told us to take cover. We dropped to the ground just as the bullets flew over our heads. We'd both be dead if it weren't for them."

That's not entirely true, but it's close. Fury called, and I took cover. I don't know what Dick was doing — checking his boogers or taking a selfie. But it's close enough to not be an outright lie.

The kids stare at us with eyes as big as saucers. Charity wipes her eyes and grabs Sabrina's hand.

"Thank you for sharing this with us. This gives me solace, and I know it helps the kids too. Thank you so much for coming to tell us about Dick."

Sabrina sighs.

She wants her hand back — she can't love the touch of Dick's wife — but puts up with it for as long as she can. Then her dark eyes catch mine, and I can smell she's ready.

"Thank you, Charity. I'm glad to meet Fury and Dick's family. I'm sorry for your loss, and I'm inspired by your bravery. But I didn't come to tell you about Dick. I came to take Viper home.

CHAPTER 45

Time freezes. The house is so quiet, you could hear a flea sneeze.

Charity drops Sabrina's hand.

"I'm sorry. You said...."

"I came to take Viper home."

The air is thick with apprehension. Sabrina dropped a bomb in Charity's lap. She has to deal with it, but she's vulnerable and unprepared. She didn't plan for this.

Sabrina did.

"Viper was my partner, and he's my best friend. I need him in my life, and he needs me too. I appreciate your caring for him, but he only spent a few weeks with Dick. Viper belongs with me."

Charity's eyes grow wide as she stares at Sabrina.

"But... But Viper was Dick's partner. He was with him until the very end and tried to save his life. That's what they said when they offered Viper to us for adoption. They said the kids were too young, but they made an exception."

Sabrina sighed.

"I understand. I appreciate your caring for Viper, and I know he does too. But Viper belongs with me."

"But he's been here for weeks. And he adjusted so well! And

we're going to do the best for him. He's is the only link to Dick we have left. We can't let him go!"

"If you want to do what's best for him, let him come with me."

Charity's troubled eyes look from Sabrina to the kids, then to me.

"But he loves it here, don't you, Viper? Don't you want to stay with us?"

I yawn like I always do when I'm stressed. I wish I could say something that wouldn't hurt her, but nothing comes to mind.

"I..."

Sabrina sighs like she's ready to jump in cold water. She's about to explain where her swollen belly comes from. She'll tell them that Dick betrayed them, and she'll destroy his memory to take me away. But these people don't deserve it. They've suffered enough.

I cock my head.

"Are you really going to do that?"

She glares at me.

"Are you kidding? I'd kill him right here and now if he weren't dead already. I'm sorry for them, but I won't let you go. I'll do whatever it takes. You are my family and my best friend. I'd lie and steal to get you back. Telling the truth is easy."

"It will hurt them."

"I'm sorry. But it's not our fault. We didn't do this; Dick did. I'd love to spare them the pain, but we both know the truth."

"I wish we didn't have to hurt Charity and the kids."

"Me too."

We're so busy talking that we forgot about young Dick.

"How well did you know my father?" he asks Sabrina.

"I knew him very well."

His eyes shine with tears as he turns to his mother.

"Mother?"

"Yes?"

"Viper belongs with Sabrina. She's been his handler for way

longer than Father was. She needs him to look after her. We must let him go."

Charity stares at him like he's lost it. He's only trying to protect her, but she doesn't know.

"Are you serious?"

"Yes."

"But why?"

"You don't want to know," he says, glancing at Sabrina's belly.

CHAPTER 46

Guinness was right. Home is where you can sleep on your back and never worry because you're with those you love and trust.

I'm finally home. Sabrina and I go for long walks without looking for IEDs. We play with my new ball and watch TV in the evenings. Well, Sabrina does. I watch her and the squirrels, and I let her know when someone passes by, especially if they're cats.

It's just the two of us, and I wouldn't want it any other way. Sabrina smells happy and content, though she gets bigger every day. I'm worried she'll no longer fit in the car. She's already tight behind the wheel. But other than that, life couldn't be better.

Until one night when she wakes me up with her screams. I jump to check on things, but nothing smells amiss. She had a nightmare, I think. But then she yells again.

I go to wake her up, but she's wide awake.

"Are you OK?"

"I think it's time."

She tries to sit up but falls back, clutching her belly.

"Time for what?"

"Time for the baby."

Oops. I forgot about the baby — sort of. I didn't really, but life was just fine the way it was, so I ignored it. You know, like when your tail is dirty, but you're too busy talking to your friends to clean it?

"Viper, I have to go. Be a good boy. I'll be back soon."

I tried to follow her, but the ambulance people wouldn't let me.

So I sat by the window and watched them take her away, wondering if she'd ever return.

They seldom do. That's what happened to Butter and Guinness. And even Sabrina. The ambulance took them, and they never came back.

What if Sabrina doesn't return?

I'll just wait until she does. When she comes back, I'll be here.

But what if she never does? Like Andrew?

Sabrina isn't Andrew. She'll come back for me.

But what if she doesn't?

Then I'll just have to wait forever. Like Hachiko, that Akita who went to the train station every day to wait for his human who never returned.

I lay by the dining room window where I can watch the whole driveway and start waiting.

The sun comes up.

The sun goes down.

What if she returns with a kid? Young Dick wasn't bad, but the other two were terrors. Sabrina's kid may be even worse. What if it pulls my tail and sticks its fingers in my ears? Phew! But maybe she won't bring it home. She might just leave it there. I hope.

I lay by the window, waiting.

The sun comes up.

The sun goes down.

The sun comes up again.

It feels like forever.

I'm still waiting when a car pulls in the driveway, and Sabrina comes out. Her belly shrunk, but she's got a package decked with pink ribbons. My heart sinks. Is that the kid?

The door opens, and I rush to meet her. She puts down the package to hug me and rub my ears.

"So good to see you, Viper. Were you a good boy?"

"Of course. Other than eating the dish sponge and the soap. The socks don't count; they were dirty anyhow. How about you?"

"Look what I brought you. This is your sister."

My sister? Really?

I'm flooded with hope. Is she like Jinx?

I check her out. Phew! This is no Jinx! It's soft, pink, and smaller than a cat. It has brown fuzz on its head, and it smells like milk.

"My sister? Really?"

"Yes."

I sniff it again, and it opens its eyes the color of a stormy sky and furrows its brow to stare at me. My heart melts. I've never seen something prettier. Not even Lovely.

"Her name is Ava."

"Ava? What sort of name is that? What does it mean?"

"It doesn't mean anything. It's just her name."

"Names have to mean something. Like Butter or Guinness or Viper."

"So, what would you call her?"

I sniff her again.

"Let's call her Poop."

To find out what happened to Lovely and the gang after Viper retired, **Read LOVELY K-9**:

LOVELY K-9

Guinness' story continues in **MERCY**, Book 2 of **ER CRIMES**, but please be advised that Mercy is a medical thriller with adult content.

MERCY

AFTERWORD

Thank you for reading my K-9 Heroes. If you enjoyed it, please take a minute to leave a review and tell a friend to help other readers find it.

Review K-9 HEROES

And don't miss the rest of the gang: **RAMBO, LOVELY, PROZAK** and **MOM** can't wait to share their stories.

Go to **RadaJones.com** to sign up for updates and freebies and to stay in touch. I love hearing from you!

Rada

ABOUT THE AUTHOR

Rada was born in Transylvania, ten miles from Dracula's Castle. Growing up between communists and vampires taught her that humans are fickle, but you can always trust dogs and books. That's why she read every book she could get, including the phone book (too many characters, not enough action), and adopted every stray she found, from dogs to frogs.

After joining her American husband, she spent years studying medicine and working in the ER, but she still speaks like Dracula's cousin.

Rada, her husband Steve, and their dog Guinness live in a cozy Adirondack cabin ruled by a deaf black cat named Paxil. They spend their days writing, hiking, and dreaming about traveling to faraway places.

Go to RadaJones.com to sign up for updates and freebies.

RadaJones.com

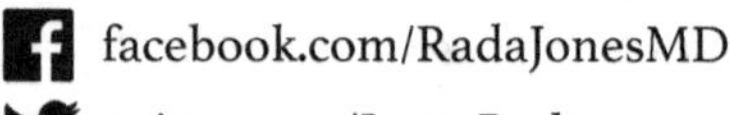

facebook.com/RadaJonesMD

twitter.com/JonesRada

instagram.com/RadaJonesMD

bookbub.com/profile/rada-jones

BOOKS BY RADA JONES

BECOMING K-9: A Bomb Dog's Memoir

BIONIC BUTTER: A Three-Pawed K-9 Hero

K-9 VIPER: The Veteran's Story

LOVELY K-9: A Prison Puppy

K-9 RAMBO: The Dutch Master

K-9 PROZAK: POW

MOM: A Dog Story Prequel to BECOMING K-9

K-9 HEROES, Books 1, 2, 3

OVERDOSE: An ER Phycological Thriller

(ER Crimes: The Steele Files Book 1)

MERCY: An ER Thriller

(ER Crimes: The Steele Files Book 2)

POISON: An ER Thriller

(ER Crimes: The Steele Files Book 3)

STAY AWAY FROM MY ER, and Other Fun Bits of Wisdom

ER CRIMES: The Steele Files

Box Set: Books 1-3

www.ingramcontent.com/pod-product-compliance
Lightning Source LLC
Chambersburg PA
CBHW070230200726
48293CB00005B/1557